BATTLE SCARS

CARA CARNES

HEARTSCAPE PUBLISHING, LLC

Cover Model: Dominic C

Photography by: Paul Henry Serres

Cover Design by Freya Barker at RE&D

Content Editor: Heather Long

Copy Editor: Jax Garren

Proofing: Ink It Out Editing

For the latest information, subscribe to my newsletter, or join my Facebook Group.

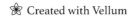 Created with Vellum

ACKNOWLEDGMENTS

It might take a village to put out a book, but when it comes to The Arsenal I'm beyond blessed to have an army behind me. I wish there were enough pages to thank everyone individually.

Thank you to my fearless editors, who never fail to knock my words into shape. And my talented photographer and fabulous cover designer for always, always providing gorgeous covers that bring the world to life.

Thank you to all the experts I've reached out to throughout this series. I have learned so much from your expertise, and I thank you for your time and insight. Any errors are entirely mine.

And to The Cohorts and all the readers who have reached out about this series...You all are beyond fabulous. Your passion for these books, the characters within and the romance genre itself is why I love writing so very much. I hope that I can do justice to the world you're enjoying.

While The Arsenal series is a romance at its heart, the fiber, blood and bone of this series is a gritty, sometimes dark, and daunting rollercoaster ride of suspense, family, team, and honor. Love isn't ever an easy road to navigate. While I've made every attempt to warn readers of possible triggers, please know there may very well be subject matter within this series that may be difficult to read.

Battle Scars contains topics of PTSD, domestic abuse, cancer, and sexual dysfunctional issues. Jesse's and Ellie's romance journey is an emotional rollercoaster which may trigger some readers.

Afghanistan
Three years ago

Jesse Mason crouched behind a stack of U.S. government rocket-propelled grenade launchers and bit back the rage rising within him. Piyale, the so-called translator who'd been his sole partner in the off-book training of village locals, conversed with a group of heavily armed insurgents.

Jesse recognized more than a few of the assholes. He'd spent most of his time in the sandbox hunting for them. Someone under a Pentagon's directive had dragged him away from the Delta team he led, however, and deposited him in the middle of nowhere with no coms. No support.

The so-called training was a joke. None of the locals wanted anything to do with the American military's ways. He'd picked up enough of the local dialect to recognize trouble when he heard it.

"One thousand."

"Two fifty," the insurgent countered in his native tongue, one Jesse barely understood. He'd kill for Cargo's translating skills right about now.

"He's well-trained, high-level American military. The best. He'll know much," Piyale countered.

Son of a bitch. Anger and revulsion rose within Jesse. The bastard was selling him like a prized cow.

The weapon he had wasn't the elite, Delta semiautomatic he preferred. Those were locked up every evening in an undisclosed location per the village chief's request—a demand Jesse had refused until the bastard Piyale explained local customs.

Piyale.

The bastard was a plant. Someone high up had either been conned or had opted to sell Jesse out.

To what end?

Coms had gone down three days before. No one on his Delta team knew where he was.

No matter. Jesse had been in worse situations. He'd handle it alone, exfil to a safe extraction point, and figure out how to get coms back.

The loose plan formed in his mind as Jesse surveilled the surging enemy force mounting outside the small village. He'd keep the firefight contained to the exterior of the clustered huts. No reason to kill innocent women and children—assuming they were innocent.

Forty-one heavily armed combatants. That excluded the villagers he'd been training. Were they part of this? If so, that brought the number to sixty-eight.

Running away into the night and drawing the enemy out of the village seemed like the smartest move. But they'd rip through the village and likely kill everyone for a chance at an American military prisoner. Thank fuck Piyale didn't realize Jesse was Delta and had far more classified intel stored in his head than the average Army grunt.

Jesse eyed the weaponry he'd stumbled across and realized the insurgents had brought it with them. Was the village one of their unknown hideouts?

Likely.

Gunfire ricocheted off the crated weaponry around him. A curse escaped him as he returned fire. So much for the element of surprise. Adrenaline surged within him, but he regulated his breathing and focused.

One target at a time.

Each bullet counted. He didn't have the luxury of unlimited ammo and a well-trained team at his six. He was alone and deep within enemy terri-

tory with no exfil, six rounds of ammo, and no idea who he could trust when he got out.

Jesse sprinted to a new location behind a broken-down truck. The firefight ignited the night with the stench of carbine and blood. Fiery booms exploded shrapnel and debris into the air as Molotov cocktails and grenades were lobbed toward him. Laughter filled the area, signaling to Jesse that they were toying with him because they expected him to be captured.

That's when he heard them. The cries. Whimpers.

Jesse cursed as dread seeped within him—an untended wound that'd get him killed.

Or worse.

"Come out and surrender or they die!" Piyale shouted. "You will get caught. There's no need for them to die."

Jesse peeked around the vehicle and cursed. The village's children were lined up. Weapons aimed at their small bodies kept Jesse still. Fuck.

Capture wasn't an option, but neither was allowing innocent children to die. Hating the only possible decision he had, Jesse vaulted from his position and fired. Three of the five armed men near the children fell. The other two fired.

Small bodies fell to the ground. The others screamed and scattered.

Jesse rolled. Aimed. Fired.

Two more down.

Gunfire from the side drew his attention. Seconds later he heard a soft thunk and looked over. Grenade.

He processed the threat and lunged away, but the explosion threw him backward. His head struck something hard. Blackness assailed him.

*P*ain *woke Jesse. The intensity demanded attention as his left thigh throbbed. Pinpricks of light above punctured the pitch-black darkness. Urine and fecal stench filled his nostrils as he shifted.*

Dirt.

His head ached as though someone had taken a hammer to his brain.

He'd been captured.

Movement to the side halted Jesse's breathing. He wasn't alone.

"You're awake," a gruff voice said. "I patched you up best I could. Their supplies were almost as pathetic as my skills, though."

"Where are we?" Jesse asked.

"The hole." The voice paused. "Once you're down here long enough, you'll see shadows if you pay close attention.

His pulse quickened as he filed away the new information. Intel was power, and he needed as much as he could get to escape. He'd assess his injuries, then form a plan.

"What are you? Army?" the voice asked.

"Yeah." Jesse kept answers short, concise. Trust no one. That was the rule when captured.

"You're lucky to be alive, Army. Most insurgents would've killed you or left you there to bleed out. But these are nasty fucks. They'll damn near kill you, then patch you up and start all over again. You must have something they want really bad."

Jesse seethed.

Someone had set him up.

"You can call me Marine, Army." Something landed beside Jesse. The man must've been trapped within the darkness a while for his eyesight to be so good. Unease rolled through Jesse at the thought. His pulse quickened.

He'd get out.

One way or another, he'd get out.

"Drink. Tastes and smells like shit, but it's as clean as we'll get." Silence ticked by for a few moments. "They'll offer you cleaner, Army. Everything has a price. You talk, you earn stuff."

"I'm not a talker."

"Everyone says that, but there's always a breaking point. They'll find yours."

Jesse peered up at the small holes of light. Fifteen, maybe twenty feet up.

"Welcome to hell, Army. Your ticket to breathe another day comes from what you'll say or endure."

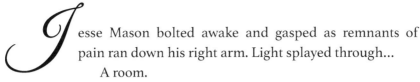 esse Mason bolted awake and gasped as remnants of pain ran down his right arm. Light splayed through...

A room.

Home.

He wasn't in the hole.

He was home.

The punch to his shoulder he'd felt ripped him from the past like it always did. Pain shot along his left leg as he sat up and put his feet to the floor. Elbows on his knees, he ran his hands through his hair and breathed.

In for four.

Hold.

Out for four.

Repeat.

Silence filled the room even though he wasn't the only one there. He looked over at Levi, then slid his gaze to Sol. Damn. "It was bad?"

"Getting worse," Levi admitted, his expression grim. "The others are in the hall. Worried."

Howie, Lex, and Brooklyn knew very little about the night terrors that had tormented Jesse since his rescue. He lectured them all about keeping no secrets, that team members knew everything about one another.

He was a goddamn hypocrite.

"I'll let 'em know you're awake. See you in drills," Sol said as he slid out the door.

Jesse rose and donned a pair of tactical pants and the T-shirt on the bed. The man still in the room remained silent, but the unspoken concern threaded within Jesse's pulse. "I'll talk with Sinclair. She'll get me sorted."

"She's done a damn good job with you," Levi admitted. "I'm not a head shrink, but your mom's accident started this. You hadn't had an episode in months before that."

"I'll get it under control again," Jesse said. "Keeping the woman who birthed me from bleeding out must've done a bigger number on me than I realized."

"Right." The man crossed his arms and stared at Jesse.

"Say it."

"Her name's not the one you're screaming every night. She wasn't the only one in the vehicle."

Jesse's jaw twitched. Ellie. She'd become a constant in his thoughts, a ghost of what could have been if he hadn't chosen to follow his brothers into military service. Bitterness, anger, and outright hostility had fueled him the first few weeks she'd worked at The Arsenal.

His little sister, Riley, had no business hiring her as the office manager. But his ex-girlfriend was firmly entrenched in his life again whether he wanted her there or not.

She'd saved his mom's life. If she hadn't slowed his mom's bleeding before he'd arrived...

Jesse rubbed his chest. An ache plagued him whenever he thought of Ellie.

"Do you talk to Sinclair about her?" Levi asked.

Nosy bastard. Jesse glared as he sat down and dragged on socks and his boots. "She's not up for discussion with anyone. Ever."

"It's time you alter your thoughts on that."

Jesse owed the man everything. Levi had led a team in a rescue mission for Jesse against orders. They'd stumbled across the encampment where he was being held and had refused to leave him behind.

Six months, thirteen days. He'd endured hell for six months and thirteen days. He'd wanted to die many times. Very few things were worth living for. He'd used them all as escapes—ways to retreat from the torture. The pain. The starvation.

His stomach growled.

Hunger plagued him after episodes—as if his brain hadn't gotten the memo that he wasn't in the hole any longer. He stayed quiet and exited the room. The long, darkened hallway offered him a bit of time to form a plan.

"Jesse."

Or not. He turned. Levi closed the distance and held out the black journal Jesse had forgotten.

"If you won't offload on me or one of the others, at least be consistent about writing it down," Levi said. "You should talk to your brothers. They'd want to help see you through this."

He didn't want to risk being sidelined. The nightmares weren't as frequent as they'd once been—not by a long shot. He no longer suffered from flashbacks—where he'd randomly slip into the past while wide awake. That shit was the worst.

Jesse expended a weary breath. Insomnia still rode him hard, but he'd refused medicine. He'd seen too many soldiers become addicted to medications to chance it unless absolutely necessary.

"Thanks," he said. The gratitude was for more than the journal. He had no clue how the kind of debt he'd run up with Levi could ever be repaid.

"For what it's worth, she's a hell of a woman, Jesse."

"That won't ever happen. It can't."

"*Can't* isn't in our vocabulary."

❦

*E*llie Travers reached under the sink and turned off the valve. Water dripped from her hair and adhered her pale pink blouse to her like a second skin. Great. She yanked it off and headed into the small bedroom off the kitchen.

Mornings weren't ever easy, but this one was starting off particularly difficult. She snagged the first shirt in the drawer and drew it over her head. One great thing about working at The Arsenal was they didn't care what she wore as long as she showed up and did her job. Her pulse quickened like it always did when she thought about The Arsenal—or more specifically, Jesse Mason, one of the six brothers who ran the private paramilitary organization.

"I'll phone Brant and get him over to fix the pipe," her mom said.

The sun rose and set around Brant Burton as far as Ellie's mom was concerned. The doctor had been one of the few they'd trusted with her mom's condition—a fact which had left Ellie in numerous rough predicaments since her mom's cancer diagnosis years prior. But family handled their own troubles, and Ellie was all the family her mom had.

"That'd be good," Ellie said. A call to Brant's brother, who actually knew how to plumb pipes, would be quicker, but Mom was having a good day. Anything she wanted to do to help out would be great. "I've gotta run into Nomad after work to pick up supplies and your meds."

"You gonna grocery shop, too? I'll text a list."

"I'll do that in a couple days," Ellie said. Mom didn't need to know her medicine was all they could afford until payday, which was thankfully the following day. "Lunch is in the fridge. Connie should be by later this afternoon."

"That woman has no business around here." Her mom's lips thinned as she shifted her frail body. "If you spent more time here and less time out at that place, we wouldn't need her at all."

"That place pays the bills," Ellie responded. Tension struck the room as it always did when anyone mentioned the Masons. "I'll see you tonight. I love you."

"You ain't gotta lie, Ellie-belly. I know I'm a burden," her mom said.

"You're never a burden, Mom. I love you." She leaned down and kissed her mom's cheek. "I'll see you tonight."

Guilt chewed away at Ellie as she left the small, one-bedroom rental and headed for work. Work was a military-like compound on the Mason ranch on the other side of Resino. Resino sat fifteen miles west of their place in Marville. Nomad, the largest town by far, was twenty miles north of both and the final location in what locals called the tri-county.

Except for a few deer here and there, the drive itself was simple. Even though Ellie had never broken a traffic law, nervousness crawled through her every morning until she crossed the county line into Resino every day. Ten miles.

The first ten miles of her commute every morning and the final ten every evening were the most stressful moments of her day. She clenched the steering wheel and silently wished for an uneventful trip into work today.

Ellie was four miles into her fourteen-mile trip when a loud pop sounded and the vehicle shook.

A blow out.

Damn.

The Arsenal vehicle she drove daily was new, but bad tires happened. She fought to get the vehicle to the side of the road. Her heartbeat thundered in her chest.

Blue and red lights flashed behind her. The siren blared.

She glanced in the rearview mirror as fear crawled up her throat. Talk about shitty timing. Although she wanted to get out and deal with changing the tire, she waited. She didn't bother pulling her identification and insurance out of her wallet.

Anger overrode her fear as Marville's new sheriff sauntered up to the window. Phil Perskins was the biggest mistake Ellie had ever made. No. He'd been the second biggest and a direct result of the biggest mistake ever—letting Jesse Mason leave.

She rolled down the window and glared at the bastard who'd wrecked her life. "I had a blowout. I'll be off the shoulder and back on the road in a moment."

"Get out of the truck, Ellie."

To most people the order would be simple enough. Law enforcement helped people with bad tires. Ellie recognized the tone, though.

Trouble.

Adrenaline surged. They'd done this dance several times since he'd become sheriff, but he'd never ordered her out of the vehicle. Thinking ten steps ahead was how she'd survived a marriage to him for six years.

"I'd rather get whatever this is over with. I wasn't speeding."

"Get out," Phil growled. "I'm searching your vehicle."

"On what grounds? I didn't do anything wrong. I'm changing my tire, then I'll be on my way." She maintained a death grip on the steering wheel as her mind raced through the possible outcomes. None were good.

Phil opened the truck's door and grabbed her arm. Fear spiked when he reached over and unclicked her seat belt. Pain shot through her body as he yanked her toward him. She kicked and heard a grunt, but pain shot across her torso when he slammed her against the front side of the truck.

"That was stupid, but you weren't ever smart, were you?"

"*This* isn't smart, Phil."

"You think that eunuch can protect you? Is that why you've gotten lippy?" Phil laughed. "Guess he's a good choice for you. He can't fuck, so he won't mind what a shitty lay you are."

"Jesse's twice the man you'll ever be. Don't you dare call him that," she spat angrily.

"Spread your legs and keep your hands on the truck. This'll go easier if you cooperate," Phil growled as he roughly searched and groped. Cilantro and onion stench filled her nostrils when he leaned in and whispered, "I miss those tits and how you mewled when I tasted them."

Bastard. She'd screamed, not mewled. "Touch me again and you'll regret it."

"I'll do whatever I damn well want, bitch." He turned her to face him. "This is my county now."

"Not for long if you keep this up," Ellie warned. "Folks won't take kindly to getting mauled by you whenever they have tire troubles."

"You've always been dumber than most." Phil coiled fingers around her throat with one hand while keeping the gun in her field of vision with the other. "You're gonna keep your mouth shut."

Ellie remained silent. Terror seized her voice, but she wouldn't give the bastard the satisfaction of seeing her fear or hearing it in her voice, even if she could speak.

"Now, you and I have unfinished business." He squeezed her neck. "You took something of mine a while back. I let you into my office to clear out your dad's old stuff you left behind, and you stole something of mine."

Her pulse quickened.

The CD.

Her mom had wanted their family Bible, which had somehow been left at the office in their family home when they'd been kicked out. A home Phil had stolen from them. Anger rolled through Ellie. The bastard had destroyed what little they'd had left after her mom's cancer diagnosis.

"Go to hell," Ellie said.

"Where! Is! It!" Phil shouted each word as he loomed in her space. "You think you're safe out there at that fancy compound, but you aren't. I'll get to you wherever you are, bitch. If I can't, I can buy anyone."

Phil's parents had come into money a while back from some good land ventures out west. The Perskins name went far but wasn't within the same league as the Masons or Burtons.

"You don't want to do this, Phil. Even if I keep quiet, they'll hear about this. They know about everything in the tri-county," she warned. "Leave me be, and I'll forget this ever happened."

Phil's eyes narrowed. "Get me that CD, Ellie. You don't want to piss me off."

"I don't have it," Ellie lied. "Let me go before it's too late, Phil. They hear about this and you'll be in more trouble than you can buy your way out of."

"I'll be seeing you real soon," Phil threatened as he released his grip.

Ellie remained frozen in place as he returned to his cruiser and left. Her hands trembled as she got back in the truck and looked at the cell phone beside her purse.

Call The Arsenal. Tell Jesse.

She swallowed.

The Arsenal had been beyond busy the past couple weeks. They'd closed for three weeks around the holidays to let the operatives spend time with their loved ones. And to give Jesse and his five brothers the chance to be with their mom while she recovered from the car crash, which had almost killed her.

Blood.

Nausea threatened like it always did when she thought about the accident. Momma Mason had been shoved off the road so assholes could kidnap Zoey. Ellie had somehow avoided serious injury and had kept Jesse's nephews, DJ and TJ, safe.

Then she'd crawled into the wrecked front and stopped his mother from bleeding to death until he could arrive. She swallowed. The Masons had been through one hell of an ordeal. The entire Arsenal had.

They were the best private paramilitary organization around. Ellie hadn't fully understood what that meant when she'd first taken the office manager job, but she'd put enough bigwigs on hold over the past couple weeks to grasp the meaning now.

Translation—they were too busy to deal with Phil and whatever this CD bullshit was. She'd lied about not having it. She'd intended to return it, then had dropped it into her safety deposit box with her mom's important paperwork instead.

Ellie forced a few deep breaths and formed a plan. She'd change the tire, get to work, and type up a memo. It'd been Nolan's suggestion on keeping them apprised of things she didn't want to bother them with. If Jesse or one of his brothers had time to read the memo, maybe they could help. Otherwise she'd avoid Phil for a few days and he'd calm down.

It wasn't the best or smartest plan, but it'd do. If Phil threatened her again, she'd contact the Texas Rangers and file a complaint. Then she'd tell Jesse and The Arsenal.

2

The Arsenal was busy despite the early hour. Kickass commandoes like Jesse, his brothers, and the hundred and seven people they employed woke up before dawn every day. By the time her lazy ass rolled into work shortly after eight in the morning, they'd been running, training, and doing whatever else badasses did.

Very fit, strong, and lethal badasses.

She rolled the truck to a stop before the newest structure beside the barn. The Arsenal had initially outsourced mechanical work to a shop in Resino, but recently heightened security protocols had resulted in all work on the vehicles either being done in-house or on-site. For the time being a few of the operatives with skills were taking shifts handling whatever repair work came around.

Ellie exited the vehicle and stilled. Medina stood near the front tire she'd changed. The glower on his typically expressionless face didn't bode well for her handling this without going through an inquisition. Spaniards had nothing on Arsenal commandoes wanting answers. Yeesh.

"I ran over something," Ellie lied.

The decision to lie her ass off about the tire trouble had come a couple miles away from The Arsenal's turn-in. They had three on-the-books missions to undertake in the next few weeks. On top of those, they had one blacked-out mission she didn't have clearance to see details for.

And those were only the official Arsenal missions. A ton more would spring up unexpectedly, thanks to Zoey's underground network. Ellie still couldn't believe her friend had run a massive operation to keep victims of abuse and sex trafficking safe.

Zoey had almost died.

Ellie shoved the memories of the accident aside. Medina's scowl was her main concern right now.

"They're sturdy tires. They aren't even available to civilians," Medina said.

"I don't know what I hit. I'm sorry." Ellie powered on. "I'll pay for the replacement myself."

"That's not happening," the man said as he wiped his greasy hands on a towel. "Leave it here, and I'll get to it next. We've got extras since most of our vehicles use the same ones."

"Thanks." Ellie turned and left before the man asked anything else.

She walked to the main building and entered her area—aka Narnia. Ellie had nicknamed all the different areas of The Arsenal grounds to help keep them straight and bring a bit more humor into the intense world she'd been thrust into.

Teaching kindergarten had been simpler.

Ellie halted a moment when she saw the large gaggle of women grouped around her desk. Then she heard the conversation and grinned. It was about time they started planning Mary's baby shower. Dylan's wife was due in a couple weeks.

Jesse was going to have another nephew. Or a niece. The couple had decided to "be surprised." Momma Mason likely knew exactly what they were having because the woman had a way of finding things out faster than anyone—even if it wasn't something she should know.

"We need to let the boys come at least," Kamren said. "DJ and TJ are both excited about having a baby cousin. They've been working on their gift for weeks now."

Ellie smiled. She'd helped them come up with the idea as part of their daily studies. Both of Dallas's sons had been through so much. They'd been raised in the woods like feral animals by Dallas's crazy ex. Zoey had said the woman was a handler for some black ops group called The Collective. The mere thought terrified Ellie. She didn't want to know anything about the assholes The Arsenal took down.

"I'm not saying Dylan shouldn't be there," Vi said. "I'm just saying he and his brothers and the other guys aren't gonna sit around and play those silly games most showers have. And if anyone comes near Mary with a tape measure for that ridiculous game, there'll be a war. One I'll help Dylan lead."

"I'm on games," Bree piped in. A twinkle appeared in her gaze when she looked up. "Oh, hey, Ellie. Just the girl we were looking for."

"When is the shower?" Ellie asked as she slid around the desk and put her purse up.

"We're thinking this Saturday. I know it's short notice," Rhea said. Her brunette hair was pulled up in a no-nonsense ponytail.

The biochemist had been cooped up the past several weeks working on some secret project. Ellie was relieved to see both her and Bree out of their labs. The two scientists tended to hole up and never venture out. She'd always made it a point to go to their work areas on the lower levels and take them cookies and other treats when she could.

"I think we should limit the guest list," Vi said. "Team leaders and family and us. It'll be easier on Ellie."

Ellie blinked. She'd assumed they were here to wrangle her help, but Saturday was a problem since today was Tuesday. Her mom had chemotherapy on Friday, so she'd be sick and would need Ellie at her side most of the weekend.

But the silent blonde sitting on the edge of her desk had taken a chance and hired Ellie when no one else would. For Jesse's sister, Riley, Ellie would make it work. Somehow. "What do you need?"

"Food," Riley said. "Mom said she'd help."

Momma Mason was a great cook. Ellie had developed her passion by helping the woman in the Mason home—the very same home Ellie had gotten Brant's brothers to renovate for handicapped accessibility. While Momma Mason's injuries hadn't required a wheelchair for long, it was now safe for future needs. Ellie had learned the importance of thinking ahead and being prepared the hard way.

"Are we talking a full meal or snacks?"

"Snacks. Sweets," Rhea said. "I bet Bubba would do barbecue."

"No." Riley shook her head. "You tell him and the entire tri-county will be out here. We suffered through thousands of people traipsing around here for Mary and Dylan's and Vi and Jud's double wedding. We aren't going through that again unless they hold a gun to Nolan's head."

Ellie winced. The double wedding had gotten way, way out of control. The Masons were Resino royalty, though. As such, everyone within the area had expected to be front and center for the first Mason man's wedding.

That would've been me and Jesse.

Her heart clenched at the thought, but she forced her attention to the women watching her. "Sure. I can do a few cakes and cookies and other treats. We can get some nuts and veggie trays made up. Meats and cheeses. Oh, I could make some homemade bread."

"Yay!" Bree clapped her hands together. "We'd offer to help, but we don't cook. We suck at it. Vi burns water."

"I do not!"

"You so do," Rhea said. "You have more than once."

"I'll help you and Mom," Riley said. "Vi, Rhea, and Zoey can coordinate the location and invites. I'll help Bree, Kamren, and the kids with decorations."

"If y'all are done planning parties, get out," Jesse growled as he entered the building.

He prowled toward the gathered group in front of Ellie. She slid her chair closer to Riley. The youngest Mason tensed at the movement, then narrowed her gaze at her brother.

"There a reason you're charging in here like a raging bull?" Riley asked.

"Leave it be, Riles," he warned.

Levi crossed his arms and leaned against the wall nearest the entrance. Ellie found Jesse's second in command to be one of the most intimidating men at The Arsenal. The door finally chose to chime its warning that someone had entered. Ellie had a love hate relationship with the stealthy way the Mason men walked. Okay, just about every operative at The Arsenal walked whisper-quiet like a ninja. While it was wicked cool, it freaked her out.

She swallowed when Jesse's gaze locked on her. Their relationship since her arrival at the compound had been...weird. The first few weeks had been downright hostile. Jesse, his brothers, his team. Anyone remotely close to Jesse not only wanted nothing to do with her—they didn't want her around *at all*.

Then they'd entered the acceptance stage of their dynamic. Jesse tolerated her existence in his day-to-day routine without surly words or growled hostility. Not that said hostility had even been a blip on Ellie's asshole radar. No.

Jesse Mason was the most amazing man she'd ever met. She was biased and didn't even care. In many ways seeing him day in and day out was a personal torment—a test of her willpower. He'd once been hers in every way conceivable. They'd been best friends since she was seven. He'd been her first kiss. Her first in almost everything.

Then he'd scraped her off like trash and entered the military.

"Out," Jesse growled.

The women stilled. Addy chuckled as she entered and leaned against the wall beside Levi.

"This isn't a show. Get the fuck out," he repeated.

"Not happening," Addy said. The redheaded operative terrified the hell out of Ellie. She was like Wonder Woman, if Wonder Woman had also been James Bond. Maybe? Either way, she was so kickass she gave every operative at The Arsenal pause.

Even Vi's husband Jud—and he'd been an assassin. Yikes.

Ellie swallowed as she processed the protective solidarity of her new friends—her tribe. The fact that she had one was a shock. She'd only ever had Jesse as a friend. Then he'd gone, and she'd had...

"There a reason you're coming in here like you're about to start World War III?" Vi asked. "Your growl doesn't scare me, Jesse."

Nothing scared Vi. All the women gathered around Ellie were amazing—each in her own unique way. The fact that any one of them had friended her was wild. All of them?

Jesse dropped something on her desk. Her pulse quickened as she watched the small object bounce a couple times then roll to a stop by her stapler. Silence descended as everyone looked at the piece of metal.

Addy and Vi cursed. Bree reached out and grabbed it.

"Why are you bringing this in and getting mad at Ellie?" The blonde looked at Ellie. "Why is he bringing this to you?"

Ellie took a moment to snap the pieces together. Someone had shot her tire out. It hadn't been a blowout. Fear crawled through her, but the anger doused it quickly enough.

Phil.

That son of a bitch.

"Medina has a loud mouth," she muttered, unsure what else to say.

"No. Don't put this on Medina. He did what *you* should've done," Jesse said.

"Actually, she should have called us when this shit went down instead of changing her tire on the side of the road after someone shot it out," Levi commented from the wall.

Riley gasped. "When?"

"I've got Cord and Zoey finding the footage now," Jesse said. "You want to tell me who shot your tire out and why?"

Ellie shook her head. "I didn't know it was shot out. I thought it was a blowout. I swear."

"What happened?" Jesse's voice was low, but gritty like he'd swallowed sandpaper. His green gaze flickered with rage. His entire body vibrated with unspent anger. She'd never fully understood how, but she could read him easily.

Ellie looked around.

"We do this here or in the whiteboard room with the rest of the crew that isn't here," Vi said.

Jesse moved to her side of the desk and grasped her arm. Though his touch was gentle, he'd grabbed the same area Phil had used to yank her from the truck. Pain sliced through her body. A sound rose from her throat.

His gaze darkened as he removed his hand and rolled her sleeve up.

Though not much time had passed, bruises were forming in a distinct pattern. Fingers.

Tension struck the room. Everyone started talking at once.

Jesse leaned down until he was in her personal space. "You and I need to have a conversation about this, Peanut. You want to do this with just you and me, or do you want them involved? Either way they'll know whatever you tell me."

She'd sat in plenty of Arsenal briefings. The Masons, the women gathered around her, and the team leaders all converged and went over every speck of detail about a case. No stone went unturned. They hacked their way into impossible-to-get intel without thought.

Mary and Vi led the discussions and used the system they'd created. HERA. Ellie didn't fully understand it, but Marshall and Nolan had both told her every government organization and country in the world wanted it.

Her stupid problems with Phil didn't need their level of intensity. He was a pissant compared to the real terrorists, drug lords, regimes, militias, spies, assassins, and dictatorships they battled on a regular basis. Nolan said Mary and Vi had never failed on a mission. While Ellie really, really wanted kickass commandoes like Jesse and The Arsenal kicking Phil's ass, more important and deserving people needed them more.

"It's nothing."

"Nothing doesn't shoot out tires," Jesse said. "Nothing doesn't leave marks on you."

"I'll handle him."

"Him? Who?" Addy asked.

"Her ex," Zoey said as she entered the fray. Her friend charged into the room from the side entrance and held her laptop out. Her gaze widened when it landed on Jesse. She snapped the laptop shut and hugged it close to her. "On second thought, let's wait to look at the footage. "Gage and the others are going to the whiteboard room. Let's move there."

Ellie didn't want a big meeting with lots of questions. There was so much she hadn't shared with them—not because she'd intended to keep secrets. There simply hadn't ever been a good time to bring up things that were technically of no consequence to them.

"Look at me," Jesse ordered in a whisper.

Heat tingled beneath her skin when his fingertips touched her chin. She leaned forward, craving the awareness igniting within her. Thirteen years. If she thought hard enough, she could recount the months and days as well. It'd been thirteen years since she'd felt Jesse's touch outside of necessity.

He'd tended her injuries at the accident. He'd remained as distant physically as he was emotionally. She couldn't blame him. He'd survived a hell she'd likely never understand because no one ever spoke facts about it. Rumors were the only morsels of information running amok in the tri-county when it came to Jesse's injuries.

Ellie would rather die than listen to what the gossipmongers said. They'd chewed her up and spat her out like gristle.

"Jesse, you all have more important things to deal with. It'll be fine."

"There's nothing more important than you, Peanut. You either walk or I carry you. Your choice."

❀

*J*esse seethed as he paced near the exit to the small room. Every debriefing they held was a tighter fit as the crew involved grew. Talk about a cluster fuck. He wanted confirmation that Marville's new sheriff was the asshole who'd hurt Ellie. He had a name.

Phil Perskins.

A growl rose from his throat. Perskins. Yeah, he remembered Phil's dick of a father having a run-in with them on more than one occasion, especially back when their father had been alive. They'd butted heads at the auction house in Nomad often when the man tried to cheat newbie ranchers with bad livestock.

Jesse's dad had always run interference and done the right thing. Jesse rubbed his chest. Pops always did the right thing, no matter what. He wouldn't have tolerated this slow-as-fuck shit show.

Mary, Vi, Cord, and Zoey had watched footage three times and had yet to share it with anyone else. If they watched one more time and didn't start this debrief, Jesse was gonna blow.

"Sit down," Dylan ordered. "You look at my wife or Vi like that one more time and you'll have issues with Jud and I."

"And me," Gage added from his new position in front of Jesse.

Jesse ignored Dylan. Big brothers were a pain in the ass. Fortunately they left him alone most of the time. People had a way of ignoring maimed head cases when they could. Nolan moved closer. Jesse felt his presence at his back.

Caged.

No.

Contained.

Riley, Bree, Rhea, and Addy had Ellie on the other side of the room. Sequestered.

"I'm a bit pissed you're wasting time controlling this situation," Jesse said through clenched teeth as he turned to face Nolan.

"You got your shit together?" Jud asked as he arrived and stood beside Gage.

"Do I need to?"

Nolan's jaw twitched.

Yeah, he needed to.

The soft swoosh of the door behind Jesse drew his attention. He inhaled the cool air from the hall and the small taste of freedom the doorway offered. Then his gaze landed on Levi and the quickening of Jesse's pulse he hadn't noted until that moment slowed.

But his mind spun.

Get answers.

Kick Perskins' ass.

Protect Ellie.

"Move," Levi ordered as he glared at Nolan and the others congregated around Jesse.

"This is a closed debrief. We'll fill you in after we're done, Levi," Zoey said from the front.

"Move or I move you," Levi repeated. He closed the short distance between himself and those gathered around Jesse.

Jesse tensed. His second-in-command recognized more of Jesse's triggers than anyone—even Doctor Sinclair. "I'm okay."

"No. You aren't," the man said. His gaze swept the room. "All due respect, you all back the fuck off or I'll level you. Don't ever cage him in. You'll trigger a flashback."

Dylan and Nolan's gazes widened. Jesse noted both because he'd been turning in small circles. His heart thundered hard in his chest, but the anxiety marching beneath his skin was burned away by rage. Someone had hurt Ellie.

Air. He breathed it in the moment the cage widened. Jud and Gage moved away. Levi stood against the wall, near Jesse's back. He breathed deeper when he saw only Dylan and Nolan remained close.

Brothers.

Most days the monsters within Jesse hibernated. They only roused when someone he cared about was hurt or needed help. They'd rode him hard when Mary's troubles hit.

And Kamren's.

Jesus, they'd damn near eaten him alive when Dallas's shit went down.

Then Ma.

Now Ellie.

"I'm gonna kick Medina's ass for showing this to you first," Nolan commented.

"Don't you dare," Jesse growled. "I should've let the girls dig into Ellie. We've all known she was hiding something."

"We've got this, brother. Whatever it is, we'll handle it," Nolan said.

"Let's go through this and what we've done so far," Mary said. She looked over at Jesse, as if assuring herself he was handling his shit.

He wasn't.

It'd been lost a few seconds after Medina showed him the bullet that'd shredded Ellie's tire.

"We've located and isolated the drone surveillance from the incident," Vi said. "We won't be showing it. Sheriff Phil Perskins appeared on scene shortly after Ellie pulled her truck over. He dragged her from the truck and an argument ensued. Threats were made."

"Show it," Jesse ordered.

"That's our call. We are all a firm no," Zoey said.

"You don't need to see it, brother," Cord said.

Assholes. Jesse paced.

"What's on the CD he wants?" Mary asked Ellie.

"I have no idea. It's in my safety deposit box at Nomad National. I put it there with the paperwork and Bible I'd picked up for Mom." Ellie's pale face drew Jesse's attention. He wanted to be across the room with her, but that wasn't a smart idea.

The woman stared blankly into the coffee he'd brought. Dark circles were beneath her eyes. Why hadn't he noticed before?

Because you've been too busy avoiding her since Mom's accident.

He'd avoided her because seeing her fussing over his mom and doing the small things he and his brothers wouldn't have considered...

She was a reminder of everything he'd lost. Survived.

Ellie Travers was his biggest regret, yet his reason for living.

Dylan moved to stand beside Mary. Big brother had set the bar high when he'd met and married one of the most brilliant women Jesse had ever met. Then Dallas met Kamren.

His brothers were happy little shits in the slop of domesticated.

Jesse wouldn't ever have a wife. Kids.

Sex.

"You cool?" Levi asked, his hand on Jesse's shoulder.

"Yeah, sorry. Must've zoned." Jesse looked around the room and noted the conversation hadn't halted, but his brothers all watched. Assessed.

He had to keep his shit reined in or they'd pull him from whatever this was. No way in hell was he letting another team take primary on helping Ellie with whatever was going on.

"We've sent a copy of the footage to the proper authorities. We expect someone will want to speak with you soon, Ellie," Cord said. "Likely the Texas Rangers, who were just in Marville. At this rate they should move here."

"We'll want to sweep the area where the shots were taken from. If we're lucky, another drone further down the road was able to catch whoever it was. The caliber used doesn't allow for distance," Bree said.

"Dallas, you want to take your team and Kamren out there?" Zoey asked. "The boys can stay with me."

"They're with Mom," Dallas said. "We'll go now."

"Riley and I will sweep through Marville. Maybe someone's talking," Jud said.

"They won't," Ellie said. "They mind their own business."

"She's right," Kamren said. "Phil's parents bleed money into that town. Everyone's pockets are lined with Perskins' green in one way or another."

"Why didn't his name come up when we were looking into Kamren's shit?" Gage asked.

"Because they're too smart to get caught," Marshall said. "Dad's suspected Herman Perskins of a lot of things over the years, but there wasn't ever enough evidence. They stayed clean."

"We'll dig," Mary said.

Jesse breathed his first deep breath. Everyone around him was rallying to get Ellie safe from whatever this latest clusterfuck was. If there was anything to find, Vi and Mary, aka the Quillery Edge, would find it.

"My team and I will rattle Phil's cage," Jesse said. "The sooner he knows she's Arsenal the better."

The sooner he knows she's mine the better. He glanced across the table. Ellie had always been his. He might never truly have her as his wife. She'd never have his children. But he'd protect her until his dying breath because he loved her more than anyone.

His world began and ended with Ellie Travers.

"Let's wait to confront until we have the CD and know what we're looking at," Nolan said. "The more leverage we have the better."

Jesse grunted. Although waiting sucked, it was the smart move.

"Though I'm in for a confrontation when you're ready. I want to be there." Nolan crossed his arms. "No one fucks with family."

Jesse swallowed. Ellie should've been the first daughter in-law. The first to carry the next Mason generation.

"We have plenty of cottages ready since Burton construction completed so many a couple weeks ago," Zoey said.

Jesse was impressed with Brant's brothers. They'd completed one-third of the first section of housing The Arsenal was building for the Warrior's Path—a program he and Dylan had created for veterans returning home from military service.

"Good idea," Marshall said. "Pick whichever one you want to use, Ellie. We'll send a few guys over to help you bring over whatever you need."

They were moving Ellie onto The Arsenal? The move was smart, but the last thing Jesse needed.

"I can't move." Ellie's eyes were wide. Terrified. She looked at Jesse from across the room. "I can't move."

"He can't mess with you here."

"I won't cower to that asshole or anyone else." She clenched her coffee cup. "I appreciate it, but you have done enough for me."

They hadn't done nearly enough. Riley had hired Ellie to take over as office manager, but everyone had been neck-deep in troubles and had ignored the front office entirely. They hadn't noticed the beautiful woman was severely underpaid and overworked until Zoey had knocked their asses down a few pegs.

They'd tripled her salary and given her a company vehicle and credit card. They were in the process of hiring an assistant for her, but Jesse knew it wasn't close to enough because the woman was exhausted.

"Why can't you move here?" Mary asked, her voice soft.

Mary saw things faster than most. Jesse wondered what she suspected.

"Mom won't agree to move here," Ellie whispered.

"Your mom?" Rhea asked. The quiet scientist studied Ellie a moment. "She's the *how*."

Jesse tightened. Son of a bitch. His mind connected the dots, but the brilliant women gathered within the room had already finished the pattern.

"What?" Cord asked.

"She's how you knew how to care for Momma Mason," Rhea said. "I'm right. Aren't I?"

Ellie curled into her chair as if warding off their perusal. A part of him wanted to carry her out of the room and away from whatever troubles she was having.

But she wasn't his.

Not anymore.

"Ellie," Nolan whispered. "I know your mom is fiercely private, but we need to know."

"Why? Why does that matter?"

"Because you matter," Jesse answered as he sat across from her at the table. "Is your mom sick?"

"Mom has colon cancer," Ellie whispered into the thick silence.

"I'm sorry, Peanut." Jesse reached over and took her hand.

He'd held her hand at her dad's funeral. It'd been simpler back then. Ten years old and masters of their know-nothing world.

"How long?" Marshall asked.

"A while," she hedged. "She doesn't need this worry, not with all the others she has."

"The debt," Zoey whispered. Red crept up her cheeks when she peered up from her computer. "I sort of started looking. We wanted to a while back, but Jesse wouldn't let us. He said you deserved your privacy."

"Thank you," Ellie said as she looked over at him. "Mom was really sick a while back and made some poor choices. The bank let her take out second and third mortgages she couldn't ever repay."

"Patterson," Dallas said, anger in his voice. "She's one of those affected by the land scandal The Rangers are looking into."

"Phil bought it after the foreclosure finalized," Nolan guessed.

Ellie nodded.

Jesse suspected there was far more lurking beneath the surface when it came to Ellie, but it'd wait. For now they needed to get her and her mom secure at The Arsenal.

"Come on. Let's go get your mom. We'll stop and eat at Bubba's first," Jesse said.

She needed time to relax and process what'd happened before handling her mother. Jesse didn't recall the woman fondly. She brought a whole new meaning to the term abrasive.

3
———

*R*iley watched Ellie like a hawk about to swoop down on a rat. Everyone in Bubba's watched Riley, while Jesse glared back at them. Fun. Times.

Ellie found the entire situation disconcerting. She'd gotten a couple hours work done in between all the drop-in visits from operatives and well-meaning friends checking on her. It was nice to know people cared, but she felt bad for wasting so much of their time.

Damn Phil for whatever petty crap he was stirring up. It wasn't like gang members were shooting at her. That'd happened to Kamren. She didn't have a crazy congressman trying to kill her. That was Zoey.

Ellie didn't even want to think about the scary shit Mary and Vi survived. It was black-in-black level classified—which meant she shouldn't know half of what she'd become privy to, thanks to the guys' lack of desire to type their own reports up.

"How did y'all meet?" Riley cocked her lead to the left as she sipped on her straw. Curiosity glinted in her blue eyes. "You and Jesse? I never heard the story."

"School. My first day," Ellie whispered. Heat rose in her cheeks as she moved a bean from one side of her paper plate to another. "Mom was a teacher, and she'd gotten a job in the elementary school. I didn't know anyone. I saw a couple bigger boys squaring off against one with the nicest, warmest smile. I got angry and clonked one of them when he..."

She'd been alone for so long with only the fond memories of him and what they'd once been to one another to keep her sane. Sharing any scrap of what she'd safeguarded so long with anyone felt...wrong. A lump formed in her throat. She forced a smile and hoped the conversation would move somewhere else if she was quiet long enough because finishing the sentence was almost as impossible as forgetting the man sitting beside her.

"Nolan pushed me to the ground. She clonked him over the head with her backpack, then stomped on his foot." Jesse smiled.

Warmth seeped into Ellie. She missed his smile. Its presence washed away some of the protectiveness within her. They weren't just her memories—they were Jesse's. And Riley wasn't just anyone. She was his little sister.

Family.

Ellie took a deep breath and let her thoughts spill out as the memory of how they met assailed her. "I didn't know they were brothers."

"The resemblance didn't clue you in?" Jesse teased.

Her stomach somersaulted and her pulse quickened when their gazes locked. The bustling conversation of patrons vanished as her awareness tunneled to Jesse. The way his full lips upturned in a smirk that didn't quite strike his eyes. Eyes haunted by a hell she no longer had the right to pull him out of—but she would anyway because her world stopped and ended with Jesse Mason.

"I reacted too quick for common sense to enter the equation," Ellie said.

Riley laughed. The sound boomed through the interior of the small eatery. Ellie looked around and noticed the curiosity ramping up to palpable levels. Although Bubba's was in Resino and the social ostracism of her troubled divorce from Phil was contained mostly to Marville, anxiety still rode her hard when too many people noticed her. She didn't need to take another spin through the gossip mill.

But the pull of the past she'd shared with the man beside her was far stronger than her fear of what everyone in Bubba's thought of her. Warmth flooded her insides and washed away the worries. Her mind drifted in the happiness they'd shared back then—back when they'd been kids with no cares in the world.

He'd been her entire world.

"We were inseparable from that point forward," Jesse whispered.

They'd eaten their lunches together and discovered their mutual love for peanut butter cups. Ellie had discovered that the teachers kept a stash in their lounge. Jesse would be lookout, and she'd sneak in and snatch a handful. Whenever she got caught, she'd lie through her teeth and say she was there to see her mom.

She smiled at the memory.

Jesse chuckled.

Did he remember the crazy things they'd done?

Life had been simpler back then. Ellie's dad had still been alive. So had Jesse's. Nothing ever touched them.

No one ever messed with them.

"We should go," Jesse said, his voice clipped as if he'd soured to the idea of remembering anything to do with her. Tension corded her muscles.

They'd had good times together before he'd gone off to war. She never allowed anger to darken those times. He'd left. She was proud of all he'd done while in the service, and she never, ever blamed him for leaving her. Not once.

Had he blamed her for not going away with him? Her mom had needed her help.

But thinking of what could've been hurt. She couldn't travel that road, not when the man she still loved so much wanted no part of it. "Yeah, let's go."

The fifteen-mile drive to Marville was quiet, except for Riley's random musings every now and then, mostly directed toward her brother. Worry furrowed the woman's brow on more than one occasion when she glanced back at Ellie, who'd insisted on sitting in the back seat.

Marville was a yawn-sized town, one business-closing from comatose. The recent oil fracking had offered a huge jolt to a lot of people's bank accounts and overall morale, but the richer had gotten richer and the poor had gotten nothing.

"I need to stop at the Sip and Spin. Dani needs to know I'll be at The Arsenal for a bit."

Jesse's gaze cut to her via the rearview mirror. "Is she your supplier?"

Riley gasped. "Don't you dare believe the shit the rumor mill says!"

From what Ellie had seen, no one at The Arsenal had discussed the drug rumors much, but Jesse had clearly put two and two together and made fifty.

"Pot for her mom's pain," Jesse whispered as he looked at his sister. "I'm not judging. You know I'd do the same for Mom."

"I would, too." Riley glanced back. "Is Dani your supplier? I didn't think she was into that stuff her brother's crew did."

"I was an exception."

Dani's brother, Dominic Santiago, was the biggest, scariest badass in Marville, bar none. The fact that he'd gone to prison for murder hadn't changed much—just made his legend even more fierce. He'd ruled the Marville Dogs from prison. His baby sister had always been on the outskirts of the operation their cousin ran for Dom.

Then Javier betrayed Dom and tried to take over the gang. Things had gone south, and Dani—who was Kamren's best friend—almost died in the attack. The Marville Dogs were no more. The few who'd escaped Dom's wrath had been carted away on arrest warrants by the Texas Rangers.

Had the gang going down been the catalyst to make Phil nervous?

No. He'd left her alone for weeks after.

She was so focused on figuring out the why to her troubles she hadn't noticed Jesse had navigated his way to her rental property without needing directions. How? "You know where I live."

Ellie winced at her accusatory tone. She stared out at the untended lawn she'd meant to get around to last weekend. Overflowing trashcans at the neighbors reminded Ellie she'd forgotten to put hers out this morning. She definitely didn't want to miss trash day.

She tried picturing the one-bedroom house from Jesse's perspective. *House* was a loose term because it was smaller than the living room of the Mason home, but the roof had been redone by Brant's brothers. He'd also outfitted the bathroom with handrails for her mom.

In truth, Brant had been a godsend in many ways. He never pushed for the rent, even though she rarely had it on time—or at all. She'd definitely seen a different side of him than Kamren. She exited the vehicle and walked up the cracked driveway. Four steps led up to the narrow porch.

She unlocked the door and entered. The smell struck her as it always did. No matter how many ways she tried, there was no way around the scent of...

Death.

The word fractured a piece of Ellie's soul—a part that still clung to hope. Her mom would push through this like she had the other times.

But they'd had to do surgery a couple months back. Her mom now had a colostomy bag—a fact the proud woman who'd raised her had yet to fully accept. She refused to change it herself—a small act of rebellion Ellie understood because she'd likely do the same.

Except she wouldn't have children to take care of her when she got ill. She wouldn't ever have children—another fact she'd accepted when she'd heard about Jesse's injury. Even if the worst of the rumors were true, she couldn't imagine ever having anyone's child but his.

It was one of the many arguments she'd had with Phil. Repeatedly. Even though she'd been very clear that she didn't want to have children going into their marriage, he'd expected her to change her mind. Provide him an heir.

"Mom?"

Rustling from the small bedroom off to the left of the living room drew Ellie's attention. Her mom shuffled into the living room with more spunk and speed than she normally had, which meant she was still having a good day so far.

Ellie hated to darken a good day with her mess, but if Jesse thought she'd be safer at The Arsenal, she wouldn't argue. Phil terrified her.

Her mom froze. Her widened gaze settled on Riley first, then Jesse. "What are you doing bringing them here?"

"We need to go and stay at The Arsenal a few days."

"No." Her mom's lips thinned. "You wanna abandon me and go live out there, just say so, Ellie-belly. Don't drag me into it. I'm perfectly fine here."

She should've called Brant first. The doctor had a way of getting her mom to cooperate when no one else could because he was kind. Patient.

"Someone shot my tire out. Phil showed up, dragged me out of the truck, and threatened me." Speak straight and leave nothing out. It was the best way to handle Mom on most days.

Her mom halted her progression toward the recliner across the small room.

"Phil." She spat his name like a curse. "You never had any sense when it came to men. Worst taste. I thank God everyday your daddy didn't live long enough to see the mistakes you've made."

Jesse growled. Riley gasped. Ellie squeezed her eyes closed and willed patience. She and her mom had always had a somewhat strained relationship, but the cancer had made it worse the past few years.

Since the marriage. Then the divorce.

"What's he want with you now?" The woman sat in her recliner. "I'm not hiding out with those damn Masons 'cause you hooked up with that yellow-bellied weasel."

"You'll have a place to yourself. None of us will enter or bother you," Jesse promised.

"You after my girl again?"

"No, ma'am, but she needs to be protected. We can do that easier at our place."

The quick reply pained Ellie. She glanced away and gave Jesse the lead because dread cemented her tongue and filled her throat. It'd been years since Jesse and her mom fought. He wasn't a kid or a young man any longer. He was a battle-hardened warrior. She was a cancer-ravaged woman.

Ellie loved them both.

"It'll be easier on Ellie having you out there. She'll be on the road less and out of danger," Riley said. "She really is in danger, Ms. Travers."

"Why's he messing with you? What'd you do this time?" Her mom glared.

"I have no idea, but we'll find out and get it sorted. Then we can come back here. Please, Mom. I don't want him coming here while I'm gone and messing with you."

"I suppose it couldn't hurt to be closer. Lord knows she spends enough time out there and flitting back and forth," her mom said. "You'll keep my girl safe?"

"I will," Jesse promised.

"I've never had much count for you Masons and I'm not gonna turn into one of those Mason-loving locals. But I'll go." Concern rushed across her mom's face as they locked gazes. "Are you okay, Ellie-belly?"

"Yeah, Mom. I'm good."

"I'll help you pack," Riley whispered.

"I shouldn't leave them alone," Ellie replied as the woman was already pushing her into the small bedroom.

"We can hear them from here. You have a suitcase?"

Ellie nodded and grabbed it from her closet, along with a duffel. Her mom's supplies alone would take a lot of room. She ran her hands down her jeans and looked around at the shambled mess of a life—one she'd kept closed off from anyone seeing. Sometimes Brant came into the bedroom to look at Mom, but in typical doctor mode, he never saw anything past his patient.

Or pretended not to.

She couldn't pack everything up and haul it to The Arsenal compound. Whittling it down was...impossible. Where did she even start? The weariness she battled every day struck hard. Her mind blanked, refusing to process an action plan.

Someone had shot her tire.

Phil threatened her.

"You two should go," Ellie said. "I'll get packed. Send someone back for us."

"We aren't in any hurry." Riley touched her arm. "It's okay, Ellie. Let me help you."

"There's too much to pack. I don't even have enough suitcases. Mom needs her supplies and lots of clothes. Then there's the other stuff."

The bedside toilet her mom peed in. The bed, which was more of a cot than a medical bed was against the wall. Boards raised the head of the cot because they couldn't afford anything expensive but needed something more positionable than a standard bed. Embarrassment crawled through her as she glanced at Riley.

"It's okay," the woman said as she studied the bookshelf of supplies. "You have everything so organized."

"It helps keep Mom..." Ellie halted the excuse. In truth, the carefully placed items were more for her sanity than her mom's. "It's the one thing I can control with Mom's illness."

"I've got an idea." Riley pulled out her cell and punched a button. "Hey, Logan. It's Riley. I'm over here at Ellie's picking up her mom. Could you call Brant and coordinate equipment and supplies with him? I'm thinking we already have most of what we need on hand. I know we have the bed and a few other things."

The woman listened a minute and smiled, as if the doctor on the other end could see her. "Thanks."

Ellie blinked. Logan Callister was The Arsenal's doctor. He was a nice man she'd chatted with a few times, but he tended to keep to himself in the medical ward. "He's too busy to deal with this."

"None of us are too busy." Riley locked gazes with her.

"Remember the night of Mom's first surgery? The day of the accident? Remember when you went into our home and started bossing everyone around? You moved the table out of the dining room and called Burton Construction to alter Mom's home?"

"I didn't mean to overstep. I was just helping."

"Now it's our turn." Riley touched Ellie's shoulder. "You've been doing this alone?"

Ellie nodded. "There's a nurse. Connie. She works a few hours a week."

"Then you come to work and handle my six brothers, all their team leads, and operatives. The geek squad. The visitors and demanding idiots on the phone. Then you took on teaching DJ and TJ.

"You do all that and then come home to this." Riley squeezed her shoulder. "You should've told us. We could've helped."

"Mom's private."

Riley's lips thinned.

"She's been hurting a long time. Pain does things to people, makes them meaner than they intend to be." Ellie slid the defense out from the recesses of her mind where it lived. How many times had she muttered it? Hundreds? Thousands?

"They aren't going to let her stubbornness put you at risk."

"It'll blow over. Phil will move on. He always does."

"One way or another you need help with her. What if she fell while you were at work? What if she got into her medicines and took too much?" Riley's gaze softened. "I have a friend whose aunt was really sick. I know it's hard."

Ellie nodded. She'd spent many restless nights worrying about her mom. The what-if trail was endless with ten thousand forking paths to even more what-if scenarios. Affordable elder care was impossible to find in Marville. Palliative care? Pft. Impossible times a thousand. Add in her mom's surly attitude toward everyone in general and it'd been a vicious rollercoaster Ellie couldn't get off.

"I promise we won't interfere too much, but you need help. Let us be there for you the way you were for us."

Ellie couldn't believe how quickly they'd reacted and offered support. Help.

But Riley and her friends were part of Jesse's world—one she never should've been a part of after he returned home. Even though a part of her was relieved to have the support and help she needed in dealing with Phil and her mom's illness, Ellie was a realist.

Her being around The Arsenal daily was a problem for Jesse. He avoided her whenever he could and kept conversation to necessary business when their path's crossed. Things had turned less awkward recently, but Ellie being around full-time with her mother took things to a new level—one that wasn't fair on Jesse.

"You never should've hired me, Riley," Ellie whispered. "It's hard on Jesse. I don't want to make it any harder on him."

"My brother can take it." Riley smiled. "Come on. Let's get those clothes packed."

Jesse knocked and entered. Lips thinned, eyebrows drawn into a scowl, he looked around the small bedroom. His hands flexed into fists them relaxed as he prowled a few steps closer, then turned back toward the bedroom door.

"Everything okay?" Riley asked.

"Yeah." The lie hung with the room a second. "I've got an errand to run. Gage is outside. He'll drive y'all back to the compound."

"Where are you going?" Ellie blurted the question and waited, even though she already knew because good men like Jesse Mason didn't sit around and wait for a confrontation. They made it happen.

"I'll see you back at The Arsenal, Ellie." Jesse glanced at his sister. "Get her whatever she and her mom need."

Ellie was unsure what to think. In a way she was glad to have someone fighting her battles and taking on Phil. But Phil was a bad, bad man and they had enough troubles without taking on hers.

*J*esse climbed into Nolan's truck and slammed the door. Ellie would be okay. He glanced back at the small house. Though it was in the worst part of Marville, it had undergone significant repair. Only one group would pour that sort of money into a wreck.

"You good?" Nolan asked.

"Burton and his brothers own this rental. They're the only ones who'd put so much work into fixing up a place. Brant knew about this shit and didn't tell us," Jesse muttered.

"He's her mom's doctor," Nolan said. "Doctor confidentiality is a tricky thing."

"You're defending him after how he treated Kamren?"

"I know good men sometimes make bad decisions. Dallas has every right to be pissed. I'm trying to remember all the good Brant's done," Nolan said. "You see someone keeping facts from you that aren't his to share. I see a man having a woman's back when she's carrying an impossible load."

Jesse grunted. Nolan always framed everything with logic and common sense. The Burtons had done a lot for Resino and Marville. None of that explained the emotion churning in him right now when he thought about Brant helping Ellie.

"I should've been the one taking care of her," Jesse commented.

"You are now. Zoey's coordinating the cottage with Logan and Brant. It'll have everything her mom needs by the time they get there," Nolan said as the vehicle pulled out onto the road heading to Nomad.

"Where's Perskins at?"

"Nomad Country Club," Nolan said.

Figured. The Perskins were flamboyant with their money. The more influence they gained by controlling others, the better. They collected power by breaking the backs of others.

Nolan parked in a reserved spot just outside the country club's private restaurant. A few people watched as they made their way in. Tactical pants and T-shirts weren't exactly the attire of choice for pretentious joints like this, but Jesse didn't give a damn. Or maybe it was the guns they wore that gave everyone pause.

Jesse went in first and was greeted by a wiry, elderly man who held two menus against his chest like a shield.

"Good afternoon, gentlemen. I'm afraid this is a private establishment for members only." The man's gaze raked over Jesse, then Nolan. "With a firm dress code."

Right. Jesse glowered at the man but didn't offer the fact that the entire Mason clan maintained a membership. Not that Jesse ever used his.

Nolan chuckled. "It's not smart business to assume someone isn't a member because of what they wear."

"Certainly, sir. If I could see a membership card or get a name, I'll gladly offer you some sufficient attire." The man looked to the side as if expecting reinforcements to come and assist.

Jesse headed into the dining area. Nolan could deal with the details. He bypassed the filled tables with the fancy linen tablecloths. Pale blue—a point his mom found refreshingly original. A few people offered smiles and waves while they watched his progression.

Phil Perskins sat in the centermost table of the large dining area. The center of attention. Two older gentlemen were with him. Jesse recognized the one to the left as the vice president of the credit union in town. They'd been trying to get Marshall to move The Arsenal's accounts for months.

The one to the right of Phil was Aaron Patterson—a slug of humanity they'd tried to take down back when Kamren's troubles had erupted. But he was slippery like rich criminal assholes typically were. Patterson had just earned a new mark in the asshole ledger, though. He'd foreclosed on Ellie's childhood home after overextending credit to a dying woman.

Yeah, Patterson would get his day in Jesse's crosshairs. But not today.

"Can I help you?" Phil asked. "We're in the middle of something."

"Stay away from Ellie." Jesse raised his voice. "Get anywhere near her or her family and I'll destroy you."

"Excuse me?"

"You heard me." Jesse gripped the back of Phil's seat with one hand and stuck the other on the table next to him so he could leaned forward until he was in the man's personal space. "Stop messing with Ellie."

"I don't see how my ex-wife is any of your business, but I assure you I am quite done with that mistake." His thin lips shrank further. "She's not worth my time."

"She's an Arsenal employee, which makes her safety my business, but I'll clarify so your pea-sized brain follows along. Ellie Travers and everything to do with her was my business before you realized she existed."

"Ah. You're the ex." Phil wiped his mouth with his napkin and set it on the table.

The Marville education system only went until the sixth grade, which meant kids were either bused to Nomad or Resino. Most went to Nomad, but Ellie had been at Resino because her mom was a teacher there. Perskins hadn't done either. His parents had enrolled him in a private school.

Their social circles hadn't collided with Phil until their final couple years in high school. Even then Jesse hadn't ever spoken with the bastard. How had Ellie hooked up with him?

"I'll admit I thought you were rather stupid for choosing war over her. Now I understand," Phil commented.

Jesse remained silent and pushed the rage aside.

"Perhaps since she's your employee now you can insist she get the help I offered. I'll pay," the man offered. "Rehab facilities are rather expensive. I'm not sure what your finances are like, but I'll help fund her recovery—despite all she's done to me."

A few guffaws and outright laughs sounded around them. Jesse ignored the responses from the tables nearby. Anyone with half a brain knew the Mason name. He and his brothers didn't tout the power it held because there was rarely a need.

"It's rather coarse to come to my club and insert yourself into my day with threats. Please leave before I have you escorted off the property."

"Go ahead and try," Jesse advised.

"I know you're a war hero, but you don't want to mess with me. It won't go the way you think."

Jesse grinned. "You're on our radar now. That's a problem for you, one your daddy can't wipe away. Activate your connections and I'll activate mine. Let's see who wins."

He stood fully and looked about the room. "I'd steer clear of Phil here. We're digging deep into him and everyone associated with him."

"Are you through?" Phil asked.

"We're just getting started." Jesse turned and left.

Nolan chuckled as they got into the vehicle. "That was more than a small nudge. Ten bucks says we get a call from his daddy by the end of the day tomorrow."

"Good." The sooner they got some answers, the better. The last thing Ellie needed was to deal with that asshole. That part of her life was through. She was Arsenal now.

4

It took longer than Jesse expected to get Ellie's mom situated into a cottage. By the time they'd finished, darkness had descended on the compound. He'd received more than one text from Mary and Vi. Their team's next mission had rolled up to the docket.

Jesse made a run through the mess hall and grabbed a protein shake from the fridge and a few nutrition bars for his pack. Then he made his way to the briefing room where his team was already assembled, along with Cord and Zoey. Nolan and Dylan sat at the table as well.

Jesse glowered at his brothers. "There a reason you're here?"

"She still as bitchy as I remember?" Nolan asked.

Zoey gasped. "You didn't just say that. She has cancer."

Nolan glowered. "Woman is ten levels of bitch rolled up into about a hundred more."

"He's not wrong," Jesse commented. He looked at Levi, then Lex, Howie, Brooklyn, and Sol. "Sorry I wasn't in touch. You cool?"

"We're solid," Sol answered. "You need help sorting Ellie?"

"Brant's handling the details. He insisted." The man had a way of calming Ellie's mom—a troubling fact since the woman had always hated Jesse. "What do we have?"

"This is for the underground," Zoey said. "Your team is up next for one of those, but Nolan and Dylan have both offered to go if you want to tap out."

"Read us in," Levi said. "Then we'll decide."

Jesse nodded his approval of the decision. Though Jesse was officially the team leader, Levi had taken the reins many times. The man was an exceptional operative and a natural born leader—a fact that couldn't be ignored much longer.

"The Dark Web crawler Cord and I added to HERA a few weeks back has snared quite a few assholes. This one took longer to ferret out. He's got deep pockets and is heavily tied to old money and big politics." Zoey motioned toward the table where a man's image flashed up.

A heavyset man in his early 60s. Gray hair. Wrinkling skin.

"Meet Oliver Tundstill of Tundstill Pharmaceuticals. He's made billions charging hundreds for drugs that only cost pennies to make per bottle," Zoey said through clenched teeth. "His perversions make him a frequent flyer in the auctions, but he's somehow avoided capture. Either he's got someone from the FBI in his pocket or he's a lucky son of a bitch."

Jesse grunted. Assholes like him needed to be taken down. Jesse picked up the electronic pad in front of him and thumbed through the data. The bastard was one state over in Louisiana. A plantation in the bayou.

"We have any details on who we're rescuing?"

"Honestly? I'd expect more than one trafficking victim. More than likely a child or children. The crawler found financial records for six transactions in the past year. Details for the auction facility he used are limited. They're smarter than most about not leaving much of an electronic footprint. We know he bought someone—just not who."

But her program had still found them. Jesse smiled at the woman who'd come into her own over the past few weeks since her ordeal. Since she'd finally come forward with the Dark Web scanning technology she'd created off-book during her downtime, she'd helped Cord merge it fully into HERA.

The results were startling. They'd unearthed nest after nest of sick shits. The Arsenal had taken them all down, gathered any evidence on-site, and turned them over to authorities with full warning The Arsenal would be watching to ensure the assholes were properly prosecuted.

Even though Jesse didn't want to leave Ellie, they didn't have enough information to proceed with her problems, and he'd be better off as far away from Phil Perskins as he could get.

"Schematics for his mansion were filed by the previous owner, but the county doesn't require it. We expect heavy modifications," Cord said. "You're going in blind."

It wasn't the first time. Most of the missions they'd run for Zoey's underground network had been blind. At least this time they had a name. He glanced over at his team, but already knew they were onboard. Go bags were against the wall nearest the entry. None of them liked the idea of leaving a kid or anyone else in the hands of a psycho.

"Let's do this." Jesse pounded the table. "Departure ETA?"

"Twenty," Levi said with a smirk. "I've already started the jet's prep. Z has a transport cache at the airstrip we'll be flying into. Arriving late night will keep us under radar longer. We can slip into recon position while everyone in the area is sleeping."

"Authorities won't be notified 'til after the mission is completed," Cord said. "We'll use our national FBI contacts rather than locals."

His team headed out with their go bags. Jesse kept an extra in a locker at the hangar so he was always ready. He waited out the silence as his three brothers looked at one another. He recognized a setup when he saw one.

"Erm, should I leave and pretend nothing awkward is unfolding, or do you need a witness? An alibi will cost you." Zoey shut her laptop and folded her arms in front of her. A purple and pink unicorn do-rag covered her head.

"You want point on Ellie," Nolan said.

"That a problem?" Jesse asked.

"We do this one by the numbers to avoid trouble later on," Dylan said. "You aren't alone. Wherever you go, one of us shadows you."

"You think I'll lose it, take the fucker out."

"I would," Nolan said. "You went code red on her troubles faster than I would have."

"I saw what Dallas went through with Kamren. I'm not letting Ellie's problems get out of control." Jesse looked at his hands. "I didn't know the mom was sick when I left."

"We figured," Dylan said. "That's heavy shit. You talk to Sinclair about it yet?"

"No, but I will." Jesse rose. "We done with the forced therapy?"

Nolan and Dylan grinned. Cord didn't comment, but Jesse hadn't expected him to. Baby brother had been quiet and withdrawn around Jesse a while. Eventually he'd have to ferret out the why, but not today. They were done.

⚜

*J*esse trudged across the well-manicured lawn leading up to the mega-mansion nestled within the Piney Woods. Gargoyles perched on light posts every fifty feet along both sides as if warning no one to tread any closer. Light splayed into the inky darkness of three a.m.

It'd taken less than two hours after landing at the out-of-the-way landing strip to make their way to the Tundstill plantation and establish a perimeter. Within half an hour they'd surveilled long enough to form a loose penetration plan.

"Security cameras on every other light post," Zoey stated into the com. Drones flitted overhead, well above the limited range of Oliver Tundstill's security system.

Jesse pulled up the scans on his display and sighed into the com. Movement on the thermal scans of the house indicated clusters on the northwest sector of the first floor. Another grouping on the second.

And two souls in separate areas on the third floor.

None of what he saw was a problem. It's what he didn't see.

"Scan again," he ordered into the com.

"There's a basement. There has to be," Zoey stated into the com.

"I agree," Levi said.

Jesse grunted.

"Are you sure your intel is right? This is the place?" Jesse asked. It was too...normal. Silence greeted the inquiry. "Right."

Amusement echoed through the otherwise quiet com as his teammates chuckled. Yeah, asking one of the geeks if they were sure of their info was a bit suicidal. But he owed it to the team fanned around the mansion to make sure the risk was worth the payoff.

"You're green lighted for entry," Zoey stated. "And yes. The intel is credible."

"Move into position one on three," Jesse said. Coms would remain silent from this point forward unless a problem arose.

No one on his team needed guidance. They'd done this song and dance more than a few times. Gain stealth entry into the domicile. Eliminate the threats by whatever means necessary. Find and secure the target.

One by one, clicks chimed on the com. Yellow lights on his display turned green with each one. Jesse moved to the first position he'd selected—the southwestern corner of the mansion. From there he slowly scanned the lower level and ground. The drones had done an excellent job providing images, but no tech would ever beat human eyesight.

Jesse had spent years in reconnaissance and recovery within the military. Countless missions had honed a sixth sense he couldn't explain to others. Fortunately no one at The Arsenal ever asked him how he managed to see what no one else could. It was a skill.

An asset.

A curse.

"Electrical panel located," Levi stated. "HERA's patched into all systems."

A glimmer of metal captured his attention. He moved a couple feet closer and crouched. Bingo. He pinged the image to the visual displays of his team. Coordinates immediately displayed. No words necessary. No orders needed.

"Alarm sensors down," Zoey commented. "Looping security feeds now."

Brooklyn appeared a couple moments later. She was one of the best ordnance and entry specialists Jesse had ever worked with. Though he could've easily gained entry into the secured hatch, she did so swiftly and without sound.

Jesse read the data feed on his visual display. Levi had entered via a second-story balcony on the east side of the house. Howie used a southern facing first-floor window, which left Lex to breach from the western side and make his way up to the third floor.

Sol would remain in his perch and snipe any assholes who got in the way.

Jesse descended the narrow stairwell first and plunged into darkness. His headgear immediately switched to night vision. A drone whizzed by him and headed into the catacombs of darkness. The display shifted as images were fed from its surveillance.

Brooklyn followed him, her movements as quiet as his.

The second display provided intel on the rest of the team's progress. Two drones had assisted Levi's takedown of the largest cluster on the second floor. He'd secured all targets there and moved to the third to assist Lex.

A second drone appeared. Jesse grunted at the unnecessary presence. Baby brother was on drone duty tonight and taking no chances. Cord never did. He was the most cautious of the seven Masons.

Pale shafts of light loomed at the other end of the narrow corridor. Wooden boards braced the otherwise earthen tunnel Jesse was in.

Concrete replaced the dirt walls when they arrived at the sconce. A red light flashed from the drone ahead. Jesse followed but kept his progression slow. Methodical.

"This is too easy," Zoey commented. "Last time I fed intel to a team for a place like this, the guy..." Zoey paused, as if measuring whether they needed to know.

"Z," Cord growled into the com, making his presence known for the first time.

"The crazy bastard had a self-destruct system," Zoey said. "He blew the house up. And everyone in it."

"I'm thinking you should've led with that before we were wheels up," Levi commented.

"You think..."

"Everyone keep eyes open for it," Jesse ordered. "Let's find our..."

Target. He hated the word, but it kept the humanity out of the mission so he could focus on whatever was necessary. If he thought about the fact that they were here to rescue a little girl...or a little boy...or a woman.

Damn.

His gut churned as adrenaline surged within him.

Find and secure the target.

"Movement on perimeter. Five, no, six vehicles inbound," Sol stated. "Permission to engage?"

Translation—could the best sniper The Arsenal had on payroll take out unknown civilians?

"Soft engagement," Zoey said. "Dispatch drones to assist."

The women had insisted they take three extra sets of drones with them. The nerd collective of The Arsenal was always prepared for World War III.

Two men stood at opposite sides of a doorway at the end of the corridor. Jesse loaded two darts into his weapon and fired before the drone aimed. He sprinted down the corridor and took the largest man while Brooklyn dragged the other. Neither would wake anytime soon, but he zip-tied their wrists behind their backs anyway. Rhea's new knockout compound lasted hours.

Sound drifted from behind the locked door, which was metal reinforced with crossbars. Brooklyn placed ordnance and nodded. Jesse covered his face and looked away. The explosion was a soft swoosh rather than a concussive boom, but the sound on the other side of the door halted.

Jesse switched back to his primary weapon and kicked the door in. The drone whizzed in. He directed his attention at the red light flashing on his display.

A fat, bald man whirled, gun drawn. The brisk movement parted his robe further, putting his hairy, round stomach on full display.

"Drop the weapon and put your hands up," Jesse ordered.

"Fuck," Brooklyn said.

Jesse ignored everything except the asshole with the weapon. Zoey wanted him alive because she thought he'd have information they needed. Moments like this tried his patience, his humanity.

No amount of focus prevented him from hearing the terrified sounds coming from behind Oliver Tundstill. The man's large body blocked a visual and the drone offered no glimpse.

"Fuck," Brooklyn said. "Drop the weapon, Tundstill, or I'll drop you." The woman aimed her weapon and positioned herself closer.

"Who are you?" The man's surly voice rose. "You have no right to come into my home. You have no idea who you're messing with."

"We know," Jesse said.

"Leave now, and I'll forget about this," Oliver offered.

"Drop the gun or you die." Jesse glanced at Brooklyn. The muffled screams were louder, more desperate. A clang of metal on metal sounded. "Secure her. I've got him."

"Don't touch her." The man growled and aimed his weapon at Brooklyn.

Jesse fired. The bullet nailed the bastard's knee. A loud scream echoed through the chamber as he fell to the ground.

And Jesse saw the cage.

Wide brown eyes so filled with terror they were almost saucer sized. Tears. Jesse's gaze followed them as his mind tried to process what he was seeing. But Brooklyn was there, looming between him and the little girl as she undid the cage.

The tiny girl crawled to the back of the confined space and huddled into a ball, as if protecting her naked body from any further harm. Round, dark, red-and-black spots marred her skin along her back and arms and legs. A tiger-striped tail scraped against the floor.

He tracked the tail upward.

Jesus.

"Likely an anal plug inserted," Zoey said. "Nolan's crew had one last week."

"Hey there, sweetie. I'm Brook. We're here to take you home."

The girl sniffled. "Daddy hates me. He said so when he gave me to the mean man."

"Oh, honey." Brooklyn motioned. "Come on out. Lots of people have been worried sick about you."

The partial lie hung in the room. How long had the little girl endured this sick hell? How long had she been trapped in a nightmare while not one single person noticed? Or cared.

If the newly enhanced tool Zoey had created to crawl through the Dark Web hadn't been installed in HERA, would anyone have ever found her? Disgust churned in Jesse's gut as Zoey's orders tumbled through the com.

The girl wasn't secure yet.

"Perimeter clear," Sol said.

"Clear on two and three," Levi said.

"Clear on one," Howie added.

Jesse assessed the young girl's condition. They were far from clear. Blood oozed from long gashes on the bottoms of her bare feet. Cigarette smoke hung the air. Butts were scattered on the floor along the cage. Burns. That's what the red-and-black spots were.

Fuck.

Bruises along her legs and arms. And face.

Urine and feces were in a shallow pan on the edge of the cage. Nausea pitched Jesse's stomach. Who would treat a little girl like this?

"Give me a reason to let you breathe," Jesse growled as he shoved the butt of his weapon against Oliver's temple. "One reason your sick ass deserves to live."

"I-I'll give you the others."

"Others?" Brooklyn asked.

"My club."

Jesse's gaze swept to the entry as Levi entered. "Take this sick shit out of my sight."

"My pleasure." Levi grabbed the man and hauled him up, despite his injury. "You cry or bitch about that knee and I'll double tap the other one."

Interrogating Oliver would wait until they returned to The Arsenal. He wouldn't be turned over to authorities until they had every scrap of intel the man had.

With Oliver out of the room, Jesse could focus on tending to the girl's injuries. Most would have to wait until they were at a hospital, but he needed to make sure she was medically secure for transport.

"There's a doctor in the network six miles down the road, but he's new," Zoey said. "Get her home if she can wait. Logan is the best option until we figure more out about this supposed club. Tundstill's too connected. Anyone could be in it."

Jesse wanted the asshole father who'd sold his baby girl into...

He bit back the disgusting thought and focused on the little girl huddled against Brooklyn. "Hey there. I'm Jesse. What's your name?"

"Sonja." The girl's voice was low, hesitant. Her expressive brown eyes never stopped moving. They wandered from Brooklyn to Jesse, then toward the door.

"He's not coming back, sweetheart."

"He hurted me."

"He won't hurt you or anyone else ever again." Jesse sat outside the cage. There was no way his large bulk would fit in it with Brooklyn and Sonja. "I know you're hurt and scared, but you're safe now."

Did the girl even understand the word safe?

Anger rode Jesse hard. His nephews had been put through hell by their mom before Dallas had found them. DJ and TJ had come a long way since their rescue, and so would Sonja. Jesse backed up when Brooklyn motioned her intent to leave the cage.

It took a fair amount of coaxing, but the girl followed Brooklyn out. Sonja's torso was covered in the same wounds. Revulsion rolled through Jesse. Most of the injuries could wait until they got back to The Arsenal.

"We'll have a female doctor onsite," Zoey said.

Blood trailed a line along the filthy concrete floor when the girl moved to follow Brooklyn farther from the cage. Jesse tracked the trail and silently cursed. She was bleeding, but he couldn't determine whether it was vaginally, anally, or both. Unshouldering his backpack, he grabbed the blanket he carried and handed it to Brooklyn.

"Sedate her, Jesse. It's the best way," Zoey whispered.

He'd already reached the same conclusion. He reached in and took out the sheaf of stickers Rhea had made for occasions like this. The fact that a scientist as brilliant as her had spent no telling how long creating stickers with a sedative safe enough for children showed how dedicated everyone at The Arsenal was to rescuing anyone Zoey's Dark Web crawler discovered.

The girl's eyes danced with curiosity as she watched Jesse unroll the stickers. Her tiny hand trembled as she reached out and stroked them. She burrowed her head deeper into Brooklyn's embrace as she crawled onto the woman's lap.

"You want one, sweetie?" Brooklyn asked, her voice soft and filled with feigned merriment Jesse and his team hadn't felt in ages. "Pick your favorite and Jesse will put it on for you."

The little girl bypassed the butterflies and ladybugs. She paused at the kitten and puppy, as if unsure which to pick. She landed on the puppy. Eyes on Jesse, she watched as he peeled it off and gently placed it on the back of her right hand. So fucking small and delicate.

He'd used the stickers three times before this. Each time it'd taken only moments to take effect. Rhea was not only brilliant, but efficient. She understood that every second in the field was a risk.

Tundstill knew where other children were, which meant the never-ending mission had now entered another leg. He glanced at Brooklyn and noted the resolve in her gaze as she stroked the girl's hair. They'd find the others. For now, though, his sole focus was on stabilizing Sonja for transport.

*S*onja's injuries had been too severe to wait. Jesse and his team had taken her into a nearby hospital where a vetted doctor within Zoey's underground network had staffing privileges. The FBI and local law enforcement had been contacted. The Arsenal carved through most red tape, but there was only so much clout to be thrown around when a little girl was rescued from a billionaire's basement.

By the time her injuries had been dealt with and the authorities had decided whose custody the girl would be in, it was well past noon. FBI Special Agent Victoria Blevins was the lead investigator on the new case and would run point with The Arsenal on the remaining recoveries—whatever they may be. They'd worked with her on a couple of the other rescues, so Jesse knew the little girl was in safe hands.

More importantly, he knew Tundstill was screwed because Blevins was as clean as they came.

The jet landed at The Arsenal's private hangar shortly before sunset. Late afternoon sunlight splayed across the landscape as if offering a promise of a better day. Jesse remained silent as he gathered his gear and followed his team off the plane.

He'd been awake too long to remember the last time he'd slept, but that didn't matter. Sleep never came easily. His gaze scanned almost a dozen people. Mary, Zoey, Cord, and Vi huddled together near the hangar's exit. Jud and Dylan stood beside their wives. The latter flashed Jesse a smirk as if to apologize for the onslaught of people.

None of them were Ellie. Was she okay?

Every recovery ended the same, no matter which team had gone. Everyone converged as if there was a reason to celebrate, even though no one ever felt like the recovery was a victory. None of those gathered thought it was. They were there for moral support because the shit they saw...

He bit back the memories of Sonja's injuries. His gaze flitted past

Doctor Sinclair. The shrink had become a given in Jesse's daily routine. She would haunt his ass until he showed up at her office.

Not today, Doc. Not today.

"You good?" Nolan asked.

"As good as can be expected," Jesse answered honestly. Big brothers had a way of sussing out bullshit.

"Tundstill's already singing," Dylan said as he joined the huddle.

Levi grabbed Jesse's gear and nodded as he followed the rest of the team to the storage vault. They'd need to inventory all ammunition and supplies before they were considered fully checked in from the op. It had been one of the newer procedures initiated and was a serious pain in the ass.

"I'm surprised they got him in a box so quick."

"Blevins doesn't mess around," Nolan commented. "Sonja has a sister. A year older. We know her location. Addy's team is on point."

Levi had flown the jet for them. Having an operative on his team who could fly helped Jesse's team be ready faster than anyone. Having a female operative on recovery missions helped more than he wanted to admit because he'd never thought a soldier's sex made a difference. It was the person's skillset and courage that made them a good operative.

The Arsenal had a pilot on call and was in the process of hiring a full-time one. Marshall had been pretty tight-lipped about the who but had said he'd only hire the best.

They always did.

"Location?" Jesse asked.

Dylan's jaw twitched. "Cuba."

Fuck.

"Mom's been asking about you." Nolan crossed his arms and furrowed his brow. An unspoken order to go see her hung between them. "She's heard Ellie's out here."

Their mom had been through a lot the past couple of months. Three surgeries later, she was on the road to recovery, but it was a slow crawl—a pace their mom wasn't down for.

Jesse understood more than anyone how difficult recovery was.

He'd been down that road so much he had his own personal lane. The sooner he filled out the mission paperwork and debriefed with his team, the better. He'd see his mom, then maybe grab a beer and try to forget the shit he'd just seen.

"And Ellie?"

Nolan smirked. "Think you can track her down and find out for yourself. We aren't in grade school anymore."

Big brothers were a serious pain in the ass.

5

*J*esse decided to stop in at the cottage Ellie and her mom were sharing before he went to the main house to see his mom. He knocked, but no one answered. Laughter he recognized drifted from inside.

He entered.

His mom sat on the sofa beside Ellie, whose mom was in a recliner nearby. Asleep. An IV stand was beside her. Jesse nodded at the two women watching him as his gaze tracked the small cottage. It'd undergone a metamorphosis. A partition separated the left section of the living room off. Except for the IV pole, you couldn't tell anyone sick lived there.

Jesse suspected that was a tremendous burden off Ellie. The other house had been...

Dismal.

He understood now why Ellie had made such a big deal about the environment for his mom's recovery. She understood the importance because she'd seen its impact on her mom. She'd given his mom what she hadn't been able to afford for hers. Jesse's mom had made huge strides in her recovery the past three months since the accident.

"You're back," his mom commented. "I thought for sure you'd let Nolan or Dylan take this one."

"It was our turn." Jesse wondered how his mom always heard about the ops even though she never stepped foot near the operations area. Someone had very loose lips—a fact that bothered quite a few operatives at The Arsenal.

A diffuser cast a vibrant scent of pine and wilderness. Though it was strong, Jesse found it far more pleasant than what'd been at Ellie's house.

"Ellie and I made chicken parmesan. There's a plate in the oven on warm. Beers are in the fridge. I had Marshall go buy some earlier," his mom said.

Jesse didn't comment on the beers or the fact that she'd had them put in *Ellie's* fridge. If the woman scented the barest inkling of interest from him, she'd be unstoppable. She was bound and determined the rest of her babies would be married and having babies of their own within a year.

He padded into the kitchen and grabbed one of the beers from the fridge. He chugged half before he made his way to the oven. The scents wafting from it activated a rumble from his stomach. He'd eaten a few nutrition bars but hadn't had anything else all day. Or was it two days?

Fuck. Exhaustion sucked.

"Sit. I'll get it," Ellie ordered.

Jesse stilled as the woman moved past him and got to work getting the chicken from the oven.

"Give me a few and I'll make some pasta to go with it. Your mom wanted to go ahead and make it, but it's better fresh." Jesse took another swig of beer and grabbed a second from the fridge. He'd need more than one to deal with the domesticity of the situation he'd walked into.

His mom was playing house with his ex.

Jesse's jaw twitched. He didn't want to give Ellie false hope that something aside from friendship could happen with them. Seeing her day in and day out was torture enough. Being friends?

Well, that was one of the epically shittiest layers of hell. Seeing a woman he'd once wanted more than anything. Never touching her. Never tasting her.

Never fucking her.

She'd been his escape. No matter how bad shit in the hole had gotten, she'd been his out.

Now she was in the kitchen of a cottage on his ranch humming as she fixed his dinner.

Jesus.

He should leave. A smart, sane man would get out while he could.

But the scents were almost more tempting than the woman. He'd gotten off the jet tormented by what he'd seen. Sonja had endured so much a little girl should never experience. Her father had sold her to a depraved bastard.

Jesse sat at a barstool and took another sip of beer.

"Pasta will take a few minutes. I'll pull the chicken when it's done. Sauce is warming, too." Ellie leaned against the counter and snagged the second beer he'd pulled out. She popped the cap and took a swig. "Not bad."

"You don't drink beer."

"I'm not the woman I was back then," she replied.

"And I'm not the man I was. I won't ever be him, Ellie."

Sadness haunted her gorgeous eyes a moment, then she looked down. Her fingernail scraped at the bottle's label. "I know. I'm okay with that. The man you are now is pretty damn impressive. Nolan told me where you were. You okay?"

"No, but this helps," he admitted. Unsure why he'd given so much of himself away with the admission, he let the silence hang a moment. "I'm sorry."

Ellie's sharp inhale drew his gaze to her. Shock resided in her gaze.

"I'm sorry for not asking why you didn't say yes to coming with me."

"I'm sorry for not telling you why." She cleared her throat. "You don't owe me an apology, Jesse. I never, ever blamed you for leaving.

You're the bravest man I've ever known. I'm proud of what you've done. Who you've become."

Jesse rubbed his chest as if he could massage away the ache. "I'm not a good man, Peanut. Some would argue I'm not even a man. Not anymore."

"Don't." Her voice was low, but angry. It drew his gaze away from his beer. She reached out and took his hand. "Don't ever put yourself down, Jesse Mason. There are too many people in this world ready to knock us down. Don't ever make their job easier."

"Ma's gonna get the wrong idea," he whispered.

"So what?" Ellie turned away and turned the burner off. She lifted the pot and headed to the sink. "We're adults, Jesse. We don't owe anyone any explanations. I know what's what."

"You do? What is what?" He took another swig of beer and watched her turn and drain the pasta like she was performing surgery.

"You've said nothing can happen between us."

"It can't."

"So it won't." She set the pot down and pulled the plate out of the oven using a hot pad. "We're mature enough to be friends."

"Ellie..."

"Friends. Nothing more." She poured the pasta onto the plate, then added sauce. Sprinkled parmesan cheese on both. "You want to pretend with a salad for your mom? Or are you adult enough to risk a no-veggie night?"

Jesse chuckled. "I think we can pass on the salad."

"Okay then." She set the plate before him and left the hot pad beside him. "Careful, it's hot."

He reached over and took a fork from the hanging utensil dispenser. "Thanks, Ellie. It's been a long day."

"Or two. No offense, but you look like hammered dog shit right now." Amusement danced in her blue eyes as she smiled.

Warmth flowed through him. He hadn't seen her smile at him in a long, long time. He tightened his grip on the fork to keep himself from reaching out and touching her cheek. Her hair. Her mouth.

How many times had he closed his eyes and pictured her smile? Damn.

He looked down at the plate of food. No one outside his family had ever cooked for him—not something like this. He cut into the chicken and ignored the woman silently watching. An awareness flowed within him. He felt...

Alive.

Connected.

For the briefest moment he'd felt...

Normal.

Maybe he hadn't died in the hole after all.

*E*llie stretched out on the double-sized bed and sighed. For the first time in a long, long time she felt...

Calm.

Her mom was asleep in a medical bed, which meant she was safe from falling out and could adjust herself without needing help. Ellie had a real bed beneath her—not some dingy sofa she'd found at the curb.

And Jesse had fallen asleep on the sofa.

He'd eaten two servings of chicken parmesan and pasta. Then she'd cut him a wedge of peanut-butter-and-chocolate pie. She'd secretly started sprinkling peanut butter goodness back into his world. It'd required her doling out enough sweets to everyone for it not to be obvious, but it'd been worth the time she'd invested because anytime she watched Jesse eat one of her creations, he seemed calmer. Happier.

They'd had another beer as they watched *SWAT* with her mom—who'd woken up in a better mood than usual.

Momma Mason had worked her magic and kept Ellie's mom calm and content. By the time the episode was over, Jesse had been fast asleep. She'd helped her mom into bed and tucked her in tight after checking her bag and dispensing medicines. Then she'd walked his mom out.

The faint chime of the alarm on the door drew her attention. Was Jesse sneaking out? He'd been fast asleep just moments ago. Her heart thundered in her chest as she left the bed and padded into the living room.

Levi froze three steps from the main door.

Shock kept her mute. She'd gotten to know the quiet man rather well the past few weeks. He was Jesse's second-in-command and one hell of an operative, from what Zoey had said. Why was he here? Was everything okay?

He sat in the recliner beside the sofa and kicked it back.

What the hell?

"Go to bed, Ellie."

"Why are you here?"

"Goodnight, Ellie."

What the hell? She swallowed the questions on her tongue because she didn't want to wake Jesse. "There's chicken parmesan in the fridge. Help yourself, but don't wake him or I'll have Addy kick your ass."

The man grinned and nodded but made no comment. His stealthy entry and quiet nature assured her he wouldn't intentionally wake Jesse up.

But why had he come in the first place?

The answers would wait until morning. Ellie went back to her room and went to bed.

❀

A loud crash woke Ellie. She bolted up out of bed, fully awake. She'd spent years tending her mom. She'd spent almost as long married to a lunatic who enjoyed terrifying her. She padded into the second bedroom and was surprised to see her mom sleeping soundly.

What the hell had she heard?

She went into the living room and froze.

Jesse was awake. He'd stripped off his shirt and pants and was in a pair of boxer briefs. Deep gouges along his back were evident, thanks to the lamp, now on. Levi stood in the corner, his focus on the man prowling the room.

Jesse stumbled on the coffee table. His lips moved, but no words escaped him. His green eyes were half open, but he was...

Asleep.

"Peanut!"

The mournful scream fractured her shock. She bolted forward, but Levi snagged her about the waist and drew her against him. Locked in his arms, she punched and kicked angrily.

"Don't," Levi growled in her ear. "He's asleep. Night terrors."

Night terrors? God. She squeezed her eyes shut and shook her head. That sounded bad. Very, very bad. She'd had nightmares since the car accident.

Night terrors?

"Wake him up. Help him."

"I will, but stay back. He's usually disoriented when he wakes and strikes out." Levi's grim expression cast pain through her. How many times had Jesse endured this? How many times had Levi watched over him?

Jesse curled into a ball in the middle of the living room floor. His gaze was...

Clouded.

Was he awake?

No. He was trapped in hell—the same hell which had left the scars.

He screamed.

The sound fractured Ellie's resolve to trust Levi. She couldn't stand there and do nothing, not when he needed someone to wake him up.

"Jesse." Tears trekked down her cheeks.

The scars. The screams. They were too much to process.

Levi knelt at Jesse's side and shook him. Jesse lunged and the two men wrestled and rolled around on the floor.

"Goddammit, Jesse. Wake the fuck up," Levi growled. Then he whistled.

The sound made Ellie wince, but Jesse froze. Blinked. Ellie sat on Jesse's other side and touched his cheek. She remembered the assurance he'd offered her the other day. "You're okay, honey. They won't ever hurt you again."

Honey. She hadn't uttered the endearment since before he broke up with her, but a part of her knew he needed to hear her voice.

He grabbed her head and breathed, as if smelling her hair. The drawn breath thundered through the tense silence. Fingers threaded through her curls, so softly and delicately the movement brought tears to her eyes.

"Just one more night with my Ellie, then I can die. Give me one more night. Don't take it. No."

She turned her head so he could bury his face deeper into her hair. Her tears fell onto his bare chest.

"Jesse, I know you're almost with us. Wake up, man," Levi said. He shook him one more time.

Ellie noted the moment Jesse was alert, back in reality instead of wherever he'd been. The muscles beneath the hand she'd splayed on his chest tensed.

"You're cool, man. We're at Ellie's cottage. You fell asleep here." Levi's voice was low and even. Calm. "You're cool."

Ellie wrapped her arm around Jesse's waist and tightened her grip when he tried to pull away. Fear and shock and worry swarmed together and stung her insides like a million pissed-off wasps. She was raw from the emotional upheaval of today. If she let Jesse pull away, he'd bolt.

"Don't. Don't pull away, Jesse. Let me hold you a minute."

"He doesn't like to be touched, Ellie, especially after an episode," Levi said.

Oh. She released her grip and moved to pull away. "Sorry, Jesse. I didn't think."

No verbal reply came, but his arms wrapped around her. Loose. Tentative. The contact offered her a small hope that he was okay. He'd be okay.

👁️

*J*esse breathed in Ellie's scent. Strawberries. He'd inhaled phantom vanilla and lavender so long the new scent burned his nostrils with an unwanted dose of reality—a reality the hazy fog of confusion blurred out.

Tendrils of the nightmare still wrapped around him and squeezed. An IED ticked in his chest—slamming in tempo with his rapid breaths. A fiery burn pulsated along his back and torso as though he'd just taken the lashes all over again. The blood he'd imagined coating his skin was sweat.

He'd fallen asleep at Ellie's.

"You're cool," Levi repeated.

He was far from cool. If Levi hadn't…

Eyes closed, he slowed each breath. In for four. Hold for four. Out for four. Repeat.

Strawberries.

Each drag of the scent into his nostrils went deeper, as if seeking each shrapnel of horror to excise them. Jesse wished it were that simple. He opened his eyes, and the cloudy haze from before dissipated.

Levi crouched nearby, silent and observant as always. "Why don't you go put some water on, Ellie? I'll run and grab some cocoa mix from the mess hall in a minute."

"I can make cocoa," she whispered. She looked up at Jesse. "Does that help? After?"

Nothing helped after, but Jesse nodded because he recognized the tactic. Levi wanted Jesse back on the established routine they'd set forth with Doctor Sinclair's guidance. The sooner the journaling process started the more he'd remember.

Ellie crawled away, then rose. Concern reflected heavily in her watery gaze and thinned lips. She ran her hands up and down her arms as if staving off a phantom touch. Dark bruises from her run-in with Perskins marred her creamy skin. The thin, pink and white, sleeveless nightshirt hung loosely on her frame, except around her ample breasts.

Back when he was fifteen, he could've jacked off for hours at the sight of Ellie as she was now—minus the bruises. The thin material outlined her hard nipples perfectly. The matching shorts were loose, but short.

"Jesse?" Her eyebrows furrowed. "Are you okay?"

"I'm good," he lied.

"No marshmallows, Ellie," Levi said with a smirk that told Jesse he'd missed at least one question.

Ellie wandered into the kitchen a short distance away. Jesse ran a hand down his face and forced a deep, even exhale, even though his heart still beat hard. A shirt landed in front of him followed by pants.

How had Levi tracked him down?

As if sensing the question, the man sat on his ass and settled his elbows on his knees. "Little brother will likely hunt your ass down tomorrow. He caught you on surveillance."

Jesse glanced up at the drone in the corner of the living room. Of course. Jesse dragged on his shirt and stood on wobbly legs. One leg at a time. He could do this.

"You got a journal with you, or do I need to run and grab one?"

Jesse zipped up and fumbled with the largest pocket along his right leg where he always kept a journal and pen. It'd taken a while to adapt to the process of "debriefing" his brain after an episode or particularly shitty day, but he had to admit it helped.

A tremble settled in his hand as he sat and got to work. It'd been at least a decade and a half since he'd had cocoa, but it didn't take all that long to make.

Fuck. I had another episode after falling asleep at Ellie's. The past few days of little sleep must've caught up with me.

No. I can't lie in this thing. That's the rule.

I felt normal. For the first time since this clusterfuck happened, I felt alive. I was just a guy kicking back and having a meal with...

Ellie. Mom.

It was like I'd dreamed. The beer was cold, the food so damn good I can still taste it. Chicken parmesan.

The TV show was SWAT and decent. The movie afterward was shit— a romantic comedy of some sort, but I didn't give a damn because I was home. Ellie was there.

I must've fallen asleep.

My heart is still banging in my chest. Sweat. For a second I thought it was blood.

Fuck. My skin burns. I can feel the whip.

My throat hurts like hell. I'm almost afraid to ask what I screamed. Whatever it was must've been bad. It's written all over Levi's face. But he won't ever tell me, and I won't ever have the balls to ask.

Ellie was here. I didn't ever want her to see this monster I've become. She shouldn't ever get tainted by this bullshit, but she is. The darkness I've fought is on her now. I'd hoped she could move on, but I know my sweet Peanut won't walk away.

How the fuck can I make her walk away when she's the only reason I fight?

Strawberries. Her hair smelled like strawberries. I can't even smell the vanilla and lavender like I always do. Is that a good thing? Deviations are progress.

Fuck if I know. How can any of this shit be good?

What am I feeling? This is the part I hate, but if Doc ever reads this, she'll drill my ass until she gets an answer. I'm pissed. I had these episodes under control.

Why now?

I had a good night. A damn good one.

I was a normal guy for a few hours. I wasn't the broken half-man.

I should go, leave the cottage while Ellie's in the kitchen fussing over cocoa I'll likely puke up. My gut's in knots thinking about a conversation with her or Cord. She wasn't ever supposed to know about this shit.

Jesse wanted to add more, but he heard Ellie's quiet approach and knew his time was up. The rest would wait. The entry wasn't the typical fare after an episode. He hadn't focused on the details because, for once, they hadn't been at the forefront of his mind. He'd felt the pain, the terror.

But Ellie had been there.

He glanced at Levi, who remained silent as always. The man had seen him through countless episodes. He'd hoped to hell they were through this patch of their friendship. The one-sidedness grated on Jesse in a way he couldn't ever forget. There were no words or actions to repay all Levi had done.

"Thanks, man."

"Anytime, brother. Anytime." Levi stood and took the tray when Ellie arrived.

She plopped down near Jesse—within touching distance but not the skin-to-skin close he'd gotten before, back when his mind had been too confused to process the contact.

He hadn't minded her touch. In fact, he wanted to haul her closer and experience it once more while his mind was firing on all cylinders. But he had no business blurring the lines. A woman like Ellie deserved a man who could be there for her in all ways.

Sex.

She deserved a man who could fuck her hard, long, and often.

"I brought some snacks," she whispered.

Jesse glanced down at the peanut butter chocolate chip cookies on a large plate. Three cups of steaming cocoa were passed out before the rightness of the moment slowed the pounding of his chest.

Peanut butter.

No matter where he'd woken, Jesse had always craved peanut butter afterward. Doctor Sinclair said it was a symbol for Ellie, what they'd shared and what he'd left behind. But Jesse hadn't ever let his talks with the shrink go too far when it came to the woman doling out cocoa and cookies in the middle of the night.

"I'd best take mine to go," Levi said as he rose with a cup of cocoa in one hand and a stack of cookies in the other. "I've got a perimeter shift starting in a few hours."

Jesse grunted. They'd increased their security presence around the perimeter back when assassins attacked the compound to try and kill Mary and Vi. "Thanks, man."

"Appreciate the cookies," Levi said. "And the cocoa."

Ellie moved to stand.

"Sit. I'll see you both later."

Jesse watched the man leave. Nervousness chewed in his gut as silence loomed. He bit into a cookie for lack of anything to say. There was so much to talk about, yet none of it came easily. She wouldn't understand.

Would she?

"If you need to finish the journal entry, I can go in my room," she whispered.

Jesse swallowed. "I'm sorry, Peanut. I wasn't trying to hide anything. When I first wake, I'm confused and still half in the nightmare."

"Do you have them often?"

Yes. No. Jesse sipped the cocoa and let the sweet, chocolaty warmth roll down his throat. The scent permeated his nostrils and chased more of the phantom tendrils away.

"I used to have them every night. They aren't as often now. I used to sometimes have them during the day, though those were flash-backs and way worse," he admitted.

"Does it help? Journaling?"

Jesse studied Ellie a moment. "I must've been loud for you to hear me from your room."

"I was awake and heard something. A crash maybe. I decided to investigate." Ellie drank her cocoa and watched him over the rim of her mug.

He recognized the haunted exhaustion on her face, the way she studied him as though he held the answers to a question she dared not ask. He'd been like that with Sinclair at first. Too afraid to ask for help. Not knowing what the hell he needed help with.

"You're having nightmares," Jesse guessed.

Her blue eyes widened. "How did you know?"

"About Phil?"

She shook her head. "The accident."

Son of a bitch. Jesse had been so wrapped up in worrying about his mom and Zoey and the boys, he'd never thought to ask Ellie how she was handling the aftermath. She'd been amazing that day. A warrior.

No. A mamma bear protected her cubs.

"You know, Sinclair will kick your ass if you don't journal it right away," Jesse said. "That's important."

"I—" Ellie's lips tipped in a forced grin despite the wariness in her gaze. The woman had always been easy to read because she never held anything back. "I know."

Jesse set the cocoa and cookies down. He reached out and ran a thumb across her cheek. "Please tell me you're seeing Sinclair about the accident, Peanut."

She looked down. "She's so busy, Jesse. Her schedule is crazy."

"You need to talk to her. She can help."

"I will."

"Soon," he said.

"She works from seven in the morning to well after nine or ten at night every day, Jesse. I can't add to that workload."

Jesus. He hadn't ever noticed, and Marshall and Nolan hadn't mentioned it. Did they know?

"Fuck. We've screwing up with her like we did with you. She needs help." He'd talk to Nolan. "You want to talk about your nightmare, Ellie?"

She shook her head. "I'm fine."

Jesse picked up a cookie and took a bite. The morsel melted in his mouth. "You're an even better cook than I remember."

"I've had lots of practice. Baking is my escape, like Vi has quilling and Rhea has music and Bree has that ridiculous game she plays." Ellie rolled her eyes and sipped her cocoa.

Jesse chuckled. "Bree is a bit scary. What game?"

"You don't want to know. She makes me farm it for her when she gets busy. She's the union leader and there's all sorts of drama and politics going on. You'd think it was a civil war instead of a phone game."

Laughter rumbled from Jesse. Ellie's eyes twinkled with delight. "And Rhea's music gets a bit creepy sometimes. She's into some Mongolian throat metal of some sort right now. I went down there one day and thought I'd walked in on some ancient sacrificial ritual."

While Jesse enjoyed hearing about her day-to-day in the present, he needed answers to some questions plaguing him about the time in between. After he'd left. The delicious cookies gave him the first question he'd contemplated often. "What happened, Peanut? Why didn't you open a restaurant like you wanted?"

Ellie choked on the cocoa she'd just swallowed. He reached for her, but she recovered. "Wow. I barely remember that."

It'd been her sole dream outside the two of them married with babies—lots and lots of babies. He forced back thoughts of the latter and waited out the silence. How could she barely remember what'd once been so important?

"You had scrapbooks of recipes," he said. "Pattern swatches you stole from my mom's sewing chest you insisted would be perfect tablecloth patterns."

Red rose in her cheeks. "I think she knew I stole those."

"She raised six boys and a hellion of a daughter. Nothing escaped her notice." Jesse chuckled. "Not that it mattered. Ma always loved you. You could've stolen everything in the house, and she would've let you slide. Heck, she'd chew me out anytime I upset you."

Ellie smiled. "She's an amazing mom."

"I'm sure yours is, too, in her own way."

"She's had a rough go. That changes a person," Ellie whispered.

"You've been too busy caring for her to live your life. That's it, isn't it?"

"She needs me. You would've done the same thing."

Probably, but he had siblings to help. A community. And his mom would've had his ass if he'd made her the center of his world. Jesse didn't want to fight with Ellie, not when he was still too raw from the nightmare.

"You're a hell of a woman, Ellie Travers," he whispered. "The biggest mistake I ever made was leaving you."

"My biggest regret was letting you go." Ellie looked away, as if she was as rattled by what she'd said as he'd been with his admission. "I didn't mean to blurt that out. I'm sorry."

"I didn't mean to make you uncomfortable, Ellie. I'm sorry."

"You didn't. It's just..." She took a deep breath he tracked as her breasts moved higher. "What the hell are we doing, Jesse? One minute we can't be in the same room without you snarling or me cowering. Then we're kinda okay but ignoring each other. Then we're chatty. And now we're..."

"I have no clue what to do with you in my life, Ellie. I can't be what I once was for you," Jesse said. "You know that."

"I know." She swallowed. "But I can't walk away like it's nothing. Whatever this is between us is something, Jesse. I can't pretend I'm not worried about your nightmares. I don't want to ignore that or anything else to do with you."

"And I can't take a backseat in dealing with your bastard ex," Jesse admitted. "Even though I should."

"So what do we do?"

"I have no clue," he admitted. "We take it minute by minute and day by day. We pave our own road, Peanut. Whatever it is, we decide it together. I won't let anyone else determine our path. I can't lose you. Not again."

"I'm not going anywhere, Jesse."

The determination in her voice offered a warmth which penetrated deep within him. For a moment he almost believed they'd find a road where they'd keep whatever this was between them.

"I should go and let you finish your journal," she said as she stood.

"I'm done, but go try and get some rest. It's early still." Jesse motioned toward the mugs and leftover cookies. "I'll take care of this and then head out."

"There are extra pillows and blankets in the hall closet if you need more than what's there and want to crash on the sofa again," she offered.

That wasn't a viable option. Another episode could happen, and he wasn't ready to share more of his darkness with her. "Goodnight, Ellie."

"Goodnight, Jesse."

6

A soft knock on the door a few minutes after Jesse left startled Ellie. Was he back? Was something wrong?

Surprised to find Cord, she opened the door. "Is everything okay?" She didn't mention Jesse because she wasn't sure if his brother knew about the episodes. It wasn't her place to say anything to anyone.

He prowled into the living room and looked around. The assessment was swift, but thorough. Adrenaline surged in her as her mind raced. Was something wrong? She tracked his gaze when it lifted to the ceiling.

The surveillance drone.

Ellie swallowed. "He's okay."

Cord's attention shifted to her. He dropped a stack of folders onto the coffee table. They landed with a thud. "You thought I didn't know."

"What he went through leaves more than scars. He's strong. He'll get through it," she said. "He's a good man. A good soldier."

He took a couple steps toward her, but she held her ground. "I lost my brother in that hole."

Tension corded her spine in steely determination even though the pain in his voice struck her heart. "You didn't."

"I did. Back when Mary's shit was going down, Riley said that bitch Rachelle was ghosting through life," Cord said.

Ellie wanted to stop the man and correct his assessment of Rachelle. Though she'd tried to kill Riley, Rachelle wasn't a bitch. She was a severely troubled woman who...

She almost killed Riley.

Okay.

She was a bitch.

"Jesse's the ghost," Cord clipped. "He's so good at faking normal no one sees a part of him is still back there. In hell."

Ellie's eyes burned. Her vision blurred as she blinked away the tears. Whatever this was, she wasn't prepared for the enormity of Cord's presence right now. "Cord, I..."

"Marshall and Nolan think you're trouble. They've been on board with kicking your ass to the curb since the first day you showed up," Cord said. "Dylan's on the fence."

Her gut clenched. Big brothers held a lot of influence, but she wondered who was influencing who. Had Jesse's initial desire to vacate her from his life driven his brothers' scorn of her, or had they instigated it?

"Dallas saw it first."

Ellie jerked at the shift in his tone. From angry to soft, confused. "Saw what?"

"The little shit I didn't pick up on because I don't remember you with him back then."

Oh God. Ellie blinked tears back and turned. She padded into the kitchen and grabbed a bottle of water from the fridge. The action gave her a second to collect her thoughts before she returned to the living room and set the extra down on the coffee table beside the folders he'd tossed there.

She opened the bottle and drank. The cold liquid didn't detract from the tension filling the room, but at least she had something to think about other than Jesse and her back then. Before he'd left for war. Before he'd been imprisoned. Before he'd almost died.

She sat on the sofa and glared up at him. "I'm not hurting anyone. He hasn't noticed. Go ahead and chew my ass out if you want, but I'm not stopping."

The little shit. Ellie admitted she'd gone a smidge overboard with the small things meant to give a piece of happiness to not only Jesse, but the other operatives as well. Homemade goodies. Personalized jars of jellies.

It'd started as a compulsion to give everyone a taste of good after a rotten day or a horrible mission. Then it'd morphed into a personal project she hadn't admitted to anyone. Yet Dallas had noticed and shared with Cord. Who else knew?

"You keep the mess hall stocked with his favorite stuff."

"Everybody's favorites are there if I know what they are," she argued.

"Peanut butter cups in the candy dispenser on your desk on the days Jesse signs checks," Cord said.

Okay, that was for Jesse. Ellie took another swallow of water as Cord sat down on the sofa beside her. She didn't know the youngest of the Mason men well. He'd chased around after them growing up, but keeping up with Riley had been a full-time chore. She barely remembered the quiet youngest brother.

"Peanut butter cookies. Peanut protein bars."

"Everyone should have a dose of home when they're away risking their lives," Ellie whispered.

"And you give it to all the teams now so you can have an excuse to see to Jesse," Cord said.

She did. The compulsion had become a reality shortly after Kamren's situation. She'd set cookies out in all the operations rooms and in the mess hall, but that hadn't been enough. The past couple weeks she'd started making little baggies of sweets and sneaking them into the operatives' personal lockers when she saw their team on The Arsenal's list of upcoming ops.

"I like baking. It's not a big deal."

"Maybe not, but it is to me." Cord took the bottle of water and uncapped it. "And to Dallas."

Ellie looked away as he drank. Jesse's brothers were almost as amazing as him. Everyone at The Arsenal was. She wished she was a brilliant computer person like Mary or Vi or Zoey. Or Cord. Heck, she wished she was a scientist like Bree or Rhea. Or a kickass operative like Addy. Or a budding sleuth like Riley.

But she was a teacher who'd lost her job and was answering phones and processing vendor payments.

"You're good with the boys," Cord commented. "Dallas watched like a hawk the first few weeks. That's why he noticed."

Of course. He hadn't been fully committed to her teaching his sons, but that's what made him such a kickass dad.

Jesse would be a kickass dad.

The thought punched her heart hard. She clutched the area and forced a breath. He wouldn't ever have a kid of his own, would he? Ellie wasn't sure. She had ten billion questions about Jesse's captivity and his injuries, but no business asking, even if someone was willing to answer.

"You're good for Jesse." Cord studied her. Ellie stayed silent, too shocked to speak. "This last mission was the first one he hesitated to take. For a moment I could've sworn he'd turn it over rather than leave you."

"Most wouldn't say that's a good thing, Cord," she commented softly.

"Then they're crazy. We put our lives on the line every time we go on a mission, Ellie. The day we don't give a damn whether we come back or not is the day we likely won't. I've watched my brother dance that line too long."

"He has Doctor Sinclair. Besides, Mary and Vi are really good. They'd spot problems if Jesse had any." Ellie prayed they would because Cord's statement terrified her. What if he was right?

She hoped he was an overly worried little brother. Nothing more.

"Jesse's a chameleon. Each of us has a skill, a unique ability in the field that makes us a bit better at one or two things than anyone else on our team or at The Arsenal. You don't get to lead without it." Cord studied her a moment. "He always blended in with whoever he was around growing up. I remember envying him that ability. Dylan and Nolan mentioned it once, back when Jesse first returned. That skill likely kept him alive."

God. Ellie squeezed her eyes shut. She couldn't take anymore of whatever this was. It hurt way, way too much. "Why are you here?"

"Because you're the first real hope I see of getting that piece of my brother back, the part of him he left in that hole." Cord tapped the files. "This is my going all in on you bringing him back to us, Ellie."

"W-what are those?"

"Answers. Horrors."

"No." She stood, too tempted by the stack Cord had assembled. Answers. "Those aren't yours to give, not without permission. I don't have a right to those."

"You do. We all do." Cord stood.

Determination shone in his eyes—eyes so like Jesse's it hurt to maintain contact, but she did. This was too important to shrink away from. "I know you mean well, but this isn't my business."

"Let me set you straight on something, then I'll go," Cord said, his voice tight and low. "This is *war*. We didn't ask for it, but we were all dragged into it the day those assholes took Jesse."

"Cord..."

"This is a war. I'll fight dirty and use anything and everything within my power to win because I love Jesse. I want him back. *All the way* back." Cord took another step closer. "I know my family and the teams we have assembled are onboard with this war, Ellie. We fight it in the trenches alongside him every goddamn day. Levi watches his six twenty-four seven. There is *nothing* The Arsenal won't do for Jesse."

Ellie loved that Jesse had so many fighting for him—helping him heal.

"We won't ever get that part of him back without you," Cord declared. "You're the key."

"No, I'm not," she denied. "He left me, Cord. You were young. You don't remember, but he chose that life over one with me. I'm not a key to anything but what could have been if he'd chosen a different path."

"'The biggest mistake I ever made was leaving you.'"

Ellie gasped. "Don't you dare throw his words back. You spied on him?"

"Clue in, Ellie. When I said this was war and I'd fight dirty and do anything for Jesse, I damned well meant it," Cord said, his voice louder than before. "You're the key. You damned well know it."

"I don't." Ellie shook her head, but the denial was bitter on her tongue. "What do you want from me? What do you think I can do?"

"*Everything.* I want you in those trenches fighting and clawing whatever monsters you get to that we'll never touch. I want you to find every scar and heal it." Cord motioned toward the pile of folders. "That's all I've gathered about what happened. It's not much, but it's a start. I've seen your Google searches, and I know you've bugged Logan a few times with questions he refused to answer. Most of what I thought you wanted is there, too, but there are a lot of holes I can't patch without alerting Mary or Vi."

And Cord didn't want to bring anyone else into what he'd been doing. God. "How long have you been gathering this stuff?"

"Since he got back," Cord said with a whisper. "A couple of my brothers went and blew shit up and kicked some asses to process what Jesse went through. One tried fucking his way through half the state. They talked it out with one another and got a bit of closure, but we won't ever heal until he's happy."

And Jesse's youngest brother had buried himself in the redaction to try and get answers he might never obtain. He was traumatized by what had happened to Jesse but had likely never spoken to anyone about it.

Neither had she.

"Cord, you should talk to Jesse about this," she said gently. She touched his arm. "He should know you're worried."

"He's not ready for us. What he went through..." Cord swallowed, visibly shaken by whatever he was thinking. "I don't even know how he survived. He returned to us, but he's not home, Ellie."

"Because he's a ghost." He was haunted by what had happened. Who wouldn't be? "That's what the therapy is for, Cord."

"Yeah, he's a thousand times better than he was before Sinclair came onboard," Cord said. "You're the key to finding the rest of him."

Ellie stood, too shocked to reply as the man left. Minutes ticked by as she stared at the pile of folders she had no business having. If Jesse ever found out…

This is war.

Tears tumbled down her cheeks. Cord and everyone else at The Arsenal were fighting a silent war to help Jesse overcome what'd happened. Turning away wasn't an option. She'd been trying to ferret out answers to mount an attack of her own because she'd seen the haunted gazes, the pained expressions as he watched his nephews play.

He'd never have boys of his own.

I want at least six babies, Peanut.

Six? How about four.

Fine. Eight.

We aren't having eight babies, Jesse James Mason.

She'd curled into him and sighed her acceptance for however many babies he wanted because when it came to Jesse James Mason, there wasn't anything she wouldn't give him.

That hadn't changed. She may have married Phil, but a part of her had always been Jesse's. She wrapped her arms around her waist and fell to her knees and sobbed.

If there was any chance at healing even one of Jesse's emotional scars, she had to try. With a trembling hand, she picked up the first folder and started reading.

*M*ornings with Ellie's mom weren't ever simple. It didn't take long for Ellie to realize this morning wouldn't be an exception.

"That Mason isn't what I expected," her mom commented.

Ellie turned from the stove and glanced at her mom, who'd taken a seat at the bar of the small cottage. The first portion of the morning routine had been simpler than expected. The bathroom was outfitted with the same walk-in tub and accoutrements that the Mason ranch house had been upgraded with. She'd known a few of the new houses were being outfitted with them, but she hadn't expected to be put in one.

"Jesse. You know his name, Ma."

Ellie continued working on an omelet. Some things never changed. No one would ever be good enough for her as far as her mom was concerned.

As much as she appreciated the sentiment, she was too emotionally raw to handle it this morning. She'd been up most of the night pouring through the files Cord had provided. Details about the assignment that'd left Jesse alone in the middle of a war and surrounded by potential enemies were sketchy, but Ellie knew the why didn't matter.

Not anymore.

"He's haunted. No one goes through what he did and comes out the same," her mom said.

Cord had said pretty much the same thing last night.

But her mom never talked with anyone and never went anywhere without Ellie, which meant she hadn't heard much about Jesse and his "ordeal." Folks in the tri-county thought they knew the Masons better than anyone else.

"He's a good man."

"Never said he wasn't. They sure moved you out here quick when Phil started messing with you."

Approval resonated in her mom's voice. Ellie paused, a bit surprised and curious what Jesse had done to win her mom over. "They're good people."

"I don't like that Phil's messing with you, Ellie-belly."

"I know, Ma. It'll die down soon. You know how he is."

"Don't gloss over his bad. You let that Mason and the others see for themselves what he's like. Don't cover for him. He never did anything to earn that from you," her mom said.

Ellie tightened. "Is that what you think? That I covered up for him?"

"Didn't you? You never let anyone see the bruises. You always took the blame for the fights. Keeping the peace isn't always the best option."

"There was only so much I could fight when up against him. You know his family, Ma."

"I know, baby girl. I was up many nights worrying about you tied up with them."

The confession startled Ellie. She cut the omelet in half and plated it. Turning, she set one plate in front of her mom and studied the woman. A light shone in her gaze that hadn't been there before, as if something had shifted.

"We've had our troubles over the years. I wasn't ever the best mother, but I tried my best. Things got jumbled in my head after your dad passed. Lots of things became your worry that shouldn't have been."

Ellie took her mom's hand. "I love you, Ma. You're the best mom I could've asked for."

"No. No, I wasn't, but the fact you think so fills my heart and soul. I've been worrying about you, what'll happen when I'm gone. Last night, watching television and seeing you smile for the first time..."

God. Ellie squeezed her eyes shut.

"Then you laughed and I knew."

"Ma..."

"I knew you'd be okay when my time comes 'cause that boy won't rest until you are. Doctors say it'll be soon, a few months at most," her mom said. "One last treatment. My body's not reacting the way it should, Ellie-belly. You know what the doctor said."

Ellie avoided any thoughts of what little time remained. Her mom had enough worries on her mind without the morbidity of that particular conversation.

"I'm sorry I was always so opinionated and headstrong. I wasn't the easiest child to raise."

"Stubborn, just like your dad."

Ellie smiled. "You think...you think Dad would've liked Jesse?"

"Yeah." Her mom patted her hand. "He would've liked him for you. But I'm worried about that boy. I heard the ruckus last night."

"He went through a lot."

"I know you think I don't hear things, but folks call enough. I've heard what people say about him. Is it true?"

"Not all, but most," Ellie said. "From what I know." She knew far more than she had before last night. Surgeries had repaired a "significant amount" of the injuries sustained during his imprisonment. The vagueness of the verbiage pissed her off.

"Then the boy's got problems of his own. He'll need you fighting those battles with him." The light deepened in her mom's gaze. "That brother is right. This is war. Don't turn and run. We don't run from a fight, Ellie-belly."

"I know." Ellie had already decided she was all in. "He's worth the fight. I love you, Ma."

"I love you, too, Ellie-belly."

7

*E*llie glanced about the crowded whiteboard room. It'd been a long morning. Jesse, along with his entire team and Marshall, had escorted her to Nomad National to empty her safety deposit box. Marshall's original plan to remove the contents himself failed because Old Man Bufort, the bank President, was out of town with his family for an extended Scottish Highlands vacation and unreachable. Translation—no one at the bank was willing to cut corners so she had to remove the contents herself.

It'd taken longer to "secure the area" than it had for Ellie to get the contents. From start to finish, the trip into Nomad had taken less than an hour. Mary, Vi, and Zoey had met them in The Arsenal's parking lot and whisked the CD and everything else away.

That'd been half an hour ago.

Jesse, Marshall, and the rest of the Mason brothers were gathered with the team leaders and Jud. Ellie overheard conversation about an upcoming mission to Cuba and hoped Jesse and his team weren't going. Anyone going to Cuba was a bad idea in her mind.

The door opened, and the women entered with matching grim expressions. Kamren entered behind them. Mary and Vi didn't even smile at their husbands—a fact which everyone in the room must've noticed because the tension went from a solid three to eight within seconds.

"We asked Kamren to help us with the video footage so we'd have a better idea of what we were looking at since a lot of the audio was corrupted," Mary said. "It was obvious, but every piece of data is important."

Kamren moved to Dallas and wrapped her arms around him as she buried her head in his neck. The two whispered, but Ellie couldn't hear anything from across the room. Dallas held the woman close and moved them side to side. Did the gentle movement calm her?

Ellie wished she'd had that sort of connection with her husband. She'd always planned to marry only once and spend the rest of her life being her husband's other half. The possibility of that had fled when Jesse left, but she'd tried hard to find it with Phil.

The relationship she'd had with the arrogant bastard had been created by necessity—a fact that had poisoned the foundation before it was even constructed. Ellie had made a lot of foolish decisions back then.

"First off, the majority of the CD is an encrypted dataset of some sort. HERA's working on it. Buried within the files were some old video clips," Mary said.

"We're gonna need passwords and user IDs for your ex," Zoey said. "People tend to reuse IDs and passwords. Anything you can remember will help speed up HERA's decryption of the rest of the files."

"Sure." Phil hadn't ever trusted her with passwords and user IDs, but she'd seen more than a few scrawled on slips of paper inside his office while cleaning.

She grabbed one of the small tablets off the middle of the table, along with a pen, and wrote down the ones she could remember. Although it'd been a while, the arrogance and strangeness of the words made them memorable. She also included the email addresses she'd run across.

"Ellie, did you ever watch this? Or look at it?" Vi asked.

"No." She shook her head. "I wasn't sure what it was. It just looked important."

"That's an understatement," Zoey muttered. "Are we really gonna have to sit through this whole thing again? Can't we just give the highlights?"

"Dylan and his brothers need to see the people in the video. It's too grainy for HERA to identify most of them, so we need to rely on anything they may pick up on if they know anyone," Mary said.

Ellie smiled at the way Mary placed Dylan first. Kamren likely did the same with Dallas. Their Mason was the counterpoint of the Mason world as far as they were concerned. Ellie did the same thing with Jesse.

The biggest mistake I ever made was leaving you.

Jesse's declaration last night had started a shockwave of conversation Ellie regretted. She'd admitted too much to him. Emotion clogged her throat when she looked across the room where he stood —literally as far away as he could get and still be in the same room. The distance may as well have been a continent away, though.

Whatever tentative bond they'd formed over chicken parmesan and television was gone. Running scared. She could almost taste the terror wafting off him, and it pained her to sit back and give him that retreat. She'd bought her all-in pass to the war for Jesse's heart, though, so she'd follow him down whatever hellholes he tumbled into.

"Let's get started." Mary punched a button on her laptop. A grainy video began on the large monitor behind them. "We cleaned it up the best we could."

Headlights and growling engines drowned out most of the anxious screams and revelry. Ellie recognized the scene well enough because she'd partaken in it more than a few times. Dallas had once been one of the best street racers in Marville. Only two had been better—Dominic Santiago and his little sister Dani.

The images cut away to black. Wind battered until the audio was nothing more than white noise as the camera zoomed in to...

A field.

A group had gathered in the distance. The video zoomed in closer.

"Oh god." Ellie looked away a moment. Her heart thudded in her chest.

Don't be a ninny. They're all here because of you.

Ellie focused on the video once more. A young girl lay motionless on the ground. A man was raping her. His bare white ass was evident as he...

Mary paused the video.

"We had to watch this more than a few times to realize the people gathered around him were saying something. Kamren was able to help."

Kamren was beyond amazing. She read lips. Ellie imagined the skill was more of a curse than a gift in times like this.

"They're cheering him on. Go, Ronnie," Kamren said. "The only Ronnie I know is Ronnie Haskell."

Ellie gasped. The former Marville sheriff was on video raping someone. Phil had the recording. How?

"This is the part HERA couldn't do much with because of the poor quality," Vi said.

Disgust consumed Ellie as the video played, then stopped as Jesse and his brothers discussed who people in the footage may have been. It'd been many years since it'd been shot. She and Jesse used to hang out at the races many nights. Most had taken place on small back roads rarely travelled after dark.

Dallas had stopped racing after Dom's arrest and subsequent imprisonment. He'd enlisted in the military—one of the last Masons to march into combat. Jesse had been the final brother to join a couple weeks later. She'd been a freshman in college. He'd been a junior.

"Are you okay?" Bree asked.

Ellie blinked. When had Bree arrived? The blonde took her hand and smiled.

"Sorry we're late. Something came up," Rhea whispered from Ellie's other side.

The video had stopped yet again. Vi and Mary were typing into the laptop. Images of people were on the screen. Ronnie Haskell and Eric Brine.

"Eric was Phil's best friend in high school, I think. They both went to the private school in Nomad after Marville Elementary. I remember folks were surprised because the Brines didn't have the kind of money needed for a private school," Ellie commented into the silence.

"Okay, we have another section of video that'll be harder to get through." Vi paused and looked over at Kamren. "Sweetie, why don't you go outside?"

"I'm not leaving." The woman shook her head and swiped at the tears escaping her eyes. Dallas drew her back into his arms. "This is my fight, too. I stay."

Mary looked around the table. "Let's contain our reactions so we get through this without missing details."

Ellie looked at Jesse. His jaw clenched as he and his brothers all nodded. Mary had looked right at them, which meant it'd affect them more than others. Why?

Worry quickened Ellie's pulse as the video started. The same grainy quality spotlighted what seemed to be the same field as before, except there weren't any headlights this time. A lone beam of light appeared. The camera zoomed in.

"Nolan?" The voice was soft, but audible. "I came alone. Dom and Raul didn't see me leave the race."

No. No. No.

The video paused. "We thought we had the timetable of these recordings, but this part confused us," Vi commented.

Nolan's jaw twitched as he glared across the table. "That's what you're having problems with? The timetable?"

"Don't growl at my wife," Jud warned.

"Nolan was on leave for half my senior year," Dallas said as he wrapped Kamren in his arms. "An injury he couldn't talk about."

The video continued. Daniella Santiago, Kamren's best friend, continued calling out for Nolan. Tears rolled down Ellie's face because, even though she had no idea what she was about to see, the pain and anger in Kamren's reaction blanketed the room.

The woman never broke down. She was one of the strongest women Ellie had ever met. Yet she was sobbing in Dallas's arms. Why didn't he take her outside?

Because he respected her need to be part of the fight even if it hurt like hell. Ellie swallowed. Dallas was so much like Jesse.

Ellie fisted her hands in her lap and remained silent as headlights flicked on from behind Dani—who looked to be around thirteen or fourteen. Ellie remembered how the girl used to shadow the Masons. Nolan had once raced the streets, way before Dallas took the wheel. Then Dom had taken the reign as street king when Nolan went off to war.

"Nolan?"

An engine growled as the headlights approached. Fast. Ellie gasped as Dani started running across the field to escape the car. Then a second vehicle appeared—a truck with running lights along the top. It cut Dani's escape off.

She fell.

The camera jumped up and down. Breathing sounded in the microphone. The person was running forward. Closer.

Disgust rolled in Ellie's stomach, but she refused to look away.

Dani was involved in something Phil had kept on a CD for *years.* Ellie had known about the CD a while and had done nothing. Guilt clogged her throat.

"Let's get to the summary," Jesse growled. "We don't need to see more. We'll review later."

"Pertinent facts: Aaron Patterson, Juan Hidalgo, and Raymond Jordan are identifiable as the attackers in this video. There are others present in the background. Images are too grainy, and HERA can't do voice recognition on this. Many of the assailants were still going through puberty. Voice patterns would've changed too much," Mary said. "We've fed it into HERA anyway in case we can clean up the footage anymore," Mary said. "We all know what the next step is."

"Christ." Nolan pinched his nose with his fingers. "This is why."

Dani had a hatred for the Masons no one had ever understood—even Kamren. She'd heard the two women arguing about it several times since Kamren had hooked up with Dallas.

"Juan and Raymond were the two Dom went away for," Dallas said.

"Now I want to give Dom a medal," Dylan said.

"I don't understand. Why didn't she tell me?" Kamren asked. "This is what happened. She wasn't the same afterward."

"Erm, guys, there's another clip," Zoey said. "I thought they were through, but there's another after the snow."

Everyone focused on the screen as the field returned. Two dead men were sprawled out and visible on the footage. Voices rose above the wind.

"Damn video jacked, man. I missed the kills."

That voice. Icy tendrils crawled along Ellie's spine. "That's Phil."

"Are you sure?" Mary asked as they paused the footage.

She nodded. A hand settled on her shoulder. She looked up and saw Jesse standing behind her.

He cupped her face. "This is going to be okay, Peanut. We'll figure out what all this is."

"Why? Why would he have recorded this and kept it and done nothing?" She swiped at the tears rolling down her face. "Sorry, I know this isn't about me. Not anymore. There's something way bigger than my ex-husband being the biggest asshole of all time."

"Look at me, Peanut." Jesse crouched down so their gazes locked. His hand rested behind her head. "You are the main focus here. We're going to figure out what the hell that CD is about and lock it down, but you being safe from your ex and his threats is the main priority."

"I didn't know. I swear if I'd known what was on there, I would've done something." She looked over at Kamren. "I didn't know."

"None of us did," Dallas said.

"There's a bit more for this footage," Zoey said.

"Play it," Marshall ordered. "Then we get to work figuring this out. Until this is sorted and Ellie is secure, we aren't taking any more cases. Addy and her team will handle Cuba as planned, but nothing more beyond that."

Everyone in the room nodded. Shock resonated within her. They were shutting down for new cases because of her. Because of the CD she should have looked at long ago.

"This isn't your fault," Jesse whispered in her ear. "Don't take blame that's not yours."

"I was married to a monster and had no idea."

"We don't know what his involvement was," Jesse said.

"He was there. That makes him a monster."

"We'll take him down," Gage said. "We won't rest until we do. Play the rest, Little Bit."

Zoey tapped a button on the laptop. The voices returned as the camera zoomed in on the two bodies. Phil's voice thundered through the speakers. "I wanted the kills on video. That'd be better leverage."

"We've got them on the other camera, man. We're solid. We own this town and everyone in it."

"Damn straight," Phil said. "What now?"

"Now I finish this. It ain't over 'til someone goes down for those two. I know just who."

The footage stopped. Vi shut off the feed and looked around the room. "The second voice?"

"Javier," Dallas and Kamren said at the same time.

"Dom's cousin? The dead cousin?" Zoey asked.

Dallas nodded. "This must've been the night Dom supposedly murdered those two guys. Now we know he may not have even done it."

"Dom had every reason to kill those fuckers. They raped his sister," Jud repeated.

Everyone in the room nodded. Street justice. Ellie was more than familiar with the term because it ruled in Marville most of the time. Sheriff Haskell had always been a waste of a uniform, which left the town and the rest of the county on their own to handle troubles.

"I'm thinking we missed taking a few dirtbags with Kamren's mess," Addy said.

"We won't miss anyone this time," Nolan said. "We need to find the other camera footage he referenced. Every prick there for those attacks is maggot food."

Mary raised her eyebrows. Everyone chuckled. Ellie knew the man had a strong dislike for worms and maggots because of an op where Mary saved his life. She'd heard Nolan's brothers teasing him about it many times since her arrival at The Arsenal.

"But we've gotta figure out how this involves Phil and why he's suddenly nervous about it. Turning it over to authorities doesn't help get Ellie safe," Jesse said.

He was focused on getting her safe. Though the focus had right-fully redirected to getting justice for Dani and the other girl on the videos, Jesse was still focused on how all of this affected Ellie. The realization spread warmth through her. She wasn't alone in this fight, whatever it was.

"We knew we missed some rotten apples with Kamren's crap. It's time we finish the cleanup," Jud said. "Even if it means gutting the entire town."

Ellie swallowed. The word gutting had an entirely different meaning when Jud said it. Marville had its problems—to be frank, it was dirtier than most small towns likely were. But it was her home, and there were good people mired in the muck of this drama.

"They aren't all bad," Ellie whispered.

"We know, Peanut," Jesse said, his hand on her knee. "You under-stand we have to investigate these rapes, right? We need to figure out how Phil's tied to all this. The more we uncover for ourselves, the sooner you'll be safe."

Ellie wasn't used to someone fighting her battles. They had kids to rescue from traffickers and terrorists to take down. They'd closed themselves off from doing all of that and all the other commando stuff so they could get her safe and find justice for Dani and the other girl on the video.

Were there more?

Her stomach soured at the thought. "He had other CDs inside a cabinet behind the desk. This one must've fallen into the box somehow."

"Then we get the others," Marshall said. "Who's our best B and E?"

"Everyone?" Zoey asked. "You're all kickass commandoes. Breaking into that asshole's place won't be a challenge."

"Fallon," Mary and Vi said at the same time. The latter added, "We don't ever assume a mission will be easy."

Everyone looked at Fallon, who was glaring at the two women. Ellie knew the man was good with explosives. He was the "boom" in missions.

"We don't want to blow the place up," Cord commented.

Mary and Vi stared at Cord but offered no explanation for their decision.

"Fallon and Jesse," Mary said. "We'll need schematics of the house as a starting point."

Ellie nodded. "I'll sketch something out."

"Jud, start applying pressure in Marville," Marshall said. "Make sure everyone knows we're leaving no stone unturned this time around. People come forward with what they know, and we'll take it easy on them. The Texas Rangers don't need to know."

"Riley will want to be in on this." Jud crossed his hands in front of him. "She's ready."

The Mason brothers regarded one another a moment, then Nolan grunted. "Watch her six."

"I'll get my team back into position in Marville in case there's chatter when you all apply pressure," Marcus said.

"You need help, let me know. My crew doesn't hang with the local populace at all," Gage offered.

Marcus nodded. "We'll need help locking Dani down. She's not a fan of protection."

"I'll put my team on standby," Nolan said.

"Maybe you'd best hang back from this one," Mary said.

"That's not happening," the man said.

Ellie tightened. "She's right."

All attention shifted to her.

"Whatever happened started because she was out there for *you*. That's why she has issues with Masons. Going to her with this and asking questions is going to make that wound raw all over again. You're not who she needs at her back," Ellie whispered.

"That so?" Nolan asked. "You'd best follow your own advice."

"Meaning?" Ellie pulled back from Jesse, who'd risen with his brother's statement.

"Stop leaning on Jesse so much. You're a raw wound that won't ever heal for him," Nolan said.

"Outside," Jesse growled. "Now."

"What the fuck?" Jesse shoved his brother against the side of the building and waited for a response.

Nolan offered no comment, nor did he push Jesse away. The pain and guilt and rage in his brother's gaze was palpable. Dani had been a shadow who followed Nolan around whenever he came home on leave.

"You want your ass beat?" Jesse asked as he eased off. "You had no business feeding Ellie that shit sandwich. She's going through enough."

"You had another episode last night," Nolan said. He pushed Jesse. "You wanna look me in the face and say it's not because your mind's twisted up in her? In her shit?"

He knew about the episodes. Cord had found out. Levi, Sol, and the rest of his team knew. No one else.

"Not much goes on around here that doesn't hit Mary's or Vi's or Zoey's radar," Nolan commented. "They brought it to my attention because they were concerned. No one else knows."

"You never said anything," Jesse said.

"You'd tell us if you wanted us to know. I've gotta admit it burns—knowing you trust Levi to have your back over one of us."

Jesse had always been tight with his brothers. Growing up they'd shared everything. He, Marshall, Nolan, and Dylan had shared the same friends through most of their formative years, despite the age differences. Since Jesse was in the middle of the pack of six boys, he'd also shared friends with Dallas and Cord.

"It's not like that, brother."

"This isn't about that," Nolan said. "Your business."

"You went after Ellie because of it, so now you gotta hear the why. Brace yourself because you won't like what you hear."

"Oh yeah?" Nolan faced off with Jesse. Hands clenched at his sides. "Bring it on, little brother."

"Levi was there," Jesse spat. He waited for the fact to work its way into Nolan's mind. He'd never told them where or when he'd met Levi.

"He pulled me out of that hole. Disinfected my entire body and saved what was left of my dick. He and his team carted my mostly dead ass through heavy enemy fire. I begged them to let me die. To kill me so they wouldn't have to deal with me."

"Fuck, man."

"Don't. You wanted it. You get it," Jesse said. "I tried, you know. More than once I tried to give you a piece of what happened. I wanted to unload on you. Marshall. Dallas. Dylan. Cord. *Any* of you."

"Anytime. Anywhere," Nolan answered.

"Right. That's why none of you came back after what I said to Dallas. Open com. All of you heard, but no one came and got in my face about it." Jesse shook his head and took a step back as the pain of the statement burned his insides.

Back when Dallas had been looking for his sons, Jesse had taken an opportunity to share a small bit of what he'd gone through to try and get his little brother to open up about his time in The Collective. Fortunately it had worked, and Dallas had worked through the intense shit he'd done for the black ops group.

The gestures Jesse had made to ask for their help had been small —too small. He'd known, but he'd put what he could of himself on the line. He'd hoped it was enough because there wasn't much left.

"Jesus, Jess. I thought you needed space. We all did," Nolan whispered. "You've really thought we wouldn't have your back with this? I would've taken your place. If I could take your pain, I would."

"Jesse, brother." Dallas's pained voice behind Jesse startled him.

"The reason Levi's there every fucking night watching my six is because he gives me no choice. That's not a hell you ask someone to follow you into."

Fuck. He turned and saw the crowd who'd assembled around him. Anger, pain, shame, and remorse filled him when he spotted Ellie, who hovered near the back of the gathered group. Tears pooled in her eyes.

"Forget it," Jesse growled. "It doesn't matter. We take down Perskins and figure out what he's been hiding and handle that. Then we move on."

"Jess, I'm sorry. Fuck, we discussed approaching you so many times I lost count," Marshall said. "It's on me. I locked them down, said you'd come to us when you were ready."

They'd all told him they were there, but Jesse had grown jaded during recovery. Add that to what'd happened in the hole and there was no way in hell he could meet them halfway. Reaching out at all terrified the fuck out of him.

Too many people offered shallow support, then vanished when real shit went down. And it wasn't like Jesse needed or wanted to share the gory details of what'd happened. He got more than enough chances to do that during group therapy and with Doctor Sinclair.

He'd wanted...

Family.

Growing up he'd always had big brothers who kicked the asses of anyone who gave him shit. He'd never spent a moment alone because in a family with seven kids, there was no such thing as privacy. Entering the military had given him that sense of family and belonging tenfold. He'd had a unit. A team.

A second family.

Then everything had gone to shit. He'd lost the sense of family, and even though he'd survived and returned home, a part of him was still back in that hole.

Or dead.

Jesse glanced at Ellie. Up until the chicken parmesan, he hadn't truly relaxed and enjoyed the family around him because he'd been too fucking terrified to lose them if he went crazy. But looking into Ellie's gorgeous eyes and seeing her smile and tasting food she'd made for him had struck his defenses like a battering ram.

Rather than fight the moment, he'd kicked back and enjoyed it. For once he'd forgotten what he'd gone through.

Then it had waylaid him when he fell asleep.

Now this.

"Look, it's cool. Doc says my mind over-processes my emotions at times or some shit. You've all had my six since I got back. Without question," Jesse said. "Forget it. Let's move on."

Nolan's gaze narrowed. Jesse recognized the look. Big brother wasn't moving on. Jesse glanced at everyone else gathered around him. None of them were.

Great.

He ran a hand through his hair. "I can't handle more right now."

"Then later." Nolan put a hand on Jesse's shoulder. "Promise me."

He'd opened a can of worms. Now he'd have to deal with the slimy fucks. He forced a nod.

Nolan moved past him and stopped in front of Ellie. "I'm sorry. I struck out because of what I saw on the video. It had nothing to do with you, Ellie. You've been the best thing to happen to us in many ways."

"Don't ever apologize for looking out for Jesse," Ellie said. "This is a war. We're all in."

Jesse froze. The determination in her voice unlocked one of the many coiled chains around his heart. His soul. She wanted to fight for him. He was a dick for letting her because he had nothing to give her in return, even if she succeeded.

"Is there a reason you're all standing around looking like you're about to brawl?" Levi asked.

Jesse tensed. His second-in-command was loyal to a fault. He'd left the service and kept watching his six. He'd faced a court martial because he'd ignored direct orders to not engage his captors. Sol appeared on the other side of the huddle, as if they'd coordinated a defense.

Marshall smirked and crossed his arms. "I'm pleased as fuck to know they've got your back, brother. We'll all sit down after this is over so you can fill in the holes."

Jesse nodded. Fair enough. He looked at Mary, Vi, and Zoey. "You three keep digging to identify the others. We'll get to work with what we know."

"Feel like taking a ride to Marville?" Dallas asked.

"Let's go." Jesse motioned toward the vehicles.

"Hold up," Addy said. "Where are you two going?"

"To talk with Dani," Dallas said. "Kamren will come with us."

"Right. And having two men with the last name Mason nearby will really help her open up," Kamren said. "You aren't going near my best friend. Not about this."

"We need some answers, sweetheart," Dallas whispered.

"I'll get them. Addy can come with me." Kamren looked at the operative. "Will that work? You're leaving for an op soon, right?"

"Not until the morning. I'm in." The woman looked at Jesse. "Me and my team are all in."

Addy Rugers was one hell of an operative. They'd butted heads the first couple weeks she'd been at The Arsenal, but they'd meshed after she fucked up and threatened to geld him during a meeting one day. Jesse had shared more of his hell with her than the others because she'd relayed more than a few of her own monsters to him.

It'd take one hell of a man to deserve Addy.

"And me," Ellie added.

"No," Jesse said. No way in hell was Ellie getting anywhere near Marville without him.

"I'm not hiding out here and letting all of you fix whatever this is. I won't cower to Phil. He needs to hear I'm out and about. That I'm not scared."

"Are you?" Jesse asked. When she didn't answer right away, he clarified. "Scared?"

"I'm terrified, but I trust you. I trust you all."

A warmth returned inside him—an awareness.

"Are we sure doing this at her work is the right play?" Addy asked.

"She'll bolt otherwise," Kamren said.

"Fine," the woman replied as she looked at Jesse. "You cover exterior, and I handle interior."

Jesse admired the fierce female operative. She'd helped take down her brother's operation when he'd orchestrated Mary's kidnapping and subsequent torture to try and steal HERA. The redhead staring at him expectantly had been Mary's, Vi's, Rhea's and Bree's primary protector before they all came to The Arsenal. Jesse chuckled. "You aren't gonna give on this."

"Nope. And you won't expect me to because it's the right play." The woman moved closer and lowered her voice. "Nothing will happen to her."

He believed her. Jesse nodded. "But Brooklyn goes in, too, before you all arrive. Bystander."

"Done," Kamren said.

⚅

Ellie was crunched in the middle of Bree and Riley in the back seat. She wasn't sure why her newfound friend Bree was riding along, but she'd learned to not ask many questions where the brilliant blonde was concerned because she was a bit different.

"You okay?" Kamren asked from the front seat.

Addy glanced at Ellie from the rearview mirror. The redhead was a great field operative. Ellie had watched her training with the rest of the commandoes a lot.

"I should be asking you that," Ellie said. "I had no idea. I swear."

"I know. Neither did I, though I should've suspected." Kamren grew quite a moment. "The ink."

"What ink?" Riley asked.

"The gang her brother ran had a tattoo of a dog chewing a femur bone. Some of the more hardcore members of the gang had blood drops dripping from the bone. She...she got the tattoo with a drop around that time. I never figured out why, and she wouldn't talk about whatever went down. I remember the timing because everyone had a fit. She was so young to get a tattoo." Kamren's voice softened. "Dom did it himself."

"We'll get some answers," Ellie said.

She glanced over her shoulder.

"They're still behind us," Addy commented.

Heat ran up Ellie's cheeks. Busted. Time to change topics.

"I heard Jud bragging about you to Dylan the other day," Ellie whispered.

"Really?" Riley looked out the side window. "That man never says anything to me."

"He was an assassin. Do you really want him to say something?" Bree asked. "I can't believe he's training you. I'd be terrified."

"No, you wouldn't. You've been begging him to train you with knives," Ellie said.

"He's training Kamren," Bree said.

"Yeah, 'cause she's Kamren. There's not much training needed," Addy put in. "Let's focus on what's about to go down. We'll let Kamren make the approach. Ellie can go up there, too, but the rest of us will fan out."

"I have a layout," Bree said. She dragged a folded piece of paper from her purse.

Addy glared at them from the rearview mirror.

"Right." Bree shoved the layout back into her purse. "Fan out."

"What else is in that purse?" Riley asked.

"Nothing."

Ellie smirked. She recognized the singsong tone. Bree totally had something else in her purse. No one made a comment, though. She grinned at her friend and winked.

The Sip and Spin parking lot was busier than Ellie expected since it was mid-afternoon on a Thursday. Addy parked the truck near a small gray Toyota Corolla that'd been unearthed from somewhere within The Arsenal compound.

Jesse's vehicle parked alongside theirs. Ellie waited to get out, since she was in the middle back. Jesse was there and lifting her out the moment she slid toward the door. Awareness beaded along her skin as it always did when he was near.

She looked up into his intense gaze. "Are you okay?"

"I'll be a lot better once we figure out what's going on. You?"

"Me, too," she admitted.

"Do whatever Addy says when you get inside," Jesse advised. "If anything goes wrong, Brooklyn has orders to get you out. She's at the small table near the jukebox. Try not to be obvious about finding her."

Ellie nodded. "This is all cloak-and-dagger, commando territory."

Jesse smirked. "You think so?"

"Maybe." She narrowed her eyes. "Are you making fun of me?"

"Never." He thumped the tip of her nose with his finger. "We'll grab an early dinner at the place down the road when we're through here."

"The place" was a Mexican food restaurant run out of someone's house. It didn't have any signage or a name. Word of mouth gave them more than enough business—too much, if the long wait was any indication. She'd stopped and ordered food a couple times for her and her mom as a treat.

Mom.

"What's wrong?" Jesse asked.

"I should've told Mom I was going to be busy for a while. If she needs something, she won't know where to find me."

"First, she's covered twenty-four seven now. There are surveillance drones in the cottage. Second, Rhea and my mom are over there this afternoon. Mary and Dylan will stop in if we're gone for longer than expected." Jesse touched her hair. "She'll be okay."

Ellie nodded. It felt odd trusting others to care for her mother. She'd been alone in the battle for so long. "She's got tests at the hospital tomorrow. They're important. I'll need to take her."

"We'll figure it out over dinner."

"You done?" Addy asked. "Half the town knows we're here now."

Right. Ellie smiled back at Jesse, who leveled an intense look in Addy's direction. The redhead just laughed and shook her head. In terms of unusual places, the Sip and Spin likely ranked at the top for most folks. Not every town could boast they had a laundromat in a bar. Or was it a bar in a laundromat?

Ellie supposed it depended on the time of the day and who was partaking in what. Washers and dryers lined the left and right walls as you entered. Tables were spread about the rest of the area in between. Waitresses alternated between tending tables and schlepping laundry for those who paid extra to have their dirty clothes tended.

The long bar took up the back area except for a narrow hall which led to the bathrooms. The dark-haired woman behind the empty bar froze when they entered. Though Dani's gaze scanned them all, it paused on Ellie longer than she expected.

Then slid to the back corner.

Weird.

Ellie glanced back there and noted three tables shoved together. Eleven guys sat drinking. They watched Riley, Bree, Addy, and Kamren. A few licked their lips. A couple grabbed their crotches.

Oh boy.

Addy headed toward them and motioned for Riley to grab a cue stick. The two women claimed the nearby pool table. Bree sat at a table nearby.

"Get out," Dani said through clenched teeth. "Whatever this is, get out."

"Dani," Kamren said, unfazed by the rude greeting. "Two beers, bottled. Don't ever trust the taps in Lonnie's bar, Ellie."

Lonnie Haskell was Ronnie's twin brother. Both were assholes. Ellie ignored the nausea pitching her stomach and forced her gaze to Dani.

But all she could see was the young Dani from the video. Scared. Running for her life.

Being raped.

Ellie hadn't watched anything beyond the chase, but she'd heard enough from the guys afterward. Jesse and Dallas had gone back in and watched the footage.

"There a reason you're darkening my bar with your new crew?" Dani slammed two beers on the bar. "Free if you get to the point and get the hell out."

Ellie tensed. She'd thought the two women were solid. Why was Dani acting like a total bitch? Ellie was about to say something about her attitude, when the woman's gaze cut to the back table—the same one she'd looked at before.

The group in the corner was trouble. Dani would do anything for her best friend—including keep her safe from those she deemed a threat. Like the cluster of guys in the corner. Ellie glanced there, but remembered what Addy had mentioned in the vehicle on the way over. The Sip and Spin was on surveillance, so Mary, Vi, and Zoey could do the geek thing and get everything about everyone in the bar.

"You getting off soon?" Kamren asked, seemingly unfazed by her best friend's act.

"There a reason you care?"

"Lots of things have gone down in the past few days. The sooner we get answers the better it'll be for everybody," Kamren commented. She took a swig of beer.

Dani sighed. Hands on the bar, she leaned forward. "What sort of things?"

Ellie wiped at the perspiration along the sides of her untouched beer. "Someone shot my tire and Phil threatened me."

"Sorry to hear that but not sure what I can do about it. I haven't heard anything." The woman scooped ice into a glass then upended two bottles until the liquid was halfway. "Why are you here?"

"They want something she has," Kamren said. "When are you getting off so we can chat?"

"I'm closing. Double shift," Dani replied. "It's not smart being seen with me. We've got a new crew over in the corner."

"I saw. Friends of yours?" Kamren asked.

"No. Half are from San Antonio, a crew Javier was tight with. Devil Horns or some stupid shit like that." Dani glared at the corner again. "Others haven't been around before."

"Do you need help handling them?" Kamren asked.

"I won't ever ask for help from Masons," Dani said.

Ellie's heart clenched. The vehemence always there stung worse now that she'd seen the video and heard the young girl's forlorn cries for Nolan—cries that'd turned to terrified pleas toward the end of what little she'd watched.

"Cut the shit. Why are you here?" Dani asked.

"I found a CD when Phil tossed me out of my house," Ellie whispered. "I hadn't ever looked at it. We did today. We need help identifying who was there that night."

That night. Dani's dark eyes flared wide as she stood straight. Tears pooled in her gaze.

"I'm guessing you know what's on the CD," Kamren whispered as she reached out to take her friend's hand.

But Dani pulled away and took a couple steps back. "You come into my bar wanting to talk about that shit?"

"No. We came to tell you we need to chat," Ellie said.

"That's not happening." Dani grabbed a rag and wiped the bar down. "Everyone's dead or hurt in a way they won't ever be a problem. It's done."

"For you, maybe. It kills me knowing you suffered and never told me," Kamren said.

"You had your own shit."

Ellie understood what the woman was saying. How many times had she told herself the same thing when she'd kept her issues from Jesse and everyone at The Arsenal? Even though the circumstances they were in were radically different, she and Dani had a lot in common.

"I get it, you know," Ellie whispered. When Dani glanced at her, she continued. "I've had problems I kept to myself because Jesse and everyone is always so busy. Mom taught me to handle my own troubles."

"That's what we do," Dani said. "Dom made them pay."

"Most of them," Kamren whispered. "He didn't get them all. Did he?"

"You don't go telling him that. I've moved on. It's done."

"For you, maybe. There was another girl, Dani," Ellie whispered. "She deserves justice, too. Help us give it to her."

The tears escaped Dani's eyes. She grabbed Ellie's untouched beer and took a swig. The bottle slammed to the counter with a loud thud. "You have a lot of nerve rolling into here throwing this in my face."

"Who led the crew? What did Phil have to do with it?" Ellie asked.

Dani laughed. "The Masons only give a damn 'cause it affects you."

"They'd never condone what went down on those videos," Kamren said. "The Masons are good men. They weren't part of what happened to you. Point us in the right direction. You know me. I'm not stopping this hunt," Kamren whispered.

"Don't kick this rock over, Kam."

"There's not a rock anywhere I won't kick over for you," Kam said.

The two women stared at one another. Ellie'd never had a good friend, one who could read her thoughts so easily.

Jesse could.

"Don't make us take it to Dom," Kamren stated.

Dani's expression changed. Anger. "Don't you dare drag him into this."

"He's already been pulled into it, hasn't he? We're short on options, Dani."

"Years. This has rotted for years. Why bring it up now?" Dani glared at Kam, then Ellie. "This is you. You found that damn CD and dragged this out."

"No. Phil threatened me to get the damn CD. He's never getting his hands on it," Ellie said. "But I'm not gonna ignore what we saw. None of us are."

Dani remained silent, but some of the rage within her stance eased. Her shoulders drooped, and pain resonated in her gaze, so raw and untended that it struck Ellie hard.

"The other choice is to turn the tape over to the Texas Rangers and let them investigate," Ellie said. "If it were me, I'd rather have someone I know looking into it."

"Think about it," Kamren said as she stood and threw a twenty on the bar. "We're grabbing grub down the road. We'll take our time in case you decide to help."

Sadness and fear reflected in Dani's gaze. "I'll go by the farm tonight. You, Dallas, and the kids only. No one else. None of those drones or the other freaky shit your crew's got. I give you what I know, you give it to them, and you leave me out of it. Love you like a sis, but I'm not going down this road with you. I don't do sentimental bonding over booboos."

"You think I do?" Kamren said with a smirk.

"No," Dani muttered. "That's why I'll give it to you."

Kamren reached across the bar and squeezed her friend's hand. "Later."

9

"*Hey, Army. Catch.*"

Jesse barely caught the flying hunk of...meat? Though his eyes had adjusted to the pale pinpricks of light in the otherwise pitch black area, he'd barely seen the object hurling toward him. Pain rolled along his side from the movement. Broken ribs sucked. He took a few shallow breaths and remained frozen in place until the worst of the pain dissipated.

Mind over matter or some shit.

"Eat. It's protein."

Jesse grunted and studied the small hunk of what Marine had declared protein. "What'd this cost?"

"Don't matter. You weren't the one who paid." The man tore off a piece of his own hunk and chewed. "How long's it been since you've eaten?"

Jesse had lost count of the days long ago. At first he'd maintained a solar-based count, but that hadn't lasted long.

"Chew slow," Marine advised.

It wasn't the first time Jesse had gone without food. If he got out, it wouldn't be the last. He tore off a small bite of the substance and chewed. Bile rose up his throat, but he swallowed and forced it back. Every morsel he ate gave him energy to get through another day.

A growl escaped him as he took another. Gamey. Like a wild animal maybe. Ellie would make it taste better. She was a damn good cook. When he got back home, he'd take her out to eat at the fancy place in Nomad, though. Someone should cook for her for a change.

"You're thinking about her again," Marine said. "What are you thinking?"

Jesse studied the man warily. Why did he care about Ellie so much? He took another bite and glared.

"You eat, you talk. That seems fair."

"She cooks," Jesse said. "Best cook around."

"Oh yeah? What's her favorite?"

"Sweets. Chocolate." Peanut butter. He kept the truth to himself.

Say nothing.

The more he said, the more he hurt. The more he kept quiet, the more he hurt. Fuck Marine. Fuck the assholes. He didn't need them.

Jesse closed his eyes and took another bite. This time he remembered Ellie's beef enchiladas. She'd made them with his mom. It'd been the best meal he'd ever had. If he held his breath and chewed slowly, he could almost taste the chile con carne and beef. The cheese.

I made green salsa just for you. I know it's your favorite.

But you hate tomatillos.

It's your favorite. I love you more than I hate them.

"Army?"

Jesse growled when Marine shook him. He'd done that more lately. Physical contact. "No touch."

"Jesus, Army. They're doing a number on you," the man commented as he sat on his ass right across from Jesse. "You gotta give them something. Anything. Then they'll leave you be so you heal for a while. That's the game, Army. Play the game."

No games. He wouldn't ever talk.

"You wanna see your girl again?"

Jesse growled, low and long. Marine mentioned Ellie too much. All the time. Why? She was Jesse's. Not Marine's. He rocked back and forth. The motion hurt, but kept him focused on the now rather than the then. It was easier to slip into the then and remember.

Remembering didn't hurt.

The now hurt so bad.

"They cleaned your wounds," Marine commented.

They'd hosed him with cold water like an animal, then poured alcohol on him as he hung from chains. Jesse growled. Never again.

"You're gonna get out of this hole, Army. Hang on. Don't ever let her go."

Jesse closed his eyes and went back to enchiladas with Ellie.

❦

"*J*esse?"

He jumped as someone jostled his shoulder. Dylan. Fuck.

His pulse pounded in his ears. His vision blurred along the edges, but started returning if he blinked hard enough. Nausea pitched his stomach.

"Is he okay?" The soft voice punctured his hazy fog.

Ellie.

Jesse looked around, not recognizing their surroundings a moment, then his brain kicked in. They were in the Marville restaurant. The eatery was inside someone's house. He studied the gathering of people around him. His brothers had all shown up shortly after he, Brooklyn, Bree, Riley, Addy, Kamren, and Ellie had sat down.

"He's fine. It's easy to get triggered by the small shit sometimes," Nolan said. "Mine's grass and trees."

"And worms?" Dallas teased.

Jesse chuckled.

"What was it?" Nolan asked. He leaned forward and set his hands on the table. Determination reflected in his gaze.

Jesse had activated that gritty determination and resolve. He couldn't back away. They weren't gonna give him space anymore. "Food. Sometimes I remember the hunger."

It was all he could say. He wasn't ready to admit to anyone—most especially Ellie—he'd survived starvation by remembering her cooking. Pathetic much?

He regulated his breathing like he'd been taught and looked at Ellie, who'd switched seats with Marshall so she could sit beside Jesse. A tingle rolled through him when she touched his hand.

"Do you want to go somewhere else?"

"No, Peanut. I'll be good in a minute."

She nodded, but doubt resonated in her gaze. She shifted to face everyone rather than him solely. The waitress came by and started taking orders. Red rose in Ellie's face when it was her turn. She chewed on her lower lip, then glanced at Jesse. Then she studied the menu again.

"What is it, Ellie?" Jesse asked, his voice low and worried.

"I-I don't want to order the wrong thing."

"Order whatever you want," he said. "Why would that be wrong?"

"Because it could trigger you," she answered, her voice soft. "What should I order? Is a burger okay?"

Jesse was floored by her statement. Too stunned to speak a moment, he was grateful Nolan suggested the waitress skip Ellie and Jesse for now. Ellie set the menu down and took a sip of her water. She was worried she'd trigger another flashback.

He cupped her face and waited. He lowered his voice and leaned in to keep the admission to as few as possible. "They only fed prisoners if they gave intel. I wouldn't ever give them anything. When the hunger got to me, I'd think about another time. I thought about breakfasts with my family. Things like that."

"Th-That sounds so...I can't imagine."

"I remembered the enchiladas you made with Mom," he admitted. "That's what I was thinking about just now. The smells in this restaurant must've triggered it."

"We can go somewhere else," she said quickly.

"No." He shook his head. "They don't get another second of my life, Ellie. If I run from something after I'm triggered, I'm regressing. That's not acceptable."

Her blue eyes flared a moment. She relaxed deeper into the contact he'd maintained—his palm on her cheek. The softness of her skin drew his attention. He'd forgotten how soothing it was to touch her. Run his fingers along her ivory smoothness and...

Jesse drew away. He had no business remembering what it felt like to touch her. He wouldn't ever have her like that again.

"Señor?" The waitress glared at Jesse.

Right. Food. The thought made him want to hurl, but he knew better than to not eat right now. "Chicken fried steak, gravy on the side."

"I'll have the same," Ellie said.

She hadn't ever been a chicken fried steak fan, but Jesse kept quiet. At least she'd ordered food. He took a sip of the water in front of him and listened as everyone chatted. He glanced at the narrow hallway across the room, which he assumed led to the bathrooms.

His mind itched. He needed to write down the flashback while it was fresh on his mind. The more he'd performed the process, the more necessary it'd become. It soothed and calmed his mind—which continued replaying the memory as though it were on a loop.

"Go," Ellie whispered.

"What?"

She reached down and tapped the pocket with his journal. "Go. Though, they'd understand."

Jesse wasn't ready to journal in front of his brothers. The act was...private.

He'd watched Mary journal many times since her ordeal, but him doing it seemed...

Weak.

Rationally he knew it wasn't, but a part of him didn't want his brothers and other operatives outside his team knowing he journaled as often as he did. Perhaps because the subject matter was so private and emotionally raw.

Jesse had started therapy at The Arsenal to support Mary after her ordeal. He figured seeing a friendly face in group therapy would help. Group therapy was something he had no issues with anyone seeing. Hell, he actively encouraged operatives to go because it helped. He'd been the same way about the journaling at first.

Then the content turned...

Raw.

Painful.

Brutally honest in a way he couldn't let anyone see. Yet a part of him wanted to give it to Ellie. She deserved to see she'd been his light.

She was right. He needed to go, or he'd be a wreck all night. Rising from the table, he motioned toward the bathroom. "Back in a minute."

❧

"*A*re you okay?" Bree asked.

Ellie glanced at her friend, then at Rhea and Zoey. They'd assembled for their weekly movie—Bree's pick, which meant it'd be a horror. She didn't want to admit the last thing she wanted to watch tonight was a bloody slasher movie or whatever other terrifying flick Rhea chose. At least it wasn't Bree's week. Her choices were always beyond terrifying.

"Of course," Ellie lied. "I'm just worried about Dani." And Jesse.

She scraped the remnant brownie batter from the sides of the bowl and worked it into the mixture. Dinner had gone well after Jesse returned.

Enchiladas. Ellie barely remembered the one time she'd made enchiladas with Momma Mason, but it'd been a strong enough memory in Jesse's mind for him to use as...

An escape.

She'd read most of what Cord had gathered. She'd puked her guts out more than once, but she'd gotten through enough of it to know there were still many questions in her mind. He'd suffered more than she'd realized. Details on how were vague.

"Ellie-belly."

Her mom's voice drew her attention. "Are you okay, Ma?"

"I'm fine, but you aren't. What happened?"

Ellie blinked. She'd never lied to her mother. It was one of their sacred promises to one another since the first cancer diagnosis. "Jesse shared something that surprised me. That's all."

"What did he share?" Zoey asked as she snagged one of the cookies Ellie had just removed from the oven and chewed. Mouth full, the woman looked around the room. "What? You were all wondering."

"They starved prisoners. You ate only if you gave intel, which he never would." She swallowed. "He'd remember his mom's cooking when he got really hungry. And my enchiladas."

"They must be good," Rhea commented.

"I only made them once, with his mom," Ellie whispered as she glanced at her mom, who'd sat next to Zoey at the table. "I barely remember, but he remembered well enough to escape into it."

"The mind's a tricky thing," Bree commented. "Why did he leave the table?"

Ellie froze. She wouldn't ever betray Jesse's trust, and telling anyone about the journaling felt like a huge breech of the trust he'd given her.

"That's something between them," her mom chided. "Best leave it be. I've seen that look many times. She'd never repeat something he shared. He could be a serial killer and she'd go to her grave with the secret."

Ellie smiled when everyone laughed. Her mom was having a good day. She'd eaten a good meal—a fact Sara had shared when they'd returned from Marville. As if summoned by thought, the woman entered the small cottage in a frenzy.

"Are you okay?" Rhea asked.

"Yeah. I-I just need a break," Sara admitted. Her eyes and face were red as though she'd been crying.

The poor girl had been through a harrowing ordeal—physically and sexually abused by her own father, a U.S. congressman. Ellie hated to think about what would've happened to Sara and her baby girl if Zoey and The Arsenal hadn't helped.

Sara had handled the situation well for an eighteen-year-old thrust into parenthood because of sexual assault. The sick bastard had bred his own granddaughter. Ellie removed her apron and went into the living room. Ariana was kicking and wailing as though she were dying. The moment she took the little girl from her mom, she quieted. She positioned the baby in a burping position and rocked from one foot to another.

"You're good with her," Sara said with a smile.

"She babysat just about every baby in Marville," her mom said. "She even diapered Riley many times, if I remember correctly."

"You'll get the hang of it," Ellie said, sensing the young mother's agitation. "You're already a thousand times better than I was when I first started tending babies. Little ones like this terrified me. I don't know how many times I called Mom crying for one reason or another."

Her mom laughed. "Too many to count."

The door opened again. Jesse entered and froze. His eyes widened. A pained expression crossed his face as he looked at Ellie.

"Hey," she said. "Come in. I was about to make peanut butter and chocolate brownies."

"I can't stay," Jesse said. He held up her purse. "You forgot this."

"Oh." She looked around as he turned as if leaving. "Wait a second, Jesse. I'll walk you out."

"Don't bother. I'm fine," he clipped. The door slammed behind him.

Silence.

"What the hell was that?" Bree asked.

"I have no idea," Ellie admitted. "It's been a long day for us all. He likely needs rest."

And time away from her and everyone else. "What movie are watching tonight?"

"*Alien*," Rhea declared.

Ugh. "Those are the bug ones, right?"

Bree and Zoey cackled. None of them understood Ellie's hatred for scary movies. They all groaned when her turn for movie night came about because she always opted for romantic comedies instead. Everyone had enough scary and tragic in their lives as it was.

"Fine, but we leave the lights on." Ellie glanced at Sara. "Why don't you stay and watch with us? There's popcorn and tons of sweets."

"Ellie stress bakes," Zoey commented. "I've gained fifteen pounds since knowing her. At this rate, Gage will dump me in a month because of it."

"As if," Sara said. "That man is head over heels for you."

He was. Ellie grinned. "So? You staying?"

"I shouldn't. Ariana needs a crib."

"There's an extra in the guest room," Bree said. "Rhea and I were in this cottage for a while before it was renovated. The furniture remained. We had the extra crib for when we watched Ariana for you."

"Oh, that's perfect." The girl beamed. "Are you sure you don't mind?"

"Not at all." Ellie smiled and snuggled Ariana closer. Maybe tonight wouldn't be so bad.

※

*J*esse paced. His mind streamed ten klicks a second, but his mouth refused to move. Doctor Sinclair sat in the seat she always used when he showed up unannounced. For the first time, though, he stepped back from his agitation because of something Ellie had said the night before.

Sinclair worked too many hours. Ellie was worried.

He assessed the head shrink with a new mindset and noted the dark circles beneath her eyes and the disheveled look to her clothing. It was well after dusk, and she'd still been in her office.

"Is your mind spinning again?"

He grunted.

"Give me a word, Jesse. Anything. Let's find a starting point."

"Ellie," he growled.

She shifted in her chair, as if surprised. Anytime she'd broached the subject of Ellie he'd shut her out, and now here he was agitated out of his fucking skull because of Ellie. She'd been holding Ariana when he entered, and seeing her with a baby, knowing he'd never give her or any other woman that...

He growled and paced again. Back and forth in the area he always chose. Sinclair had even bought a small runner carpet that looked like a road. Appropriate since he felt like he'd been hit by a Mack truck.

"You're agitated. What happened?"

"Lots."

Sinclair hated when he regressed to short sentences, but he couldn't help it. She remained quiet as he calmed his breathing. Again. But the sight of Ellie holding that baby...the little girl had been cooing. Happy. That kid wasn't ever happy for anyone.

Except Ellie.

And his mom.

And him.

Fuck.

"Have you been sleeping?"

"No." He paused, forcing the first admission out. "Fell asleep at Ellie's last night."

"Okay. That's different. I'm sure it was a surprise to you. Had you been there long?"

"Dinner. Her. Mom. Her mom. Movie. TV Show." The night appeared in his mind like a list at first. Order within the jumbled chaos.

"What did you have?"

"Chicken parmesan. Ellie's a good cook."

"I know. I've had her chicken parmesan before," Sinclair commented. "You do know it's okay to enjoy spending time with her, right?"

Jesse glared.

"Is that what's wrong? You had a good time?"

"Then I had an episode. Levi had to handle me like I was a crazed animal." Jesse breathed deeper as the words flowed easier. The tightness in his chest eased a bit.

"Ellie saw the episode," Sinclair said, her voice soft. Soothing. "That must've been scary."

Terrifying. The realization thundered through Jesse. He stilled. "I didn't want her seeing that."

"How did she handle it?"

Jesse rubbed his eyes. "Amazing. She...Levi had her fix cocoa so she'd leave the room and I could..."

"You didn't want her to see you journal."

He shook his head. "She brought cocoa and peanut butter chocolate chip cookies. For a second I almost forgot, Doc. Then she told me to finish my journal. She'd known."

"How did that make you feel?"

Jesse hated that fucking question with the heat of a thousand suns. He rubbed his chest and paced some more. He needed to go beat up on the bag downstairs some. That'd purge some of the excess energy. Maybe then he'd pass out tonight.

"Jesse."

"Good. I felt...comfortable." Safe.

Loved.

A glimmer of a smile appeared on her typically expressionless face. He recognized that glimmer. Progress.

Jesse growled.

Ellie wasn't progress. Sinclair didn't understand. The freaking baby.

"What else?" The woman nudged like she held an electric cattle prod.

Jesse offloaded the rest. The restaurant. The enchiladas. The baby. By the time he'd finished, the pressure in his chest was mostly gone and his breathing was normal. He sat on the sofa and expended a weary breath.

"You ready to take sleeping pills yet?" She asked an already answered question.

Jesse wouldn't ever pop pills to fix a problem. He'd seen too many soldiers eat a gun or waste a second chance they'd gotten after almost dying because of pills. While he understood the need for medication, he wouldn't ever choose it for himself. He shook his head anyway.

"You've never been ready to discuss this, Jesse, but last night leads me to believe you are."

Jesse braced. There was only one topic Sinclair had tried to broach that he'd refused to listen to. He glanced at the door but knew better than to bolt. She'd track his ass down.

"You suffered tremendous damage to your sexual organs, Jesse, but the majority of the functional damage was repaired," Sinclair whispered. "There's no medical reason for you not to have some form of sexual relationship—even if it's limited in scope because of your psychological trauma."

His dick looked like it'd been chewed up and spat out by a meat grinder, but the doctors had assured him he could get an erection "naturally." Whatever the fuck that meant. He'd masturbated a few times, but rarely tried anymore. It always reminded him of what he'd lost. What he'd endured. He'd lost one testicle, but the other still worked. Kind of. Jesse rolled the medical diagnosis he'd heard multiple times through his mind, but remained silent.

"Even if you never have sex with Ellie, there's no reason you couldn't have a loving and fulfilling relationship with her."

"She won't ever have my kid, Doc. She needs kids. She'd be a good mom."

"There's adoption. Surrogacy. You're a smart man, Jesse. You recognize excuses when you hear them."

"That part of me is dead, Doc. It wouldn't be fair to her."

"Why? Just because you may not have an erection or achieve an orgasm doesn't mean she can't. There are a multitude of things you could do." She fell quiet a moment. Jesse braced. "I think a part of you wants to try, and that terrifies you. But why?"

Shit. Jesse rose and returned to the road. Paced. Damn Sinclair for planting the thought in his brain. His mouth watered at the thought of tasting Ellie again. Her lips. Her breasts.

"I can't lose her," he admitted. "I can't risk it."

"Will you at least talk to her about it?"

The woman was nuts. He froze and stared at her as though she'd grown ten heads. She may as well have. No way in hell was he talking about *sex* with Ellie. "She knows that's not happening."

"Right. Because you both agreed only you and Ellie would define your relationship."

Jesse narrowed his gaze.

"Stop defining, Jesse."

He paced. Was he setting boundaries? Yes. Were they necessary? Maybe.

The *maybe* made him halt again. He'd never answered *maybe*.

What if Doc was right? What if he could...

He ran a hand through his hair and glanced at the doctor once more. She was good, the best he'd ever spoken with. But he'd come here and delayed her departure. How many others did that to her every day?

"Thanks, Doc."

"Anytime, Jesse." She folded her hands in her lap. "I mean that. I'm proud of you. You've made tremendous progress."

"Because of you. The journaling helps."

"Have you considered sharing them with her?"

Jesse looked over at Sinclair, too startled by the thought to respond.

"You're worried about losing her. Why?"

"I'm a fucking mess. She sees too much, she'll bolt. Besides, she's got her mom to deal with."

"She's not bolting from that, is she?"

Jesse shook his head. Ellie wasn't a runner. She entrenched herself in a problem and stood her ground. She always had. "What if it's too much for her? I can't lose her, Doc."

"Think on it. We'll take it slow, Jesse, but you're ready for the next step."

10

*E*xhaustion plagued Ellie through her first two cups of coffee. Early morning light spilled into the windows across from her desk. A part of her wanted to escape her current project and take a walk outside. Remembering the home she'd been raised in—the one Phil had stolen from her mother—was painful.

"You're tired," Mary said. "Rough night?"

She nodded. "Mom had a good evening. We did movie night, but she woke shortly after midnight with an upset stomach. Those nights aren't ever good."

"You should call Logan when you have those nights. There might be something he can do to help," Dylan said as he sat on the side of the desk where Jesse typically perched while signing checks.

Ellie nodded. For once she wasn't alone in dealing with her mom's cancer. Maybe Doc Logan would have pain medication to help ease her mother's suffering. Legal or otherwise, she'd accept whatever made her mom's remaining time more peaceful. Rather than mire Dylan and Mary in the muck of her grim reality, Ellie focused on the horrible rendition of her childhood home that she was trying to sketch.

"This was your home," Mary commented.

"Dad built it for Mom. He spent hours with the designers to get everything just right."

There was a long porch with four sets of sliding glass doors to offer ample breezes. The main living room paralleled a formal living area which could be separated by recessed sliding doors. Windows along the far wall of the formal living space offered cross breezes and ventilation.

The kitchen was large—far bigger than in most houses of its time. Cabinetry crouched a bit lower than standard because her mom was "vertically challenged." Ellie smiled at the memories of her parents' arguments about her height. It'd been a simpler time.

"The house is ranch style, so everything is spread out on one floor," Ellie said. "The office is by itself on the northwest side of the house. There's a window at its southern wall, but there are cacti growing in a bed below there. Or there was."

It'd been a while since she'd actually seen her family home. How much of it had he changed? They'd renovated the master bathroom and bedroom for her mother shortly after they'd been married. Phil had been a different man back then.

"This is exactly what we needed," Mary said with a smile. "We'll be able to dispatch surveillance drones to cover Fallon and Jesse's entry much more easily now. Did you and your ex live there with your mom the entire time?"

"When she was sick. She gave him free rein of the office since she didn't need it, but there were a couple drawers of her paperwork there. That's what I was packing up when the disc must've fallen into my box." Ellie flipped the page. "This is what the office looked like last time I saw it."

Not that it mattered. Ellie suspected Mary and Vi could've handled this simple break-in without any assistance, but it was nice to help. "I'm rambling."

"Not at all." Dylan crossed his arms. His right leg swung back and forth. "We'll need to hit this afternoon, around the time you're in Nomad with your mom. His shift starts then. We have some people who will follow him around while Fallon and Jesse are inside. Do you know of anyone else who'd be at the house?"

Ellie's gut somersaulted. "I haven't been out there since the divorce. I'm not sure who he's hanging out with."

"We'll get some answers, Ellie," Mary promised. "I'd better get to ops before baby here drop-kicks my bladder."

Dylan grinned, leaned down, and kissed his wife. Ellie loved watching the two of them together, but moments like these hurt. That could've been her and Jesse. A tightness formed in her chest.

"Do you have names picked out?"

"We have a few ideas, but haven't committed to anything yet." Mary looked up at Dylan.

She admired them for not finding out the sex of the baby. Whether he or she was healthy was all Mary and Dylan cared about.

"You and Phil never had children. You were together awhile."

"He wasn't the one I saw as the father of my children," Ellie whispered. "That chapter of my life won't be opening."

Sadness glinted in the couple's faces. The unspoken *why* hung in the room like an unwelcome visitor.

"Riley's taking you into Nomad this afternoon," Dylan said as he stood and draped an arm around his wife. "Medina and a couple of other operatives are going along to assist."

Ellie nodded. It was a simple trip to Nomad, so the security wasn't necessary, but she appreciated having someone around just in case. Everyone had relented to her mother's determination that one of Jesse's brothers was not leading a team to haul her into the doctor.

Kamren and Dallas entered. Ellie's stomach dry-heaved as she noted the woman's exhausted but enraged face. She unshouldered the backpack she always wore and reached inside as she arrived at the desk. Dallas's grim expression matched one Jesse wore often.

"Are you okay?" Ellie asked.

"No, but I will be once we skin every asshole involved with this," Kamren said. She handed over a notebook and a laptop. "I didn't record what she said when she came over. I know this is important, but she's my friend and she doesn't trust any of you enough to let me record what she said."

Dallas drew Kamren close and kissed her head. "We got a couple more names from her. Tattoos and birthmarks on a couple more spectators. That's what Javier called them afterward. Dickheads paid twenty bucks to watch."

Ellie swallowed as Mary took the laptop and notebook. "Why didn't she tell her brother Javier was there?"

"She blocked out a large chunk of what happened that night. She remembers going out to meet Nolan. She remembers being chased. The rapes. Nothing after," Dallas said.

"She didn't find out about Javier's involvement until after Dom had admitted to the murders," Kam said. "She's hiding something, but I don't know what or why."

"Do you think Dom took the rap for murders he didn't commit?" Dylan asked.

"Yeah." Dallas sighed. "We need to keep digging and find the other recording."

"Dallas and I made notes after she left. Between the two of us I'm pretty sure we retained about ninety-nine percent of it. He has a wicked good memory," Kamren said. "The laptop is Javier's. It was in his vehicle. Dani said he didn't have any CDs or anything lying around that she ever saw, but he and the other Marville Dogs recorded things constantly. They used a cloud-based storage of some sort. Some underground vault."

"Asking her about videos was smart," Dylan said.

"Information is power," Kamren said. "I learned that from you all."

🐚

"Is it always this busy?" Riley asked.

Ellie noted the filled parking lot. "Most days, no. The clinic is around the back, near the emergency room exit. There's a smaller area nearby to park."

She glanced at her mother, who'd refused to let the Masons send a large squadron of commandoes to watch over her. Despite the long and very heated discussion as to why it wasn't a good idea to go with just a few, her mother had been insistent.

Don't need no one making a big deal about this, Ellie-belly. I've taken enough kindness from the Masons. I'm not spending my last days anymore indebted to them than I am now.

While Ellie appreciated the protectiveness and concern Jesse and his brothers expressed, the only thing that mattered today was getting her mom's treatment done so they could get her back to the cottage and comfortable.

Riley navigated the SUV back there and glanced in the rearview mirror. "I'm not telling those overprotective lugs, but I'm glad they insisted on coming along."

Four operatives led by Medina and not assigned to Arsenal teams had insisted on coming along rather than "lazing around." Ellie recognized them as frequent visitors to her desk, where she always kept assorted candies and homemade goodies on hand.

Riley pulled up against the curb near the entry and turned the vehicle off. "Stay inside until I come around."

Ellie had been impressed with Jesse's little sister so far. She'd taken to her investigative work around the area with gusto and had already solved a few petty thefts in Resino. Jud was helping her work a couple of bigger cases, but neither of them had shared details.

"Everything has to be a big production with those Masons." Ellie's mom unlatched her seatbelt in the back and moved to open the door, but Riley was already there with the walker. "I can get my own damn self out."

The blonde smirked. "Good to hear, Ms. Travers. I'll help Ellie instead."

Ellie exited the vehicle but was crunched between it and Riley as the blonde waited for Medina, who was prowling toward them. Three men exited The Arsenal vehicle which had followed them from the compound. Backup. Riley and a team of five men were all her mom would agree to—and only because Ellie had insisted to appease Jesse.

The Arsenal's truck headed toward the smaller parking area. Two of the operatives who'd exited the vehicle headed around the side of the building, which the other made his way around the other side. A shiver traveled up Ellie's spine when she noticed holstered weapons on their hips.

They were not messing around.

"We'll cover the three exits and the parking lot," Medina said. "You good for the interior? I can call for more."

The man was tall and wide and exuded lethal confidence like all the Arsenal personnel did. Riley sized the man up. "You know I can kick your ass."

"I know you'll try."

"Jud's been training me."

Medina smirked. "There's only so much kick in a pint-sized package. Are you clear for the inside or not?"

"What would you do?" Riley asked.

The man smiled. A glimmer appeared in his gaze. "Bonus points for being smart enough to recognize when you're in over your head."

"Stow the smartass," Riley growled. "Ellie's mom needs to get inside. Standing isn't likely simple for her."

The man's light brown complexion darkened with a blush as he looked around. "Call Zoey and have her patch into the hospital's security system. We've got gear with us. That'll give the five of us and you additional eyes on the areas we can't physically cover. HERA can scan for anyone near Phil's size and warn us if anyone is spotted."

Riley nodded. "Right. Right. Okay. Do it."

"Already done," Medina said with a grin.

The blonde's gaze narrowed. "Are you humoring me, Medina?"

"I wouldn't be suicidal enough to mess with my bosses' little sister," the man said. "Get Ms. Travers inside. We'll get patched into the security feeds."

"Stay close," Riley ordered as they made their way into the congested lobby of the cancer clinic.

The progression halted long enough for Riley and one of the operatives to sweep the interior of the small clinic. Ellie stood beside her mom and watched the methodical way Jesse's sister helped ensure the location was safe.

Riley returned and offered Ellie's mom a smile. "We're clear."

Ellie's mom continued to the right and down the narrow hallway leading to where she'd be treated. Ellie flashed an apologetic smile at the nurse behind reception. "Sorry, she's having a bad day."

"No worries. It'll be quieter back there anyway. You know the rules. One person only in the treatment area. Your friend can wait in the room nearby. I'll put her in number two."

Ellie nodded.

"I'm not leaving your side," Riley said.

"They're close." Ellie caught up with her mom, who was already sitting where she needed to be. "You shouldn't go wandering off by yourself today, Mom. Riley's trying to keep us safe."

"No one's messing with us in here. Not everything's about a Mason. I can't even die in peace without you bringing that boy and his notions into it." Her mom's voice rose. "Not everything's about you."

Ellie kept quiet and glanced across the narrow hall. Riley had dragged a chair from the small consultation room and was sitting in the doorway. She'd see straight into the room without issues. The woman's gaze was narrowed. She'd lip-read every harsh word Ellie's mom had spoken.

A nurse shuffled into the room with a blood-draw kit. "I need to get some blood, Ms. Travers."

"Damn vampires. You've got enough."

Ellie smiled. "I'm Ellie. I don't believe we've met. Are you new?"

"I started a few days ago," the young woman said. A deep bruise along her eye drew Ellie's attention. She tied off her mom's arm and started working on finding a vein. "That blonde across the hall with you?"

"Yeah. She's a friend," Ellie said.

"She shouldn't be back here."

"It was cleared. I'm having a few...security issues."

"You'll have more if you don't listen," the woman said, her voice low.

"Excuse me?" Ellie tightened and glanced at Riley.

"You call out to her and I'll push this into your mom's vein." Ellie looked down at the empty syringe. Air?

Fear clamped around Ellie's lungs. She looked at the woman, then down at her mom, whose eyes were wide.

"Leave her alone," Ellie said.

"Keep quiet and listen," the woman whispered. She angled to the side and looked at Ellie. "They've got my kid. I do this or my boy dies."

"Do what?" Ellie asked softly.

"You've got something they want. A CD. Where is it?"

The CD. Ellie let anger roll through her a moment. "The Arsenal has it."

"My boy's gonna die if I don't get that CD." Tears appeared in the woman's eyes.

Ellie glanced at the hall and noticed Riley watching. The woman's body hid the empty syringe. Ellie needed help. But how?

She swallowed and recalled the hand signals she'd watched Jud and Dallas train Riley on. She held her left hand up in what she hoped to hell translated to "enemy."

"Marshall Mason has it," Ellie said. "You don't have to do this. They'll help you find your son."

Riley prowled forward, gun drawn. The woman's steps were so quiet they were unheard by the nurse threatening her mom. Ellie's pulse quickened when Riley shoved the gun against the woman's head with one hand while the other grabbed the syringe. A second later the woman was on the floor and Riley was straddling her.

"I think we need an assist back here, Medina," Riley said into the Bluetooth she was wearing. She glanced up at Ellie. "Are you okay?"

Ellie glanced down at her mom, who'd yet to move or speak. She untied the band around her mom's arm and nodded. "We're okay. Thank you."

Riley nodded as she pulled the nurse up. "Let's step into the hall and have a chat while we wait for someone to come pick you up."

"What was that, Ellie-belly?" Fear clung to her mom's words.

"We're safe, Mom. Riley handled it."

"What have those Masons gotten you into?" Ellie sighed and realized her mom didn't remember the multiple conversations they'd had about why they were staying at the Mason ranch for a while. Days like this made her want to cry.

The woman who'd raised her was slipping away a little each day. All Ellie could do was make the best of the situation and ensure she had everything she could possibly want. Keep her comfortable, safe, and happy.

"Nothing, Mom. This is Phil."

"Phil? That woman didn't say anything about Phil."

"The CD she was asking about was in the Bible. Remember I mentioned there was one stuck in with my things, and I said I should return it?"

"The one I told you to burn because that bastard ain't ever getting into heaven no matter how much scripture he read?" Her mom's eyes narrowed. "I told you he was trouble."

"I know, Mom." Ellie patted her mom's arm.

Her mom coughed, then cleared her throat. Face pale and hands trembling, she looked up at Ellie. "I need some juice."

Ellie peeked around the corner at where Riley and Medina were with the nurse. "I'll get you some in a minute."

Her mom coughed again. Guilt overrode the concern about safety. The nurse had been caught and the area had been swept earlier. Surely getting juice from the breakroom would be safe. "I'll be right back."

She stepped into the hall. Medina and Riley were talking. The man had taken possession of the nurse a short distance away. She flagged them to get their attention. "I'm gonna grab my mom some juice."

Riley's gaze narrowed. "Don't go far."

"I won't. It's just in that room." Ellie motioned toward the second door to the right where the nurses kept juices and other beverages for the patients to sip on.

The room was empty when she entered. She moved toward the refrigerator along the back wall, but movement in her peripheral vision caught her attention as a door squeaked open.

The emergency exit.

A scream rose in her throat as she took a step backward—away from the man dressed in scrubs. He closed the distance and latched a hand across her mouth.

She punched and kicked. Screamed against the hand.

"Bitch! You're gonna learn not to fuck with us. You should've kept your mouth shut."

Pain ripped through her body as she was slammed to the floor. He struck her head. Her face. A fist? No. It was harder. She punched and scraped her nails on his arms. His face. He slammed her head against the floor. Once. Twice.

Blackness assailed.

11

*J*esse glared at Howie as the man drove to Nomad Memorial. The vehicle had hit ninety-five, but it felt as though they were standing still. The search of Phil's house was a bust. Nothing of value had been found. Frustrated, he and Fallon had wired the entire house while Jesse's team patrolled the perimeter with drones. A mouse couldn't fart or take a dump in that place without being seen and heard.

While they'd been wasting their time at Phil's, some nurse had threatened Ellie.

"Riley neutralized the nurse," Vi said over the vehicle's speakers.

They'd already been on their way to the hospital because staying away from Ellie was like blocking out the sun—impossible. Jesse had been worried.

The truck slowed as they entered Nomad.

"Second assailant on scene," Medina growled into the com. "Fuck. Stay with me Ellie. I've got you."

No. Howie gunned the engine again and turned onto a side road that paralleled the congested main highway leading to the hospital.

"Suspect down," Riley said into the com.

"Ellie? How's Ellie?" Jesse's voice rose, making the word more a scream than a question.

No response.

The vehicle turned into the back entry of the hospital parking lot on two wheels. Jesse vaulted out and sprinted inside. Only ten minutes had passed since Riley had called in the nurse incident.

Ten minutes.

He followed the shouts and bustle of activity. Medina, Riley, and three other operatives were in the hall. A swarm of people filled the area. Tears trekked down Riley's cheeks as she leapt into Jesse's arms.

"I'm sorry. I'm so, so, sorry. I shouldn't have let her get the juice. I thought we were secure. We swept the area and had the nurse detained. No other threats were picked up."

Jesse didn't care about the how. Not now. He pulled away from his sister and tried to enter the room but froze.

Blood pooled around Ellie's still form. A man in a white coat was shouting at the people gathered around him. They hoisted her onto a nearby gurney.

"Ellie-belly!"

Ellie's mom was clutching the entryway. Pale and terrified. He shifted his attention, even though it pained him to leave Ellie's side for a second. She'd want her mom secure and calm.

"She's going to be okay, Ms. Travers." He put a hand on her shoulder. "Let me help you to a seat."

"That nurse threatened her."

"In a minute, you tell Riley everything you heard, okay?"

The woman nodded. "She'll be okay?"

"I won't rest until she is."

"She's in this mess 'cause of you and me. She never would've married that mangy mutt if you hadn't left and I hadn't gotten sick again."

Jesse tightened. The woman had a way of carving out a heart without leaving a mark. "You're right. The biggest mistake I ever made was leaving her. I'm guessing one of yours was around the same time—when you told her not to share your illness with anyone.

We've both done wrong by her, but I mean to make it right. You're either with me on this or you aren't."

The woman regarded him a moment. "She's better off without you."

"Yeah, she is." Jesse let the fact settle between them because all he wanted was to make sure Ellie was okay. Worry worked his breathing into shallow, quick pants. His vision blurred. Sweat beaded along his brow.

"Deep breaths. Focus on me."

Nolan. Jesse rested his forehead against his brother's and forced deep breaths in. Fear choked him, kept the words tumbling in his brain from escaping. Ellie couldn't...

Die.

Just the word sent a shockwave of new emotions to the forefront of his mind. He stumbled as his vision tunneled a moment. Blackness swept across his peripheral vision, but he focused on his brother's steady voice.

"Deep breaths, Jesse," Nolan said, his tone calm and determined. "It's just you and me."

But it wasn't. Ellie's blood ran like a river a short distance away. If Jesse breathed deep enough, he could smell the coppery scent in his nostrils. Doctors and nurses were working on her right now. He'd failed her.

He should've taken her to the hospital himself. Then maybe she would've been okay. His breathing steadied and the blackness in his vision dissipated. He squeezed his brother's arm and forced a deep exhale.

"I've got you, Jesse," Nolan said. "She'll be okay. Head wounds bleed like crazy. You know that."

He glanced at Ellie's mom, realizing he'd freaked out right in the middle of a conversation with the woman. She'd likely been terrified. Still was. "I'm sorry, Ms. Travers."

"Don't be." She looked at Riley when she approached. "I wanna see my girl."

Jesse turned his attention back to Ellie, who'd only been moved a few feet as the doctor continued his assessment. Tests.

Why wasn't she waking?

"The doctors and nurses are with her right now," Riley said. "Let's go back in and see to you. Ellie wouldn't want you worried. She's gonna be okay."

Nomad police appeared and swarmed around Medina, who'd already raised his hands and begun speaking. The man had saved Ellie.

Riley had saved her.

Jesse should have been there.

"This isn't on you," Nolan said. "None of this is. The man snuck in through a side entrance. HERA didn't flag him as a problem because he was a part-time employee at the hospital. Riley cleared this room and all the others before she took position to watch over Riley and her mom. She did everything by the numbers."

Phil Perskins would pay for this.

Jesse woodenly followed the gurney. A couple nurses tried holding him back, but Levi and Brooklyn were there. Talking. His mind didn't process the words. None of them mattered.

Ellie wasn't awake yet.

Her blood was on the hospital floor.

❀

"*Y*ou should eat." Riley shoved the untouched tray of food closer.

Jesse glanced at the offering, then returned his attention to Ellie. Six hours in surgery. The procedure had lasted longer than he'd expected, but she'd pulled through.

The doctor expected mild traumatic brain injury, but they wouldn't know until she woke.

Which would hopefully be soon. Soon was a screwed-up word. It'd been a day and a half.

"Mom's gathering troops to haul you out of here. You should

shower and clean up before she wakes," Riley said. She dragged a chair closer to the bed on the other side and sat. "You look like hell. Ellie will worry if she wakes and sees you like this."

He didn't want to leave her alone, but Riles was right. Ellie would have enough to worry about when she woke. A shower would do him wonders, and a debriefing would as well.

"Call if you need to leave," Jesse ordered.

Riley pulled an electronic tablet from her purse. "I'm not going anywhere. I just started a book I think Ellie will enjoy."

Jesse headed out of the room before he changed his mind. The hospital had been more accommodating than expected, given the sheer number of Arsenal personnel who'd drifted in and out of the facility. They'd commandeered a small waiting area near Ellie's room.

Nolan and Dylan glanced up from their seats. Sol and Levi were stretched out in two corners of the room. The latter had become Jesse's constant shadow, more so than he'd already been.

"Oh, there you are." His mom shuffled forward and touched his bearded face. "The nice nurse said there's a shower down the hall you can use to clean up."

"Why don't you go sit with Riley, Ma?" Nolan rose. "We'll sort Jesse out."

He didn't need sorting, but remained quiet because he needed a debrief and some time away from his well-meaning mother. He noted her slight limp as she made her way out of the waiting room.

"She needs to rest," Jesse growled.

"She will once Ellie is awake," Dylan commented. "You aren't the only one worried."

"Debrief."

Dylan reached down, grabbed a duffel from the seat, and headed toward the bathroom, Nolan with him. "Shower while you debrief."

Jesse avoided showering around others most of the time, but he didn't have the energy or patience to give a damn today. His big brothers had already seen the damage.

The bathroom was larger than expected, with a full walk-in

shower and handlebars at the back. He shucked his clothes and tossed them in a pile and got to work.

Silence ensued a few beats, but Nolan recovered first and tossed a bottle of liquid soap his direction.

"A low-level thug named Benny with a local gang called the Nomads shot Ellie's tire. The girls found him on camera. Benny's address is nearby," Nolan said.

"Anything else on the bastard Medina shot?"

"Low-level thug with a group based out of San Antonio," Dylan said.

Jesse stilled. "Not the same crew as the first attack?"

"No." Nolan's jaw twitched. "A different one. Southside Raptors. Mary and Vi are digging. Texas Rangers are taking the lead on investigating Phil for the traffic stop on Ellie. Tying him to this will be a problem. So far he has a rock-solid alibi. He was buying drinks for everyone at the Sip and Spin when the hospital attack happened. And the footage of the first incident is excessive force at most at this point."

Jesse grunted. The attack was planned. A second crew meant it was a far more coordinated effort than he'd first suspected. "Why more than one crew?"

"That's the question of the hour. Add in the third crew at the Sip and Spin, and this shit sandwich is getting hard to chew," Dylan said. "The girls are digging. They'll figure it out."

They always figured it out. He kept his back to his brothers. The less they saw of his groin, the better for everyone. His gut clenched. It hadn't gotten any easier—letting others see the damage done during his captivity.

"Marshall wants us to extend the investigation. Maybe this isn't Phil," Nolan said.

Phyllis and Herman Perskins had money—enough to keep their precious son out of the slammer until enough evidence was gathered against him. Jesse would rather put a bullet between his eyes, but that'd be too quick.

Too painless.

"Herman is a grade-A loon," Jesse commented. "They're after the CD she got from Phil. He has to be involved."

"Did the nurse say anything more?" Jesse asked.

"Nothing useful. We found her boy wandering a back pasture outside Marville, near the gin," Nolan said.

"Sinclair is worried," Dylan said.

Doctor Sinclair had two settings—worried and more worried. Jesse had avoided conversations with the woman so far, but he had to admit he wouldn't mind having a few minutes with her. "I'm fine."

"You'll be better when Ellie wakes and we get her home," Dylan said.

Home. He had no business wanting to make The Arsenal her permanent home, but he couldn't let her go. "Thanks for the update."

Jesse took his time showering off the hospital stench after they left. He hated the antiseptic smell burning his nostrils and the way sickness and death clung to his skin. Desperation. Pain.

Fear.

He'd woken alone in the hospital the first few times after his own rescue. Unsure where he was. If he was even alive.

The pain.

Jesus. He still remembered the violent burn and constant stabbing sensations as Levi and the rest of the team carted what was left of him out of that hellhole. Levi had kept what was left of his dick and balls clean.

"Let me die."

"Not happening, Mason. You didn't stay alive for me to give up on you now. My name's Levi, by the way. Figured you'd wanna know since me I'm gonna be up close and personal with your dick until your medevac arrives."

"Don't bother. It's gone."

"We don't ever give up. You know that, Mason." Levi grinned down at him. "I'm getting you home to Ellie."

"Ellie?"

"She's your girl, right? You keep talking to her."

Jesse forced the memory back as he shut the water off and towel-dried himself. No good came from going down that road, but a part of him refused to turn away. Ellie had almost died.

What if Sinclair was right? What if he could salvage a relationship with Ellie? Maybe he'd ask Sinclair or Logan about...

No.

That'd wait.

Right now he needed to get dressed. The sooner he got back to Ellie the better. He didn't want her waking alone. Nothing was worse than waking up in pain with no clue where you were.

He eyed the electric razor.

I like the new look.

Ellie's confession from a couple weeks ago halted Jesse's movements. He ran his hands along his jaw. He'd leave scruff for her.

D isinfectant. The stench filled Jesse's nostrils. Pain radiated from his groin and along his left leg, but it was different than before. *He floated, as if shrouded from the worst of the pain.*

Yes.

He sank deeper into the hazy fog consuming him.

Beeps. Voices. The foreign sounds didn't belong in the hole. He breathed deeper and smelled...

Clean.

No urine stench. No shit.

No blood.

He flexed his fists and fought the confusion clouding his mind. Something had changed.

The rescue. Levi.

Jesse jerked awake with a gasp.

Freedom.

His throat felt as though it'd been rubbed raw. Tubes stuck out of both hands. A heavily bleached white sheet covered him. Pain. He closed his eyes and inventoried the sensation.

Light blinded him a moment.

Jesse's eyes burned as tears seeped from them. A hospital. That stubborn son of a bitch and his team had gotten him out.

He blinked until his vision cleared enough to assess his surroundings. His pulse pounded wildly. He was free, yet terror gripped him hard.

Get out. Get out. Get out.

He pulled at the tubing. Beeps sounded around him.

Get out. Get out. Get out.

A metal rail prevented a simple roll from the bed. Jesse didn't understand why, but he was still in danger. His mind screamed the fact, even though his body refused to cooperate.

Pain exploded as he impacted with the floor. Okay, that wasn't smart.

"Get the doctor!" a female voice shouted. "He's awake!"

Jesse crawled and scurried beneath the edge of the bed. The darkness swallowed him up. Maybe they wouldn't see. He curled into a ball, but the movement knifed pain along his left leg. The fuckers had hurt him while he was asleep.

"Fuck."

Jesse froze. A growl rolled from him. Levi. They'd gotten him and his team. "Leave them alone!"

"Mason, look at me," Levi ordered.

The man was on all fours and peering into his hidey hole. Jesse uncovered his head and blinked until the man unblurred.

"You remember me." It wasn't a question, but a statement. "You're safe. You're in Germany. We tracked down most of your brothers. They're spread all over hell's half acre, man. Leave it to you to have five brothers in spec and black ops."

Brothers.

Jesse tightened. "Not secure."

"You are. I swear you are secure, Mason. I have your six until your brothers arrive. My team and I took leave."

Leave. They had his six. Jesse grunted. Strangers.

No.

Brothers in uniform.

They'd carried him out.

He'd survived.

☙

*J*esse jolted awake when something grazed against his arm. Nolan stood nearby, concern on his face. "What's wrong? Is it Ellie?"

He glanced at the bed. She rested peacefully. Vitals were good.

"Benny Vale was taken into custody but has already made bail. I figured you'd want to come along as I pay him a visit."

Benny Vale. It took Jesse a few heartbeats to recognize the name of the man who'd shot Ellie's tire. He rose, then froze. What if she woke while he was gone?

As if sensing the dilemma, Nolan took two steps outside and motioned. Riley and their mom entered. Both carted large bags of paraphernalia as though they were settling in for a long stay.

"You go see to business so our girl's safe when she wakes," his mom ordered. "We aren't going anywhere."

"You shouldn't be here so much. It's not good for your recovery," Jesse argued.

"I'm where I want to be, son. Ellie is the reason I'm up and about as well as I am. I'm almost fully recovered because she saw to me while she was tending her own mom and everything else." His mom's eyes watered. "I need to do this, Jesse. I wasn't there for you when you woke. I need to be here for her."

Jesse's heart swelled as he looked at his sister and saw the determination there. They had his back like they always did, but this was more.

They had Ellie's back.

He nodded and kissed both women goodbye before following Nolan to the truck. The intercom rang the second they were in motion.

"Vale's got a small place a couple blocks south of the grocery store," Zoey said. "He's been running with the Nomads. Talk about a lazy name for a gang operating out of Nomad."

Jesse couldn't help but grin. The woman was so unlike Mary and Vi. The fresh, often gut-wrenchingly open dynamic she had with the team was the touch needed to balance out the intensity of the Quillery Edge.

"Southside Raptors hit her in the hospital. Nomads hit her on the side of the road, and Devil Horns are circling in Marville. Let's get some answers before they make their move on our girl," Zoey ordered.

Nolan clicked the connection off as they pulled up outside a small house at the tail end of a long row. Large dogs barked and ran freely within yards cordoned off by fences too small to contain them if they chose to leap over and attack.

Jesse didn't bother knocking. Let the fucker call the cops. He kicked the door in and entered with his gun drawn. Nolan swept to the other side.

The asshole cowered behind the sofa. Nolan hauled him to standing. The house was three rooms grouped together with thin walls separating them. Jesse swept the rest, then returned to loom in Benny's personal space. The man puffed up like a swollen puffer fish facing off against a shark.

"You fucked with the wrong woman, Benny," Jesse said. "You're gonna tell us what the hell is going on and what Phil's endgame is."

The man's bravado crumbled beneath the rage within Jesse's voice. "I don't know nothing. And I don't know no Phil."

"Let's hope that's not true, Benny," Nolan said as he grabbed the man's neck from the back and squeezed. "We get very, very cranky when people don't have answers."

"Did you tell the police who hired you?" Jesse asked.

"They didn't ask," Benny said. "My attorney took care of it."

"Right. Like your stupid ass could afford anything more than a one-dollar candy bar," Nolan commented. "You running with the Nomads?"

"What if I am?" Benny sneered. "They're gonna fuck you up for messing with me."

"That so?" Jesse took the final step and loomed in Benny's personal space like he belonged there.

Wedged between Jesse and Nolan, the man whimpered.

"Who hired you?" Jesse asked.

"I dunno. Some rich mark from Marville. Said there'd be a connection to a bigger gig if we proved ourselves," Benny said.

"Yeah? You got a name?" Nolan shoved the man onto the sofa. "Talk."

"I was a lookout for the meet, but I heard most of it."

"Where?" Jesse asked.

"Some water tank between Resino and Marville." Benny shrank backward when Jesse sat on the coffee table. "I don't want no part of this shit, man."

"You know anything about the Devil Horns and the Southside Raptors?" Nolan asked.

"Yeah, they're horning in. Paco is pissed, said the bastard didn't say nothing about competition for the gig. Now he's pissed at me for fucking it up and not getting the CD."

"You saw the guy who hired y'all?" Jesse leaned forward and rested his elbows on his thighs. When the man nodded, he continued. "This is how it's gonna go, Benny. You're gonna have a conversation with the Texas Rangers when they arrive in a few minutes. You'll tell them everything you know about the bastard who hired you and your crew and the crews in San Antonio. Anything about everything. You hear me?"

The man nodded.

Nolan held out his phone. "That the man?"

The guy nodded. "Yeah, I seen him."

"Is there another meet planned?"

"Yeah. Tonight. Same place. All the competition is supposed to be there," Benny said. "I-I heard you've got someone out there who skins people for fun."

Jesse chuckled. The rumor mill was apparently good for something after all. "We've got more than one. Skinning isn't anything compared to what I'll do to you if anything else happens to my girl."

The man gulped. Jesse rose and left the house. Zoey would coordinate with The Rangers.

Nolan clapped him on the back and held out the keys. "Go. I'll hitch a ride with The Rangers out to the hospital once they're done here."

"Thanks, man." Jesse ran his hand through his hair. "She's gotta be okay."

"She will be."

"I want lead on the meet tonight," Jesse said.

"You know that won't happen. You can pick which team takes lead and you can be secondary, but that's the most I see Mary and Vi agreeing to." Nolan crossed his arms. "You talk to Sinclair about this?"

Jesse shook his head. The shock of seeing Ellie so pale and bandaged up had brought too much to the surface. "She didn't deserve this, man."

"No, she didn't. He'll pay, but we do this by the numbers. The bastard is going down."

One way or the other, he'd pay. Jesse wouldn't stop until he did. He got into the truck and headed back to the hospital.

12

*P*ain. Ten million hammers pounded inside Ellie's head. Nausea. Her stomach heaved.

"It's okay, Peanut. I've got you. Let it all out."

Jesse. She opened her eyes and peered up at him as he swept her hair back.

She puked.

Violent spasms racked her stomach. The pain in her head increased. She reached out and grabbed Jesse. What was happening?

"You're okay, Peanut. I'm here."

Memories drifted forward as if in slow motion. The attack.

Light penetrated the ambient darkness. She winced.

"Turn that off," Jesse growled. "She's light sensitive."

"How would you know? She just woke," a female voice asked.

"Because I've been in that bed waking up and puking my guts out," Jesse answered.

Ellie reached for him and squeezed his arm. Why was she in a hospital? Was her mom okay? Riley! She'd been there. Had she been hurt, too?

"Everyone's okay," Jesse whispered.

That's when Ellie realized she'd been whispering names. Ma. Riley. Jesse.

"You'll need to stand back so we can assess her," someone said.

"Leave the room, sir," the same angry female ordered.

"He's not leaving," someone said. "He's been here since she was admitted. They all have been."

Calm spread through Ellie. She wasn't alone. Jesse was there. So was someone else. She was okay.

"Ellie-belly, we're here," her mom said.

"You need to sit," Momma Mason said.

"So do you," her mom replied.

Ellie listened as the two women argued over which of them should take the seat. Neither wanted to. The mundaneness of the conversation kept Ellie from thinking about the ten thousand things she desperately wanted answers to.

She bit her tongue to stifle the groan when a bald man with a very bright light leaned into her personal space and attacked her eyeballs with a beam of torment. There was no other way to describe the pain which swept through her.

A deep breath did little to ease the pain. Her vision fuzzed along the edges.

"*Thsee.*"

Confusion overwhelmed Ellie. The bald man was saying something, but everything blurred.

Ellie looked around, aware time had passed since she'd awakened, but she didn't know how long. Jesse leaned down and ran a hand across her cheek.

"Welcome back," he whispered. "Just relax, Ellie. You had a seizure, but those are common from head injuries. You're okay. You're safe."

It took a few moments for her movements to return fully and for the fog in her brain to clear somewhat. She still felt as though she were floating above her body—there but not quite connected.

"She's awake, Elena," Momma Mason whispered.

"Ellie-belly." Her mom shuffled to the other side of the bed from where Jesse sat. "You gave us a scare."

"I'm okay." She repeated what Jesse had said, even though she wasn't sure what injuries she'd sustained.

"Hi, Ms. Travers. I'm Doctor Hobbs, the neurological surgeon on call when you had your incident."

Incident. Ellie pursed her lips and clasped Jesse's hand. She'd been attacked by some asshole while in their facility. That wasn't an incident.

"You sustained quite a concussion and experienced some internal head injuries. We operated to alleviate the pressure and kept you sedated until the swelling decreased. We'll run some tests, but I expect you'll be out of the hospital in a few days' time. We'll sit down and discuss the after-effects of an injury such as yours after I've reviewed your test results."

Ellie blinked. She hadn't processed at least half of what he'd said. Not fully. She nodded, though. Someone would help her understand when she needed to.

Jesse leaned down and kissed her forehead. The contact cast warmth through her entire body. He pressed his forehead against hers and sighed heavily, as if breathing for the first time in a long while.

"I'm so glad you're awake, Peanut."

"The guy who attacked me?" She swallowed.

"He's not a problem. Medina handled him."

Ellie didn't ask what *handled* meant since her mom was there. It didn't matter. If Jesse said he was handled, she wouldn't worry.

"Is your stomach still upset?" her mom asked. "They said your injury would likely cause nausea."

Ellie nodded a little.

"Here. Jesse said it would be. Sip on some ice chips. Rebecca will go get those pills the nurse said you could take for nausea. She's supposed to have them on standby. Jesse made sure earlier." Her mom smiled. "You rest up, Ellie-belly. We aren't gonna let anyone near you."

Ellie closed her eyes and rested.

❦

*J*esse waited until Ellie fell asleep to exit the room and meet with the Texas Ranger waiting outside. Dalton Coleman was a middle-aged man who listened and rarely spoke unless necessary. Jesse admired that the man shot straight when asked a question and didn't try and shut them out of the investigation into Phil Perskins. He understood The Arsenal was involved and had no issues accepting the intel they gathered as part of his investigation. In return, Jesse hadn't let anyone but himself coordinate with the man because there was only so much red tape a man at the end of his rope could tolerate.

Ellie was awake.

Relief filled him. Seizures had been a possibility he'd braced for —one he hoped would resolve itself soon enough. Either way they'd get through it. Whatever happened, he'd make sure she had anything needed to recover fully.

"I heard she's awake," Coleman said.

"She's resting."

"We can wait to speak with her. I'll be honest. Everything we have on Mr. Perskins' involvement at this point is circumstantial at best."

"And the gangs?"

The man shifted and crossed his arms. "Officially, we'll open an investigation into the Southside Raptors. Medina's testimony is enough to serve search warrants for the attacker's domicile and the gang's primary compound and related properties. We'll likely coordinate that with the SAPD and DEA. If we're lucky, that'll lead to links between them and Perskins."

DEA. The Southside Raptors were under investigation for drugs, weapons, or both. Jesse filed the information away, even though the geek squad likely already had it. Warrants took time—time he sorely didn't want to waste. Phil Perskins needed to get behind bars for his own safety. Jesse was one bad day away from killing the asshole himself.

He glanced at the entry to Ellie's room where Cord and Sol leaned against the wall as if they'd become adhered to it. Big brother Marshall must've issued an order of some sort because no matter the time of day or location, there were always two people at Jesse's six.

"Tell me what you need from us." He remembered the man's first word and added, "Unofficially."

"If it were my woman in that room, I'd cut through as much red tape as I could. Get the bastard behind bars, even if it isn't for the attack. A slippery son of a bitch like Perskins will have more than one reason to be taken down."

Jesse grunted. "We're working on an older case—sexual assaults. The victims were minors, so there is no statute of limitations. Video footage done by him was located, but that's all we have so far."

"Good. Whatever you get will help. In the meantime, I'd apply pressure to those gangs. Catch Perskins with them somehow. Bring in the DEA or SAPD to make it official, though I know your crew has a knack for legally inserting yourselves into just about any situation."

"Did Vale mention the meet tonight?" Jesse asked.

"Yes. We can try and organize surveillance for it, but I'll be honest. I can't coordinate something that fast without more evidence of its importance." The man shifted his stance. "You have an idea how to move that along?"

"We'll be there gathering evidence with our equipment," Jesse said. "All we need is you there to make the arrests. We'll handle the muscle."

"I'll make a call, see if that can work. The DEA will want to be there as well."

"I don't give a damn who takes the assholes down as long as it sticks and they never breathe the same air as Ellie ever again," Jesse said. "Coordinate the details with Vi or Mary."

He returned to Ellie's room. Cord and Sol appeared within moments.

"The Rangers are gonna contact Vi and Mary about tonight. Make sure they do," Jesse said.

"I'll call the girls. They've been running the gangs through HERA," Cord said. "Marcus and his crew are running down Paco from the Nomads. Marshall wants him on ice until we coordinate our plan. We'll likely commandeer another room. The hospital administrator has been very accommodating."

Jesse wondered how much money Marshall had donated to grease the way for *accommodating*, but didn't make any comment. He was grateful his brothers and The Arsenal teams were working out a plan because, when it came to Ellie, his judgment was skewed.

"Take care of Ellie. We'll handle the details," Sol said.

Jesse returned to Ellie's side and watched her sleep a long while. Fortunately, neither of the mothers watching him watch her made a comment or struck up conversation. Everything fell into his brain and mixed together. She was going to be okay, but he had no idea what that meant for them.

Was there a them?

Dare he take a chance at moving further than just friendship? Would Ellie be okay with that?

She deserved a real relationship, one where the man could make love to her however and whenever she wanted.

"Have you eaten?" His mom put a hand on his shoulder.

Tension ran along his spine, but he never moved away from his mother's touch. She wouldn't understand. Since his return home after physical rehabilitation, he'd learned to tolerate touch when necessary. As long as he saw it coming, he was okay. It was one of the unaddressed issues Doctor Sinclair hadn't broached yet.

Even if you never have sex with Ellie, there's no reason you couldn't have a loving and fulfilling relationship with her.

The doctor's words from their last session had echoed in his mind a lot since Ellie's assault. After almost losing her, he was lost. Confused.

Scraping sounds echoed within the room. Jesse hoped the loud sound didn't wake Ellie. When it didn't, he leaned back in the seat and looked over at his mom, who'd pulled her chair up beside him.

"You've got that look your dad always got when he was lost in the weeds of his thoughts."

Jesse smiled. Mom had spent a lot of time talking about their father since the accident. He enjoyed hearing the stories she'd rarely shared since his passing. "Moments like this make me miss him the most. He'd know what to say.

"I made a lot of mistakes after he passed, Jesse. You boys had to step up a lot, especially Marshall. I never expected to outlive him," she whispered.

He rubbed his chest and massaged away the ache he often felt when thinking about his dad. He'd passed in the dining room while reading the newspaper early one morning. Their mother had been in the kitchen making homemade biscuits and gravy.

He'd died alone.

Fast.

"Don't waste a second of life. That's what I learned from his passing." Sadness resonated in her voice. "You can't stop living to prevent a scar, Jesse. Love cuts us up. It's the times in between that heal those wounds."

"I'm not what she needs," he whispered.

"Bullshit." Jesse glanced back at Ellie's mom, whose statement startled him.

The woman hadn't ever been a big supporter of his. She'd actively attempted to come between them on multiple occasions before their breakup.

"I made a lot of mistakes, but asking her to choose caring for me over going with you was the biggest. I can't ever give that time back to her. Or you." The woman's voice broke. "But I can make damn sure you don't turn tail and run now. My girl never stopped loving you. Never."

Jesse swallowed. Ellie's hand was warm in his.

"I've been worried. I'm not making it past the cancer, not this time."

Damn. Ellie would take her mom's loss hard. It'd been just the two of them for a long time. No. Asshole Phil had been a part of the mix as well.

"Promise me you won't ever let her go," the woman ordered. "I've seen you with her. I know you won't ever let anything touch her. Promise me."

"Elena," his mom said gently.

Jesse already knew the answer. It'd fanned out within him in an awareness he couldn't deny, not after almost losing her. "I swear."

*D*arkness cloaked the area, but the stillness bothered Jesse as he got into a standby position with his team. The meeting at the hospital to coordinate tonight had been brief yet necessary. Nolan and his team would be primary, with Gage's and Jesse's on standby.

"You cool?" Levi asked.

"Yeah." Jesse forced the word out despite the frenetic energy coursing through his system. What the hell was taking so long? "If Vales lied about this, I'll skin his ass."

"The girls confirmed the meet," Brooklyn said. "Communications have been intercepted from the Raptors and the Horns. Both are under surveillance and en route. We've got a good half hour before anyone nears the zone."

Right. Jesse had let everyone else handle the details so he could focus on Ellie. Damn. He should've stayed at the hospital with her. At least she wasn't alone. Medina and Riley had arrived to handle security while everyone else at The Arsenal was either following one of the targets, onsite for the meeting, or on standby to assist.

"Figured you'd be crawling out of your skin about now," Dallas said as he arrived and got on Jesse's other side. "When I was going through my shit, you were always there, hovering in the background ready to pounce if I needed you. Pissed me right the hell off."

"So you're returning the favor."

Dallas smirked. "Something like that."

Levi chuckled. "You always have been the craziest of his brothers."

"We've got enough operatives in position to take down a third world country," Dallas commented as he got on his belly and settled his rifle into position. "I damn near had to tie Kamren to our bed to keep her from coming here tonight to have your back."

Kamren was one hell of a marksman and a perfect match for Dallas in every way. Jesse swallowed. "Glad you're here, brother."

"It's not the time, but we should chat about what you said to Nolan."

Jesse had opened more than one can of worms, and he wasn't anywhere close to ready to handle them. As if sensing that, Dallas made no further comment. Of all Jesse's brothers, Dallas was the one with the darkest, nastiest past. He'd been in a black ops assassination squad for The Collective.

"I didn't mean to call you out."

"You should have," Dallas said. "I put you on the back burner because of Kamren and the boys, and I shouldn't have. Family doesn't come around only when it's convenient, and we sure as fuck don't ignore a problem because we don't have time. We make time. I fucked up."

"No. It was on me, too. I should've been in your face about your shit, making sure you processed it all."

"Why weren't you?"

"Kamren. I saw the way you two were, the way she remains at your side and whispers in your ear. It's..." Jesse heaved a breath. "I had that once."

"Wish to hell I remembered you with her the way the elders do," Dallas muttered. "But not remembering helped me see the way she is with you now—even when you and the others were being dicks to her."

A rumble rose from Jesse's throat at the reminder.

"Best not poke the bear, little brother. He's mighty touchy about that particular subject," Levi advised.

Smartass. Jesse hadn't taken Ellie's presence at The Arsenal well at first. His brothers had followed his lead. Even though they'd moved past it, guilt still bothered him.

"Heard you carted his ass across the desert to safety," Dallas commented.

"I might have been around."

Tension coiled within Jesse. He didn't want this particular conversation going down when an op was about to get underway. He glared between the two men and noted his brother's grin before Dallas glanced through his rifle's site.

"Anything you need, man. Without question," Dallas said.

A weight lifted off Jesse's shoulders. Levi had been such a huge part of his daily life for so long—one he'd kept from the most important people in his life. The shame of what the man had seen and the secrets he carried had kept Jesse from merging Levi with his brothers. Jesse had needed the two parts of his life separated.

Now?

Jesse glanced between the two and realized they'd seamlessly merged somehow anyway. He hadn't wanted his brothers hurt that he'd trusted someone else to have his back when the night terrors struck. Or when flashbacks happened.

It wasn't because he didn't trust them. It was because Levi had always been there. From the start, he'd been a guardian of the gate.

"He's never told me why," Jesse commented. Dallas glanced up. "Levi flushed his military career to get me out of that hellhole. He walked away from it all to get me out."

"Told you a thousand times, there's no deeper *why* than because it was the right thing to do. The day I take an order to leave a man behind is the day I deserve a bullet." Levi's jaw twitched. "But it's chewing away at you, so I'll give you the why. My sister's in the service —best damn pilot you'll ever meet. She's had a hard road proving herself—one she shouldn't have had because she's a woman."

"That's the why?" Dallas asked.

"No. She was in a black ops group a while back, ran across some bad shit she couldn't share with me. All I know is she made the call I did with you and got kicked out for doing the right thing. That'd just happened. It was fresh on my mind when I came across you." Levi's jaw twitched. "I wasn't about to walk away when the best woman I know didn't."

"Sounds like one hell of a soldier," Jesse commented. Levi hadn't ever mentioned a sister. He'd held details close to his vest to keep the road clear for whatever shitstorm blew in from Jesse's ordeal. A one-way road. "She'd be proud of you."

"I landed on my feet. She's currently flying supply runs in a third world country. Can't say I feel too good about sharing how my life's turned out when hers should be a fuckload better than that." Levi commented. "We done with the bonding?"

Dallas chuckled. "Yeah. Though, just to say, Marshall's been scouring the spec ops theater looking for a pilot. Might be worth having a conversation with her because the second I hit the compound, I'm having a word with the geek squad."

"Fuck." Levi muttered the word, but Jesse noted the man's smirk.

"We've got incoming," Nolan said through the com.

Jesse shifted into position and forced a deep, even breath. Drones were in position, and the entire area was locked down tight. Phil Perskins wouldn't walk away from this. One way or another, Ellie was getting her justice.

13
_____

*a*uthorities from the DEA and FBI were positioned in deer blinds a short distance away. The idea had been Marcus's and inspired by the time Kamren had kicked their asses hard by using them. They'd wait until the transaction closed to move.

"Things go south and they don't take him in…" Jesse hesitated.

"We've got your back," Dallas commented. "He's going down tonight. One way or another. No one hurts family and gets by with it."

Vehicles arrived over the next fifteen minutes. The different gangs faced off but tolerated one another's presence better than Jesse expected. The drawn machine guns brought into play by the Flores cartel quieted everyone else.

"What do we know about the Flores leader?" Jesse asked.

"That's not the leader," Zoey said. "I've wrangled with this cartel before, by the way. They're huge in the underground."

"And you're just now mentioning it?" Cord asked.

"It's not relevant. Besides, every cartel worth their weight in product handles drugs and the sex trade these days. It's expected for them to diversify. It's pretty disgusting."

"Maybe we can jump to what we need to know for now," Mary suggested.

"Right. Their leadership story is interesting. Mrs. Flores staged a coup and killed her husband after catching him raping a set of twins they'd just kidnapped for sale on the black market as virgins. That was six months ago. No one has contested her leadership because she kills anyone rumored to be so much as disgruntled."

"Sounds like a real ballbuster," Levi commented.

Jesse grunted. "Hard to see which of them was the bad guy in that scenario."

A hummer-style limousine pulled up. The four machine gun-toting men closed in around the vehicle as doors along both sides opened. Phil Perskins exited from the driver's side of the back while a tall, muscled man exited, then helped a middle-aged woman out.

"No fucking way," Dallas said.

Jesse looked over at his brother. "We got a problem?"

"Depends. Raul Santiago just exited that fucking limousine."

"I'm sorry, what did you say?" Vi asked.

"Raul Santiago is in play. I barely recognize him, but that's him," Dallas said. "You said something about a CIA asset being in play. Get some fucking answers, Quillery. He's been AWOL since the night of Dani's rape."

Jesse remained silent. Now wasn't the time to hash out his brother's relationship with Dom and Raul. Both of them had been extremely close to Dallas. Their loss had been the catalyst for him joining the military he'd always sworn never to be a part of. He'd intended to remain at home and help their father with the ranch.

"How well did Phil know him back then?" Mary asked.

"Passing acquaintances at most," Dallas said. "Perskins was a hang-around at the street races, but Dom and Raul didn't give him the time of day. Any recognition would be easily passed off as a spoiled, rich, white boy thinking all Mexicans look alike."

"Let's hope you're right, or this op is going south quickly," Vi said. "If Javier was there that night and so was Phil, how did he not immediately recognize Raul?"

"I barely recognized him. Dom and Raul didn't hang with Javier or his crew back then in public. When Dom and Raul were at the races, they were royalty. Javier wasn't part of that," Dallas said.

The small drones high overhead were easily masked by the darkness cloaking the area. The sensitive microphones picked up the conversation without interference. The man Dallas had identified as Raul pulled a device out of his pocket.

"Couple of problems. One, the man Dallas says is Raul is identified as Sandoval Jimenez, Clara Flores's main henchman and fuck buddy," Zoey said. "Oh, and he just turned on a frequency scanner— a very high end one that likely caught the edges of our com's transmission ban."

"I thought our equipment was undetectable," Marshall growled into the com.

"Everything is technically detectable if the equipment is sophisticated enough," Vi said. "HERA modified the communication range immediately. We were detected for less than a second."

The man's gaze swept the area, but he nodded to the machine gun-wielding man beside him as the others gathered everyone's cellphones and searched them for weapons. Everything was set in the center of the clustered group.

"CIA had confirmed presence of their asset and instructed us to ensure the Flores cartel escapes the raid without injury to anyone," Vi said.

"So the fuckers refuse to identify which of them is the asset so they all walk to keep their op in play," Jesse said.

"And interestingly enough, we just received the same order from the DEA agents on-site," Zoey said.

Dallas chuckled. "Jesus. I wonder if they know about each other's ops."

"That's not our problem," Mary said. "Looks like we're starting."

Phil stood in the middle of the gathered group and preened like a peacock. He pulled on the suit blazer he wore as though he'd never worn one and flashed a tooth-filled smile at Clara Flores as the woman joined him. She stroked the man's chest, then repeated the motion with Raul, aka Sandoval.

"Thank you for joining us tonight, gentlemen. We'll make this brief. As you know, we're currently accepting applications for distribution in this area. Assets will be..." Phil paused and smiled. "Varied. Requirements are a strong presence within not only this area but at least one of the larger cities within transportation distance. Trucks capable of handling live cargo are required, as are secured facilities to temporarily house the assets."

Disgust rolled through Jesse. This was far worse than they'd expected.

"Flores is known to transport illegal immigrants into the States and force them into cheap labor within the cartel's stateside operations," Vi said.

"They handle sex trafficking, too," Zoey said. "I've helped free more than a few from their auctions."

Jesse wasn't surprised they'd run across a trafficking ring. The region bordered Mexico and was so large that policing the flow of traffic back and forth was difficult at the best of times. Those were rare, given the recent corruption issues. Marville's problems left the entire region ripe for asswipes like the Flores cartel to move in.

"I've been quite displeased with your efforts to impress me, to be honest." Phil looked around. "My instructions were simple and concise. All you had to do was handle my ex-wife and get a CD back from her. How can we trust any of you with the level of business Ms. Flores has to offer if you can't handle one simple request?"

Everyone looked at one another.

"You didn't tell us the bitch was tied up with The Arsenal. No one fucks with them," one of the men spat. "We've heard intense shit about them throughout our network. Raptors are in a lot of the cities. The Arsenal's made a name for themselves in the underground, too."

"Did I ask for your opinion?" Phil growled.

"Shut up, Phil. I tire of your preening." Clara walked over to the man. "You're a Raptor."

"I am. All due respect, you chose a shitty middleman. He's got a target ten miles wide for the shit he's pulled the past few weeks," the man said.

"Really?" Clara cocked her head. "I do like a drama-free distribution channel. What exactly has Phil done?"

"Targeting his ex-wife brought trouble. She's tied up tight with The Arsenal. They won't stop 'til everyone associated with hurting her is six feet under." The man spat again. "You threw us into the middle of that shit. And for what?"

"Excellent question." The woman turned and regarded Phil. "Do we have a problem I should know about, Mr. Perskins?"

"Of course not."

"You'd tell me if we did?"

"Of course, Clara." He lifted her hand and kissed the back of it. "You are my one and only focus. I was merely tying up some loose ends left by the Marville Dogs. They were sloppy and left too much evidence of past...situations."

"Ah, I see." The woman regarded Phil, then the outspoken Raptor. A malevolent smile spread across the woman's face.

"Shit," Jesse said. "This is about to go south."

"Hold," Mary ordered. "We do not interfere. We see this through until we have the evidence needed to shut this shit down."

Jesse couldn't agree more. He didn't give a damn if the crazy bitch killed everyone.

"San, dear, handle this for me. You know I hate dealing with this sort of thing." The woman walked past Raul. Her hand ran down his chest until she cupped his cock. "I'll reward you later."

The man grinned as he pulled out a gun and shot the Raptor. Angered shouts rose from the man's counterparts, but San pointed the silenced weapon at the unarmed men and killed the remaining three.

"Fuck," Dallas growled into the com.

Silence descended as the Devil Horns looked at the Nomads. Both groups took a step back.

"Well, that was rather distasteful of them," Clara commented. "To clarify, the one thing I loathe more than drama within my network is rats. You aren't paid to have an opinion. You're paid to handle product. Understood?"

Everyone nodded.

"Excellent. Now, I'll admit neither of your groups have the reach we need. I'm not sure why Phil even bothered adding you to the possibilities. We have a few other interested parties, but I suppose we can set up a temporary agreement with you both—assuming you'll work with one another?"

The two groups looked at one another. Both nodded.

"Excellent." Clara clapped her hands together and smiled. "We'll administer a test. We'll deliver the first batch of cargo tomorrow night at this spot. Have sufficient transport available. Half of it will be handled by the Nomads while the remainder will go to the Horns. I'd caution you both to handle the assets with care. Those in the best sellable condition at the end will win a three-month contract with us. A trial run."

"Fuck," Jesse said into the com. The immediacy of the first delivery left tonight's op on pause. Arresting the players present with real cargo was an unquestionable guilty down the road. "Fuck."

"Hold positions." Vi's order was expected.

Dallas rolled away from his rifle and tapped something into his personal communicator. A ping sounded on Jesse's. All team leaders wore them in the field in the event of an emergency situation where coms weren't a viable option. They rarely required private communication where everyone on the com wasn't privy to the op. That's not how The Arsenal worked.

Raul signaled for a meet tonight. 2 a.m. At the track.

Jesse read the note Dallas had sent to Vi and the rest of the team in the operations theater.

Understood. Everyone cover Dallas's exit upon target's departure.

Jesse grunted. With the DEA and CIA involved, they had to assume everyone at The Arsenal was under heavy surveillance. Dallas disassembled his gun and had his gear packed in less than a minute.

"You cool?" Jesse asked.

"No," his brother admitted. "Been wondering what happened with him a long time. Never thought this is where we'd find him."

Jesse studied his brother a minute and realized he couldn't leave him to go to the meet alone. Losing an entire team from the site would be noticed, but two brothers going to have a couple beers afterward would be an easier cover to play off.

Beers. Me. Dallas. Levi. Jesse typed the suggestion in and waited.

Dallas's jaw twitched but he nodded his agreement as the assent came back from operations. Whatever was going on, Jesse wasn't about to let anyone face trouble alone. Likely the women had already come to the same conclusion and had planned to dispatch assistance from one of the teams returning from San Antonio.

But Jesse needed to see as much of this through himself as he could for Ellie.

❀

*J*esse waited until he, Levi, and Dallas were in a vehicle and offsite to mention the biggest trouble they faced. The connection to Arsenal operations was answered the first ring.

"There's a problem," Mary surmised.

"Yeah. That limo is headed toward Marville. I don't know what game Phil is playing or what Raul's cover is, but if they show up at the Sip and Spin, we need Dani contained," Jesse said. "Phil may not know he's Raul, but Dani sure as hell will. And there's no telling who else might recognize him."

"Fuck," Dallas said. "Phil's suspicious. That's why they're going there. If it's Raul, he'll get called out by the locals and Phil gets his confirmation. I can call Kam, get her there."

"No," Vi said. "Jud is there. He and Riley both are. He'll handle Dani. We'll contain the rest."

Jesse wasn't sure how the hell they'd manage, but he trusted Mary and Vi without question. Add Zoey to the mix, and they would do the impossible if necessary.

"The files are buried deep," Zoey said. "Like really, really, really deep. But there was a sting on a local drug ring back when the rapes happened. The warrants were redacted, but the Marville Dogs were listed. The sting took place less than a week before the attacks, based on the video footage's dating tags. Sandoval came into existence the day after the sting."

"They flipped him into being DEA," Dallas said. "There was a couple weeks between Dani's attack and the other girl we haven't identified."

"Yeah and there were likely others. DEA would be more interested in whatever intel they could get from the bigger fish—i.e. the Flores cartel," Vi said.

"So the connection between Phil and the Flores cartel has been around a while," Jesse said. "He was a young-ass punk back then."

"We all were," Dallas said. "Barely out of high school and thinking we were the shit. Dani was still a kid. Fourteen. There's no way he knew what went down with her and Dom. No way he would've turned and abandoned them like that."

"Guess we'll find out tonight," Levi commented. "When did he get roped into the CIA?"

"A couple years ago the CIA began suspecting someone high within the DEA was feeding intel to the Flores cartel and a Russian-based organization," Zoey said. "The files are thin and vague as hell, but the few reports filed indicate an asset was acquired to investigate DEA officials via bogus information leaks."

"Damn. That's dangerous ground to tread alone," Dallas commented.

"It is, but so far four high-level DEA personnel have been quietly removed as a result," Vi said. "I don't know what happened to get him inside, but he's done stellar work from what we can see."

Jesse clicked off and let the silence speak for itself. He and Dallas were alike in many ways. They both needed solitude to think through whatever ate away at their minds.

By the time they'd made it to the Sip and Spin, it was just past midnight. The limo was parked right by the entry.

The entire situation was rife with trouble, but Jesse wasn't about to walk away. If Raul was deep, deep undercover, he'd likely want help because reentering the area he'd grown up in after so many years would prove difficult. Had he heard about Dom's arrest? Did he know Dani worked at the bar?

Jesse couldn't imagine returning to Resino deep undercover. It'd be damn near impossible to contain. He clicked on the com. "We may need unknown operatives in the bar to help contain this cluster fuck."

"They're en route. Jud will help until then. Levi can go in alone and assist," Vi said. "Dani has been removed from the situation. Don't flip your shit, Dallas, but putting Riley in as bartender would've sent everyone in the area on alert."

"Tell me Kamren's not in there," Dallas growled.

"We had no choice," Mary said. "She has more than enough protection and is known by the populace since she used to work there. She's tied to us, but in a way that still makes it plausible she's there helping out a friend."

The argument made sense, and Jesse suspected Dallas agreed because he offered no rebuttal. Levi slid out of the vehicle and headed into the bar. By the time they entered moments later, the man had ghosted entirely.

"Jesus, Levi's a ninja, too," Zoey said.

Jesse chuckled. The women declared operatives who were beyond exceptional in all skills to be ninjas. Few of the operatives had the designation.

He and Dallas sat at a table near the bar but across the room from where Clara Flores and Phil Perskins held court.

His brother came in to the Sip and Spin enough for locals to not think twice about their presence. Kamren covered shifts for Dani on occasion and made no qualms about not wanting to be bothered by anyone—most especially her overprotective man. She was all business when on a job.

The Devil Horns leader and Paco from the Nomads sat with Perskins and Flores. A few others Jesse didn't recognize had joined as well, but they wore the distinctive colors of Devil Horns and Nomads. Jesse sauntered up to the bar and waited his turn.

"Two Bud Lights," he ordered.

Kamren glared at him as she uncapped the cold beers and handed them to him. She said nothing, but anger and confusion were evident in her gaze. Fuck. They'd thrown her in so quickly she hadn't been warned.

Jesse took a chance the woman would keep herself composed. Or maybe she hadn't recognized him.

Raul Santiago is here. Deep cover.

Kamren's gaze widened as she lip-read his statement. She nodded, then glanced over at the corner. Jesse couldn't blame the woman for being confused.

He set a ten down on the bar and returned to the table with Dallas.

And waited.

When the two gang leaders left, most people departed the table within moments. Once it was Phil, Raul, and Carla, conversation began. The small surveillance cameras they'd installed months ago picked up the conversation easily. It flowed within the coms Jesse and the rest of the team wore.

"You still remind me of someone, Sandoval," Phil commented.

"Told you twice already, white boy. Back off. I don't know you. Don't want to know you." Raul's menacing glare was evident from across the bar. "You want to continue this chat, we can do it outside, but it'll end with you not breathing."

"Confirmation on the situation. Everyone prepare to contain as needed. Intercept anyone approaching them."

Kamren approached the table and smiled. "Evening. Sorry for the delay. What do y'all want to drink?"

"You don't work here," Phil spat angrily. "Where's Dani?"

Raul's eyes flashed wide a moment. His gaze cut to Jesse and Dallas. Jesse nodded, confirming they had his back. The man's attention shifted, and he flashed a smile. "Hello, beautiful. What's your name?"

"Kamren." She smiled and tapped the ring on her left finger.

"Afraid I'm taken though, sexy. Wish I would've met you before, though. You look like you'd be a fun one to know."

"Doesn't he remind you of someone?" Phil asked.

"What's that supposed to mean?" Kamren asked, hand on her hip. "Cause he's Mexican?"

"Watch it, bitch," Phil growled. "I'll bury you."

"Ha. You can try," Kamren taunted. "But, no. He doesn't remind me of anyone. You, on the other hand, remind me of a thieving, lying sack of shit who beats women and rapes little girls. I guess we all have our doppelgängers." She smiled prettily and looked at Carla. "I just learned that word last week. I'm getting my GED soon."

"Good for you. I admire a hard-working woman who stands up for herself. I was once like you." The woman smiled. "Don't let any man break you down."

"Oh, I don't. My man builds me up and puts me on a pedestal." Kamren laughed. "Another of my new words. Now what can I get you all?"

"Bottled water for me," Phil said.

"And?" Kamren asked. "This isn't a daycare, Perskins. Order alcohol or get out."

The man rose. His hand raised, but Raul clasped the man's wrist. A cry rose from across the room. The chair tumbled as Phil landed with a hard crash to the floor.

"Touch a woman in anger around me again and I'll bury you alive," Raul warned.

"Ah, yes. I see the similarity you mentioned earlier," Carla commented when she looked at Kamren. "Tell me. You do not like this man. Why?"

Kamren's gaze slid to Jesse and Dallas, then back to the woman. She had no com and no idea the woman was the leader of one of the largest cartels in Mexico. Fear spiraled through Jesse.

"I don't like men who steal their wives' homes and accuse them of being an addict. I don't like men who take advantage of the poor because their parents have money." Kamren shrugged. "We all have our pet peeves, though."

"Ah, well that explains it. Sandoval and I will take two Tecates with extra lime," Carla said and then pointed to Phil, who remained on the floor clutching the hand Raul had released. "Bring some ice for his broken wrist and whatever you have on tap for him. We'll need some privacy. Clearly there's a lot we must discuss."

"Carla was born in Brooklyn. She went missing during her freshman year of college," Vi said. "We're looking into the time period after that."

Damn. Jesse watched as Kamren walked away from the table as though nothing had happened. Nerves of steel. He glanced over at Dallas, whose gaze remained on her.

"She's a hell of a woman," Jesse commented.

"Yeah, she is."

Jesse's gaze swept the bar and settled on Jud, who'd taken position at the pool table nearest the trio. The menacing don't-fuck-with-me aura he cast easily radiated from him as he handed a cue stick to Riley. Laughter tumbled from Jesse as he realized the former assassin was the only containment they'd needed because no one would approach that side of the room with him around.

Everyone within the tri-county had heard about him single-handedly taking down an assassination team who'd come to kill Vi while they were all overseas rescuing hostages. They'd likely heard he'd once skinned a man alive. Moments like this made Jesse thankful as fuck he'd landed on solid ground with his brothers and the men they'd brought in. Without The Arsenal, life after the hole wouldn't have been worth living.

14

The track was a narrow, straight section of farm-to-market road south of Kamren's farm. Jesse cut off the truck lights and sat. Dallas seethed in the passenger's seat. Levi had remained behind in case blowback from the night arrived late.

Phil had left. Riley and Jud had followed him to Nomad Memorial, where he was currently being treated for a broken wrist. Jesse owed Raul a beer for taking him down a peg.

"She intentionally goaded him," Dallas said into the silence.

"Yeah, she did."

"She could've been hurt."

"She knew you wouldn't let that happen. None of us would have. She went into the situation blind because she got a call she was needed. She handled herself better than a lot of soldiers back in the service would have. Arsenal, through and through." Jesse leaned back and glanced at his watch. "He's late."

"He's likely having to fuck and tuck Carla," Dallas said. He pounded his fist on the console between them. "What's the play here, brother? We're mired in more shit than we expected."

"Ellie is the play. Whatever we need to get her safe and take Phil down."

"And Raul?" Dallas glanced over at him.

"We decide that after we find out what's going on. Either way, we'll do what we can because he had Kamren's back at the bar." Jesse paused. "For you."

"That wasn't for me. He had no way of knowing she's mine."

"Bullshit. You broadcast that fact every time you enter the place. The glares when men flirt. The way you watch her walk across the room." Jesse chuckled. "He knew, so he protected you because that's what he and Dom did for you back in the day."

"You know it wasn't y'all, right? I was young and stupid and wanted my own crew. Something away from being a Mason."

"I get it. Nolan did the same thing. Street racing. He was Dom. Hell, Dom learned most of what he knew from Nolan."

"Dom never told me," Dallas said. "We were standing in the prison and neither acknowledged the other. Acted like strangers."

"Because what you and Dom had transcended the brief relationship they had. Nolan wouldn't undercut that. We all knew those two were important to you."

"Never more important than you all were," Dallas said. "Cuts me deep I didn't follow through with you. I should have."

"You will. When all this is done, we'll talk."

Before Dallas could respond, a set of headlights appeared as a vehicle pulled behind them. A lone shadow formed as he exited the driver's side. Jesse and Dallas exited as the figure stepped into the beam of light.

Raul.

Jesse hung back and let Dallas take the lead.

His brother stood woodenly for the first couple of seconds until Raul dragged him into a hug. The anger and distrust crumbled quickly, though, and the two shared hard back slaps and smiles.

"Christ," Raul said. He ran his hand through his hair. "Gotta admit, I've sweated bullets more than once since this started the other day."

"Fill us in. We know you're DEA and CIA," Dallas said.

The man froze. "Where did that come from?"

"It was easy to figure out," Jesse added. "There's nothing our crew can't uncover. Your cover is solid."

"No offense, but my ass is the one on the line here."

"Yeah, and we covered it and will continue covering it, so tell us what the hell is going on," Dallas ordered.

"You tell me. Where's Dani? That's why the bastard dragged me there, right? And Dom?" Pain radiated on the man's face a moment. "He went down for that shit, didn't he?"

Dallas filled the man in on what they knew and explained that they were investigating the gaps—including his disappearance.

"That bastard. I should dig Javier up and kill him again," Raul said. "He sent Dom down so he could take over the Dogs. I was collateral damage he'd intended to take out, but the DEA snatched me up first. I didn't have time to tell Dom I'd been taken. They wanted me in deep and fast."

"Were you there that night? Did you know? About Dani's rape?" Dallas asked.

"No." Raul shook his head. Pain shown in his gaze. "Fuck, how is she? Dani?"

"Cold steel," Dallas said. "We removed her from the bar before you arrived."

"Your woman, man. She was straight sass," Raul said with a grin.

"Owe you huge for having her back."

"My pleasure to break the bastard however I could. Gotta admit, I've been weighed down with evil so long I can't find my way out."

"Then we'll help. How much longer?" Jesse asked.

"We're close. This operation should do it. Tomorrow night. Carla doesn't usually come to the meets, but she wanted to meet Perskins. Tonight made her nervous, though. Your girl has her questioning whether we should do business with the bastard. We lose this, then I'll be in longer."

"We need him to go down tomorrow. Ellie's laid up in a hospital with a TBI because of him," Dallas said. "And he's got evidence from that night. We found one CD, but it didn't have the kills."

Raul's jaw twitched.

"There's another copy running around. Javier made a recording."

"Son of a bitch," Raul growled. "Did he rape her?"

"Don't go down that road, man."

"Did he rape her?" Raul thundered.

"We don't know. A large section of the footage was damaged. It's grainy, and she's not talking. She doesn't trust us."

"Why not?" Then Raul's eyes widened. "Nolan. He lured her out with Nolan."

Jesse nodded.

"Where is she? I'll have a word."

"After we take the bastards down tomorrow night," Dallas said. "She's safe, man. We've had a crew on her since Kamren's bullshit stirred up Javier's shit."

"And Dom?"

"He's solid," Dallas said. "We'll get him out."

"Fuck, yeah we will."

❀

*J*esse was worn out by the time he'd showered, changed, and made it to the hospital. The digital clock on the truck read 3:49 a.m. when he turned off the vehicle and headed inside. His mother was asleep on the chair that made into a bed. Seeing her warmed his heart but awakened his concern. She had no business staying with Ellie overnight. He glanced at the woman asleep in the other chair.

Bree's new hair growth was evident without the coverings she'd been wearing around the compound. Jesse admired the hell out of the woman for what all she'd done to make Zoey's recovery easier. He dragged his feet along the floor to alert the woman to his presence. When it came to the brilliant scientist with the freaky ability to create dangerous weaponry, a man was smart to make his presence known.

"Jesse," she said as though affirming he wasn't a ghost. "She's asleep."

He smirked as the woman sat up in her chair and fidgeted with Ellie's blankets.

Ellie.

Her long, blonde hair had spilled out onto the pillow, but bandages still covered the bulk of her head. He walked to the other side of the bed where the tubes and poles weren't in his way and leaned down. He feathered kisses along her forehead.

"How is she?" Jesse asked.

"She's had a rough night," Bree said. "She woke up a few times. Confused. The doctor said that's to be expected for a couple of days. He's a bit annoyed because I've made him come in and check on her quite a bit."

Jesse smiled. "Where's Medina?"

"Food. I made him go, so don't get angry he left his post. He needed to get out of this place. He's at Whataburger. He'd better hurry back though because I'm craving a chocolate shake really bad." Bree glanced up at Jesse. "It's not my business, but it'd go a long way if you told him Ellie's attack isn't his fault. Or, I dunno. Say something to him."

Jesse ran a hand down his face and sighed his exhaustion. He hadn't realized the man needed confirmation, but he nodded. "Go home. Get some rest. Thanks for staying with her."

"Erm, you need to tell your mom to leave. She won't listen to us." Bree smiled. "She said Ellie was gonna wake with family here, one way or another."

Damn. Jesse loved the idea of Ellie being family. As far as Jesse was concerned, she was. But he didn't need to confuse the issue with his mom. She had a way of cutting corners.

"Jesse, you're back." He turned and helped his mom rise from the chair. She drew him into a hug. "I'm sorry you didn't get him, dear, but you will. There'll be a lot more evidence tomorrow night."

He shook his head, then glanced at Bree. Red rose in Bree's cheeks as she picked up her phone. "I cheated and got the Cliffs-Notes. Sorry. I didn't tell Ellie, though. I swear."

Jesse was relieved the woman hadn't shared the operation with

Ellie. She needed to focus on healing, not worrying about him or Phil or anything else beyond getting better.

"You need to go home and rest, Ma."

"I'm not the one burning the candle at both ends. You won't do her any good if you're too exhausted to see straight." His mom patted his cheek.

"I'll sleep better here with her than I will at home," Jesse admitted. Not that he'd dare sleep in the hospital.

Medina entered. "Sorry, boss. Bree wouldn't leave me be until I left and ate."

Jesse waited as the man doled out milkshakes to Bree and his mom. "I'm glad you did. Thanks for watching over Ellie," Jesse said. "And thanks for saving her life, man."

"I should've done more," the man said.

"You saved her. You and Riley both did," Jesse said. "Go and get some rest. Take Mom and Bree with you. I doubt either can drive, as tired as they likely are."

"And you? No offense, but you look like shit."

Jesse laughed and motioned toward the convertible bed. "I'll sleep here."

The man paused, as if unsure whether it was the right call, but nodded and guided both of the women out. Jesse repositioned the chair closer to the bed and closed the hospital room door so the sounds from the hallway wouldn't wake Ellie.

The temptation to take her hand, to caress her, overrode his common sense. The glide of her soft skin beneath his fingertips calmed him. He leaned down and kissed her hand.

"We'll get him, Peanut." He rested his head alongside her hand and closed his eyes. Antiseptic and hospital stench overrode her scent and reminded him of his recovery.

"Jesse."

He sat up. Smiled. "I didn't mean to wake you."

"I'm glad you're here. Bree wouldn't tell me where you were. I was worried."

. . .

*E*llie hated the possessiveness within her tone. The fear. Jesse wore exhaustion like a second skin. He didn't need her drama on top of whatever he'd been handling.

A nightlight on the other side of the room was the only source of light with the room's door closed. She shifted on the bed until she was fully against one side. She patted the area beside her. "Can you lie with me? Please?"

"Ellie..."

"Sorry. I shouldn't have asked. I just..." She swallowed. "I hate this place."

"Me, too." He crawled into bed and stretched out beside her.

The space was too small for the two of them, but she didn't mind being crunched in with him. Heat spread through her as their gazes met. "I'm sorry, Jesse. You don't have to lie here with me. I don't know why I asked."

"It's okay."

"No, it's not. I know better. I swear I do. Don't be angry."

"Hey," he whispered, cupping her face. "It's okay, Peanut. You're safe with me. You can't ever say or do anything to upset me, okay? Injuries like yours sometimes lower your filter."

"Filter?"

"You'll be more apt to say what you think."

"Great. I'm a blurter now."

Her stomach somersaulted when he smiled. All the Mason men had killer smiles. They smoldered. Some of the tension in her melted away beneath the intensity. He settled an arm around her so she was partially lying atop him with her head on his chest.

"Are you okay?" The question tumbled from her.

"I am now, Peanut. Close your eyes and rest. I'm here. You're safe."

She was safe because he and everyone else at The Arsenal had made sure of it. Every time she woke, someone was there. It'd taken her a few moments to recognize some of them. The guilt of not remembering her new friends had caused more than a few anxiety attacks.

"Will I get better? Be honest."

"Yeah, Ellie. I swear you will," he whispered against her forehead. "Sleep, Peanut."

"Only if you will." She watched his jaw twitch as he glanced about the room. "You're too worried to sleep."

"Yeah," he admitted.

Ellie interwove their fingers. She rested both atop his chest beside her head. Calm and relaxation would lull him to sleep. "Close your eyes. Remember when we used to sneak out to the tree and watch the stars."

"I remember we did more kissing than stargazing," he said with a grin, but his eyes were closed.

She relaxed and basked in the warmth of his body near hers. "I was always worried we'd get caught out there and you'd get in trouble. I was terrified your parents would call my mom and tell her I was over there instead of wherever I'd told her I was going. Remember what you'd say?"

His muscles flexed as she rubbed his chest, then stroked his face. And waited. He'd remembered the scent of her shampoo. She had no doubt he remembered everything they'd shared beneath the tree.

"Nothing can come between us. We face everything together, head on," he whispered.

She interwove their fingers once more and relaxed against him. "Nightmares can't come between us if we face them together. You aren't the only one afraid of sleep."

"He's not gonna hurt you ever again, Peanut."

"And those bastards aren't ever touching you again, honey. I'll kick anyone's ass if they even breathe wrong around you." Ellie grinned at the thought. She was a short, curvy woman with no ninja skills while he was one of the most well-trained operatives at The Arsenal.

Everyone needed a champion in their corner because there was no such thing as on-duty twenty-four seven. Her head throbbed from the thoughts rolling around. Jesse was too important to not consider. She closed her eyes and evened out her breathing but remained alert.

The early morning hours were rife with constant ins and outs from the door, but shift change wasn't for another couple of hours. With a bit of luck, Jesse would get an hour or so of rest before Nurse Grumpy came on duty and threw him out of the bed.

A brief shaft of light splaying across the floor was the only signal she got that someone had entered. Her pulse quickened when she realized she faced away from the door and couldn't see who. Some operative she was.

Tension coiled within her. She remained locked into place alongside Jesse, who slept as though he were comatose. How long had he been awake? Levi prowled into her line of vision and sat in the chair beside the bed. Though silent, his assessing gaze spoke volumes, as did the nervous tick in his jaw and the quick widening of his eyes.

Ellie locked gazes with him and drew the hand interlocked with Jesse's closer. Levi was one tough operative, but she'd go toe-to-toe with him if she had to. He wasn't waking Jesse up or pulling him away from her. No way. No how.

Levi's grin fractured the tension hanging between them. He stretched his long, muscular legs out, leaned his head back and closed his eyes. Although Ellie didn't want him intruding on the moment she and Jesse were sharing, she wanted the man she loved safe more than anything. Until she fully understood how to handle the nightmares, flashbacks, and terrors he experienced, Levi and anyone else more familiar with how to handle everything were a necessary part of Jesse's sleeping routine.

She waited a few moments before she surrendered to sleep.

❀

*J*esse glared at Levi. The bastard had spent most of the day grinning or outright laughing. He hadn't made a comment, though. Nolan and Dallas were crouched in the same locations as yesterday while they waited for the meet time to come around. Lookouts from both gangs were already in position and heavily armed. Two transport vehicles were parked near one another in the open field near the water tank.

None of that bothered Jesse.

Levi's humor, however, pissed him off.

"Say it," he growled.

"Nothing to say," Levi said.

Nolan and Dallas looked at one another. "We miss something?"

Levi remained silent but raised his eyebrows. The silent dare hung between them a moment. Times like these made Jesse wish the man wasn't such a good friend. Killing him was way simpler than admitting what'd happened. Though it seemed like nothing on the surface, Jesse recognized its importance.

"I fell asleep with Ellie at the hospital," Jesse said.

"That's not a surprise. You've been running on fumes," Nolan commented.

"We're entering a new phase of life, man." Levi settled on his belly and peered through the sites of his rifle. "That woman would've gutted me had she had a knife. No one was gonna get close to you, much less wake you."

"I might know someone with a knife or two to spare," Dallas said with a grin. "We need to get her trained in hand-to-hand and basic weaponry. She's alone at the main office entry a lot. We've got security and defense drones there, but it'll give her peace of mind to know she can take an asshole down if needed. Plus it's hotter than hell when your woman can handle herself."

Jesse grinned. His woman. He was liking the sound of that more and more.

"First time I didn't worry," Levi said. "I could've turned around and left because there was no way she was letting anything you dreamed or did hurt you."

"If I have an episode, she can't control me."

"You slept like the dead. Didn't move once," Levi said. "Her in your arms, pressed snug against you. I'm thinking that's the best medicine to keep those nightmares away."

"Getting her ex behind bars will help, too," Nolan said. "We can talk with Logan and Sinclair, see what they recommend. Maybe one of the cottages. We can put defense drones in. They can knock your ass out if there's a situation."

"I don't want to hurt her."

"You won't," Levi said. "That woman is fierce. Bandaged up like a mummy, likely drugged out of her mind, and she stared me down like a lioness. She would've figured a way to hand me my ass if I'd tried waking you."

Nolan grinned.

"She's good for you," Dallas said. "Whatever comes of it, she's good for you."

Jesse kept the what-ifs to himself. He wasn't ready to share that he might be able to have sex. He wasn't sure how to navigate his way down the path—if it was even possible.

A comfortable silence fell among them as they waited for the meet to go down. Both gang leaders arrived at the same time with the rest of their crews. They fanned out farther than Jesse had expected.

"They're preparing defenses in case Flores goes after them," Mary commented. "Everyone expand your perimeter."

Jesse noted the new perimeter formation on the headgear they wore. None of the changes affected him, so he kept his attention focused on the readout displaying where everyone was. Darkness had descended and cast the area in shadowy darkness. The sliver of moonlight did little to help visibility.

The grumble of a large engine sounded from the road as a large semi pulled off the paved highway and slowly wound its way down the narrow strip of terrain carved out from the overgrown shrubbery and weeds. Mesquite tree limbs scraped the sides of the semi-truck as it exited the road and came fully into the field near the water tank.

The two gang leaders stood beside one another with armed men behind them. Raul exited the truck, then made his way to the dark blue Escalade that'd parked alongside the truck. Phil exited the driver's side and made his way to the gang leaders without pause.

Raul helped Carla from the car and followed behind the woman with his weapon drawn. His gaze swept the area, but he didn't bother scanning with the surveillance device like he had the night before.

"Gentlemen," Carla greeted. "I see you came prepared for transport. Very good."

"Let's talk about our cut," Paco said. "It costs to feed and secure these *assets*."

"Yes, it does, which is why you are getting the amount we agreed on up front." Carla walked across the field in her high-heeled shoes as though she were on a runway. "Once the sales have gone through, you'll receive fifteen percent. That's your incentive for taking care of the cargo."

The leaders looked at one another and grinned. Idiots.

"That's too much. Five's more than enough," Phil said.

"They're taking the risk," Raul said. "You get five percent, they get fifteen. Take it or leave it."

Phil glared at Raul, then Carla. Tension coiled within Jesse as the situation played out. He'd spent the afternoon reading the intel the women had gathered on the Flores cartel. They left a body trail wherever they went—far more now than when the husband had been in charge.

"Primary directive is to secure the asset," Vi said.

The asset. Raul.

Jesse remained silent as the transaction got underway. Raul and two gunmen who'd exited the truck opened the back. Two other men exited the back and shouted in rapid Spanish as women and children were moved out of the vehicle. Their clothes and appearances were far cleaner than he'd seen with most of the traffickers they'd been taking down, but their captivity had likely been brief at this point.

Revulsion locked all thoughts beyond freeing them aside. The children wrapped themselves around the women. Tears streamed down their little faces, but they remained quiet as the men herded them into two groups.

One of the men handed one backpack to each of the gang leaders. Carla smiled at them both. "Three days, gentlemen. Care for them as though your lives depend on it. We'll be in touch with each of you with a drop location."

The men nodded. Neither opened the backpacks.

"The other product you've purchased is here," Carla said as two large duffels were deposited at their feet. "Prove you can handle this, and we'll increase your supply."

"And mine?" Phil demanded. "Where's my fee?"

"Jesus, he's an idiot," Dallas mumbled.

"Right. Raul?"

Raul tossed a smaller pack to Phil. The man caught it with a malevolent glare, but he remained silent.

"We're a go," Mary said.

"DEA. You're under arrest." The broadcast statement thundered through the area.

Panic ensued as gunmen drew their weapons and frantically searched for a target. Drones, which had already honed in, darted them. They crumped to the ground where they stood. Carla, Phil, and Raul ran toward the Escalade, but Gage's team had already swarmed the area.

Marcus's team moved in on the trucks as Dallas separated from Jesse and instructed his team to assist with the women and kids. There'd been more than expected. Jesse remained at a distance as he'd promised, but his rifle remained sighted on Phil.

Gage shoved the bastard to his knees and zip-tied his hands behind his back. Raul and Carla were secured a few feet away. Anger radiated from the woman as she watched the takedown unfold. The Arsenal had provided the tech and the backup, but everyone hung back as the DEA agents took control of the arrests.

A tall brunette with a DEA vest walked up to Phil. "Phil Perskins?"

"I want a lawyer."

"Come with me, sir."

"Why is he being separated?" Carla asked, rage evident in her voice. "You sold us out."

A slight smirk appeared on Raul's face as the female agent dragged a screaming Perskins away from everyone and placed him in an SUV that'd just arrived on scene. The moment he was in, she got into the driver's seat and left.

"Damn," Nolan commented. "That was slick."

"Definitely put a target on Phil," Jesse said, not the least bit sorry. "That should loosen his tongue nicely. What about Raul?"

"He's not our problem. They'll untangle him when the time is right. They'll want his cover maintained for use later if needed, but from what I see—he's done," Mary said.

15

The Nomad Police Department was the nearest detention facility available and nowhere near prepared for the shitstorm that rolled into its small building shortly after midnight. Carla, Raul, and everyone associated with the Flores cartel had been taken away by the DEA and FBI, who'd been briefed about the operation because of the human trafficking angle.

While Jesse was relieved the headache was not an Arsenal problem, he'd hoped to get a few moments alone with Phil Perskins before he lawyered up like the pretentious prick he was. None of the alphabet soup was interested in Perskins or anything he might know because the cartel had been caught red-handed.

They'd relegated his detention to local authorities until the alphabet soup got around to him, which would likely be tomorrow at the earliest. Nolan and Dallas remained Jesse's appointed handlers as he paced the small patch of Chief Lyon's office.

The middle-aged man entered with a huff as he shoved past a stack of paperwork that nearly toppled as his large belly scraped against it. Jesse fisted his hands and noted the closed door. Confined spaces sucked.

"You boys must be something else. I thought I'd have to send half my officers home because everyone was hanging around to see what brought the mighty *Masons* in. I would've been here sooner, but I got stopped at least five times between here and holding so people could tell me what they knew about *The Arsenal*."

Tension struck the room as Jesse froze in position and braced for the man's surly attitude as he fumbled with a file on his desk.

"I'm gonna shoot straight because I was told that was best with you boys. This isn't the military. And this isn't the FBI, CIA, NSA, or whoever else you're used to steamrolling over. This here's Nomad County, and we don't have time to deal with the Marville messes you're uprooting." The chair creaked as the man leaned back and ran his dirty fingers across his mustache. "I've had calls from a lot of my constituents protesting Mr. Perskins' incarceration. More than a couple of them mentioned an altercation out at the country club."

"He was caught with a drug cartel and two gangs—one of which operates here in Nomad," Dallas said.

"I'm aware of the gang arrest. We've had to assist in executing search warrants on their houses and their headquarters," the man said. "You boys really should've brought us into the loop on this."

"He's tied up with the attack at the hospital," Jesse said. "He hired the bastard who attacked Ellie Travers."

"You have evidence?"

"Funny, I thought that was your job," Nolan commented.

"There's pressure to arraign him quickly," the man admitted. "All evidence I'm seeing is circumstantial at best."

The man was nuts. No, he was in Perskins' pocket. Son of a bitch.

"He'll be arraigned in a few hours and will likely make bail." The man shut the file. "You don't have jurisdiction to question him, so go on back to Resino where you belong. Stay out of Nomad. I don't take kindly to local vigilantes getting in the way of real police work."

The man wouldn't know real police work if it knocked him in the face. Jesse pulled out his cell to contact the girls and see what strings they could pull, but the door opened and the brunette DEA agent from the scene entered.

"You can't just walk in here," Lyons said.

"Sorry, Chief. I'm Special Agent Moana Rice. I'm here to pick up Phil Perskins."

"On what grounds?"

"He's a material witness on more than one federal investigation. As such, he falls outside your domain and within mine. Notify whoever's in detention that I'll be taking him into custody immediately." The woman thumped a piece of paper down on his desk. "There's the paperwork you need. Now, should I make the call myself or can you handle it?"

Jesse rocked back on his heels. Nolan chuckled. Dallas covered his mouth as his shoulders shook. Red rose in the police chief's face as he glared at the woman. He picked up the phone and made the call.

Moana left the office. Jesse and his brothers followed. A text arrived on his phone.

The old rest stop. Twenty minutes.

He left the building and his brothers followed.

"There a reason we're leaving?" Nolan asked.

Jesse tossed his phone to his brother. "I'm thinking someone pulled a string for us."

"Looks like," Dallas said as he read the text when Nolan passed it to him. "You wanna call the girls? Verify?"

"No. They've got enough crap to deal with thanks to the cartel and the gangs," Jesse said.

The old rest stop was ten miles east of Nomad on the highway to San Antonio. Though the place had been closed down by the state, the building remained. Jesse parked behind a burgundy SUV and noted the license plate, just in case.

Dallas exited and headed to the west of the building, while Nolan went around the back. Jesse unclipped his weapon, but kept it sheathed as he approached the woman leaning against the entry to the men's bathroom.

"Special Agent Rice."

"You're surprised," the woman commented.

"I am."

"My asset refused to cooperate with us or his CIA handlers until we secured Perskins. He didn't say why, but here I am. Securing Perskins." She crossed her arms. Anger rolled through her small frame. "You want to tell me why?"

"You knew he was CIA?" Nolan asked.

"Not until night before last when they steamrolled through years of work," the woman spat. "You've got twenty minutes, then I'm hauling Perskins to the federal facility."

Jesse cracked his knuckles and entered the men's bathroom. Phil was handcuffed to the first urinal. The man's eyes widened. "Hello, Phil. I think you and I need to have a conversation."

"I want a lawyer."

"No, you don't. Besides, I'm not law enforcement. I don't give a shit what you want."

"She is. I'm gonna sue."

"No, Phil. You won't because you're likely gonna be dead in a few hours anyway. In case you didn't notice, the Flores cartel thinks you're the one who sold them out."

The man paled. Eyes wide, he yanked on the wrist manacles attached to the pipe. "No. I didn't. She'll know."

"How? You're the one who was gonna walk without so much as a blip on your jacket by the time Daddy got through greasing palms. That's what you expected, right?"

"What do you want?" Phil glared. "Is this about that cunt?"

The urge to punch the bastard rode Jesse hard, but Rice had put her ass on the line to give him time alone with Phil. Any injury would support the bastard's claim that this happened. Nothing else would. Jesse would make sure there was no evidence of the altercation.

"Here's what's gonna happen. You're gonna tell me everything about the night on the CD. Then you're going to tell me where the rest of your stash is."

"I don't know what you're talking about."

"You get three strikes, Phil. I'll secure protective custody for you. Otherwise you're gonna find yourself in a world of hurt very, very soon. Word will spread you're talking to the feds about Flores. The

Devil Horns. Then I'll make sure folks know you were tied up with the Marville Dogs going down."

"I wasn't!"

"Doesn't matter. A pretty little rich white boy like you won't last long behind bars. Add in the fact that everyone assumes you talked, and you won't last the first night." Jesse leaned in. "If you do, I'll be there. I'll make sure you hurt until I get what I want from you."

"You're crazy."

"You hurt her. You stole from her. You tried to destroy her."

"She deserved it!" he shouted. "I knew she didn't love me, but she said yes to save her mom. Ellie was such a sweet fuck, too. I'd spread her legs and slide in and lick her tears away. She always cried, you know. At first. I made her look me in the eyes when I fucked her so she couldn't pretend I was you."

Jesse punched the man's stomach. "Don't you ever speak her name again."

"I'll do a lot more than that if you don't let me go, Mason. You have no idea what I can do to that cunt." The man laughed.

Unease crawled through Jesse. There was more in play than they realized. Perskins thought he had a hidden card left to play, which meant he likely did—one which involved Ellie somehow.

"Where's the CD?" Jesse asked, opting to switch back to the subject at hand. The sooner they got the evidence they needed, the better.

"I'd rather talk about Ellie. I heard you can't fuck anymore." Phil smirked. "She wasn't ever good at it anyway, you know."

A growl rumbled from Jesse, but he didn't physically react. That's what the bastard wanted.

"Leave," Nolan ordered as he clicked on a Bluetooth he wore. "Z, I'm taking over. Give me what you have on Perskins so far."

Jesse turned. "This is mine."

"No." Nolan shook his head. "We don't have time for him to mess with your head. This is mine. I'll get what we need."

Jesse couldn't argue because rage consumed him. Images of Ellie crying as the bastard... He punched the nearest wall beside him. Sheetrock crumbled beneath the impact.

"Lock it down," Dallas growled in his ear. "For Ellie. Walk away. Nolan's got this."

Jesse turned and left. He trusted his brothers with his life on a daily basis, but this felt bigger. More important. Because this was about Ellie. This couldn't get fucked up.

❀

*E*llie sat in her hospital bed and watched the women gathered around her. Frustration rose within her, but she kept quiet because she recognized well-meaning diversions when she saw them. Momma Mason had just left with Ellie's mom.

Now that it was only Bree, Rhea, Riley, Zoey, and Vi, the time for answers had finally arrived. She waited until the four women had hooked up the laptop they'd brought to the small television. They positioned themselves on the chairs and floor beside the bed.

"Where's Jesse?" Ellie asked.

Bree's eyes widened as she looked at the others. Vi, in typical badass brilliance, offered no visible response. She paused the video they'd started and glanced up. "He's taking care of something but should be back soon."

"What's he taking care of? A mission?"

"He'll be here soon," Vi said.

"What if it were Jud? You'd want to know."

The woman rubbed her lower stomach, a habit she'd developed, no doubt from watching Mary do the same. Ellie smiled. Vi was going to make an excellent mom. Everyone at The Arsenal was thrilled to see the next generation of the Quillery Edge being born so close together. Was she having a boy or a girl? Would she find out or be like Mary and wait?

"I told you we should tell her," Rhea said. "She deserves to know what's going on. She's got a head injury, but she's not an idiot. She knows something's up. Isn't not knowing more stressful?"

"Jesse, Dallas, and Nolan are overseeing search warrants the DEA and FBI obtained on all Phil's properties and financial holdings," Riley said.

"Riley!" Vi looked at the woman. "We agreed to wait until after it was over."

"I'm with Rhea. She needs to know. As Jesse's little sister, I'm glad she cares enough to want to know. Y'all didn't see her this morning being all protective and growly with the nurse who was getting too loud. I did."

Heat rose in Ellie's cheeks. Riley and her mom had walked in on Jesse sleeping in Ellie's hospital bed. He'd slept for a solid five hours, despite numerous nurse visits and foot traffic. While she was glad he'd finally rested, she was more than a bit concerned about him working too hard.

Mary and Dylan entered the room. Ellie smiled as he helped Mary get situated in the chair Bree vacated. Red tinged the woman's cheeks as she looked at Ellie.

"The seizures went off without a hitch. Everything was exactly where Phil said it'd be," Mary said. "Nolan was quite thorough in a rather alarmingly calm fashion. Clearly we've underestimated his interrogation skills."

"He was terrifying," Zoey admitted. "He never even touched Phil. I took notes."

"Of course you did," Ellie said. The woman had piles of notebooks filled with insights and facts she'd learned while working at The Arsenal. "If you fill one more bookshelf, Gage will have a fit."

"No, he won't," Vi said. "He's totally whipped."

Zoey smiled. "I am, too."

Ellie chuckled. The couple was adorable together. "I'm ready to go home. I miss Harry and Hermione. I even miss Dobby."

"Poor Dobby. No one names him first," Bree grumbled.

Vi's kitten and puppy were growing rapidly. Zoey's cat, Dobby, was the newest addition to The Arsenal's pet collection. All three had become Ellie's companions in the office area over the past few months.

"You don't miss them. You just hate hospitals," Rhea said. "I don't blame you, though. You've likely spent too much time in them with your mom's illness."

She had. Guilt kept her fidgeting in the hospital because she knew the people gathered around her had added everything she usually did for her mother to their own daily routines. No one had commented, much less complained.

"Thank you," she whispered. "Thank you for looking out for Mom and making this look so easy when I know it isn't."

"I'm glad we're finally able to help you," Riley said. "You've done so much for all of us. And Mom. God, we would've been totally lost without you there to get everything sorted before she came home."

Heat rose in Ellie's cheeks as her gaze flitted to Dylan, who stood against the wall with his arms crossed. A smile crossed his face when their eyes met. "She's right. I'm glad you're back in our lives, Ellie. I'll admit I had my reservations, but I'm glad to see I was wrong. You're good for him."

Ellie swallowed. Dylan was the first of Jesse's older brothers to approve of her with him in any capacity. She wasn't sure what to say. Then a flash of pain crossed Mary's face. The brief, barely discernible glint of discomfort startled Ellie. Had she ever seen the woman hint at anything remotely painful?

She remained silent and studied the woman as everyone around them spoke. Mary had positioned herself in front of Dylan so he couldn't see her face. The tall back of the chair hid the brief flashes of tension moving through her body. Ellie had gotten good at reading pain, though. She'd had years of reading her mom's varying levels of discomfort.

Mary had come to check on Ellie and give her an update even though she was hurting.

No, she was in labor! The realization thundered through her as the conversation continued. Ellie reached down and punched the nurse call button.

"The FBI has possession of all the financial records and recordings, but they've agreed to let us process them all through HERA,"

Mary said. "They're bringing everything to us in a secured transport once it's been logged in at the San Antonio facility. It'll take a few days to get."

"Damn red tape," Zoey muttered.

The nurse entered and glared at everyone in the room. Nomad Memorial had given up on enforcing the "one visitor" rule with Ellie before she'd even woken up. "Did you need something, dear?"

Well, this was going to be awkward.

"Do you have a wheelchair you could bring in here, please?" Ellie asked. She looked at Mary. "I'm sorry, but you should really go check in."

Everyone's attention shifted to Mary, who winced with another flash of pain. Dylan cursed and moved around to crouch in front of his wife. "You're in labor?"

"I think so. For several hours."

"Sweetie, you'd know if you were in labor." The woman laughed. "No doubt it's just back pain. I had that a lot with my first one."

Ellie realized the nurse meant well, but women as tough as Mary didn't respond to pain the same as mere mortals. She'd once been beaten and tortured and had still not given up any information on the security system she and Vi had created. Anyone who endured that level of brutality wouldn't think twice about enduring a few contractions without comment to make sure everything was running smoothly before she delivered her child.

"How long?" Dylan asked.

"A few hours," Mary admitted. "I'm fine. These things take forever. The contractions aren't even that close. I'm still a good four minutes apart."

"You've been in labor for hours and didn't say anything?" Dylan asked as he stood and lifted her into his arms.

"Put me down, Dylan!"

The man laughed and kissed her. The fusion of mouths was hot, hungry, and filled with enough love and joy for Ellie to feel across the room. "Hush, wife. We're going to go have our baby."

"Oh. My. God!" Riley exploded. She yanked out her phone and

started punching like a mad woman. "Yay! I'm going to be an aunty again."

Ellie leaned back and smiled, despite the sense of loss rolling through her. That moment wouldn't ever be hers with Jesse. Her eyes burned from the pain ravishing her as she watched the man carry Mary out. Who needed a wheelchair when you were married to a Mason man who loved you senseless?

"Is it hard?" Bree asked in a whisper.

She and Zoey watched Ellie as if expecting an answer.

"Is what hard?"

"That could've been you. With Jesse," Zoey said.

"I'm thrilled for them. Jesse's going to be a terrific uncle, but yeah. I'll admit knowing he'll never be a father kills me because he'd be a great dad."

"And you'd be a terrific mom," Bree said as she wiped her eyes. "Sorry, I don't mean to be a downer, but I see how much this must suck for you. Yet you're sitting there happy as a clam."

"I can live with never having Jesse's child. I can live without a lot as long as Jesse's in my life," Ellie said.

16

I *can live with never having Jesse's child. I can live without a lot as long as Jesse's in my life.*

Jesse paced.

"Jesse."

He expended a breath and turned to face Sinclair. The woman had a knack for showing up when his thoughts tornadoed. "Mary's having her baby. Phil's on ice. We've got the evidence we need to figure out what happened years ago and put him away a lot longer."

"I heard. Congratulations." She sat in the seat nearest him in the small waiting area he'd found. "Everyone's wondering where you slipped off to. I think half of Resino is in the hospital's waiting room."

Likely more. "We wanted lots of kids. The more the better," he commented. "I always hoped we'd have girls who looked like her. Boys, too, if they had her smile."

"How does Dylan having a baby make you feel? We've never chatted about Dallas's boys."

"I'm happy for them both," he said. "This isn't about that."

"Then why are we here?"

"I slept," he blurted. "In her hospital bed. With her. Hours. Nurses went in and out and I slept like I haven't in years. I know my nightmares aren't fully under control, but I woke up feeling hopeful. I'm terrified, Doc. All the excuses I've had for staying away are gone. She's burned every single one down without pause. She told them she could live without having my child. She could live without a lot as long as I was in her life."

"How does that make you feel?"

"Terrified."

"Is that all?"

"I don't deserve her," he whispered. "I don't deserve..."

"Love?"

Love. Jesse sat. Shock rolled through him as the truth smacked him in the face. Sure, he'd known she still loved him because he loved her more than he ever had.

"I need you to promise me something, Jesse. I don't take this request lightly." The woman paused, as if measuring his ability to handle what she was about to say. "I've read the journals you've shared with me. I know there are more you've kept to yourself. Nothing in them concerns me when it comes to you pursuing a relationship with Ellie. And when I say relationship, I mean a sexual one because I'm certain you can get that part of your life back in some capacity."

Jesse swallowed. He wanted to try. For the first time since he'd escaped, he wanted to try and be the man he'd once been with Ellie. "What are you saying, Doc?"

"What I *haven't* read is what concerns me," she said softly. "I read the medical reports from when you were first admitted, Jesse."

He stood. Paced.

"Have you had nightmares about what was done to you? The rapes?"

Jesse stilled. She'd known. Likely all along because Sinclair was good at sussing out what wasn't said. What wasn't written on paper. No, it'd been in the medical reports—the unredacted ones he'd given permission for her to obtain. Only one other copy of them was on file, and it was in hard copy. No one got them unless he gave his permission. It was the sole consolation he'd been given by Uncle Sam, except for a medal.

"I'm not asking you to talk about it, Jesse. I know you aren't ready to trust me with the details, but I need you to promise me you'll go slow with Ellie."

"I wouldn't ever hurt her," he growled.

"Have you talked with her about your captivity?"

"No, but I want to." Jesse ran his hand through his hair. "I brought my journals."

"Good. They'll be difficult for her to read, but they're a step in the right direction."

"She's in a hospital recovering from a brain injury. I don't have the right to burden her with this," Jesse said.

Silence. Translation—he already knew what he needed to know, and she expected him to work through it on his own. He loved Ellie and wanted a relationship with her—in whatever form it could take. From everything he'd seen, experienced, and overheard, she wanted the same.

So she needed the ugly truth about everything that'd happened to him because those monsters reared their heads whenever they wanted.

The door opened. Cord stepped in and stilled. He glanced between Sinclair and Jesse. "Sorry, didn't meant to interrupt."

"No. We're done," Jesse said. "Any word from the parents-to-be yet?"

"The doctor was paged," Cord said with a grin. "You ready to be an uncle again?"

"Yeah." Jesse chuckled. "Come on. Let's go."

Pandemonium had broken out in the large waiting area they'd taken over. Bubba had most of the locals who'd dropped in corralled off on one end of the room, while operatives and family had taken over the other. Ellie was sitting with his mom and her mom.

"Ellie," Jesse said. He crouched in front of her and cupped her face. "Are you okay? Should you be out of bed?"

"The doctor said it was okay." She smiled at him and stroked his face. "I wanted a dose of happy. I'm bored off my ass. I want to celebrate with everyone."

Jesse smiled. "I'm so glad you're here with us. I can't believe she waited so long."

"The doctor said she was already dilated six centimeters when they admitted her," his mom said.

Jesse wasn't exactly down for the details, but he laughed and smiled with everyone around him. The only thing that mattered right now was celebrating the new life about to enter this world. Ellie winced a couple of times and kept her head angled downward. He shifted slightly to pull the sunglasses he always carried with him out and slid them onto her face.

She looked ridiculously cute in them. The large lenses swallowed her face. He chuckled, leaned forward, and kissed her cheek.

"I can't wear sunglasses inside, Jesse," she said with a laugh.

"You can do anything you want. No rules, Peanut. Remember? We don't set boundaries," he said.

"It's a girl!" Dylan said as he entered the waiting area, his voice a soft whisper Jesse somehow heard over the din of conversation. "Come with me."

Then he motioned and headed out of the waiting area and down the hall. Silence echoed through the area as everyone followed.

The room was small, but accommodated the crowd. Jesse rolled Ellie's wheelchair through the group. Mary smiled, but exhaustion was evident on her face as Dylan kissed her, then took the small bundle from her arms.

Dylan was on a trajectory course for their mom, who teared up and fanned her arms as she stood alongside Ellie's mom.

"A baby girl," she whispered.

Jesse chuckled because she'd been quilting a pink and pale purple throw for the past few days. Not much escaped his mom's information network. The tiny bundle was swaddled in a pink and white blanket. She slept peacefully in the crook of her dad's arm.

Dylan's mile-wide smile made Jesse tear up as he passed the small bundle over to their mother.

"Oh, she's perfect."

"And how are you, dear?" Ellie's mom moved to Mary's bedside and patted her hand.

"I've never been better," Mary said, her eyes clouded with tears.

"I'm so happy," Ellie said. "Did you pick out a name yet?"

The celebratory conversation around them died once more. Dylan looked around and rocked back on his heels as if deciding whether he should wait to tell everyone. But his gaze moved from his daughter in her grandmother's arms to Jesse.

"Jessie Jeanine Mason," Dylan said, his voice low enough for only the immediate family and friends around him to hear. "We'll switch it to Jessica if you'd prefer, but we both wanted the name Jesse in one form or another. She's named after one of the strongest, most amazing people we know."

Tears fell from Jesse's face as his mother moved Jessie into his arms. He leaned down and inhaled the baby scent he barely remembered from when he'd held Riley shortly after her birth. His heart swelled in his chest.

He glanced down at Ellie and saw tears spilling down her cheeks. The wide smile on her face wrapped around him like a warm hug. He looked down at the tiny bundle. "Welcome to the family, Jessie. You're going to be the most amazing little girl because you have the best parents in the world."

His gaze swept across the gathered family as he returned Jessie to Dylan. "Love you, man."

"Love you, too," Dylan whispered.

⚜

*O*ne week later...

Mild traumatic brain injury. Ellie mulled the diagnosis over in her mind as she shifted the sunglasses on her face and looked about the small cottage. Bree and Rhea fussed over which set of blackout curtains looked best with the furniture while Riley and Momma Mason were in the kitchen fixing lunch. Her mom was asleep in her recliner. Vi and Zoey were on the sofa side by side, tapping away on their laptops.

Mary and Dylan were tucked away in a cottage having quality baby bonding time as Mary was put on Dylan-enforced rest before she helped pour through the intel gathered from the raids on Phil. HERA was sifting through information on the CDs that'd been seized, but no one had shared anything found so far.

"You'd better go and rest your eyes for a while. If Jesse comes in and sees you sitting up, he'll ask how long it's been since you've taken a nap," Bree said. "And we all know it's been too long."

Naps. Visual rest breaks. "I'll handle Jesse if he asks."

"You're good with him," Vi said. "With Jesse."

"He makes it easy. He's the most amazing man I've ever met. There's nothing I wouldn't do for him."

The intensity within the statement blanketed the room. Suddenly Ellie was self-conscious because she'd offloaded too much about her feelings for Jesse. The filter between her brain and her mouth wasn't firing on all cylinders right now, which had made for more than a few awkward moments.

"I'm bored out of my skull," Ellie said. "Let's watch a movie."

The two women froze. Looked up in perfect synchronicity. Blinked.

"You two freak me out when you do that," Bree said as she pointed at Vi and Zoey. Then she looked at Ellie. "As for you, no movies anytime soon. You can't do anything on computer screens, phones, or televisions. Nothing with blue light or anything else that'll cause those headaches to get worse. And we certainly don't want any more seizures."

No. No they certainly did not.

Aside from a battered face and a couple shaved spots on her head, she was physically okay. Headaches and an occasional seizure were the biggest pains in the ass. Doctors were relatively sure they'd both go away.

Eventually.

Minor pains in the ass included the random, weird shit she'd kept doing since coming home from the hospital yesterday morning. She'd put her toothbrush in the freezer. Why? No clue.

She randomly carried objects around. The soap dispenser from the hallway bathroom. The dish scrubber from the kitchen.

Ugh. Ellie was a mess and bored off her ass.

Work was a hard no, mandated by the doctors, everyone around her, and Jesse.

"Where's Jesse?" He'd been the constant focus of her thoughts. Nervousness and anxiety attacked her if she didn't know where he was and what he was doing.

Riley looked at Vi, who looked at Zoey. The three glanced at Bree and Rhea, whose widened eyes were on Ellie. "Ugh. I've asked before. Right?"

"Just a few times," Riley said as she headed into the living room. She held out a pad and a pen. "Tell you what. Let's write important stuff down, just in case."

Memory lapses were expected until her mind healed. Portions of her short-term memory might never return. But she was alive, her mom was more comfortable than she'd been at the rental, and Jesse was...

Ugh. She really wanted to know where he was.

"He and Nolan ran to Bubba's to grab some grub. We're all having lunch together and spending the afternoon hanging out," Sara said as she wandered into the living room with baby Ariana in her arms. "Here. You want to hold her again?"

Again?

Ellie swallowed and held out her hands as Sara passed the gorgeous baby girl over.

"She's growing so fast," Vi said.

"Vi, are you going to find out if it's a girl or boy, or wait like Mary did?" Sara asked.

"I'm married to a former assassin. He's insisted we know everything about everything."

Everyone laughed. Jud took *intense* to an entirely different level.

"We're going to be covered in babies. My heart is full," Momma

Mason said as she came into the living room and set a tray of warm cookies down. "These aren't as good as Ellie's, but you girls had best grab what you want before my boys get back. They fall on desserts like starving animals."

Which was hysterical since they were all seriously fit. Ellie took a chocolate chip cookie and nibbled. The nausea she'd endured the first couple of days had slowly eased to tolerable levels. Ariana cooed and reached for Ellie's long hair. Her big blue eyes peered up in the curious merriment she always had. Ellie clutched the baby close and leaned down to inhale her scent. For a second she could pretend.

Mary had named her daughter Jessie. The name was perfect in so many ways and a beautiful testament to the couple's love for Jesse. They'd given him what he'd never have for himself, and while a part of her was sad, Ellie was overwhelmed by the love the Masons displayed so easily every day.

Her gaze swept to her mother, who was napping in a recliner in the corner of the room. The past few days with her had been... wonderful. The woman wasn't the same as she'd been before Ellie's attack. She was...

Loving.

Ellie hated the thought. Her mom had sacrificed a lot to raise Ellie alone after her father died, but that level of stress had taken its toll. They'd never had a relationship like the one Jesse and his siblings had with their mom. It'd been strained most of the time.

The cancer had shifted their dynamic. Now Ellie was the caregiver. It'd been a difficult transition—one neither of them had been prepared for. Being out at The Arsenal—surrounded by so much love and family—had somehow changed her mom.

And Ellie.

It made her thankful for the time she still had with her mother.

"I wasn't trying to snoop, but I sort of found something in your room when I was changing the sheets the other day," Rhea whispered as she sat at the coffee table in the living room. "I probably shouldn't say anything with everyone here, but I put them in the top dresser drawer so they'd be safer."

"Them?" Bree echoed Ellie's question.

"The files." Rhea blinked. "Oh gosh, you don't remember?"

"What files?" Vi closed her laptop.

"I took a peek, just long enough to see what they were." Red rose in Rhea's cheeks. "They were about Jesse. His capture. His injuries."

Cord.

The memory returned with a vengeance. He'd come by the cottage after Jesse's episode and given her files. She'd stayed up and read a lot of them, then she'd cried herself to sleep thinking of everything Jesse had endured.

There hadn't been much in the way of details. She hadn't understood half of the medical stuff.

"Where did you get them? Do you remember?" Vi asked.

"It doesn't matter."

"It does," Vi said.

"Cord," Ellie whispered. "He told me to not quit the fight to get his brother back."

"Good." Riley plopped down. "He's right. Once you're on your feet, Jesse's gonna bolt. He'll stay as far away as he can. I know fear, and he reeks of it."

"Riley Mason! Don't you go saying that about your brother." Momma Mason came in and sat on the loveseat beside Ellie. "But she's right, dear. My boy's had a rough go of it. I suspect he's got a lot to process. He and Nolan are like their daddy. They hole up alone and mull things over."

"Marshall's the worst," Riley replied. "They're damned animals with a sore paw. They'll run to ground and growl if you get near."

"You need to talk to Doctor Sinclair," Vi said. "About what happened to you. About Jesse."

"She's right," Rhea said.

The door opened. TJ and DJ burst into the room with loud shouts as the little boy chased his big brother through the living room. Ellie winced and curled deeper into the sofa as Dallas and Kamren entered. Little Ariana slept peacefully on Ellie's shoulder.

Where had Sara gone? She looked around but didn't see the young girl. Maybe she'd gone to take a nap.

"Boys, what did I say about the volume?" Kamren asked.

Both boys froze and looked at Ellie. DJ walked up and climbed up between her and his grandma. He put a little hand on the unbruised side of her face.

"You hurted like Auntie Z was."

"I am hurt like Auntie Z was," Ellie corrected. "But I'll be okay. Have you been studying your letters?"

The boy nodded with a smile.

"Your numbers?"

"I'm real good with those. Uncle Cord said so."

"Well, Uncle Cord would know," Riley said. "He's always been the best with math of us all. I flunked."

"Jesse did mine," Dallas admitted. "That old coot who taught Algebra used the same tests every year. Jesse found Nolan's and passed them down to me."

"Is that where they went to?" Ellie asked with a smile. "He used to let me see them in exchange for kisses."

Everyone laughed. Recovery the past few days had left a lot of contemplation time. She'd stifled any fears of pursuing a relationship with Jesse because the man hadn't left her side. While everyone else appeared and disappeared regularly, he'd remained the constant guardian at her side—her own private gargoyle. But way sexier.

"Mom's been studying, too," TJ said. "Dad's been helping. When she gets something wrong, he tickles her."

"What'd we say about not listening when your mom and I are alone?" Dallas asked.

"Sorry, Dad." TJ's bottom lip curled outward. "I don't mean to snoop."

"When are you going to take your GED exam?" Bree asked.

Kamren looked at Dallas and chewed her lip a moment. "If you don't mind, I'd like to get my diploma before the boys transition to public school. I...I want to be able to help them with their homework."

Wow. Ellie's heart clenched with the passion and conviction in the woman's voice. She loved Dallas's boys without hesitation. TJ wasn't even Dallas's biological son—not that anyone even considered him anything other than family.

"With you helping them, they'll both be valedictorian," Dallas said. He wrapped his arms around Kamren and kissed her mouth.

The door opened again, and Nolan and Dylan entered with large paper bags. Cord and Jesse entered next.

Jesse's gaze swept the room, then halted on Ellie. His jaw twitched as a look she hadn't seen before settled in his eyes. Then she looked down and remembered she was holding Ariana.

Damn.

Ellie looked around for Sara again, but she still hadn't returned.

"Here, dear, I'll go put her in the crib. She'd sleep on you all day if you let her." Momma Mason rose and took the baby. Riley grabbed the bags from Jesse and followed her brothers into the kitchen.

Jesse sat beside Ellie. "How are you feeling?"

"Better. I'm bored."

"Bored is a good sign," he said with a grin. He knocked the side of her sunglasses with his finger. "You're still rocking the cool look."

"I'm always cool," she teased.

"I know it's late, but the sun is down and you've been cooped up in here all day. You want to eat outside?"

"Yes. Please."

"Great. Give me a few and we'll go."

17

*E*llie knew where Jesse was taking her when he made a right at the stump. The truck bumped along the worn path. The large oak tree had once been a focal point of their romance. Whenever they'd been at Jesse's house—which was often—they'd snuck away from everyone and come out here.

Anticipation beaded along her skin as he grasped her waist and lifted her down to the ground. Her pulse quickened when she peered into his eyes and saw...

Intensity. Awareness.

She swallowed and touched his biceps. Strength. Her breathing increased. She should pull away, but she was drawn to him—a magnet to its counterpart.

"Come on, let's get the blanket set up. I'm starving." He smiled.

A breeze flowed from the open field and rustled the leaves of the mighty tree. Jesse made quick work of spreading a large quilt out on the ground. Ellie walked over to the thick trunk and ran her hand along the bark until she found what she was looking for. It'd been so cliché, but teenagers hyped up on hormone-driven love didn't care. They'd wanted to immortalize their love for one another in his great-grandfather's tree.

I want to make you part of us, Ellie. You're a Mason because I love you, heart and soul.

Jesse's fingers brushed against hers, then he clasped her hand, interlocked their fingers, and traced the letters. E. She was always first with Jesse. J. Because he was always beside her.

Damn.

"You okay?" Hot breath fanned the shell of her ear.

A shiver traveled from her neck and down her body.

"Vanilla," he whispered. "You changed your scent again."

"I—" She cut off the admission. What could she say? She'd changed because he'd mentioned vanilla and lavender. He'd remembered for years how she smelled. "I liked that you remembered."

Jesse turned her around and grasped her face so his palm was against her cheek. The contact sent a shockwave of awareness and need through her. Guilt stilled her thoughts of what they used to do beneath the tree. The way they'd attacked each other, so hungered for the taste and feel of one another they weren't satisfied until they were one.

"Don't ever hide what you feel, Peanut. Not with me."

Tears escaped her eyes. Sadness and confusion reflected in his gaze.

"I'm okay with this...nothing more. I feel more with your touch than I ever have with another man," she admitted. "Whatever this is, whatever it can be, I'm all in."

"Ellie," Jesse whispered. He leaned in and feathered his lips across hers.

The contact was the single most amazing thing she'd experienced. Soft, raw, hesitant. So many emotions in one light sweep of mouths. She firmed her grip on his arms and deepened the kiss. A glide of her tongue along the seam of his mouth.

A groan escaped her. Or him. The world tunneled to the two of them. Everything else ceased. Pleasure coursed along her skin as her pulse quickened.

Jesse wrapped an arm around her and guided them to the ground. Anticipation ignited her pulse as she severed the kiss for a raspy breath. Then she took his mouth again, too needy to risk his retreat. He grasped her hair and took control. His tongue delved, attacked with a voracity that left her breathless.

Years.

The last time she'd felt this hunger had been with Jesse before he left.

The emotional dam she'd controlled ruptured. Tears slid from her eyes as the kiss softened to a slow but carnal fusion. Jesse severed the contact and kissed her cheeks.

"Ellie." The intensity in his gaze made her heart stop. "Tell me what you need, Peanut."

"You. Just like this," she whispered. She wrapped her arms around him but noted the tension in his body. "Tell me what you need, honey."

"You. Just like this." Pain filled his voice.

Her sweet Jesse was lost and confused. "We pave our own path. Lie down with me?"

Jesse stretched out on the blanket. Ellie settled alongside him and rested her head on his chest. Questions listed in her mind, but the silence blanketing them was a warm cocoon of comfort she didn't want to lose by asking the wrong thing.

"Does my touch bother you?" Ellie asked.

"Not as much as when others touch me. I..." He swallowed. "I like your touch."

Good, because she loved touching him. She splayed a hand on his chest and looked up at the stars. "There are so many of them."

"Dylan and Mary come out here sometimes and name them. It's something she and Vi started when they were kids at MIT. I caught them out here once, so lost in the moment he'd lost all sense of security."

"Because he knew y'all would watch out for them," Ellie whispered. "They'd do anything for you."

"I know, but they shouldn't have to."

"That's what family does."

Jesse traced a finger along her cheek and palmed her face. "You need to talk to Sinclair about the accident, Peanut. And your mom. The hospital attack. Don't let it simmer in you. It's a lot harder to contain when you leave it be too long."

"Did you leave it too long?"

"Probably." His voice turned husky. "There's a lot I haven't told her that I know she'd want to know—things too dark and depraved for her to understand. They eat my insides."

"Jesse." The whispered plea escaped her before she could stop herself. She feathered kisses along his cheeks, then across his lips. She took his free hand and wrapped her pinky around his. "There's nothing too dark and depraved for me to hear. Remember our vow?"

"Everything. Forever." He stroked her arm and stared into her eyes.

The haunted expression within his steeled her determination. She'd vanquish the dark and depraved he mentioned. That was the real battle in the war for Jesse's heart.

"She thinks I should let you read the journals," he whispered.

Ellie relaxed against him and looped her leg between his. "I want to read them. I want to know what happened, Jesse."

"You won't understand."

"I will because I love you. I will because you and I were connected heart and soul before you went over there. That hasn't changed." She feathered a kiss along his mouth. "That won't ever change. There is *nothing* you can say or do that will *ever* change that."

"I can't lose you," he whispered against her mouth.

"You won't ever lose me because I was lost in you long ago." She peered into his eyes as she kissed his mouth softly. The tension within his body pained her. She sensed the internal war he waged and prayed she had enough fight to see the war through.

To win.

"I'm not ever letting you go, Jesse James Mason. Not ever again."

"I'm not the man you knew."

"I'm not the woman you knew."

Jesse groaned and kissed her. Hunger. The carnal need overpowered her as he flipped them over so he was on top. His weight rested atop her, and for the first time in a long while, she felt...complete.

❀

*D*inner.

Jesse had thought a dinner alone under the tree was a perfect idea, but he'd underestimated his compulsion to touch Ellie. To taste her sweet lips and feel her come apart beneath him. He deepened the kiss, guiding her tongue with his.

Fuck.

He was a bastard for staking a claim on her when he couldn't...

"Jesse," she cried out as she writhed against him. She clawed at his shirt, but he was too lost in the taste of her to give a damn. She'd already seen the scars.

His pulse quickened when she stripped his shirt off, then hers. The soft glide of fingertips along his skin sent shivers of anticipation down his spine. He froze, too confused by the pleasurable sensation to do anything but relish the contact.

"Relax," Ellie whispered against his neck. She nibbled his earlobe. "It's just you and me."

But he couldn't relax. The wrong touch or word could send him into a flashback, and he was alone with Ellie. He could hurt her. His breaths grew labored as he severed the contact and drew back until he was an arm's reach away from temptation.

Fuck, she was beautiful. Her full breasts were tucked inside a deep blue bra with lace along the edge. He swallowed as his gaze remained locked there. Her creamy skin would be softer there, more sensitive to his touch. His mouth.

"I can't help if you don't talk to me, Jesse."

"This isn't a good idea." He looked around and ran his hand through his hair.

This had been an epically shitty idea. They were too far away from help if he went nuts, but she couldn't read his mind. As much as it pained him to share the why, she deserved to know it wasn't her. It wouldn't ever be her fault he was screwed up.

"I-I don't want to hurt you. I haven't done this since..." He swallowed and forced a deep breath, even though his gut churned with nervousness that left his entire body humming like a livewire. "Touch triggers flashbacks sometimes. I don't want to hurt you."

"Then we'll watch the stars and enjoy the quiet," she said as she slipped her shirt back on.

Shocked, he watched as she curled up on the blanket where she'd been before. Her light blue eyes were barely visible in the light he'd put on the edge of the blanket, but it was enough for him to see adoration and concern. A calm spread through him, brushfire swift. He lay beside her but kept a small distance between them, just in case.

His heart thundered hard in his chest, but he continued his breathing exercises and focused on the stars above him rather than the beautiful, quiet woman who owned his soul. No one deserved to put up with the shitstorm that was his thoughts. A woman had needs he couldn't fulfill. Tonight was the perfect example.

Sure, it was easy enough in intention. He could pleasure her orally—make her come all night.

But that plan didn't take Ellie's reactions into account. Her touch. Her smell. Her groans.

He closed his eyes and inhaled the vanilla scent she'd worn for him. It mingled with the grass and earthen smells of his family ranch.

Home.

"I need your help," she whispered into the silence.

Jesse tightened. "What's wrong?"

"We'd planned to have a baby shower for Mary, but then the hospital incident happened. And now she's already had the baby."

Jesse smiled. "Of course, you're worried about still giving her a baby shower."

"She deserves one. She went through a lot," Ellie whispered. "Your namesake deserves to be pampered."

"That kid will be spoiled rotten. Does the name bother you?" Jesse asked.

"No, I love it," she whispered. "It hurts that we'll never have a child together, but I'm okay, Jesse. You're what matters."

"Why didn't you have a kid with him?"

"He wasn't you," she admitted.

Damn. Jesse rubbed the ache in his chest. Ellie always shot straight with him. No lies. No hesitation. That's what they'd been for one another. She was lying beside him offering an all-in he shouldn't take, but he couldn't pass up. This moment with Ellie beneath the tree. Alone under the stars. Yeah, this was why he'd survived in the hole.

His mother's words from the other day resonated in his head. She was right. He couldn't waste a second of life. Ellie was worth the risk.

"You're gonna be a great mother," Jesse whispered.

She tightened. He scooted over and drew her against him so her weight settled along his side. "You're my one, Jesse. I'm stuck to you like glue."

He grinned and looked at her. Pleasure danced in her eyes. "Good, because you're my one, too, Ellie."

Jesse felt as though he'd vaulted more than a few steps forward, but he was still behind where they'd been before he'd left her. He'd had a ring. Memories flooded him, but he focused on the woman curled against him and the stars above them. He stroked one of the bare spots on her head. He'd come close to losing her.

Never again.

Death had a way of carving through red tape. When you'd inhaled the grim possibilities and kneed them in the nuts, you couldn't help but race toward your reward. Ellie was his reward.

"Will you talk with Sinclair?"

"Yeah. I know I need to." Her hand ran up and down his chest in slow, methodical sweeps. His mind raced between pleasure and fear with each touch, but he craved more. He loved her touch.

"I'll let her know you can ask whatever you want," he whispered into the silence.

She kissed his chest. "I'm all in, Jesse."

He hoped to hell so because he couldn't keep the things bottled up in him from her. They'd always shared everything, and a part of him refused to hide from her now. "I don't know what the hell I did to deserve you."

"I think the same thing about you," she admitted.

Jesse's cellphone rang. He reached into his pocket and pulled it out. Anger spiked within him when he read the text. Sitting up, he cupped Ellie's face, which reflected concern. "We need to get back to the compound."

Ellie's eyes rounded. "Why?"

"Addy's team is in trouble."

18

*E*llie looked around at the gathered teams as apprehension crawled through her insides. The Arsenal didn't use the large meeting room often, but when they did, the operation was huge. It'd taken her a few meetings to grasp why they insisted she be here when something big happened. If an emergency call pertaining to a mission came through, she needed to know exactly who to forward it to. Information was power, and they wanted her armed to help them be successful with their missions.

She swallowed her nervousness as Jesse entered with his brothers. Vi and Zoey set up a computer with the massive overhead.

"This briefing will be exactly that—brief. Addy's team has run across some trouble." Vi paused. "Addy, you're connected. Everyone's here. Read us in."

"It took us longer than expected to track the bastard down, but we found Monte Carlito's domicile on the outskirts of a village. Surveillance raised several red flags. First, none of our equipment works within a quarter klick of his damn compound. And we use that term as an understatement. It makes The Arsenal look like Bubba's."

"What do you mean *none of the equipment works*?" Bree asked. "That's not possible."

"Well, since I'm calling from my cellphone while sitting my ass in a shitty dive bar, I'm gonna respectfully disagree," Addy said. "Anything using HERA or its energy source is dead weight whenever we get within range of that compound."

Vi typed furiously on the computer. "Monte Carlito has diversified assets, but nothing HERA flagged."

A list appeared on the overhead.

"Carlisle Industries," Rhea said. "That rat bastard."

"Carlisle? As in Stan Carlisle? Your college boyfriend? The one who stole your thesis?" Bree looked at the screen then Rhea. "He stole more than that. Jesus. He's got our initial blueprints. That's why the energy source isn't working within HERA's equipment."

A man's image came up on the screen. "Carlito has controlling interest in Carlisle Industries. HERA didn't flag it because it isn't a known black ops supplier or facility."

"I remember him. You two dated while you and Bree shared a room," Vi said. "First priority—can we get the equipment operational? How deep is this breech?"

"I-I dunno," Bree said. "I'll need to look through our initial schematics, but the energy source is reprogrammable. We can theoretically use a different transmission frequency and change the security. We've wanted to upgrade anyway."

"How soon?"

"I have some experimental models of upgraded drones, but they haven't been tested."

Nolan sighed and crossed his arms. "How experimental? Is this like the exploding ones from Iraq or the energy cannon from the roof?"

"We can do a trial run in a couple hours."

"We need to be wheels up in two hours," Jesse said.

"Then we use what's ready and make modifications to send through to the others," Vi said.

"That assumes we can establish a satellite connection for long enough," Addy said. "We'll need to do the system update before we near the compound. Otherwise we're fucked."

"Are you still under their radar?" Marshall asked.

"So far, yes. They've got a shit ton of security, heavily armed. I'm uploading what we have so far from the perimeter scans." Addy sighed heavily into the phone. "This is bigger than the girl at this point. Do we pull back and reevaluate the mission objective or go in and get her?"

God, Ellie wanted to leave. She was the office manager. This was way, way above her pay grade. But this was Jesse's life, and anything to do with him was her concern.

Would he be one of the ones to go? There were so many teams. Surely he wouldn't go.

Mary, Vi, and Zoey decided which teams were best suited for missions. Sending the wrong one could get someone hurt—or worse —killed. Loving Jesse meant not only accepting what he did but supporting it. Cheering him on because he saved lives.

"What's the scope of our exposure here?" Dylan asked.

"It's hard to say," Vi said. "Either way, we need to investigate Carlisle Industries. Anyone and anything connected with a bastard who'd buy a kid for sex is a problem."

"The bastard stole our schematics," Rhea said. "We steal them back."

"After we gather more intel and surveillance. No way in hell are we ready to take these bastards on right now," Addy said. "This is a slicker operation than Hive was."

"Understood. I'll text you once we establish which teams are en route. Are you secure?"

"For now."

Ellie shifted in the seat she'd taken nearest the door. Out of the way. She'd heard everyone say Addy was one of the best operatives in the private paramilitary world, so she'd be okay until help arrived.

"Hang on the line for a minute. Sol has resources there," Jesse said. The man made his way to a phone Zoey held out.

Any hope she'd had that Jesse and his team weren't one of the ones going died. Her pulse quickened as a new shockwave of fear and nervousness crawled along her spine. Sol had resources in the area. Ellie swallowed.

Jesse was good at this. The best. He'd be okay.

"The remainder of the debrief will happen en route once we know more. Bree and Rhea, get busy organizing the new drones," Vi said. "We'll need a sidebar after the teams are on their way to determine our future security implications. That bastard could've sold those schematics to anyone at this point. We'll need a deep dive investigation into him, everyone he's worked with—everything."

"I'll get to work. Cord can help," Zoey said.

"Jesse's and Gage's teams are primary. Dallas, your team is on perimeter. Departure in two hours," Vi said. "All gathered intel from the field has been forwarded to everyone's data tablets."

"And the girl?" Zoey asked.

"We aren't forgetting what our primary objective is," Marshall said. "We'll need to assess our options once we have good intel."

Ellie remained seated as the teams who'd assembled filed out. Sol, Brooklyn, Lex, and Levi all offered smiles as they shuffled past her and headed out. Jesse sighed heavily as he approached and squatted so they were at eye level. He took both hands in hers and rubbed her palms with his thumbs.

"Peanut."

Ellie forced a deep breath. An unfocused operative was bad. She'd heard Mary and Vi and Zoey all say as much when they were talking amongst themselves or with Kamren. The four women watched their men go into danger all the time. They powered through and remained strong because they were the most amazing women she knew.

She could emulate that bravery and strength for Jesse. Emotion threatened to overwhelm her, though, so she kept her focus on where their hands interlaced.

"Talk to me, Peanut."

"This is good. We'll have the baby shower after you get back. That way Addy will be here, too," Ellie said. The mundaneness of the statement hung like a lead weight between them. So much for being strong and courageous.

Then the fears listing in her mind spilled out in one terrifying question. "How dangerous is this? With the stuff not working? How bad is this?"

Jesse placed a hand on her neck and used his thumb to lift her chin. Emotion churned within his gaze, but she was too busy controlling her own to delve into his.

"I won't ever lie to you, Peanut. It's not good." He firmed his grip on her face. "But we practice for this every day. Most of us spent years in the service without the tech we've been using. Sure, the slick gadgets make our work a fuckload safer and give us a huge leg up, but we can and will kick ass without it."

Ellie nodded.

"I survived hell once because I wanted to get back to you," he whispered. "Nothing will keep me from you. Nothing."

A tear escaped and rolled down her cheek. "I love you, Jesse James Mason."

"I love you, Ellie."

She cupped his face and kissed him. A groan escaped him as he firmed the contact and swept his tongue along the seam of her mouth. Anticipation and need rose within her.

Jesse broke the kiss and pressed his forehead against hers. "I owe you a dinner under the tree when I get back, Peanut."

"Good. Then we can pick up where we left off," she whispered. She traced her hands down his arms.

"Even if we don't ever..." He swallowed.

"Even if."

❦

*I*t'd been years since Jesse had been in Cuba. From what he'd seen so far, not much had changed. They'd rendezvoused with Addy and her team at the edge of forested area fifteen klicks from the target's location. It'd taken half an hour to upgrade all the drones Addy's team had.

The enemy drones' perimeter sweeps were in half klick bands starting at twelve klicks—an unheard of distance that left Jesse a little more concerned than he wanted to admit.

Everyone fanned out in teams of two without comment and made their way toward the compound. They'd brought along two sets of the new drones Bree had designed. Jesse hoped to hell they worked. Protein bars and bottled water were their meals, which they ate as they trudged through the thick forest without pause.

Two klicks away from the facility, they activated HERA and sent the drones up. The sooner they tested the new design the better. Bree had said the surveillance cameras offered a wider range and better-quality images.

"Signals are strong," Zoey said. "Images are freaking killer. Nice upgrade, Bree."

"Let's hope the rest is as good," the woman commented.

Dallas's team remained in a lookout formation half a klick from the target. Armed personnel in protective gear patrolled the perimeter in frequent intervals that made the approach slower than Jesse preferred. Images from the drones Cord flew ahead of them flashed through the display of the headgear.

His body tightened as the compound's bustling interior came into view. A row of armed vehicles surrounded four large flatbed trailers. Shock stilled his movements as massive cone-shaped missile tips came into view.

What the fuck?

"Those weren't there before," Addy said.

"We spotted the flatbeds rolling in, though. I guess we know what was inside the buildings now," Johnny said.

Jesse respected the hell out of Addy's team. They reminded him a lot of his own. A couple of them had even been in Hive with her. The two teams had worked together on a lot of missions—so much so it felt as though they were one seamless unit.

"Carlito's domicile is a quarter klick northwest of the Carlisle

Industries compound," Zoey said. "Heat signatures indicate sixteen souls, ten of them armed. Two-story structure with a secondary one-level building in the back with four guards in sentry positions. I'm thinking that's our target."

"Moving into position," Gage said.

That'd leave Addy's and Jesse's teams to assist with exfil of the girl if needed. But he'd already realized their objective had just changed. Carlisle Industries had missiles. Given that Carlisle had stolen biochemical concepts of some sort from Rhea and schematics for Bree's energy source, the threat was too high for them to not gather as much intel as they could while here.

Sol and Johnny were in sniping positions within the canopy overhead. The remainder of the two teams would control the perimeter while Jesse and Levi penetrated the compound. The two of them moved undetected around the patrols thanks to the drones, which were functioning without issue.

"Three enemy drones have been detected overhead. Standby for intercept," Cord said.

Jesse crouched in position and waited as little brother did whatever geeks did to take down unwanted drones.

"You're greenlit. We've gotten control of their security feeds," Vi said. "Z, I'll need your help looping the feeds. Hand what you're doing off to Cord."

"Erm, HERA is pulling up identifications for all the men loading the truck. They're affiliated with a terrorist cell operating out of Russia. There're enough alphabet soup flags on these guys to drown us," Zoey commented.

Jesse scaled the ten-foot chain-link fence along the forested edge to the southeast of the compound. He tumbled into a roll as Levi followed him up and over.

"We're in," Jesse said. He unshouldered his backpack and pulled out the crawlers they'd brought along. The ground-based drones would sweep through the area and retrieve what data they could via their wireless tech—a new addition Bree had assured him worked because she'd field-tested it at The Arsenal. He activated the first one and set it on a trajectory path for the flatbed trucks.

The geek squad back at The Arsenal would handle their movements so he and Levi could focus on breaking into the buildings undetected. They navigated their way toward the nearest building and slid between the exterior wall and a stack of crates. The protective cover wasn't ideal, but better than the alternative.

"I'll override the bio-entry system, but there are two guards on either side of the door. You'll need to take them out and use their clothing. From what I can see, their internal security operates off a chipping system. Everyone has an established perimeter and access level for their individual chips. Anyone who deviates from their zones..." Vi paused. "Shit. They've got detonation collars on all the personnel inside."

Images from the compound's security feed filled the display on Jesse's headgear. The view flickered a few times.

"We have intermittent interference," Bree said. "It appears to be a modified EM pulse of some sort. I'm reprogramming HERA, but coms could go down for a bit."

A bit. Great. Jesse looked over at Levi, who grinned and shook his head.

"Interior security relies heavily on the chips. Once you're inside and have the guard's gear on, move along the walls as much as possible. We want to use the electronic readers you both have to copy all hard drives you find. Photograph or scan any schematics or other papers that seem important, including whiteboards and the like. Formulas. Anything geeky," Vi said. "I've overridden the locks. You're greenlit for entry."

Levi entered first. Jesse attacked the guard on the right while Levi took out the other one. They dragged both into the small room on the side of the entry. It took only a couple minutes to strip and don their gear. They left the guards restrained, blindfolded, and gagged.

Jesse and Levi each dispatched another crawler as they entered the large, warehouse-style structure. The bulk of the building was open within the middle. Offices spanned along the exterior walls of a second floor, which bordered the open-mouthed area with a narrow walkway. Guards patrolled along the upper corridor.

He needed to get up there.

They made their way into the first office. Though the sun had begun to set, the building still bustled with activity. The visual display from the surveillance cameras filled Jesse's headgear once again. People working on the first floor wore underwear only. Thick, red and yellow collars engulfed their necks. Rage rolled through Jesse when he saw little boys and girls along the back wall, all in small white shorts and nothing else but the thick collars. They worked an assembly line of some sort that ended with vials of liquid packed into a crate.

"We need a vial," Rhea said.

Jesse clicked his understanding with a punch of the com button and let his mind process the how for a moment as they swept the first office. Levi pulled out one of the many small plug-ins Zoey had given them. If the computers were networked, she could hack into the mainframe from any computer. Nothing was ever that simple, though, so they were prepared to locate every computer they could.

The headgear flickered. Then died.

Jesse stifled a curse.

They'd get HERA back online soon enough. His mind wandered to Ellie's question from earlier. Her fear had been palpable, a sour and horrid thing he still felt bone deep. But she'd kept it together.

He snapped images with the digital camera he had. Very little of value was in the room, though.

They continued on along the right wall where a narrow set of stairs wound up to the second floor. Jesse signaled for Levi to continue along the bottom floor while he took the top.

The first few offices were vacant and easily searched. He removed hard drives from the computers and snapped images of all the walls and any paperwork he found. The longer a search took, the higher the risk of capture.

A small shaft of light emanated from the back corner office. Jesse took out the nearest patrol guard and continued into the room with his weapon drawn. A woman with waist-length black hair in a thick braid sat at a long counter riddled with microscopes and assorted lab equipment. Rats ran in a wall-length glass enclosure along the left wall. Small monkeys jumped up and down in cages along the back wall.

The woman wore a bright blue bra thin enough for him to see her hard nipples underneath. The lace panties did little to conceal her. The thick red and yellow band around her neck blinked and flashed every few seconds—an item he hadn't noted on the other workers from the headgear display. Cold air from a vent overhead fell directly on her, but her full attention was on whatever she worked on.

Jesse prowled closer, careful to remain as far against the wall as possible. He halted and positioned himself immediately in front of the woman. Crouched mere feet from her position with weapon drawn, he waited a couple seconds for her to notice his presence. Her eyes flashed wide, but she didn't scream or cry out as he'd expected.

Her eyes darted to the left. He tracked the movement but remained silent as her attention returned to him. Intelligence resonated within her gaze. Her lower lip trembled as moisture pooled in her eyes.

Help me.

The mouthed plea left Jesse stunned. What the fuck had they stumbled across?

He breathed a sigh of relief when HERA came back online.

"Status?" Vi asked.

One by one everyone flagged themselves in with their personal devices. Jesse waited until everyone else had checked in to bypass the expected non-verbal response. "Need your help."

He gave the women on the other end of the line a moment to focus on the images his headgear provided. The woman continued the work she'd been doing, but her gaze flicked to him and the camera in the corner every few seconds. With slow, deliberate steps he approached the woman and lowered his weapon. Wide, terrified, coal-black eyes watched his progression.

"It's okay. I'm here to help."

"American." Not a question. A fact stated with a low but southern-accented voice.

"American," he affirmed. "Quillery, I need the collar off to extract her."

"Fallon's here. We need a better view of it. I've located the security files for each one, but I'm not sure which is hers. We need to make sure there's not a tripwire on it. Even if I deactivate it, there's a chance it'll still go off."

Jesse wasn't leaving the woman behind. She trembled as she stood beside the stool. He approached and made sure the headgear got a full visual of the device.

"There'll be a clasp on the back somewhere. You'll need to clip the red wire first, then the blue," Fallon's deep voice boomed over the com. "These are Russian chokers."

And the guys near the trucks were Russian.

Fuck.

Jesse clipped the wires as instructed and removed the collar from the woman, who'd maintained her terrified silence. "I'm Jesse. We're going to get you out of here. What's your name?"

"Nikki. Nikki Everly." She motioned toward a pile of paperwork on the side of the area she'd been sitting at. "You'll want to get that."

Jesse shoved the papers into his pack and shouldered it. "We'll get you some clothes in a minute. What's the easiest way for me to get computer access to their systems here?"

"Over there. That's the workflow coordinator. It hooks this sector with the others and feeds everything to the overseer," she whispered. "I don't know the password. I'm sorry. Please don't leave me."

"We aren't leaving without you," he said.

The woman nodded. "And the others?"

Fuck. "How many?"

"Ten, maybe twelve. We came together for course credit. They work a different shift. I haven't seen them in weeks," Nikki said as she swiped at tears on her face.

"Where are you kept?"

"The house up the road."

"On it," Gage said. "We'll need backup at this location."

Three double-clicks sounded on the line. Jesse trusted the operatives to coordinate the details for the house operation. "Let's go."

The woman froze. "You weren't here for us."

"No."

"Why are you here?" The woman cocked her head. "You knew about Carlisle?"

Jesse remained silent. Rescued hostages tended to be more difficult to manage if they were civilians. Few had questions. The woman stayed out of the way as he put the device into the computer's USB port.

He removed the exterior shirt from the uniform he wore and handed it to the woman. "Put this on. We'll find something more suitable later."

Jesse shouldered his pack, unholstered his weapon, and headed toward the door. The woman latched onto his belt loop without needing instructions. He froze.

"Nikki and ten others disappeared seven weeks ago," Zoey said. "Media coverage has been extensive on the east coast, but not in our area. Her older sister is FBI."

That explained how she knew to stay out of his line of fire. Jesse filed away the information and hoped to hell they'd figure out a way to get everyone out. He dispatched another two crawlers and guided the woman back down the stairs.

"You're clear for exit. The crawlers will get what they can," Vi said. "Let's get her out."

*E*llie hated feeling useless. She'd brought caffeine and snacks for her friends, who'd been sequestered in the operations theater all day. The clock ticked into the midnight hour as Ellie sat beside Rhea and listened to the rescue operation. It'd started for one little girl and had uncovered a secret facility with missiles, strange compounds, and a group of kidnapped college kids.

"This is my fault," Rhea said. "I should've realized he'd stolen from us."

"That's not on you," Fallon growled as he turned and looked down at her. "None of this is on you. Get your shit together before they land because we'll want to know what those chemical compounds are before the FBI or some other government agency seizes them."

The woman glared at the man but remained silent. Ellie took her friend's hand and squeezed. Bree, Zoey, and Cord were navigating the floor drones, or whatever they called them, around the compound and gathering what intel they could. The small devices could fly high enough to perch on tabletops and counters, which made it possible to photograph and access electronic equipment.

"You are all amazing," she said. "What you can do."

Watching them in action helped her feel better about Jesse being out there.

He was deep within forested terrain in *Cuba* and surrounded by heavily armed men—some of which were affiliated with a ruthless Russian crime syndicate. Ellie wished she could ignore the chatter between Vi, Zoey, Cord, and Bree as they worked.

"Come on. Let's go check on my mom. Sara was there with the baby. I'm sure she'd like to get some rest," Ellie said.

Vi looked over her shoulder and mouthed a thank you as Ellie guided Rhea out of the operations theater and toward the cottage. Exhaustion plagued Ellie, but she was determined to help her friend. She'd never seen the brilliant scientist so upset.

"We'll get it back," Ellie promised, using the term "we" loosely since she couldn't help, aside from offering comfort and food.

"They'll never forgive me for all the mistakes I've made," Rhea whispered.

Ellie assumed the *they* were Mary, Vi, and Bree. The four brilliant women had gone to MIT together. Mary and Vi had graduated before they were old enough to drive. "You are their friend first and foremost. Nothing will ever change that."

A lone lamp was on in the living room when they entered. Ariana was crawling around on the floor, hellbent for the kitchen. Sara was asleep on the sofa. Rhea headed the curious baby off while Ellie slipped in to check on her mother.

The colostomy bag was empty and the area well-cleaned. The sheets were clean, and a fresh pine scent filled the room, rather than the sickness she'd constantly smelled at the rental.

"Ellie-belly," her mom whispered.

"I didn't mean to wake you." Ellie ran a hand along her mom's forehead and smoothed her hair out. Someone had brushed it. "How are you?"

"Better. I had a rough go a few hours ago. That nice man came and gave me something."

Logan. The doctor had a way of slipping in and checking on her mom. "I'm sorry I wasn't here to help you get ready for bed."

"Rebecca told me what was happening. Are they out?"

Out. Her mom knew about the rescue op. Ellie wasn't sure her mother needed particulars. "There were some problems, but they're good at what they do."

"I was wrong about him. He's a good man. They all are."

Ellie smiled.

"It does my heart good seeing you with him, Ellie-belly. I stole too many years from you with this cancer."

"I love you, Mom. I wouldn't change a thing, even if I could." She kissed her mom's cheek. "It's you and me. We can do anything."

Her mom squeezed her hand. "Love you, Ellie-belly. Get some rest. Don't worry about me."

But she would. She slipped back into the living room and found Rhea curled up in the recliner. Asleep.

Ellie peeked into the second bedroom and found Ariana sleeping. How did such a sweet little girl come about from such a violent act? She'd have a good life. Ellie and everyone else at The Arsenal would make sure of it. Sara wouldn't ever be without whatever help she needed.

Exhausted, Ellie went to her room, closed the door, and sat on the bed. Although Jesse had been gone for almost a day, she hadn't had the courage to begin reading the journals she'd found on her bed shortly after he'd left. He must've left them there while she was helping her mom shower.

She was worried about what was on the CDs and other evidence the FBI had finally delivered to The Arsenal earlier in the day, but everyone was busy saving people in Cuba. Phil was behind bars and no longer a threat.

She kicked off her shoes and crawled into the bed. There wouldn't be any sleep tonight, not with Jesse and so many others in Cuba rescuing girls and doing other commando stuff. She picked up the first of the journals and began to read.

⚅

*T*he obnoxious ring wouldn't stop. Ellie blinked the sleepy haze away and grabbed her cellphone. What if it was Jesse?

He's in Cuba, idiot. Remember? He wouldn't be calling you.

"Hello?" Ellie used the silence to recall where she was. Asleep in the cottage. The late afternoon sun struck the draperies across the room. The room was in darkness otherwise. "Hello? Is anyone there?"

"Call your dogs off," the voice warned. "Things could get very embarrassing for you otherwise, Ellie."

Herman Perskins. Phil's father had always made Ellie apprehensive. She squeezed her eyes shut and ignored the chill running through her body. "It's not a good idea to call and threaten me."

"They're stirring up a hornets' nest you'd best not kick over, little girl. I let you crawl away from my son with your dignity. Don't make me get ugly."

Ellie could practically see the man's reddening face—one of the many things Phil had inherited from his father. His temper had been the ultimate gift, however. "Ugly? You don't think spreading lies about me being a druggie was ugly?"

"You cavorted with a known gang member. It's not my son's fault you chose drugs over the love he offered so freely."

"Right. I guess I missed the lesson on punches and kicks being proper ways to express love," Ellie clipped. She stood beside the bed and wobbled as dizziness assailed her. "Thanks, by the way. I appreciate the asshole pounding my head into the hospital floor. A TBI is exactly what I needed as the final parting gift in scraping your crazy asses off."

"That's what you get for associating with the wrong people, Ellie," the man said. "Call them off before I get angry, little girl."

"Call me that again and I'll hunt you down and kick your ass. Let's get back to the ugly, Herman. You don't think getting me fired was a low blow? You don't think that was ugly?"

"You got away easy. Clean. Call off your eunuch and I'll stay out of this. Otherwise I'm gonna make sure everyone in the tri-county sees exactly what you are, *little girl*."

The threat hung between them, and even though she didn't want to hear the details of what he meant, she knew HERA likely recorded the line to the cottage. Evidence. Proof Herman Perskins was as bad as his bastard son.

"What do you mean?"

"A picture's worth a thousand words. In this case, video's worth so much more." The man chuckled into the phone. Icy tendrils of fear slithered through her and squeezed until the breath swooshed from her lungs. "I didn't ever think you were worth the effort to bag, but I gotta admit, seeing you all teary-eyed, begging on your knees while my boy took what was his—what he *owned*..." He trailed his statement off and smirked.

"You sick son of a bitch. He never owned me."

"He did. Bought you lock, stock, and dying mom." The man laughed. "Call them off or I'll make sure everyone sees how you whored yourself out to my boy. By the time I'm done with you, you'll be wishing that gangbanger had killed you."

The line went dead. Ellie let the phone land beside her as she sank to her knees and curled into a ball. Nausea pitched her stomach, but she didn't move. Frozen into place, her mind processed the threat.

Phil had recorded their "sessions."

Revulsion rolled through her. Jesse couldn't ever find out what she'd endured. What she'd done. A good, kind, loving man like him wouldn't ever understand. A brave, strong, courageous soldier like him wouldn't understand.

No one would.

Voices drifted around her as she shivered. She glanced up and blinked until the hazy fog closing off her vision dissipated. Dylan and Nolan stood in the bedroom.

No. No. No. They couldn't know. They'd tell Jesse.

She rocked on her ass and buried her face into her knees. They'd leave. They had to leave.

Herman had won this round. She'd figure out how to call them off Phil. Then they wouldn't see.

"She's in shock." Nolan crouched beside her. "Ellie, look at me."

She turned her head away and blinked back the tears. Why couldn't she be strong and kickass like Mary or Addy or Zoey or Vi or Riley? Even Bree and Rhea were pretty damn tough. Bree had shaved her freaking head to stand in solidarity with Zoey. That took guts.

"Ellie." Nolan grabbed her chin and forced her gaze to his. "What's he threatening you with?"

"It doesn't matter."

"It does," Dylan said. "Tell us."

Mary shoved past Dylan and stood in front of Ellie. Shock and worry pulled Ellie out of her terror and self-pity as she frowned at the new mother. "You can't be here. It's the middle of the night. You need your rest."

Anger rolled through the woman's gaze. Mary rarely displayed emotions like the rest of the makeshift friendship tribe Ellie had become a part of.

"No one calls my friend in the middle of the night and threatens them. Read me in. If you don't want Jesse's brothers to know, they'll leave."

"To hell I will," Nolan growled. "She's family. No one fucks with family."

"I don't need any of you," Ellie said through clenched teeth. The lie hung there a moment as she forced a breath. She had no idea how to battle a man like Herman Perskins.

His son was in jail—a fact that'd likely been a direct result of everyone around her weighing in on her troubles. She breathed freedom from Phil's bullshit because of them.

And now she was gonna pay the price.

If Phil had recorded things…

Ellie powered through the what-ifs and accepted that he had. Otherwise Herman wouldn't have threatened her. He'd watched. Gotten off on watching.

Her stomach pitched again. She clasped her hand to her mouth. Nolan rose with her and steered her to the bathroom. She heaved the contents of her stomach into the toilet as he held her hair. Dizziness assailed her when she stood, but he was there supporting her with a hand at her back.

"Mouthwash," he said as he handed her a small cup of liquid. "It'll get the taste out of your mouth. Some TBIs heighten your senses. You don't want to get sick again."

Right. Ellie clung to the matter-of-fact explanation and swished her mouth out with the mouthwash. She spat in the sink and watched through the mirror as he turned on the water and rinsed out the sink.

Intensity resonated within Nolan's green gaze—a gaze so like Jesse's she almost collapsed beneath the emotions emanating from him. "It's not going away. It'll fester beneath the surface whether you do what he wants or not. It'll rot away inside you."

"You don't know," she whispered. "He can't ever know. None of you can."

"Jesse will rip the entire tri-county apart for answers. He'll hunt the bastard down and get what we need, Ellie."

"You don't know that."

"I do," Nolan said. Determination and anger flashed across his face. "I know because that's what I'd do if you were mine. If a woman I loved was threatened, I wouldn't stop until the danger was gone and the bastard was six feet under."

"He's right," Mary said. She took Ellie's hand and guided her back into the bedroom.

Ellie sat beside the woman on the mattress. "Phil was verbally abusive. He must've recorded some...things."

"I'm taking it you aren't going to be more detailed," Dylan said.

"It wouldn't be good for anyone to see what he..." Ellie swallowed. "What he made me say and do. What he said and did."

"Jesus." Nolan paced and dragged his hand through his hair. "We'll get the tapes, Ellie. No one will see them."

"Please don't tell Jesse. He has enough to worry about."

"We don't keep secrets from one another," Dylan said. "Not something of this magnitude. We'll tell him when he returns. I promise we have his back and yours on this. Okay?"

They had no idea how horrible those videos would be, but she nodded. For now she had no choice but to trust them with it.

19

*E*llie carted the *Doctor Who* tote bag holding Jesse's journals and Cord's files with her as she tramped down the winding corridors leading to medical. She hadn't bothered doing more than yank on a pair of shorts and a T-shirt before sliding on a pair of flip-flops and heading out.

It was a few minutes after ten the next morning, and she'd stayed up all night reading after the horrible phone call had woken her up. She'd managed a couple hours sleep, but nightmares created by the haunted words she'd read and the threats Herman lobbed demanded she remain awake. Since she couldn't do a damn thing about Herman Perskins, she'd directed all her focus on Jesse's journals. There were questions to ask. Answers to get.

Doctor Logan Callister was a handsome man. His semi-long, unruly hair tumbled around his face in a messy warning that he wasn't the sort of doctor most folks were used to. He glanced up from the clipboard he'd been holding as she walked in and plopped down on the nearest examination table. The tote bag was heavy in her arms, but not from weight.

The enormity of the contents left her...

Confused.

Pained.

Determined.

She'd win the war to get Jesse fully out of that hell. One way or another.

"Ellie. This is a surprise." He set the clipboard down and sat on the small stool near her. "Are you okay? Is your mom?"

"Mom's fine, thanks to you. Never better actually. What's in those shots, Doc?"

A sad but resilient spark flared in his gaze. "Something to make her comfortable. Brant knows."

"Thanks." Ellie had fed her mom pot-filled cookies before she'd been moved to The Arsenal, so she was fully onboard with whatever helped ease the suffering.

"You've been under a lot of pressure caring for her alone as long as you have."

"That's what family does." Ellie thumped the tote bag down on the small step up to the examination table. "Let's talk about Jesse."

"I'd rather chat about you a few minutes. Have you spoken with Doctor Sinclair?"

"No, and I won't." She crossed her arms. "She's Jesse's."

"Excuse me?"

"She's his sanctuary—where he goes when he needs to get dragged out of whatever nightmare has him in its clutches. She sorts his head and keeps him here with us rather than in..." Ellie cut the words off. She wouldn't ever share what she'd read in Jesse's journals. He'd trusted her with the contents. "She's his."

"From what I've seen and heard, you're his sanctuary. Amanda is the light guiding Jesse's path to you."

Ellie gasped as the steely admiration in the man's words appeared in a faint smile on his face. Maybe coming to chat with him hadn't been such a good idea. What did she really know about the man? He'd been a Ranger in the Army, then did a stint in the CIA. Somewhere before or during those two, he'd become a doctor. Details were vague, but she'd heard enough to know Mary, Vi, and the Masons respected and trusted him.

Which meant she would, too.

She reached down and pulled out the two sheets of carefully constructed questions she'd listed out. "These are the most important of my questions. I filtered out the stuff that can wait a while."

Logan's eyebrows rose. Amusement flickered across his face as he took the papers. His brows furrowed as he read, then flipped. Read, then flipped again. The stool creaked beneath him as he shifted his large, muscular frame.

"This is quite a list."

"It's quite a problem I'm solving." She reached down and dragged out the folder of Cord's data. Color-coded sticky notes matching the ink colors in the list stuck out amongst the papers. "Help me make sense of this, Doc. I'm a teacher turned office manager. This doctor-speak is above my head. I need this in laymen's terms."

"May I?" Logan held out his hand.

Ellie turned the file over. He was Jesse's doctor and likely had the medical portion of these records—if not all of it. Maybe even the unredacted version. Her pulse quickened with nervousness as she waited. A stillness settled within the open area. Only a small curtain separated the examination bay from the rest of the large room.

He thumbed through the file, going to the sticky notes as though the confusion in her brain that'd drawn her to color-coding the questions made perfect sense. She ran her hands over her thighs as she waited. By the time he'd set the file aside, she was a wreck.

"Take a deep breath, Ellie," he advised.

She obeyed, remembering the "in for four, hold for four, out for four" method Jesse used. A temporary reprieve of calm filled her, but she felt the need already building up again. The compulsion to demand answers.

There had to be answers. Why had that shit happened? Her eyes burned.

Why had those monsters carved him up? Tears spilled out.

Why?

She blinked and swiped at the tears. "I need to know why."

Logan took her hand but rested his fingers at her wrist. "There's not always a why, Ellie. I know you've spent a lot of time taking care of your mother. You're a fixer. You want to make everything that's wrong around you right."

She did. She totally did. Starting and ending with Jesse.

She forced a watery breath and took a tissue from the box he held out. Jesus, talk about being a mess. "Sorry. I didn't intend to come here and erupt. I'm gonna get stronger, like the others. I can handle whatever you tell me. I promise."

"The others?"

"Mary. Vi. Zoey." Ellie sighed. "Bree. Rhea. Riley. Addy."

"Ah." He folded the papers she'd given him in half. "Everyone has a superpower, Ellie. An inner or outer strength stronger than others have. For Mary it's her steely determination, her resolve to solve every problem and avert any danger using her intelligence and forward-thinking."

Wow.

"You're trying to attack this like it's a mission," Logan said.

"*It is.*"

"You aren't an operative or a handler. You're Ellie. His Peanut."

A gasp escaped her. What did that even mean? It sounded so right, yet her mind refused to process it.

"Your superpower is your heart. The way you make this compound feel more like a home than most of the operatives here have ever had. Mary and the others are the bone—steely strength. You're the heart."

"I'm his heart."

"You're more than that," Logan whispered. "There won't ever be any sense made of what he endured. We'll likely never hear it all. All that matters is what lies ahead."

She shook her head. He'd given her the journals for a reason—so she'd understand what he went through. Crap like that changed a man, had changed *her* man. There may not be a why, but she damn sure needed the how. "How do I make this right for him, Doc?"

"By doing what you've always done," Logan answered. "Love him."

Ellie swallowed.

"Your mom says you aren't sleeping. Want to tell me why?"

She chewed on her lower lip.

He sighed. "Jesse's got Sinclair. If you won't talk to her, you need to talk to me. You've been through a lot, Ellie."

"The accident," she whispered.

"The hospital attack," Logan said. "Assaults are scary and often leave residual side effects. Post-traumatic stress."

"The car accident," she clarified. "I can't get it out of my head. The blood. Seeing Momma Mason's blood on me. Stopping the bleeding so she'd live, so Jesse wouldn't arrive and find the most important woman in his life dead. I can't get it out of my head."

"That's why you need Sinclair." Logan leaned forward. "For the record, I think you're the most important woman in Jesse's life, and he's finally getting into a position to accept that."

Ellie swallowed. Her heartbeat accelerated at the idea.

"I can't talk about Jesse's injuries with you, Ellie. I'm sorry." Logan wrote on a prescription pad. "Here's something to help you sleep. It's not a sleeping pill, just a mild anti-depressant."

"I'm not depressed."

"No, but you're traumatized. Your mind needs help relaxing so it can heal. Staying up all night and reading those journals likely left you with some horrible headaches. Right?"

Heat rose in her cheeks. Her head still hurt.

"Go get some real rest and then talk to Sinclair. She can help you through this, Ellie. She may be helping Jesse, but that doesn't mean she can't help you, too."

Ellie wasn't sure what to think by the time she left the doctor. She went back to the cottage and secured Jesse's journals. Then she went into the kitchen and did the one thing guaranteed to make her feel better.

She baked.

*J*esse entered the cottage and inhaled. Sugar and chocolate wafted through the air. His stomach rumbled an angry protest he couldn't ignore. He went into the kitchen and stilled.

Jesus.

Piles and piles of cookies. All were covered with plastic wrap. Containers were stacked up with sticky notes on the sides. His heart expanded as he read the names. Levi. Sol. Brooklyn. Lex. Howie.

Jesse's team.

The other three teams were there as well.

But the massive plate of cookies on the counter drew his attention. His pulse quickened when he picked up the note labeled with his name.

Honey,

Welcome home. Milk's in the fridge.

Love, Peanut

Warmth flowed within him as the tension he'd carried around since finding out Addy's team was in trouble melted away beneath the aroma of Ellie's cookies. He undid the wrap at the side and snagged two cookies, then bit into both as he turned to grab the milk from the fridge.

Another note was stuck to a foil-covered plate.

In case you're still hungry after those cookies. :)

Meatloaf and homemade macaroni and cheese. He grabbed a fork, leaned against the counter, and ate. Though the meal might seem ordinary to most people, it was the best thing Jesse had ever tasted—even if it was cold. The cottage door opened. Jesse glanced up and watched as Dylan made his way into the kitchen. He reached toward the plate of cookies.

"Touch those and you die," Jesse said, his mouth full of meatloaf.

Dylan smirked, but folded his arms and leaned against the island. "She baked all day. The girls finally got her into bed a few hours ago."

Fuck. Ellie baked when she was stressed or worried. "She okay?"

"She will be."

"There a reason you're darkening my dinner by being here?" Jesse shoveled macaroni and cheese into his mouth and chewed.

"Depends."

"On?" Jesse sat his plate down and studied his brother. Dylan was the most cautious of them all, except Marshall. "She's not okay."

"Herman Perskins phoned her."

"What the fuck? How?"

"Vi and Zoey are looking into that. The call went directly to the landline here in the cottage, so they suspect one of the subcontractors Burton Construction used."

Son of a bitch. Jesse ran a hand down his face. "What'd the bastard say?"

"He threatened her. Told her to get us to back off."

"Or?"

Dylan's jaw twitched. Anger spiked within his face—red tinged his cheeks as his lips thinned, eyes flashing with unspent rage.

"Or?" Jesse repeated as he took a step forward.

"There's video footage," Dylan whispered. "We don't know of what, but Ellie's terrified of it getting out."

"I should've killed Phil at the rest stop." Jesse ran a hand through his hair and paced.

He'd known Ellie had been abused by her bastard ex-husband. Videos.

"We'll find and destroy them, man. You know we've got her back on this," Dylan said.

"Yeah. We'll find and destroy them." Jesse glanced back at the hall.

"Marshall, Nolan, and I have been thinking. We'd like to switch things up around here and expand operations," Dylan said. "I have a proposition for you."

"I'm listening."

"The women need more help with strategic operations, and we need a full-time presence in training and skill development. We need operatives more diversified in field tactics than they are," Dylan said. "You interested?"

"You want me out of the field." Jesse fisted his hands and looked away. "I'll get my shit under control."

Silence ticked by as they faced off.

"First, I wasn't aware your shit wasn't under control. From what I've heard, you're having nightmares and occasional flashbacks like we all have. If I benched every operative with those problems, we wouldn't have anyone in the field," Dylan said. "Second, this isn't just for you."

Ellie.

"She held it together well, but she's not an operative or handler, man. You fought like hell to come home. I'm thinking it's time we make it so you don't have to leave."

"I'm an operative. That's what I do," Jesse argued.

"Think on it." Dylan pushed off from the island. "You're one of the best soldiers I've ever worked with, but you're my brother above all else. That woman back there's ripping herself apart trying to figure out how to fix you, how to make sure she never loses you again."

"Something happened."

"Mary was taking Jessie to her checkup with Logan," Dylan commented. "She overheard a few things."

"The journals." Jesse ran his hand through his hair. "I shouldn't have given them to her."

"I'm glad you did. It'll help having her in your corner, listening to the stuff you can't share with people."

"You talk like you know something about it."

"I do," Dylan admitted. "We all came home with our own rucksack of skeletons. Yours are a fuckload heavier than mine, but mine weighed me down. Mary's had her share, too. I promised her I'd have a word."

"She talked to Ellie?"

"Not yet. That'll likely happen soon, though. She's a momma bear ready to adopt anyone who smells like they need her." Dylan grinned. "She's a hell of a mom."

"Pleased for you, brother. You set the bar high with her."

"No." Dylan smiled. "Ellie set it first by knocking Nolan on his ass for you back when we were kids. I'm glad she's fighting her way back into your corner. I'll do whatever I can to get her there, man."

Jesse picked up the plate of food and continued to eat as his brother left. He rinsed the dish off, then went back into the bedroom. He'd only intended to peek in on her, make sure she was sleeping okay. Hearing she'd had troubles while he was away left him anxious.

"Jesse?"

"Hey. I didn't mean to wake you."

"I'm glad you did." She sat up and flipped on the lamp.

Breath swooshed from his lungs. Her hair was in disarray. Pink tinted her cheeks a rosy shade that matched her full lips. Her generous breasts peeked out from the thin, spaghetti-strap top she wore.

Vanilla.

The scent filled the room.

He glanced over and noticed the candle near her bed. She'd wanted her bedroom to smell like vanilla. For him?

"Lie with me?" She scooted over and patted the bed beside her.

Jesse had no business agreeing, but was sprawled out with her pressed against him before he realized what was happening. He kicked his boots off and swallowed as she settled into the same position she'd been in in the hospital bed.

He'd thought about that time a lot the past couple of days. Having her pressed against him felt right, like a part of him had been returned after a long absence.

"Are you okay?" she whispered.

"I am now, Peanut. Thanks for the cookies and the meatloaf," he whispered. "Your macaroni and cheese was so good I almost licked the plate."

She giggled and splayed her hand out on him. Ellie had always been full contact—a fact he didn't mind, even though everyone else's touch bothered him. He stroked her hair and relaxed deeper into the bed.

"The girl?"

"Safe with her sister. Gage and his team remained behind with the rescued college students to coordinate with the FBI. It's a freaking media circus." Although Jesse didn't want to ruin the moment, he needed to know she was okay. "You did lots of baking."

She tightened against him. "I've watched you leave on tons of missions before, but this time was different. I don't know why. It just was."

He caressed her face. "Because we're starting something good, Ellie, and got interrupted."

"We did." Her eyelids fluttered shut.

Anticipation ignited within his pulse as their mouths met. Her taste was a drug he craved. He shifted so she was beneath him. The soft moan she emitted quickened his heartbeat.

"You're beautiful, Ellie." He nibbled her earlobe and ran his hands along her sides.

It'd been too long since he'd made out with a woman. Nervousness crawled through him, just beneath his skin like an itch he wouldn't ever scratch. Ellie claimed his mouth once more as she ground herself against him. Legs wrapped around him, she was lost in the moment.

Shame consumed him. He couldn't give her what she wanted, but he could give her the release she needed. He kissed a fiery trail down her neck and along the swell of her breasts. The thin barrier spotlighted her hardened nipples. He licked and scraped his teeth across one tiny bud. Rising up, he dragged the thin chemise off of her and threw it to the ground beside the bed.

His pulse thundered in his ears.

Fiery need shone in her gaze. Pupils dilated, breathing labored, Ellie was in the throes of passion.

Shame consumed him a moment, but Ellie drew him closer and took his mouth. Her soft caress moved along his arms, then beneath his shirt.

Tension coiled within him when she started dragging the material over his head. She didn't need to see the ugly scars.

"Jesse," she whispered against his mouth. "Let me love you."

He'd once vowed to give Ellie anything her heart ever desired. His eyes burned as a rush of emotions assailed him. Love. Anger. Remorse. Yearning. Fear.

Why couldn't one of them be lust or arousal?

The T-shirt he'd worn fell beside him on the bed. His heartbeat accelerated as he watched. Waited for her gaze to roam the minefield of scars along his torso. Moisture pooled within her eyes as she traced each scar. Heat spread through him with each kiss against his skin. Her tongue was a fiery whip that traveled along each wound.

A burn resonated in his gut. The need to take control rode him hard. He claimed her mouth and cupped her breasts. Her nipples hardened more beneath his touch. He licked and sucked each one. She tasted sweeter than honey and smelled like the vanilla he'd craved so goddamn long.

Tears burned his eyes and spilled out down his cheeks.

"Ellie." The name was a plea and a cry for help rolled inside of a whisper.

Goosebumps formed along her skin wherever he touched. Kissed.

He lifted her up with one hand on her hip and removed the small shorts she wore.

Fuck.

She was more beautiful than he remembered.

"Jesse."

"I thought about tasting you every day, Peanut," he whispered against her stomach. He rested between her thighs, inhaled her arousal and the soft skin of her thighs against his cheek. He grazed her slit with his fingertips and relished in the wetness.

She wanted him.

Scars and all, Ellie needed him.

"So fucking beautiful," he whispered.

He slid two fingers into the wet heat and imagined it was his dick, like it'd once been before. She'd be tight around his shaft and so lost in pleasure she'd squeeze tight. Soft moans filled the room as he feasted on her, alternating between his fingers and mouth as he teased her clit and fucked her slow and sweet with his fingers.

Her arousal was ambrosia he'd imagined savoring. Ellie tightened around his fingers and cried out as an orgasm overtook her.

Jesse hung on and continued feasting, so desperate to sate the carnal desire he remembered from before that he couldn't stop. Not yet.

Moans turned into screams as he brought her over the edge once more.

When her entire body quivered from the releases he'd given her, he kissed his way up her body until he claimed her mouth.

Home.

"That was amazing," Ellie whispered, breathless.

Jesse situated them back into position. "I love you, Ellie."

"I love you, too, Jesse."

But was that enough? Jesse kept the worry to himself. Would what they did be enough to keep her? He hoped to hell so because he couldn't imagine a life without her in it.

"Dylan told me about the videos, Peanut. We'll find and destroy them. Phil isn't going to hurt you ever again," he whispered.

Ellie tightened against him. "I didn't know he'd recorded those things. Jesse, promise me you'll never watch them."

"Nothing on them will change the fact that I love you, Ellie."

"Promise me."

"I swear."

20

---

*B*lood dripped from an open wound along Jesse's eyebrow. His gaze clouded with every other blink, likely thanks to the blows he'd been dealt earlier.

Five days.

He'd gone five days without a session.

Why?

The chains rattled as he shifted so the blisters along his wrists didn't scrape against the cuffs. Footsteps echoed, but he continued the physical inventory. His back burned, but not as bad as it once had. The nerve endings had died long ago. Too bad the rest of him hadn't followed suit.

His chest was no better.

And his dick...

Anger rolled through him.

The footsteps halted a couple feet away. Jesse lifted his head to glare at the bastards as he always did, but shock overcame him.

Marine.

"It's unfortunate I'm going to have to do this myself," the man said. "Everyone always breaks. You messed up my routine, Army."

The bastard snapped on a pair of gloves. This wasn't happening. He was injured in the hole and locked in a night terror. It'd happened before.

"Last chance to give us something before I get creative."

Jesse remained silent and closed his eyes. As long as he had Peanut, he could withstand anything. Maybe Marine would finally be the one to end the pain. Jesse craved death almost more than he craved one last day with Ellie.

A scream ripped from his throat as the lash struck his groin.

A feral scream punctured the night. Ellie woke. Heart thundering in her chest, a scream escaped her when pain exploded along her upper cheek and eye.

"I'll kill you, Marine!" Jesse shouted.

Nightmare. The word ricocheted within her mind as she rolled off the bed and away from the man thrashing about. She dragged on a T-shirt and a pair of shorts. The angered shouts continued, but she couldn't understand his words.

Jesse had punched her.

Fear struck her a moment. She'd survived physical confrontations with Phil many times, but Jesse wasn't her bastard ex-husband. She clung to the facts she knew. Each one melted away a bit more of the terror freezing her into place.

Jesse was the best man she'd ever met.

Brave.

Kind.

Jesse Mason loved her.

He was locked in a nightmare, and she needed to rescue him from whatever horror had him within its clutches.

"Jesse! Wake up." Ellie approached the bed, but vaulted backward when he lunged for her.

Jesse flung himself back and forth and screamed. The raw pain within the sound was unlike anything she'd ever heard. "No! No! Marine, no!"

Jesse jerked off the bed and landed on the floor. He punched and kicked. The lamp on the bedside table crashed to the ground, but he continued the violent brawl with his past. How had Levi handled it the last time?

They'd fought.

"Ellie-belly?"

"Stay in the hall, Mom. It's okay. Jesse's having a nightmare."

"I'll call Logan."

"I'll kill you for this, Marine!" Jesse screamed as he doubled over so his knees touched his chest. And he sobbed.

"No, I've got this." Determination overrode the fear and shock. Ellie had read the journals, yet had never read anything about someone named Marine. She grabbed the candle that'd fallen to the floor when he struck the bedside table. The lighter was beside Jesse.

She lit the candle, then grabbed another. And another.

If someone walked in, they would've likely thought she was attempting an exorcism. In a way, she was. She waited a couple minutes for the scent to permeate the immediate area, then she shook Jesse. He struck out, but she moved back.

"Jesse, wake up." She kept her voice low and imploring rather than a shout. "Wake up, Jesse. Wake up."

She touched his face when he started rocking back and forth. He froze. His eyes opened as he tensed.

"You're okay, Jesse. Take a deep breath." Ellie curled up on the floor beside him so she was the only thing he'd see. "You're safe. They aren't ever going to hurt you again."

"Peanut?"

"I'm here." She ran a hand down his arm. A sheen of sweat coated his entire body, but it was the confusion in his gaze that broke her heart. "I love you, Jesse. You're okay. You're safe."

"Where's Levi? He can't leave you alone with me," Jesse said. "Fuck. I fell asleep, didn't I?"

"You're okay."

He clasped her face gently and angled her head to the side so the pale shafts of light from the downed lamp spotlighted the pained area.

"I hurt you." The horrified pain in his voice made Ellie tear up.

"It wasn't your fault," she defended. "I'm okay."

"I hurt you," he repeated, his voice rawer than before. He stood. Tense silence blanketed the area as he assessed the damage to the room. Then he leaned down and picked her up in his arms.

"What are you doing?"

Jesse remained silent and headed into the living room. He set her on the sofa, then headed into the kitchen. Ellie forced deep, even breaths, despite the rapid pounding of her heart.

He crouched in front of her as he placed a bag of frozen corn against her face with one hand and pushed a button on his phone with another. "Yeah, I need you at Ellie's cottage."

The cellphone landed on the sofa beside her. "I'm okay, Jesse."

"To hell you are," he growled. "I hit you, Peanut. You have a head injury, and I *hit* you."

"Ellie-belly? Are you okay?"

She nodded, unsure how to explain things to her mom, who'd followed them into the living room.

"Logan will be here soon," Jesse said.

"I don't need a doctor, Jesse," she whispered.

"You do. I hit you."

She cupped his face and peered into his teary eyes. "Are you okay?"

Sweat dampened his exposed chest. His breaths came out in labored pants as his gaze continued sweeping the room. Was he fully here, or was a part of him still trapped in the nightmare?

His journal.

Ellie rose.

"Sit down," he ordered.

"You need to journal, Jesse. The sooner you do it afterward, the better, right?"

"Can we maybe make sure you aren't bleeding inside your brain from the blow you just took first?" Jesse clipped. "You don't get to worry about me right now."

She narrowed her gaze and put her hand atop his as he gripped the corn bag. Her other stroked his face. "I'm okay, Jesse. I'm not made of glass."

"Never should've fallen asleep," he muttered. "This can't work, Peanut."

"No. You aren't running from this, Jesse. You aren't running from *me*."

"I hurt you," he repeated, this time low and terrified.

"There's no war we can't win together, Jesse. You're helping me with my troubles. Please let me help with yours." Ellie wasn't an idiot. She recognized and accepted the risks because she'd read everything Cord had provided. She'd done her own research. But there was no way in hell she was giving Jesse an inch to escape. "Breathe deep. I've got you."

Ellie rested her forehead against his. The door opened, but she kept her focus on Jesse. His entire body vibrated, as if he was ready to bolt if given half a chance.

He severed contact and rose. "Doc."

Logan stood a couple feet away. His gaze slid from Ellie to Jesse, then to her mom, who'd sat in her recliner.

"Let me get you back to bed, Mom. You need your rest."

"Don't worry about me, Ellie-belly. You'd best let the doc tend to you so Jesse knows you're okay."

Right. Okay, that made a lot of sense. Jesse would relax once he realized she was okay. No harm done. She'd figure out a better way to handle the nightmare episodes. Levi would have tips.

Logan, too. She looked at the doctor warily. He'd yet to offer a comment or an assurance, as he remained a couple feet away. Then she noted Jesse's defensive stance in front of her. His hands fisted, then opened. Fisted again.

Had he forgotten he'd called Logan?

"Jesse?" Ellie took a step forward and splayed her hand out on Jesse's scarred back. Tension radiated from him in thick waves. "What's wrong?"

"I should've called someone to sit with you while he examines you."

"You're here and so is Mom."

"I should go."

"You leave and I'll follow, Jesse. You aren't running from this. Or me."

"I hurt you," he growled.

"Let's take a look at Ellie," Logan suggested.

Jesse warily stepped aside. He prowled the area like a caged animal looking for an escape, but remained close as Ellie sat on the sofa and let the doctor assess her.

"Looks like you're already doing most of what I would recommend," Logan said. "Take a couple Tylenol if you haven't already."

"She's got a TBI," Jesse argued.

"I'm aware. She's been healing nicely. The accidental blow she took isn't to the same region." Logan glanced at Jesse. "We can take her to the ward and run a scan to make sure."

"Good. Let's go." Jesse walked toward the door.

Ellie's heart hurt. Jesse's sole focus was on making sure she was okay. He didn't have on a shirt or shoes. She looked down at her hastily donned clothes and realized she'd put on Jesse's T-shirt inside out. Her shorts were on backward.

"Let me get dressed."

"It won't take a minute. You're fine," Logan said. "Jesse, get some shoes. Then we'll go."

He grunted but headed back toward the room.

"Are you okay, Ellie?"

"I'm fine."

"Nightmare?" Logan asked.

Ellie nodded. "We fell asleep."

"I can message Sinclair."

Ellie wanted whatever was best for Jesse, but she didn't want a lot of people involved. Too much of a big deal was being made about what was clearly an accident.

"He has every right to be worried, Ellie. Soldiers suffering from PTSD battle this issue a lot. It's one of the most prevalent reasons why the Warrior's Path participants are here recovering. Soldiers like

Jesse were trained to kill. Waking up unaware of where they are with those skillsets is dangerous," Logan said softly. "You need to chat with Doctor Sinclair about this."

"I will, but I'm not letting him use this as an excuse to run away from me." She glared at the doctor. "I'm not losing him to that hell he survived."

⚜

*E*llie was okay. Jesse let the relief burn out the worry as they returned to the cottage. Her mother was no longer in the recliner—a fact he filed away as Ellie clutched his hand and steered him back toward the bedroom.

His heart thudded hard in his chest as they approached. He should've made an excuse and left her back in Medical, but he'd needed to see for himself she was okay.

Then he'd leave.

Until his nightmares were back under control, he couldn't risk spending nights with Ellie, even though he craved them like a drug. Anger and self-loathing rode him hard. He'd lost enough because of those monsters. He deserved another shot at the dream he'd once shared with Ellie. Or half the dream.

He could live without having kids with her.

And sex...

As long as he could make her come and fall apart in his arms, he'd die a happy man.

None of that was possible right now because he was a ticking time bomb every time he shut his eyes and slept. There were zero guarantees he wouldn't have another episode—one that could eventually hurt her far worse.

The bedroom was in shambles, but Ellie didn't seem to notice. She slid her flip-flops off and leaned down to blow two candles out. The movement hiked up her shorts in the back. A groan escaped him as he admired her gorgeous ass and the strip of soft inner thigh now visible. He wanted to strip her bare and feast on her once more.

Maybe then he could forget the bruises developing around her face—a mark she'd wear for days because he'd hit her.

Damn.

"Stop thinking about it," she said.

"I can't control what I think," he said.

"You can do anything." She turned and smiled as she stripped off his T-shirt, which fell to the floor.

Anticipation zinged beneath his skin as she shimmied out of her shorts. Totally bare, she smirked and headed into the bathroom. Jesse hadn't felt this alive around anyone since he'd returned home.

Damaged.

He'd left the cottage without a shirt. The realization had come a few moments after Logan put her into testing and returned a few moments later with a T-shirt. Nothing had mattered except making sure Ellie was okay.

The light pelting of water against tile sounded from the bathroom. The shower.

"Come shower, Jesse."

His mouth dried. The bathroom was eight steps away, and the bedroom door was only six. Another twenty-one and he'd be outside —where she'd be safer. But leaving was impossible when the temptation of a wet and loving Ellie was so...

"Jesse." She appeared in the entryway to the master bathroom. "Come wash my back."

He stood frozen into place as she disappeared again. Wash her back?

Confusion drew him into the web of temptation. Steam rose from the warm water. Ellie stood beneath the spray, head tipped back so the drops hit her neck and trickled downward to slope off at her breasts. The smile she offered when she turned demanded he approach.

"This is nuts," he declared.

"Why?"

"Ellie, I hit you. We can't..."

"You didn't hit me, Jesse. You struck out at whatever was in your nightmare. I happened to be in the way." She squeezed shampoo into her hand. "Now, are you going to get undressed and get in here, or am I doing this alone?"

"This is serious," he said through clenched teeth.

"I know, but I refuse to focus on the negative of tonight a second longer. I want to take a shower with the man I love, then crawl into bed and sleep a little more. Later we'll wake, eat breakfast with Mom, and then we can sort through a solution for this problem. And that's all this is, Jesse," she said as she lathered up her hair. His fingers itched to handle the task. "A problem, just like all the others we solve every single day. I've said it before. There's nothing we can't figure out or conquer together."

"I don't deserve you."

"Bullshit." She stepped under the spray. Soapy water cascaded down her body. His skin heated. His heartbeat accelerated.

Dare he give into the temptation? She'd seen his scarred back and torso and most of the damage to his legs the first time he had a nightmare at her place. Few had seen what was left in his groin. Scar tissue covered the majority of the area. He'd lost his left testicle. Skin grafts had replaced the worst of the damage on his shaft, but his dick was...gross.

Not that any cock was pretty. His was...

"Jesse," she whispered.

He startled at her proximity. Wet and impatient, she rose on her tiptoes and drew his face down. Fiery tingles burst within him when their mouths touched. The kiss was deep and commanding—an all-in fusion of tongues and lips.

"That's more like it," she commented, her lips scant millimeters from his. "Now let's get you undressed so we can enjoy this hot water. I have to admit I'm in love with the water heaters out here. It'll be hard to return to the rental."

Ellie wasn't ever returning to the rental, but Jesse kept the thought to himself. They had enough between them right now. Awareness marched along in a trail of goosebumps wherever she touched. The delicate trace of her fingernails along the scars on his upper chest didn't register physically as it once had. Too much nerve damage would prevent him from ever experiencing the physical sensation fully, but the feather-soft contact was enough.

Jesse swallowed. "I'll feel it more if you touch harder. Nerve damage numbs most physical contact."

Her eyes widened. A fiery glimmer of anger swept across her face. The protectiveness made his heart swell. If given half a chance, the beautiful woman who owned his heart and soul would kill every single bastard who'd hurt him.

Ellie leaned forward and kissed the deepest gouge along his chest. He froze a moment, then relaxed as his mind processed where he was. The reminder was enough. She reached for the button to his jeans.

"I'm not..." Jesse paused. "I'll keep them on."

"No." She undid the clasp of his jeans and dragged the zipper down. "You're mine, Jesse James Mason. I want to see you, memorize every inch of you. Love every inch of you."

"There's nothing worth loving, Peanut. I'm a heap of scars and gnarled flesh."

"You're so much more," she whispered. "We all have scars. They're the reason you are the incredible man I love today. Don't you dare hide a single one from me. You earned them surviving, staying alive to come back to me and your family. I love every single one of those scars, Jesse, because they're proof of your love and a testament to the strength and resilience it took to come back to us."

"You got me through," he whispered into her ear. "When the darkness and pain threatened to consume me whole, you were there."

Jesse kissed her as she helped him pull his pants and boxers past his hips. He severed the kiss long enough to remove them completely and then claimed her mouth quickly as the need to taste her overrode any latent concerns.

Ellie loved him.

He was safe with her.

She laughed when they moved beneath the warm spray. Raised

on tiptoes, she lathered up his hair, then filled her palm with a large dollop of soap. She washed and massaged her way across his shoulders, down his arms and chest. Every inch of him received the Ellie treatment—stroke, massage, cleanse, and kiss.

When he moved to do the same with her, she intercepted with a shake of her head. "Next time."

Yes. There'd be plenty of next times. Just because he couldn't sleep in the same room as her didn't mean he was letting her go— even if that would be the smartest move.

Their kisses turned molten—a fiery tango that danced beneath his skin and pooled at the base of his dick.

What the fuck?

Jesse froze a moment, but Ellie continued. She lathered his lower stomach and knelt as she repeated the methodical treatment his upper chest had received. Eyes closed, head back, he fought the fear and apprehension within him.

Peanut.

The name was a whispered plea between them as tingles burst beneath his skin and across his stomach in an arrowing path downward. She caressed along the scar that started beneath his naval and angled downward, where it ended in a half dozen circles of puckered skin.

Cigar burns.

She touched each one, kissed it. Then continued.

Weakness plagued him a moment. His knees buckled beneath the onslaught of sensations crawling within him. His dick twitched.

Jesse tightened, unsure what was happening. If he didn't know any better, he'd think...

"Jesse," Ellie whispered against him.

He glanced down where she knelt, eye level with his crotch. Tears glistened within her gaze—a fact he noted because his back blocked water from hitting her. Her hands splayed on his thighs. Massaged.

Then she leaned forward and kissed his shaft.

Doctors had made tremendous progress in restoring most of the skin there, but scar tissue made the area less sensitive than it'd once been. Ellie took the semi-hard cock in her hand and pumped. Once. Twice.

Fuck.

Jesse gritted his teeth as his entire body swayed beneath the contact. Fear spiraled through him a moment, but he kept his gaze on Ellie. He wasn't in the hole. He wasn't in the hell room.

He was with Ellie.

Arousal.

Need.

She licked along his shaft, but he felt nothing. Resentment flashed through him. He'd once shot off like a rocket at the slightest flick of her tongue on his dick.

No response didn't halt Ellie's attentive ministrations. She continued massaging his thighs, then stroked his abdomen.

"Tell me what you need," she demanded as she wrapped her hand around his semi-hard cock.

"Harder." He panted with shallow breaths as his awareness honed in on where she gripped his dick firmer than before and stroked. Hard.

A groan escaped him. She stood, claimed his mouth. Her hand continued working him. Need consumed him as he thrust forward. This wasn't how he wanted it.

Jesse had never expected to have a hard-on again. Sex wasn't an option.

But it was.

"Inside you," he said, too consumed with the carnal lust attacking him to say more.

With a groan, Jesse lifted Ellie up until her legs wrapped around him. He ran a hand between them to work her clit and found her aroused. Ready.

"Peanut," he groaned as he thrust into her.

"Jesse."

She clung to him as he pumped inside her slick, tight heat. The sensation was a fraction of what he'd once felt, but a million times more than he'd ever expected to have back. Tears burned his eyes as he kissed her.

"I love you," he said, his voice low with raw emotion.

"Jesse."

He held onto the release longer than he expected, but nowhere near long enough. He wanted to spend an eternity buried deep within Ellie. He thrust one last time and gave into the sensations. Ellie's entire body tensed with her own orgasm moments later.

He somehow remained standing despite weak knees. His entire body was mush—so relaxed he damn near floated with the sensation. Ragged breaths sawed from him. He rested his forehead against hers and smiled when she smiled.

"You're amazing," he declared.

"Funny, I was about to say that about you." She wrapped her arms around him. "I love you, Jesse James Mason."

"I'm sorry it wasn't..."

She placed two fingers over his mouth and shook her head. "Don't you dare apologize to me for anything we share or do."

"I didn't think I'd ever..."

"I'm all in, Jesse. Whether we ever do this again or not, I love you. Nothing matters but having you in my life again." She smiled. "That was amazing."

Jesse grinned. It'd been way beyond amazing for him.

"I know we've got a lot to work through, Jesse, but this proves we're on the right path. Nothing is keeping us apart this time. Nothing."

"Until I get the nightmares under control, I can't sleep in the same bed as you, Ellie. It's too dangerous."

"We'll work something out," she whispered. "Come to bed and hold me. Besides, you need to decompress and journal that dream out."

Jesse nodded. He'd stay awake and watch her sleep. Right now he couldn't imagine leaving her alone.

*E*llie remained quiet and napped off and on as Jesse scribbled in his journal—the only one she'd yet to read. Tension coiled within his arms whenever they rested around her a moment, then he'd return to the book he'd placed beside them on the bed.

They'd had sex.

Ellie's entire body still hummed with the release. Euphoria kept her from sleeping. Despite the unexpected and extremely pleasurable turn of the evening, there were a few things unresolved. Things she couldn't leave until later because she suspected one was very, very important.

"Jesse, who is Marine?"

He tightened beside her. "Doesn't matter."

"Is it a person?"

"It doesn't matter," he repeated, his voice higher than before.

"I love you. Nothing you say or share will ever change that, Jesse. None of the journals mentioned someone with that name," she broached. "Cord shared files with me. None of them did either."

"Cord needs to mind his own damn business," Jesse clipped.

"He loves you." Ellie repositioned herself to be behind Jesse. One of his journals had mentioned no one having his back when he needed it. It would be her new mission when they were alone—to have his back while he slept.

And they would sleep together. One way or another, she'd excise the nightmares keeping them apart. They'd lost far too many nights as it was. She wasn't about to let some phantoms stand between them.

"Then he'd best leave it the fuck alone."

Ellie wrapped her arms around Jesse's middle and rested her head on his shoulder. "I love you, Jesse. I'm here to listen whenever you're ready to share. Don't keep it bottled up inside you. Those bastards don't get another second of your life."

21

*E*llie opened The Arsenal office and waited as Harry, Hermione, and Dobby entered. The three headed to their favored positions along the full-length window near her desk. Sun splayed into the area.

Ellie doubted she'd be allowed to stay for long, but there were things to do and commandoes didn't do paperwork. She sat at her desk and groaned when the chime above the door went off. Glancing up, she watched Bree and Sara enter with Ariana in tow.

"What are you doing here?" Bree demanded.

While Ellie found the instant reprimand annoying, she was thankful they didn't ask immediately about her black eye. For once she was thankful The Arsenal's rumor mill worked with a proficiency the tri-county gossip mongrels could only hope to attain one day.

"Are you okay? I should've stayed at your place—crashed on the couch or in the spare room." Bree reached for Ellie's face, then pulled back.

"I'm fine. The bruising will go away in a few days. Now, I have emails to check. Invoices to enter. Payroll to process." She glared at her friend. "I literally just walked in. You can't yell at me for at least half an hour."

"Is that so? Is that in the TBI manual?" The blonde crossed her arms and looked at Sara. "She's stubborn."

"She's bored," Sara said. "I can help with stuff. I can file and whatnot."

"Thanks," Ellie said. "That can wait. I just want to process a couple checks and payroll, then I'm done. I swear."

"Good, because none of us want to piss off your man. He almost snapped Cord's head off earlier. The two headed downstairs into the gym only Jesse's team uses. Your man was unhappy." Bree winced. "Then we found out why. Now I'm worried about both of you."

Her man. Bree had used the term twice. Both had cast joy within Ellie, but she didn't want her dear friend worried. "Jesse has a lot of healing to do. A lot of the operatives and veterans here do."

"I know. Still." Bree bit her lip. "He's so good with you. I hate seeing him still fighting his way out of his head. It's not fair."

"No, it's not."

"I won't risk it happening again. I'm gonna get Rhea to switch out the drones in your house. We have special ones that can knock people out with drugs. We'll program them to react instantly under certain conditions." Bree's eyes widened as she stared off into the corner at the office drone. "Yeah, we can make this work."

"Bree, I'm fine. I don't need drug drones in my bedroom," Ellie said. "We're gonna figure this out."

"Yeah. We are." Bree studied Ellie's face a bit longer before taking a step back.

Ellie wasn't used to so many people worrying about her. It hadn't even occurred to her that they'd be worried about Jesse hurting her again. He'd never, ever intentionally hurt her.

"She's fine. You can barely see it with makeup," Sara said. "Besides, Jesse is a nice guy. He's not a monster."

Sara knew monsters better than anyone her age should. Ellie willed a shift in the conversation. "I promise I won't be in the office long."

"No, no you won't. You have a clear mandate to do nothing on electronics," Bree said. "Don't even get me started about all the reading you've been doing lately."

"I didn't read for long," Ellie argued. "Besides, you never said why you came over earlier."

"I didn't want to upset your mom. They're starting a debrief of the evidence from the FBI seizure. HERA's finished with her analysis of the documentation. They figured you'd want to be there."

"When?" Ellie looked at the clock on her desk. "Damn. It's now, isn't it?"

Bree nodded. "Go. Sara and I will figure out the payroll. I did it last time and only one commando has yelled at me, so I must've done most of it right."

"Thank you." Ellie stood and made her way to where they stood at the door. She leaned in and kissed Ariana's forehead. "She's getting bigger every time I see her."

"She's not sleeping through the night anymore," the girl said. "She's always crying."

Ellie noted the exhaustion on the girl's face. "Bring her over tonight, and I'll babysit. Maybe you can head into Nomad and catch a movie."

"Thanks! That'd be great."

Ignoring the you-shouldn't-have-offered glower Bree cast her direction, Ellie headed toward the conference room in the other building. Anticipation ignited her pulse. Jesse would be there.

Smiling, she entered the room and froze. Fallon, Rhea, Nolan, and Jesse sat at the table with Vi and Zoey, who whispered to each other at the head of the table.

"Hey," she said. Ellie pulled her hair down to partially cover her eye. Apparently the makeup job she'd attempted hadn't masked the bruises as well as she'd thought if Bree had seen them.

"Come sit, Peanut," Jesse said. He stood and pulled the chair out next to him.

When she sat, he ran his hand down her hair and gently pulled it back. A feather-soft caress around the bruise awakened her pulse.

Their gazes locked, and she felt the remorse and guilt within him as though it were her own.

"Don't, Jesse," she whispered. "I'm okay."

"Never again," he promised. He leaned in and gently kissed the area. "You need any aspirin or anything?"

"I took some earlier." Unsure what was happening, but more than ready to move past the incident last night, she looked around. "Where is everyone else?"

"We've already set a few things into motion," Vi said. "First up for discussion is Carlisle Industries. HERA spewed out a ton of classified documentation. He's been involved in black ops organizations for other governments for years now. How deep is our exposure with your work, Rhea?"

The brunette glanced around the room, then paled as she pushed a thumb drive across the table. "Here's what I know for a fact he took. I was a bit darker in my studies back then, heavily into genetic manipulation and how to affect it on large swaths through gaseous distribution."

"So, a dirty bomb," Fallon said.

Red rose in the woman's cheeks, but she nodded and kept her gaze away from the man. "In a manner of speaking, yes. There were flaws with the work, though. I hadn't learned a few critical components."

"But he could have by now," Jesse said.

"And likely did," Zoey added. "He's got more clout in some circles than The Arsenal does."

"Then why haven't we heard of him?" Nolan asked.

"Because these circles don't venture out of their caves until they're ready to push the kill switch of whatever they've concocted," Fallon said. "I've spent half my career taking down clusters of government-funded tech firms who go rogue."

"We're adding Carlisle Industries to the list," Vi said. "I got a call from Bob an hour ago. I let HERA's searches be seen to discover who rose to the surface. He has requested we shut Carlisle down, seize all research, and destroy it."

"And their work is?" Nolan asked.

"That's what we need to find out first, but all indications lead to a genetic weapon of some sort," Vi said. "Rhea, we'll need you with Fallon and his team in the field."

"No," Fallon growled. "She's not field-trained."

"Then you'd best keep her safe," Zoey said. "Until we figure out exactly how Carlisle's tech affects HERA and our equipment, we can't risk it going down when you and your team are in the middle of a lab trying to figure out what's important and what isn't."

"Think I can read," Fallon said.

"When do we begin?" Rhea asked.

"The sooner the better," Vi said. "This isn't up for discussion, Fallon. Make it work."

Ellie tensed. Rhea wasn't an operative. Ellie couldn't imagine how terrifying it'd be to be out in the thick of dangerous operations without any training. What if something went wrong?

"Now onto Phil Perskins and the FBI evidence we've analyzed," Vi said. "Dallas and Marshall are assisting the FBI with arrests and search warrants on two Marville residents, Lonnie Haskell and Oren Macavoy."

"Neither are a surprise," Nolan commented. "They're part of the underground gambling ring and heavily into drug running lately, based on what Marcus's team has uncovered."

"Yes. Marcus and his team have gone back undercover with the remnants of the Flores cartel. They've reorganized under the leadership of Carla's uncle. The DEA is running point."

"And Raul?" Jesse asked.

"He's clear," Zoey said. "He tapped out of service and refused to continue the assignment. That's why Marcus and his team are taking over."

"And Dom?" Ellie asked. "Did we find anything more about that night? The deaths?"

And Phil's videos of me.

Ellie looked about the room and paused on Nolan. Had they told Vi? Mary and Vi never kept secrets from one another, but the thought that everyone might know was embarrassing. She hoped the videos never came to the surface. Every evidence seizure terrified her.

Other more important issues were on the forefront right now. Dom might not have been guilty, and she might have had evidence to clear him. Her stomach somersaulted at the idea.

"Videos on Javier's cloud showed he'd meant to set Raul up, but he disappeared. Dom was the replacement," Vi said. "We've forwarded all the evidence gathered to Dom's new defense team—one funded by us."

Thank God. Ellie breathed a relieved sigh. The Arsenal always protected the innocent, no matter what.

"Why?" Nolan asked.

"Dom wasn't down with hooking the Marville Dogs up with the cartel," Zoey said. "It was greed."

Greed had stolen years of Dom's life. Put him in prison. She'd had evidence in her possession that could've exonerated him.

"Don't blame yourself, Peanut," Jesse whispered. "You had no way of knowing how deep this went."

"Deep is an understatement," Zoey said. "It took a bit of time to weed through all the videos. We'll need to turn evidence over to the FBI to get arrest warrants for a few more people for unrelated crimes done in concert with the Marville Dogs, but we were able to access Javier's videos off the cloud."

"Did you find what you needed?" Ellie asked.

"Yes and no. The files received in the raids gave HERA enough to break the code Phil was using," Zoey said. "It's a series of transactions, bank accounts, and a detailed listing of assets sold. Guns. Drugs. People."

Ellie watched as the list streamed on the overhead monitors. Long. Extensive.

"Phil did all this?"

"No," Vi answered.

"What?" Jesse asked.

"It goes back further than is possible for him to have been at this alone. It's a large network, larger than we expected. We used the crawler program and tracked all the accounts down," Zoey said. "Phil's father was the initial contact for the cartel."

Shock rippled through Ellie. Herman Perskins was a monster—one far more dangerous than most because he seemed...

Normal.

He went to church every Sunday and attended all the local events—not that there were many. He sat on the school's board of directors and was always one of the main donors to fundraisers in Nomad.

"He got me fired," Ellie whispered, letting the anger fill her. "When Phil accused me of drug addiction, his father vilified me with the board. Said I wasn't fit to teach the future leaders of Marville."

"This will clear your name," Jesse said. "We won't stop until it does. You'll get your job back if that's what you want."

Was it? She'd loved teaching, but she loved The Arsenal more. Unable to think beyond the revelations flashing up on the screen, she shoved the thought aside. "And Dani? And the other girl? Do we have that closed out? Is there enough to get the others?"

"Yes. Addy is going to establish contact with the other woman after everyone is taken into custody. We'll offer her protection until everyone's in prison. She's..." Vi's pause drew Ellie's attention.

Vi and Mary never paused. They shot straight and never hesitated because every second could mean life or death when in war. This was most certainly a war. "What?"

"It's Natalie Steele," Zoey said.

"No." Ellie shook her head. "It can't be Nat. She's the sweetest, shyest woman I've ever met. She lives across from the school and works there only because she hates leaving her house."

She never left her house unless she had to.

"God, I'm an idiot. It all makes sense now."

"You had no way of knowing," Jesse said as he turned her chair to face him. He rose, lifted her up, then sat with her on his lap.

"Jesse, you can't put me in your lap!"

Nolan chuckled. "I think he just did."

"I should be the one to talk to her," Ellie said. "She knows me. We used to eat together at lunch sometimes."

"That's why you need to *not* be the one. Dani has a confrontational, defensive personality," Vi said. "That made Kamren the ideal choice for approach because they are friends. Natalie is shy. She has very few friends from what we've seen. She only has one friend she sees regularly."

"She used to have two. Me. I abandoned her when I got fired," Ellie said. "I knew she only had me and Rose, but I holed myself up with my mom and my problems and ignored her."

"Don't," Jesse growled. "None of this is on you, Peanut. None of it."

Ellie felt the weight crushing her, though. The woman had been her friend even though Ellie was married to the monster's son. Jesus. How had she stood to watch Phil pick her up or drop by and visit? He looked just like his father.

"We'll keep her safe until this is over. She'll be on solid ground," Nolan promised.

Ellie nodded. "I need to be the one. She'll need a friend there. She won't handle strangers confronting her with this."

Everyone looked at one another.

"Okay," Nolan said. "You aren't going in alone, though."

"Jesse and his team will be helping the FBI take Phil's father down," Vi said. "This is almost over, Ellie."

"I can't ever thank you all enough. None of this would've been possible without you. And all the help with Mom." Ellie sniffled. "Thank you."

"Don't thank us," Jesse said. "I love you, Ellie Mae Travers. You're family. You've been family since you knocked Nolan on his ass for me."

"Hey now," Nolan said with a grin. "But he's right. You're family."

The ride to Marville was quiet. Ellie sat up front with Kamren, who headed straight to Natalie's house like she'd been there a hundred times. Riley, Brooklyn, and Addy were in the back. It'd taken more than a little convincing for everyone to let a woman-only crew go speak with the woman.

Not because Jesse and his brothers didn't think the female operatives could keep Ellie safe. They'd wanted to be there because sitting on the sidelines for a single second of whatever this was went against everything the Masons stood for. Although Herman's threat still concerned her, she trusted Jesse and everyone at The Arsenal.

Ellie fiddled with the earpiece hidden by her hair.

"Stop touching it," Zoey said through the earpiece. "Every shift is like a jackhammer over here."

"Sorry."

"You're going to do fine," Doctor Sinclair said. "I'll hear everything said and will help guide you if needed. From what I've seen, though, you'll do fine. Be yourself. Be open and honest with her. Be a friend."

A friend. Right.

Ellie remained silent as the vehicle came to a stop at the small house. Pale blue paint peeled along the old wooden siding. Spots along the angled roof showed bare spots where shingles used to be. Overgrown shrubbery hid most of the structure—which squatted beneath huge pecan and oak trees. With some work it would be a beautiful home.

Addy, Brooklyn, and Kamren fanned out around the house as though they'd discussed the maneuver. They hadn't. Ellie's pulse quickened as she fell into step beside Riley, who stepped in front of her at the last minute so she was the first to take the stairs leading up to the shaded porch.

Riley opened the screen door and knocked on the wooden door. No answer came.

Ellie knocked. "Natalie. It's Ellie Travers. Riley and I were in the area and I wanted to check on you."

"You don't live here anymore." The thick door muffled Natalie's response. Ellie strained to hear it. "I'm fine. You can go now."

"Natalie, honey. We need to talk." Ellie paused a moment. "Open the door."

Moments ticked by. Each one ratcheted up the nervousness crawling through Ellie. A loud grating of metal against metal sounded. A deadbolt.

Then another. And another.

Ellie's heart squeezed as the final of six deadbolts sounded and the door opened an inch. Then two. Another couple later, wide brown eyes gazed at Ellie, then darted to Riley.

"Hey, Natalie," Ellie said. "Can we come inside?"

"Why?"

"We need to talk, sweetie," Riley said. "Ellie needs your help."

The door opened wider. Natalie Steel swiped her tongue along her thick lips and ran a hand down her straight, dark brown hair. "I'm not sure how helpful I can be. I'm not good at much."

Ellie took the backhanded, self-depreciating statement hard. How many times had she said something similar when she was with Phil? He was always good at making her feel like less than everyone else.

The woman stood aside. "Come in. I'll pour some iced tea."

Riley and Ellie sat in a living room adorned with white lace doilies on pristine furniture. The interior was immaculate in every way, and nothing like what she'd expected to see. Natalie returned from the back corridor with a silver tray holding three glasses of iced tea. A spoon inside a sugar bowl sat beside them.

Ellie took a glass and sipped. "Have you heard about Phil's arrest?"

"It was mentioned at work," Natalie said. "I'm glad you're finally getting the justice you deserve. I never believed the things they said about you."

"I know. You've always been a good friend to me. I'm sorry I haven't been around lately." Ellie swallowed. "Truth is, Mom's been pretty sick for years now. She didn't want anyone to know, but I'm thinking it's time I shared that with you."

"I'm sorry to hear. Can I help?"

"No, we're out at the Mason ranch for now. They've got a doctor out there who's really good with Mom. Doctor Burton drives out every other day and checks on her. She's...comfortable. Happy."

"That's nice." Natalie smiled.

"Natalie, we found some videos," Riley said. "From a few years ago."

The woman paled. "Videos?"

"Assaults." Ellie reached out and took Natalie's trembling hand. "We think one of the women was you."

She shook her head and stood. "You're mistaken. Please leave."

"Nat..."

"Go!" Tears poured down the woman's face.

"Lonnie Haskell and Oren Macavoy were taken into custody," Riley said. "They're not going to ever hurt you again."

The woman sat on the sofa. Eyes wide and teary, she stared at Riley and Ellie like they were aliens.

"They're going to arrest Herman Perskins today," Ellie said, eyes watery. "It's over, honey, but you're gonna need to help and make a statement. That'll make sure all three of them stay away for a long, long time."

Natalie shook her head. "They'll come back."

"She's in shock," Sinclair said. "Repeat what you said."

"Lonnie, Oren, and Herman are going to pay for what they did to you, Natalie." Ellie spoke each word slowly and watched the woman's expression.

Natalie squeezed Ellie's hand. "I-I can't talk about it."

"You won't be alone. I'll sit with you if you want. We'll keep you safe," Ellie promised.

"You should go." The woman looked at the door, then Riley and Ellie. "They're too powerful. No one cares what I have to say. They'll get off."

"Not this time, Natalie," Riley said. "We've got them dead to rights. There's video."

"Too strong," Sinclair said.

Natalie paled. "People will see."

"No." Ellie shook her head. "I promise you aren't alone, Natalie. You aren't the only one they have videos of. There was another woman. She's already made a statement."

"She's stronger than me." The whispered words startled Ellie.

"She knows about Dani," Zoey said. "That was unexpected."

"How do you know about Dani?" Ellie asked.

"Th-They made me watch the video." The woman licked her lips. "She talked? Told them about that night?"

"Yeah," Riley said. "We've got someone protecting her. You aren't alone in this, Natalie."

"Y-you'll stay with me?" Natalie asked Ellie.

"I'll be there when you talk with the authorities."

"O-Okay."

22

"Authorities are en route to take Natalie's statement," Zoey said. "FBI should be at your location in twenty."

Jesse looked around at all the Arsenal operatives who'd arrived at Natalie's to help. Ellie was secure and they were closer to having the troubles handled.

"Copy," Jesse responded. "And Ellie? How is she?"

"Good. She's got Natalie calmed and talking," Sinclair said.

Jesse clicked off. He hadn't liked the idea of Ellie going to chat with Natalie, but he was glad she'd been there for the woman. Ellie was a strong, beautiful woman who always put others first.

"She's good for you," Nolan stated.

Jesse strapped on his tactical vest and glanced at his brother. Levi chuckled. Brooklyn whistled. Lex, Howie, and Sol wisely remained silent. "There a reason you're a tagalong?"

"The bastard is wrapped up in what went down with Dani," Nolan said.

Jesse froze. "That's not on you."

"It is. My name got her out there. That's mine to carry."

Dani was younger than Nolan by enough for the two not to have been close growing up. She'd been an unseen shadow to him. "It's not a good idea to follow that road, man."

"I'm not, but she deserves closure," Nolan said. "I want to make sure anyone remotely connected to that shit goes down. That's the least I can do. Then maybe she can move on. Besides, when the FBI is on scene, I figure having an extra set of eyes to watch out for those videos he threatened Ellie with would help."

Jesse's jaw twitched. He glanced at his team.

"I take it there's more than we know going down today," Sol commented.

"There's more," Jesse affirmed. "He threatened to release footage of Ellie. Not sure what, but it's bad enough to scare her. That doesn't go into evidence today."

"Understood," Lex said. "We've got your girl's back."

"You weren't in your room last night," Levi commented.

Jesse's jaw twitched as he looked at the team gathered within hearing distance. This wasn't how he wanted the 411 to go down, but when in Rome... "I'm pursuing things with Ellie."

"Think we sussed that out, boss," Sol commented.

Brooklyn chuckled. "I think it's sweet. She's adorable."

"Pleased as hell, man," Lex said.

"It's about time," Howie commented.

The teammate who knew him better than anyone remained silent. Assessing. Fuck. Jesse heaved a sigh and glanced at the clock. They had a solid half hour before the FBI would arrive and drones were monitoring the perimeter.

"It'll wait," Levi said.

"No," Jesse said. "We don't go in with our heads elsewhere."

"Yours isn't here," Nolan commented. "Is it? I heard there was trouble last night at Ellie's. You okay?"

"No." Jesse admitted what he'd yet to fully realize until that moment. He glanced at his brother. "But I will be. I spoke with Sinclair and Logan. They're putting me on sleeping pills until I get my nightmares under control better. They aren't a solution, but they'll help. Cord's adding more drones to Ellie's cottage."

He hated that his baby brother had to put safety measures in place to keep Ellie safe when he spent the night with her. But he couldn't continue relying on Levi to watch over him—not with the woman he loved in the mix. Jesse would rather never sleep again than risk repeating last night.

"Talk it out in the next group," Levi suggested. "Lots of the Warrior's Path folks are here because of these problems. You'll get through this. We'll get through this."

Everyone gathered around Jesse nodded. Once again, his team had his back.

And Nolan was in the fray. Jesse recalled his brother's words—he'd heard there was trouble last night. "That's why you're here. To keep my head on straight," Jesse said.

"And to dispense Dani's justice," Nolan said. "You're solid. We can't always leave our home behind. That's why we have a team at our backs. Yours is rock solid."

Levi remained silent, as if he'd read between the lines.

"They're the best. I owe them more than I'll ever be able to repay. They've had my back more than anyone will ever know."

"Because you've had ours," Lex said. "That's what team does."

Which was why a part of Jesse hated the decision he knew must be made. If he wanted Ellie in his life, in his heart and soul, he couldn't go out on missions. He couldn't lead a team into overseas missions and be gone long term because he wasn't that man anymore. Truth told, he hadn't been for a long while, but the thought of spending weeks away from her...

He rubbed his chest and willed the burn away. Yeah, handing the team he loved over to Levi made sense. That'd free Jesse up to take stateside missions only and train the unteamed operatives. They could take over the work with the underground for Zoey's system. It was a solid plan—one close enough to the one Dylan had pitched earlier for Jesse to know his brothers would agree.

They'd agree to anything, though, because they loved him.

"We've got movement on the southwest perimeter," Cord said into the com.

Everyone moved into position. Jesse closed the distance between his location and the primary entrance to the home. Camera images showed the lone man who'd attempted to flee through the side exit was down, thanks to the knockout drug in the drone.

A diversion.

Lex and Howie took the rear door while Nolan and Levi penetrated the primary entrance with him. The furniture in the entryway was as grandiose and obnoxious as the man who owned it. Their booted footsteps struck the marbled entry without sound as Levi went right and Nolan went left.

Jesse moved forward and through the living room. Music drifted in from the back area where the office was. He met Lex in the corridor leading to the room. Where was the man's security?

A voice replaced the music.

"Phil, no. Don't."

Ellie. What the fuck?

"Stay in position," Vi growled through the com. "Dispatch a drone."

"Say the words, bitch!" Phil shouted. A moment ticked by before the voice thundered. "Say it!"

"Jesse never loved me."

"And?"

"I wasn't woman enough for him." Ellie sobbed.

"Such a sad, worthless cow. You're lucky I married you," Phil said, his voice low and derisive.

Boiling rage spiraled through Jesse, but he locked it down and forced the numb, the lethal calm he honed like a weapon. There'd be time for the rage later—after they took down the monsters who hurt Ellie, Dani, and Natalie.

"Everyone's in position. Go," Cord ordered.

Jesse exploded into the room. Herman sat in a leather high-back chair facing a massive screen. Ellie's onscreen tears fractured his lethal calm. Phil had her hair in his fists and was...

Fuck.

A live gunshot pierced the recorded pleas and cries echoing

within the room. Nolan stood in the entryway behind Jesse, gun aimed at a sparking computer.

Herman stood, hands raised. Laughter tumbled from him. "You have no idea the firestorm I'm about to unleash."

"Shut your mouth, you sick fuck." Jesse holstered his weapon so he wouldn't use it on the smirking bastard.

"FBI is making entry," Vi commented.

"Fruit of the poisonous tree. You illegally entered my domicile. Nothing here will be admissible." The man chuckled. "I knew you idiots wouldn't wait."

"Whoever gave you your intel should've done a bit more research," Jesse said. "We're contracted on behalf of the state of Texas. We weren't support for this takedown. We were primary."

The man's grin disappeared. Red rose in his face. "I won't ever see the inside of a prison."

"If I had my way you wouldn't," Nolan said.

"Walk away now before it's too late," Herman said. A gleam sparkled in his gaze. "She was on the list, you know. Back then. We voted on who we'd initiate into our club. Javier wanted his cousin to take dick, though, said she needed to get ridden hard. Otherwise Ellie would've been a prized pig."

Jesse lunged, but Levi and Nolan dragged him back.

The bastard chuckled. "No way this holds up in a court. Not that it'll matter."

"It won't," Nolan promised. "Matter that is. Rich white ass like yours won't last long where you're going."

"I'll last longer than Ellie will," Herman said. His laughter echoed.

Tension struck the room. Jesse turned and left, trusting his team to contain the crazy bastard.

"Stay where you are. Addy and them have Ellie protected," Vi ordered.

"We're missing something. He's an arrogant ass, but he's not stupid. Something else is in play," Jesse said as he got into the truck. "Show me as en route to Ellie's location."

Across town by the school. Jesse knew it'd take less than five minutes, but it may as well have been five hours. The door to the truck opened. Nolan got in.

"You good to drive?" he asked.

Jesse didn't dignify the question with a response as the engine growled to life and they got on their way to Ellie.

❀

*S*omething was wrong.

Ellie watched Natalie flit back and forth in the room as if nothing was wrong. As if she wasn't waiting for authorities—strangers—to show up and ask her questions about the horrific things she'd endured. Ellie knew people responded to shock and trauma in different ways, but this was...

Wrong.

"Ellie, I need you to listen to me very carefully," Doctor Sinclair said. "Where are you in the house?"

Ellie blinked. Confirmation there was something wrong hung in the silence. Sinclair wouldn't have asked if something wasn't wrong. "Natalie, are you sure I can't help you chop all those onions?"

"No, I'm fine," the woman said from her position between Riley and Ellie. "I know how they should be cut. Too big and they're gross. Too little and they disappear. They need to be just right because tonight is a special night."

"It is?" Riley asked.

"We can finally be together," Natalie said.

Oh God.

"Natalie, let's go back into the living room and wait for our friends. We don't want to smell like onions," Ellie said.

"But he likes onions. He likes when I cry," the woman commented. "He said you wouldn't listen. You never, ever listen. Phil was right about you. Nothing but a loud, crass pig. I'm glad they didn't choose you."

"Ellie get out," Sinclair ordered.

Glass broke in the living room. Natalie halted her chopping and glanced over her shoulder. Riley launched herself at Natalie and toppled the woman's chair. The knife went flying across the room as the two women wrestled. Angry shouts and screams rolled from Natalie.

"Get the door open," Zoey said.

The deadbolts. Ellie sprinted into the living room. Her hands trembled as she unlocked the six barriers keeping Addy, Kamren, and Brooklyn outside. God. Riley.

"I swear I'm learning how to kick ass after this. Never again will I be useless," Ellie muttered.

"Deep breaths, Ellie. You're okay. Riley has her secured," Doctor Sinclair whispered.

She turned the knob and stood back. Addy entered first, weapon drawn. Brooklyn swept in second. Both closed in on the kitchen but froze in the entryway. Riley had the woman pinned with her hands at the small of her back.

"Restraints?" Riley asked.

Addy smirked and pulled out a zip tie from the pocket of her cargo pants. "Guess those extra lessons with Jud have paid off."

"You helped, too," the blonde said.

"Teach me," Ellie blurted.

"No way in hell are you teaching my woman to fight," Jesse said as he entered the room. "That'd be my honor."

"Jesse." Ellie wrapped her arms around him. "Natalie. She's…"

"It's okay. She'll be okay."

Natalie rocked back and forth and mumbled to herself. Her gaze was vacant as she peered out into the room. "He's going to be angry. I was supposed to hurt you. I couldn't hurt you."

Ellie blinked back tears.

"Get her home, Jesse. I'll meet you both in my office," Sinclair said into the com.

Ellie didn't want to meet Sinclair in her office, but she burrowed deeper into Jesse's embrace and left Natalie's with him. Nolan closed the distance between them.

"Just heard from Levi. He has the recordings," the man whispered. He looked at Ellie. "They aren't seeing the light of day, Ellie. No one will ever see them."

"Thank you," she whispered. "Thank you."

"Come on, Peanut. Let's get you home."

She climbed into the back of the truck when Jesse opened it. He entered with her. Surprised, she faced him and was hauled onto his lap. Jesse claimed her mouth. The kiss was hot, deep, and filled with so much need her entire body turned molten.

She shifted and straddled his powerful thighs. Anticipation beaded along her skin as she reclaimed his mouth.

"Okay, wow. So not wanting to spoil the moment, but coms, people," Zoey said. "Geez. Why can't any of you ever remember they're live?"

Jesse chuckled and drew Ellie's hair back. The panty-melting grin on his face almost made the interruption worth it. "Sorry, Z. Bye, Z."

He pushed a button on her ear thingy, then did the same with his. The engine growled to a start. Ellie tensed.

"Eyes on me, Peanut." He put a hand at the back of her neck and traced his tongue along the seam of her mouth. "I love you."

"Love you, too," she whispered against his mouth. "Any chance we can skip Sinclair and go to the cottage? Or maybe your room? I haven't seen it yet."

"I have somewhere better in mind," he whispered in her ear. "I want to make love to you under the stars. My dick willing, I want to make love to you, Ellie Mason."

Ellie. Mason.

She repeated the name she'd scrawled on so many sheets of paper as a kid and sank into the kiss. Joy leaked from her in hot tears Jesse wiped away with his thumbs. She tasted his on her tongue. Although she longed for more, she severed their mouths and rested her head on his shoulder.

A heavy sigh escaped him as he wrapped his arms around her. "I've dreamed about this moment for a long time, Ellie. Likely I should've waited until tonight, under the tree where we shared our first kiss. But I couldn't waste another second. We've lost so many."

They had. Years apart.

"Yes," she whispered. "I want to be Mrs. Jesse James Mason. Tomorrow. We'll go to a JP."

"Mom would skin me," Jesse said with a chuckle.

"Mom's really sick," Ellie whispered. "I want her there."

"This weekend," he said. "That'll give Mom a couple days to do whatever she wants. We'll keep it small. Family and immediate friends only."

"That's perfect." She smiled. "You know her definition of 'immediate friends only' will be the entire tri-county."

"As long as you are mine at the end of it all, I don't care," Jesse whispered.

"I'm already yours," Ellie said. "I always was."

❦

*J*esse waited outside Doctor Sinclair's office where Ellie was already speaking with the woman. Though Ellie had wanted him to remain, he understood that the two women needed time to form a connection and bond without him around.

Nolan rounded the corner and drew him into a hug. "Pleased as fuck for you, brother."

Tears filled Jesse's face as he saw the rest of his brothers approach. "Big mouth."

They all chuckled and dragged him into hugs. After a couple moments, Nolan held out his hand and dropped into Jesse's the small box Jesse hadn't seen since...

"Mom kept it in the same spot you've left it all this time," Marshall said.

"This should've been Mary's," Jesse whispered, too overwhelmed with emotion to speak any louder. "Shit."

Dylan chuckled as Jesse swiped at his face. "It's always been Ellie's."

Jesse glanced at Dallas, who held up his hands. "It's Ellie's."

"Did Mom see you get this?"

"Yeah," Cord said. "She teared up and went into her room."

Jesse rubbed his chest. For once there was no ache there. It felt as though a final piece had been returned from the hole. "I imagined putting this on Ellie's finger a lot when I was in the hole. It was so fucking dark I couldn't see anything. I'd close my eyes and think of her—what I should've stayed home and had."

"You picked a day?" Nolan asked.

Jesse smirked. There wasn't any way big brother hadn't heard the conversation they'd had in the back of the truck, otherwise he wouldn't have known to get the ring and bring it to Jesse. "This weekend. We want her mom there and healthy enough to enjoy the moment. Try and keep Mom contained."

"We're on it," Dallas said. "Though keeping the operatives under control might be harder. The whole compound's heard. You getting her back, making her your wife…"

"It gives us all hope we'll find our way back from whatever hells we've escaped," Nolan commented. "We'll get the tree ready for when you're done here. Truck'll be parked and stocked with what you need."

"I've thought about the offer," Jesse said. "I want to turn the team over to Levi. He's more than ready, has been since he arrived. It's time he has a team. I'll chat with him."

"It's a good move, one that'll strengthen us," Marshall said. "Having you on strategy will help."

"A lot of the unmatched operatives want to help with protective recovery for Z's underground. I thought I could do live training using those missions. That'd keep me in the field, but stateside for small absences only."

"Ellie is stronger. She's not an operative, but she'd acclimate to you being gone if you want to keep your team," Dylan said.

"This is for me," Jesse said. "She's the most amazing woman I've met. I know she'd handle whatever we decided together, but you're right. I fought too hard to come home not to be here now. Now that I have this."

He fisted their grandmother's ring closer. It symbolized everything he'd fought to return home to.

"Pleased as hell for you, brother," Cord said. "I'll chat with Z and the girls. We'll coordinate a plan going forward. Bree suggested training Ellie on running the dots."

"That'd be perfect. She's good with people," Jesse said. "Then we'd get to work together."

"Get your ass in that room before Sinclair drags you in," Marshall ordered.

Jesse smirked at his brothers and headed in. There was still a long road until he was fully healed, but he was damn close to seeing the light.

23

They'd spent over two hours talking with Doctor Sinclair. The woman was a great listener and had given each of them action steps to see them through their recovery program. They had sleeping pills to take to help Jesse and Ellie both sleep better for an evening.

Speaking with the woman about what'd happened with Jesse helped. While Ellie knew he'd never, ever intentionally hurt her, Ellie was terrified for him. What if he didn't ever get a firm grip on the nightmares? God, he'd been through so much. He deserved peace.

Cord was right, Ellie. You are the key to him fully healing. We'll get there as long as you're alongside him. He needs you just as much as you need him. This isn't a fairytale romance movie where all the problems go away. Life is ugly and fraught with challenges. With a love like the one you two share, though, I have every confidence you'll both recover fully.

They would.

Together.

Ellie finally accepted that she had just as many wounds to heal as Jesse did. She would meet with Sinclair privately once a week and with Jesse as a couple once a week. Jesse would continue seeing her three times a week until he felt ready to taper down.

Anticipation pebbled along her skin and tightened her nipples to achy nubs as Jesse drove them out to the tree. A couple of lanterns hung from the lowest branches and bathed the area in pale light. Blankets had been spread under the tree. She waited until Jesse came around, not because she needed his help but because she wanted his hands on her. And hers on him.

The truck door opened. She turned, wrapped her legs around his waist, and claimed his mouth. Desire burned along her skin where he touched her arm, then beneath her shirt along her back. Up. Up. The bra she'd worn flicked open.

His tongue delved deeper, pillaging her mouth as though he was ravenous. A groan escaped her when he severed the contact. Her shirt swept over her head along with the bra. She craved his touch, writhed forward in anticipation of his hands at her breasts.

Jesse slowed the contact. Gentle strokes, followed by soft kisses and exploratory kisses down her neck, then back up again to the shell of her ear. Tingles burst beneath her skin as the need increased, a rapid pulse in her ears and arousal pooling between her legs.

No one had ever affected her the way Jesse could. One touch undid her faster and deeper than Phil ever had. Years. She'd fantasized about having Jesse like this again for so long. One taste the other night had fueled the need, turned her carnal.

They weren't about sex. They'd never been about the mere physical.

But God she needed him deep inside her.

"Touch me," she growled as she nipped his earlobe.

Amusement tumbled from him in laughter she hadn't heard in so long the rumble spiraled within her. Jesse. He kissed her neck and stroked her back. Long, slow, and confident sweeps down her spine and into her pants. Her panties.

"You wore blue."

"Yes. For you," she whispered. "Surprised you noticed the bra."

"I notice everything about you, Peanut. Everything."

Muscles bunched and flexed beneath her touch as he stooped

and rested her in the center of the blanket. A sexy smile spread across his face. "Someone's showing me up. They brought a mattress."

Ellie laughed and stretched out on the blanket-covered mattress. "I guess we'd better spend the night out here to make it worth the effort."

His smile faltered a moment. She nibbled along his lips and pulled at his shirt. "Love me, Jesse. No rules. No boundaries, remember? We set our own destiny."

He removed his shirt, then leaned down and continued the sensual torment in slow kisses across the swell of her breasts. Caresses up her sides made her shiver and rock against him. His weight atop her was everything she'd craved.

A growl escaped her as she pushed him away enough to taste his skin and score her nails lightly down his back as she licked and scraped her teeth across his nipple. She sucked and tormented the flesh until he grasped her head and claimed her mouth.

"Minx," he said into her ear. "We've got all night, Peanut. We aren't rushing this."

"Jesse."

He palmed her breasts. The contact sent a shockwave of awareness through her entire body. A firm pinch made her moan in response. Ellie leaned back and relished the heat of his mouth as he mimicked the torment she'd done to him. Pleasure arrowed from her nipples downward to the juncture of her thighs.

Jesse kissed and nibbled his way to her other breast. By the time he'd navigated downward and removed the rest of her clothes, her entire body trembled with need. She reached to remove his pants, but he moved downward and kissed her mound. Hands on the inside of her thighs to keep her in place, he licked and taunted her until she writhed upward.

He alternated rubbing her clit and licking the sensitive bud as he thrust fingers deep into her wet pussy. A release ignited through her faster than she expected. She rode the waves of white-hot pleasure as she clung to Jesse.

"I could feast on you all night," he murmured as he kissed his way up her body. "I love you, Peanut."

"I love you, Jesse." Their kiss was languid as she helped him remove the rest of his clothes.

Ellie didn't want to rush Jesse or put any pressure on him. "Tell me what you want, Jesse."

"You." He nibbled her earlobe. "Touch me, Peanut. Like you did last time."

Ellie sank into the kiss and wrapped her hand around his shaft. The damage was extensive. Rage flashed through her every time she saw the damage the monsters had reaped. It'd be easy to surrender to the nausea and anger, let it eat away at the moment until it died beneath the weight.

They wouldn't get another second of Jesse's life. He was home. He'd survived.

For her.

She firmed her grip until he groaned against her lips. Although she wanted to taste and lick and suck him like he had her, she focused on working his cock with her hand like he'd asked.

Jesse thrust into her hand. Breaths labored against her neck, he clenched his fingers in her hair. "Feels good. Never thought I'd have this again."

Tears tumbled from her cheeks at the raw emotion within his voice.

"Harder. Please."

Ellie strengthened her grip and moaned as she claimed his mouth in a kiss. His cock hardened within her grip.

"I can't wait. I might..." He groaned as she wrapped her legs around him and guided him to her entrance. "I love you, Ellie."

"Show me, Jesse." She kissed him again as he slid inside her. She clenched her muscles around his cock with each thrust, savoring the feel of him inside her. Nothing mattered but the fact that they were together.

One.

Ellie cherished every second she had with Jesse, no matter what they could or couldn't do. As long as he was in her life nothing else mattered.

Jesse reached between them and found her clit. She groaned as his thrusts quickened. Pleasure spiraled through her once more. Close. So close.

His release came on the heels of hers. She collapsed into the mattress and relished his weight atop her. Legs and arms wrapped around him, she let her ragged breaths escape in time with his.

Jesse reached over and grabbed his pants. He pulled something from a pocket.

"This has been a long time coming, Peanut." He slid a ring on her finger. "Marry me?"

Ellie grinned and kissed him. Tears escaped her eyes. "Is this..."

"Grandma's ring. Gramps gave it to her right under this tree," Jesse whispered. "We all agreed whoever married first would get it. Dylan and Dallas both said it was yours long ago. They knew I'd intended to propose before..."

"It's perfect, Jesse," Ellie said. "And yes. Yes. A million times yes."

"I'll chat with Logan. He'd mentioned some medicine that might help with my..." Jesse swallowed. "I might be able to get more function back."

"Don't you dare worry about that, Jesse," Ellie said. "I love you. I just came twice. What we shared right now was amazing. All I need is you. Nothing else matters."

"I woke up in the hole. Marine was there. He'd patched up my leg and kept me alive," Jesse whispered.

Ellie put her head on his chest and ran her hands along his stomach. His heart thundered beneath her ear. Dread crept within her gut. Whatever he was about to share was important. The enormity of the moment hung between them.

"You never mentioned not being alone," she whispered.

"I wasn't ready to share Marine." He threaded his hands in her hair. "I escaped into my memories of you and my family. Resino. As long as I was here, I wasn't there suffering. He'd chat me up, keep me focused. Kept telling me to give them something, anything to make the pain stop. But I was Delta. I wasn't gonna break for those fuckers."

God. Ellie let the tears fall. Silence seemed like the best response because what could she say?

"I started letting my guard down. Little by little I'd let him in. Then one day I passed out while they were beating me. The pain was..." He paused. "I couldn't take any more."

"Jesse," she whispered. She tightened her grip and kissed his chest.

"He was a plant," Jesse growled. "He'd AWOLed and joined them. When they couldn't break me, he crawled out of the hole and took his turn."

"Oh my God," Ellie whispered. "Jesse."

"He hurt me the most." His voice was a barely audible whisper against her hair. He caressed her cheek with his thumb, as if seeking comfort in not being alone with the memory. "He raped me, Peanut. I'm not ever sharing that with anyone but you. I was tested when I was in the hospital, then again a few months later. I'm clean. I should've mentioned that before, but I never thought I'd ever..."

"I love you, Jesse," Ellie whispered. She peered up into his gaze. "Thank you for telling me about Marine. I want to hear whatever you want to share. I'm here for you. You know that."

Ellie swallowed and studied his expression. Wariness and shame resonated in his face, the way he looked to the side of her rather than at her. She grasped his face until their eyes met.

"Nothing you share with me will ever change that I love you, Jesse. You are the most wonderful man I know. The bravest, strongest man I've ever met. I love you."

"I don't deserve you, Peanut," Jesse said. "I never should've left you."

Ellie smiled. "We're together again. That's what matters. You made it back home to me."

"You kept me alive," he whispered. "You were my reason to continue."

Ellie kissed him. She'd likely never hear everything he endured, but she knew he needed more than her to heal. "You should tell Sinclair, Jesse."

"She knows. It was in the file she got that I had injuries that indicated..." He halted. Cleared his throat. "She knows."

"Okay," she said. He'd broach the subject when and if he was ready.

If not, Ellie would listen whenever he needed. She'd do anything for Jesse. She shifted deeper into his embrace and looked up at the stars. Nothing could be more perfect.

*D*awn crept along the horizon as Jesse made his way downstairs to the basement gym he and his team used. Most operatives used the large facility on the second floor, but he preferred the privacy of the lower-level area.

Brooklyn and Lex were sparring on the mats across the way. Howie and Sol watched, offering friendly banter as they sipped coffee from large Styrofoam cups. Levi sat on the bench near the bag Jesse typically used every morning for at least half an hour before they arrived.

The man raised an eyebrow and chuckled when Jesse sat. "I guess you had a good night."

The best. He'd stayed under the tree with Ellie for hours. Though he hadn't been able to get another erection, he'd made sure she came twice more before they'd gone back to the cottage and showered.

Sleep had eluded him most of the night, but for once he hadn't minded. Because he'd had Ellie in his arms. He'd opened up more about Marine and how Levi had killed him rather than let the bastard get off with a cushy prison cell courtesy of the U.S. government.

"I'm pleased as hell for you," Levi said. "I see now why you fought so hard to get back to her. A woman like her is a treasure."

"She is." Jesse leaned forward and rested his elbows on his knees.

"Never would've had this without you, man. I owe you more than you'll ever know."

"You would've done the same."

"In a heartbeat. Whatever you need," Jesse affirmed. "Whenever."

"Appreciate it."

"Spoke with my brothers briefly. Details need to be worked out, but I'm handing the team over to you," Jesse said.

Levi froze beside him. The man's jaw twitched as his gaze slid over to the four operatives.

"You've been more than ready for your own team. With Ellie in my life, I want to pull back and focus on her. I'm gonna take over strategy planning with Mary and Vi and training of the unmatched operatives," Jesse said. "And I'll likely use them to run stateside recovery missions for Zoey."

"It's a solid plan." Levi looked over at him. "You sure that's what you want?"

"Yeah. I lost too much time with her. I can't risk losing more if a mission goes sideways."

"That could happen with those underground recoveries."

"True, but they're no more than a couple nights usually. Zoey wants to train Ellie on running the dots." Dots were the assets hidden within the underground network. Zoey, Bree, and Rhea had taken on the daily task of checking in with the women and children to ensure everything was okay.

Though it sounded simple enough, the network was massive with caches of hidden supplies and professional contacts—doctors, police officers, anyone who might be of service to the people Zoey protected.

"They need the help. She'll be good at it," Levi said.

Jesse let his gaze settle on the team he was turning over. "We'll wait until after the wedding to tell them, if that works."

"Yeah."

"I'll chat with my brothers, but just a head's up..." Jesse paused. "Feel like a dick saying this, but you and Brook..."

"It's done. She was scratching an itch." Levi looked down at his fisted hands.

"That gonna be a problem?"

"No." Levi glanced at the lithe blonde. She body-slammed Lex to the mat. "She's too good to let anything or anyone stand in her way."

"There's more to life than the ops," Jesse said. "There's more to life than duty."

"Seeing you with Ellie reminds us all of that, man. It's a shot of happy for us all."

Jesse chuckled. Heat crept up his face. "I'd best get my ass to the parking lot. We've gotta get on the road. Later, man."

Levi rose with him. They exchanged back slaps, then Jesse headed to the parking lot to meet Nolan. The sooner they got to the prison and got Dom the better.

24

"Why are we having a baby shower in a bar?" Ellie whispered not so quietly as she followed Vi and Zoey into the Sip and Spin.

It'd been two days since Herman Perskins' arrest. Natalie had been taken into a private hospital in San Antonio for evaluation. From what Brant Burton had shared, the woman had extensive psychological trauma that she'd need help overcoming.

The bruising around Ellie's eye had darkened but was slowly fading away. Riley had shown her some makeup tricks to help cover the area better. Though it was a crappy way to bond, Ellie was looking forward to having a little sister.

"Would it be better if we considered it a laundromat?" Rhea asked.

"First, Mary will never expect it," Zoey replied.

"Second, the guys demanded it," Bree said, "in a don't-ask-questions-just-do-it kinda way. It was hot to hear Nolan get all growly. I thought he was the vanilla Mason man, you know?"

"I know you aren't going there about my brothers with me right here," Riley said.

"Oops," the blonde responded. "My bad. Ixnay on the sexy bosses."

Ellie chuckled. Each of the women had carted in a different section of the cake she had stayed up most of the night baking and decorating. Though Ellie had tried to convince her mom to rest, she'd insisted on helping get all the decorations just so. Thanks to Cord gathering all the pictures needed, they'd be perfect.

She entered the Sip and Spin and noted Dani's glower from her ever-present position behind the bar. Rhea, Bree, and Riley took all the sections of the cake into the back along with the other supplies.

"Hey, Dani."

"Don't 'hey Dani' me," the woman muttered. "Those two women have been back in the kitchen with Bubba for two hours."

Those two women were Mrs. Mason and Ellie's mom. Ellie worried her mother was trying to do too much. She bit her lower lip but remained silent because she was glad to see her mom finally connecting with people. There was no guarantee on how long she had, but Ellie was glad to know she was living it to its fullest.

"Mrs. Mason's been keeping her seated. There's a recliner in the office—nastier than hell since Lonnie doesn't know how to clean worth a damn. But Bubba and Mrs. Mason scrubbed it down and covered it with a blanket from his truck. She's been asleep for a couple hours," Dani said. "I may have slipped her a few cookies Bubba and I baked while Mrs. Mason was scrubbing down the tables out here."

"*Mrs. Mason* is more than willing to make special cookies for a woman who damn well deserves not to suffer," the woman said as she exited the back area. "I'm glad to know you and Bubba have her covered. I was going to call Logan and get him out here with something."

"May still want to do that," Dani advised. "The cookies won't last long."

"Good to know. I'll make sure he brings something a bit stronger with him." Mrs. Mason patted Ellie on the shoulder. "She's doing well, dear. I know you're worried, but sometimes being useful is the best medicine around. You made sure to remind me of that when I was down. Don't you worry. I've got her covered. You go and do whatever you need to do."

"Why the hell is a baby shower for a Mason being done in a bar? *My* bar?" Dani asked, her voice pitched high enough to broadcast into the entire area.

"Why not?" Riley asked as she plopped onto a stool. "There's ample seating. Tons of liquor and music at the ready. A kitchen in the back to cook. And...we even have washers and dryers if little Jessie pukes all over us. Or Ariana. They're both a bit pukey."

Ewww.

Ellie smiled when she realized Ariana would now have another baby around. Another girl. DJ and TJ were great with her, but they were boys who enjoyed hunting and roughhousing. By the time little Ariana was ready for dolls, Jessie would be, too.

They'd likely be robotic dolls she'd programmed because the girl would be beyond brilliant, but Ellie was confident Ariana would hold her own. She glanced over at Kamren, who entered with mounds of helium balloons. The boys ran around in hyperdrive as always.

"Let's get to it, sons," Dallas said, his voice a loud boom within the area. "Operation balloon battalion is underway. First one finished with their appointed color gets an extra thirty minutes of game time tomorrow."

"Yippee!" TJ shouted.

Ellie laughed. "Oh dear."

"I've learned to accept that my man will incentivize our sons," Kamren said as she appeared. "I'm surprised we're doing this today. Why not wait a week or two? We have a wedding in, like, two days."

Wedding.

Ellie beamed. She touched the ring on her finger and felt heat creeping up her cheeks.

"Someone is happy," Dani said, a grin on her lips. "I'm thinking some of the rumors I've been hearing about your man are way off base."

"Dani!" Kamren reached across the bar and punched her friend in the arm.

"No way in hell she's beaming that smile and not getting a happy ending whenever she wants," the woman said. She looked at Ellie. "The Masons and I haven't mixed well in a long while. All this shit going down—the way they threw down and ripped through half of Marville's high and mighty to set things straight—I'm pleased as hell you have him back."

"Some little birdie told me an emergency meeting of the Marville School Board was called for next week. They'll be appointing a replacement. And there have already been more than a few demands to return you to your rightful position as the kindergarten teacher," Vi said. She sat on the stool.

"Little birdie, huh?" Riley took a beer Dani handed to her. "Jud isn't that little, and he sure as hell isn't a birdie."

"Are you going to take it?" Rhea asked as she entered the fray with a mound of small baggies. Party favors. Thank goodness. Ellie had totally blanked on needing those.

"Sit down, girlfriend. You're looking pale and tired. Jesse will kick my ass if you have a seizure," Bree said.

"Seizure?" Dani froze. "You still having those?"

"I haven't had one in a while, but they're a possibility. The injury will take some time to fully heal. Until then, I might do randomly weird things today. Just go with it."

"Good to know," Kamren said. "Speaking of *know*, the GED exam is next week. If you've got time, I'd appreciate another practice test."

"OMG. We need to plan a party," Bree said.

"Let's make sure I pass first," Kamren said.

"Have you thought about what you'll do after?" Vi asked.

"Well..." The woman drew the word out and looked around and over her shoulder at Dallas. "We'd talked about spending the summer up north and helping the guys up there restore the cabins they're not using. It'd be a great hideout for Z's families."

It would be. Ellie and Jesse had talked about the program and his desire for them to help with it. Ellie loved the idea—so much so she wasn't going to return to teaching, even if the school board offered her her job back.

"I was under the impression you and Jesse are spearheading all that," Kamren said. "Looks like you've got more big decisions to make than I do."

"Big decisions?" Riley lowered her voice to a shout-style whisper as she looked back at the swinging doors leading to the kitchen. "Wait, you aren't going to move up there, are you? Mom will have a fit."

"We're going up there for the summer if I can convince Dallas it's okay. The boys are looking forward to hunting and fishing and tracking wild game. I am, too."

"Why wouldn't he be on board with that?" Rhea asked.

"Baby Jessie's getting another cousin soon."

"OMG!" Riley wrapped the woman up in a hug and started dancing up and down. Tears streamed down the blonde's face. Kamren smiled and looked back at Dallas. He chuckled when she mouthed the word "sorry."

Ellie beamed. Another baby Mason on the way. Things couldn't be any better.

Operatives and locals from Resino who were close to Dylan drifted in. Momma Mason swore the guest list was small, but the place was packed within minutes. By the time the happy couple arrived with baby Jessie in tow, everyone had forgotten they'd come to a bar for a baby shower.

Momma Mason and Bubba appeared from the back. The woman shuffled Mary, Dylan, and Jessie to their appointed seats in the middle of the revelry. Bree followed the woman and passed a tiny set of earmuffs to Dylan. The man grinned his thanks and put the pink and purple ear protection on his little girl.

Drinks flowed, music played, and the revelry was set to high. Ellie walked over to where Jesse stood with his brothers. The men glared at the swollen crowd as if they expected a terrorist strike any moment.

"Relax," she whispered.

"It was only supposed to be family," Jesse grumbled. He glanced over at Nolan. "This could go sideways."

"It won't. If it does, it's on me." The man clapped Jesse on the back. "Go spend time with your woman. I'll handle the rest."

"The rest?" Ellie looked between the brothers, but Nolan was already heading outside. "He's leaving?"

"He'll be back. Let's go get a drink. It's been a long day." He kissed her softly. "I missed you."

"I missed you, too."

"You were up all night baking. The kitchen looks like a tornado struck." Jesse grinned. "I heard you recruited Cord to help."

"Images. He didn't bake anything, I swear."

"Good. I'm not sure our liability insurance covers mass food poisoning," Marshall muttered.

Ellie chuckled as Jesse guided her toward the bar. Dani opened and passed two beers to them. Lost in the merriment of the moment, she didn't notice the silent hush that fell over the crowd until the woman behind the bar froze.

And paled.

Jesse had risen and made his way around the bar. He caught her before she tumbled to the ground.

"Dani?" Kamren rose off her stool, concern evident.

Ellie tracked the woman's gaze across the congested bar, which parted as two men approached. With Nolan. The latter remained close, but behind...

Raul and Dominic.

Shock struck Ellie as she looked at Jesse. That's what he and Nolan had been doing?

"Oh my god!" Bree said. "I didn't think you'd pull it off, Vi."

"I made a few calls," the woman said.

"More than a few," Jud commented as he appeared and wrapped his arms around his wife. "We aren't having this shit when it's our turn. We'll do it at The Arsenal where it's more controlled."

"You don't dictate a baby shower, Judson Jensen. That's momma country, not daddy world."

"Everything in momma country is daddy world," the man said.

But Ellie's focus remained locked on Raul and Dominic as the two brothers made their way to their baby sister—whom Jesse had navigated from the other side of the bar. The woman stumbled forward as though dazed and fell into her brothers' arms.

Ellie sighed in contentment as the music started up and the gathered crowd returned to their conversations. The reunion continued a few moments, then Nolan approached. He paused at Jud.

The former assassin unlatched himself from his wife, reached into his pocket, and pulled out a folded envelope. Nolan nodded, then turned to face the three Santiagos, who all watched with mixed reactions.

Dominic looked around as though ready to bolt from the crowded room. Raul was far worse. And Dani looked...

Confused.

"How?" she asked.

"We expedited his release," Jesse said. "Vi made a few calls. Nolan and I went and pushed the warden to not drag his ass. Marshall and Cord handled Raul's extrication. We've hit reset."

"We can't undo the wrongs those bastards did, Daniella. We can't give any of you the time back you lost. I wish to fuck we could because I'd gladly give it back to my brother and Ellie, too," Nolan said. He handed the envelope to Dani. "But this will get you started on the path to a new life—whatever that may be. Everyone gathered here today donated in lieu of a gift for baby Jessie because that girl's already got enough."

Everyone laughed.

"I can't take this," Dani said, her voice soft but edged with pain. "I can't."

Dom reached around and took the envelope from his sister. He leaned down and whispered something in her ear. Tears glistened in the woman's gaze.

"Thank you," Dom said.

"It's not much, but it'll give her what she needs to buy Lonnie out of this place. He's now incentivized to take whatever offer you make,"

Nolan said. "Or start over with what you want. Either way, you're free."

"I don't..." She looked down at the envelope in Dom's hand, then up at Nolan. "I can't..."

"I won't ever be in your world. We orbit the same people, but I'll remain far enough away so you breathe free. Seeing me shouldn't ever rip you from whatever orbit you set for yourself. Don't leave Kam's world simply because I share it now. I won't ever be an issue," Nolan promised.

The woman visibly tightened in her brother's embrace. "Thanks."

Ellie sensed the tension thickening the air. She shifted her attention to Jesse. "I need to get the cake put together. I'll be back."

"Want some help?" A glimmer appeared in his gaze.

"You go back there and we'll never get the cake put together." She patted his chest and kissed him on the lips. "Later."

Ellie entered the kitchen and was relieved to see Bubba had already begun removing the pieces of the cake from its holders. He glanced up. Tears shimmered in his eyes.

"This is perfect. A work of art. Rebecca was here helping, then she saw the artwork and excused herself."

"It's beautiful, Ellie-belly," her mom said. She entered the kitchen, leaning heavily on her walker. "You have such a gift. It breaks my heart you never followed that dream of yours to open a shop. I think you could give Bubba here a run for his money."

"I wouldn't want a restaurant, Mom," Ellie said. "I love baking more than anything."

Bubba's eyebrows rose. "No one ever mentioned you wanted to open a place. Fuckhead's in jail. There's no reason you shouldn't."

Ellie could think of more than a few reasons not to—most of them financial. The risk. Ugh. The investment. What did she even know about running a business? Nothing. She'd gone to school and gotten a teaching degree. She'd taught babies not to eat their boogers and to play nicely with one another.

"I'll make room at my place for you," Bubba offered. "We'll put your sweets and whatever else you want on the menu. The Burtons owe me more than a few favors. I've been meaning to expand the seating area anyway. The way Rebecca's boys are going, one reserved table for the Mason brood won't be enough."

Did Bubba just offer to go into business with her?

"Stand around with your mouth open in this place and you'll catch a fly," her mom commented. "Give her a moment. I've had the poor dear so withdrawn from everyone she gets confused when people make such generous offers. You're a good man, Bubba."

"You raised one hell of a daughter," the man said. "Pleased as hell we're finally getting her last name right."

Ellie smiled. "I'm thinking it's about time you get a couple things set to rights yourself."

The man glared. "That's rule one if we're working together. Don't meddle."

Her mom smirked. "She meddles. That whole bunch out there are nothing but professional meddlers. You'd best accept they mean to see you set a couple things straight. I agree."

"Not you, too. Lord save me from meddling women."

"What are they meddling in?" Momma Mason asked as she entered the area.

"Nothing." Red rose in the man's face. "You'd best set your soon-to-be-daughter-in-law straight. She's opening up shop with me."

The woman's eyes widened. A wide smile appeared. "Why, that's a great idea. As long as you keep your cobbler."

"I'll always keep the cobbler. It's a Mason favorite."

Translation—it was a Rebecca Mason favorite. Ellie smiled. The two were adorable together. Rather than tease the man any more than he could tolerate, she got to work assembling the cake. She'd figured it'd take at least forty-five minutes. Fortunately she had more than enough help.

By the time she and Bubba rolled it out on the cart he'd thought to bring along, the gifts had been opened. Pictures had been taken. Mary was more than ready to leave.

Ellie had forgotten the woman was about as good with crowds as

Ellie's mom was—not at all. A hush fell over the crowd until DJ blurted, "I'm on the cake, Mom!"

Everyone laughed. Mary and Dylan stood, their eyes on the cake. Tears glimmered in the woman's gaze as she studied the bottom tier. The base of the cake was the largest, the roots of the mighty family tree. Images of Resino and its residents and the operatives of The Arsenal made up the area around the sides. Dylan's and Mary's parents and grandparents covered the area around the base of the oak Ellie had painstakingly recreated. Hearts with the initials of the Mason men and the women they loved were displayed along the trunk as it spanned upward onto the second tier. Images of the six Mason sons and Riley spanned around the smaller tier. Images of Dylan and Mary together with their closest friends and family covered the area around the trunk as it moved upward to the final tier.

Pictures of DJ and TJ surrounded the top tier, where baby Jessie's picture sat atop the mighty tree. Branches shot outward from along both tiers, just enough to dangle leaves with people's names.

"Ellie," Mary whispered. "It's beautiful."

"Congratulations," she whispered back as they embraced. "I'm so happy for you. Thank you for naming her Jessie."

"Thank you for loving him. He's a good man, and I'm thrilled you'll be my sister now."

Ellie let her tears fall as Dylan drew her into a hug. By the time she'd separated from the couple, a crowd had gathered. Flashes filled the room. Ellie winced and made her way to the side.

Jesse was there, drawing her against him. Sunglasses appeared on her face. "They'll help. Is your vision spotty? Clouded?"

"No, I think I'm okay."

He kissed her forehead. "It's beautiful, Peanut."

"You should've told me about Raul and Dom. They aren't on there."

"I think they'll forgive you."

"Bubba offered to go into business with me. Said we could talk it out. I could bake. He's been looking to expand," she said with a grin.

"Would you be okay if I said yes? Maybe just part-time? Because I still want to help with the underground."

"You can do whatever you want, Peanut. I love you."

"You okay?" Riley asked as she approached.

Ellie nodded.

The woman reddened. "We've been a bit crazy lately, and I keep putting this off, but I have to say something. I'm sorry."

Ellie looked at Jesse, then Riley. "For what?"

"I didn't know," Riley blurted. "I didn't know he called you Peanut. He'd been gone and Dallas and Cord had both just left, and Dad knew I was distraught and missing them so bad. So he got me a horse, and I don't know why but..."

"Jesus," Jesse muttered.

"Riles," Nolan started.

Ellie looked around and realized the Mason men had all swarmed in. "I'm confused."

Dallas laughed. Kamren swatted at him. "Hush. This has been really bothering your sister."

"It's hysterical," Dallas argued, laughing harder.

"What's so funny, Dad?" TJ asked.

"Jesus," Jesse repeated. "Riles, don't. It doesn't matter."

"It does. She needs to know I didn't know you called her Peanut."

"Okay," Ellie said, dragging the word out. Cord stepped away. His shoulders were shaking. Even Mary was smiling. "What am I missing?"

"Dad got her a horse after we all left. She named her Peanut," Jesse whispered.

Oh. Wow. Ellie blinked. Then laughed. She drew Riley into a hug and laughed harder. "I love you, Riley."

"I'd better take you out of here before you decide to not marry me," Jesse whispered.

"Nothing will stop me from becoming Mrs. Jesse Mason."

25

The wedding would take place at the same spot as Dylan's—beneath the tree where their grandfather and great-grandfather had proposed to their women. Unlike the other posh affair where most of the tri-county had come, the guest list was limited to family, Arsenal personnel, and whoever else happened to show up.

The latter proved to be more than Ellie expected because, as it typically did in Resino and Marville and Nomad, word got around pretty quick that Ellie Travers was finally marrying Jesse Mason. Another of Resino's most eligible bachelors was biting the dust.

Ellie wore her mother's wedding dress, which had been altered by one of Momma Mason's friends in Nomad. A friend of Riley's had come out and done Ellie's hair and makeup. She stared into the full-length mirror and almost cried.

"Don't you dare," Bree hissed. "We've fixed your makeup three times already."

"Leave her be," Mary ordered as she appeared with baby Jessie in her arms.

Any hope of containing the emotional dam imploded at the sight of Jesse's namesake. Tears spilled down Ellie's cheeks as she offered a watery smile to the woman.

"I have something for you, but you probably shouldn't mention it to Jesse until later."

Oh boy. Ellie tried not to chew her lower lip. She wrapped her hands in the old lace of her wedding dress and waited as the woman handed Jessie off to Rhea. Mary pulled something off her neck and held it out.

"Vi, Zoey, and I chatted. We disagreed on what we should get you, so I went rogue and did this anyway." The woman smiled as Ellie took the long chain.

Two identification tags were attached at the end. The Arsenal logo was on one side. She flipped them over and swallowed as she read the inscription.

Ellie Mason

Peanut

Jesse's calm

Ellie blinked past the tears. "It's perfect."

Jesse had told her about Riley getting him and Dylan to brush her hair after they'd returned injured from war. The action had given them calm. Riley had been Jesse's steady presence whenever she sensed the darkness dragging him under.

"No one knows about the calm Riley brought to Jesse and Dylan except them, me, and now you." Mary wrapped Ellie in a hug. "Thank you for being his calm. I'm thrilled to have you as my sister."

God.

She squeezed the woman tighter. "Thank you for always having his back."

"You realize this shindig will grow in size as the day progresses, right?" Mary asked with a laugh as she pulled away. She dabbed at her watery eyes. "Dylan and Dallas have increased security around the perimeter, but containing Resino residents when a Mason event happens is like parting water."

Ellie slid the gift over her head. "I don't care who comes as long as I'm Ellie Mason at the end of the day."

Mary smiled, but her attention shifted to Jessie when she started to fuss. "It's feeding time. I'd best get to that before she starts screaming."

Ellie chuckled because the baby had a set of lungs that rivaled everyone's. She wasn't shy about crying out when needed. The little girl's bright green eyes held an intelligence Ellie hadn't ever seen in babies before. She was destined for brilliance.

"By the way, Kamren apologizes in advance. She's tried to keep DJ and TJ dressed for their part in the wedding, but they're not fully onboard with the ties. Or the 'squeaky shoes.'"

Ellie laughed. She couldn't care less what the two boys wore. The woman left with a wave and shut the door to the cottage they'd procured for preparation. Ellie looked over at the two silent women sitting on the sofa.

Bree and Rhea both dabbed at their eyes. All three of them burst into laughs.

"The makeup is useless," Ellie said.

"He won't even notice," Rhea commented as she stood.

Another knock on the door got a groan from Bree. "I swear you aren't ever going to finish getting ready at this rate."

Ellie chuckled because there wasn't much else to do. She wasn't the sort of woman who fussed over hair and makeup for hours. Both were semi-done, though the latter was likely a mess right now.

Cord entered when Bree opened the door. His gaze danced with amusement as he surveyed the room. As always, the youngest Mason saw more than most but made no comment. Ellie knew it'd take one hell of a woman to wrangle him.

Without a word, he stepped up and ran a finger along her cheek. His lips upturned in a smirk as he showed her the black on his fingertip. Then he fractured the silence when his gaze settled on the tags Mary had just given her. "Figured she'd go ahead and do that."

"They're perfect," Ellie defended.

"Almost," he replied as he pulled them off. Ellie almost reached for them but froze when he reached into his pocket and pulled something out.

He palmed whatever it was and undid the end of the chain.

Something small slid down and landed alongside the tags. Ellie swallowed as he redid the clasp and put the gift back on her. "Now it's perfect."

Damn.

Ellie's eyes watered as she lifted the tags up. A platinum key with E & J inscribed.

Damn.

"Thank you for bringing him home to us," Cord said. He clasped the back of her neck, pulled her forward and kissed her forehead. "Welcome to the family, Ellie."

Ellie hugged Cord. She couldn't speak beyond the lump in her throat, but no words were necessary. The man knew how thankful she was for him and everyone else in Jesse's life.

By the time he was gone a few moments later, Ellie was ready to be married. She'd never been a patient person.

Bree sauntered up and looked at the gifts draped around Ellie's neck. "The tags are cool, but what's with the key?"

"A private story," Ellie said. No one needed to know it symbolized the battle they'd waged for Jesse. That was something she and Cord would share. Perhaps at some point she'd tell Jesse it symbolized the war his little brother had started.

The door opened a few moments later, and Ellie's mom entered. She wore a curly, dark-haired wig and makeup. For a moment Ellie could almost forget her mom was terminal. The smile on the woman's face struck her eyes with a twinkle as she made her way into the room and sat in the seat nearest the door. A box was perched on the step of the walker.

"You look more beautiful than I imagined, Ellie-belly."

"Mom." She blinked back tears. "I wish Dad were here."

"He is. No way he'd miss his baby girl marrying the man who won her heart long ago." She looked over at Bree. "I told Rebecca earlier, but you girls should know I appreciate all the work you've put into pulling this together so quickly."

"It was nothing," Bree said, her voice soft.

"It was everything."

Ellie took a deep breath and focused on the happiness of the day —the fact that her mom would see her become Ellie Mason. She'd worn a royal blue dress that brought out the color of her eyes.

"I'm proud of you for standing beside him. You're one of the strongest people I've ever known. I'd like to think I had a hand in that, but a lot of it came out of necessity because I didn't do the best job raising you," her mom admitted.

Ellie closed the distance and crouched. She took her mom's hand and squeezed. "You are the most amazing mom. I love you so much. Don't ever doubt that."

"I'm finally at peace." The whispered statement struck the room with its finality. Ellie didn't fight the tears spilling from her eyes. Makeup didn't matter. "For the first time since the diagnosis, I'm at peace because the wrong I committed has been undone. You're finally getting the life you deserve to live, the love you deserve to enjoy, Ellie-belly."

"Mom." Ellie leaned in and hugged her mother. "I'll never regret the choice I made. That wasn't a wrong you committed. It was a decision I made because I love you and family comes first. I could've gone against your wishes and told Jesse why I was staying."

"You never would've stifled that boy's dream."

No. "Everything happened as it should have, Mom. We're together again. We've learned the hard way that tomorrow isn't a guarantee, so I'm not wasting a single second looking back at what could've been— not when I'm staring into my happily ever after."

"I'm finally at peace because that boy will give you everything your heart desires and keep you safe at his side where you belong." Tears fell from her mom's watery gaze. "I can't wait to tell your dad all about him."

Oh God.

"I love you, Mom."

"I love you, too, Ellie-belly." She patted Ellie's hand. "Enough of the waterworks. I need you to make me a promise."

"Anything."

"Don't waste a second more hiding from your dreams. You make them happen because that boy will move Heaven and Earth to help you." Her mom pointed to the box. "I found that in the trash bin a couple months after he left. That's when I knew I'd broken you. I broke my sweet Ellie-belly's heart."

"Mom. Don't. You needed me more than I needed what was in the box. That's when I learned we don't always want what we think we do."

Ellie didn't look at the box. Her mind listed all the things she'd thrown away years ago. Her scrapbook of recipes. Her swatches of tablecloth patterns and wall colorings. Sketches of possible restaurant layouts and logos. Names.

"The day your dad put a ring on my finger, he swore to give me the world. And he did." She stroked Ellie's face. "I took that away from you, but you're finally getting it back today."

She was. Jesse was all she wanted. She didn't need a bakery as long as she had the man she loved.

"Promise me you'll see your dream through. Bubba will be asking about that box. I told him so someone would hold your feet to the fire. Love you, Ellie, but you're a might stubborn about putting yourself first. Bubba and Rebecca are gonna see to it you get your bakery up and running."

Ellie didn't want her mom worrying about anything right now. But the woman's gaze glinted with the same stubbornness Ellie had inherited. "I promise, Mom."

"Good, now let's get your makeup fixed. I'm thinking they'll send drones in after you if you're late."

Ellie laughed because she could picture exactly that happening. But there was no chance she'd be late because she was about to become Mrs. Jesse James Mason.

 ou're holding up better than I expected," Doctor Sinclair commented.

Jesse looked around at the packed area around the large tent they'd constructed and grumbled, "Half the county is here."

"A few thousand less than at mine. Be glad," Dylan said dryly as he took a drink of his beer.

Jesse was finally married to Ellie.

Ellie Mason. She wore the dog tags proudly around her neck. He'd have to find out who gave them to her and thank them. It was the perfect gift. His heart was so full it'd almost burst when the ceremony ended and he got to kiss his wife.

His face hurt from smiling. He hadn't been able to contain the elation.

Love. He looked at Dallas and Dylan, who'd stayed close to his side most of the day. Nolan and Marshall had tackled crowd control while Cord worked security with Gage and Fallon.

"How do you two ever get anything done? I can't stop thinking about Ellie. I want to drag her away and spend my life with her wrapped around me."

Dallas smirked. "Sounds like big brother's sorted a couple things out since we last spoke."

He had, but he wouldn't ever speak to them or anyone else about it. Except Logan.

Because he'd made love to Ellie more than once. That first erection hadn't been a fluke. He'd never dared dream he could have that aspect of his life back, but he did because Ellie was the most magnificent treasure in the world. He wouldn't go a single day without telling her and showing her however he could.

Sex wouldn't ever be a huge component of their marriage because their relationship was so far beyond the stratosphere of the physical. But damn, he loved making love with her. The gentle stroke of her hands, the way she took control and brought just the right amount of firm to her grip when she...

Wow.

Jesse ran a hand through his hair and chuckled when Dylan's gaze swept downward. Big brother's eyes watered, but he made no comment. He glanced at Dallas and saw the same emotion in his gaze.

Doctor Sinclair stood there silently and watched the byplay. Doc always saw more than most.

"Thanks for everything, Doc. I couldn't have made it to this day without you."

"You and everyone here at The Arsenal make me glad I do the work I do." Doctor Sinclair looked over her shoulder at Sara, who approached with Ariana. "Actually, I need to speak with you and your wife a moment."

Wife. Jesse grinned again.

Ellie appeared at his side. He snaked an arm around her waist, leaned down and nibbled at her ear. She shivered against him and sighed. "I can't wait to get you home."

She splayed a palm on his chest and rested her head against him. "Hey Doc. Dallas. Dylan."

"Hey, sis," Dallas said with a grin. "Never gonna get sick of saying that."

"Never gonna get sick of hearing it," Ellie whispered.

"I know this may not be the optimal time to do this, but Sara is insistent."

Jesse tensed and looked at the young woman. "Are you okay, Sara?"

"I'm fine." The girl's eyes were watery. "I just..."

Doctor Sinclair wrapped a protective arm around Sara. "Go ahead, sweetheart. It's okay. If you're sure..."

"I am." The girl took a deep breath. "I've watched you two. I didn't know about you being together before or anything, but I saw the way Ellie looked at you. And the way you looked at Ellie. I knew you would get together even though..."

Even though everyone—including him—hadn't ever thought that was possible. Marriages were about far more than a sexual relationship, though. He'd be eternally grateful for learning that firsthand. He couldn't imagine a life without Ellie at his side. In his bed. Wrapped around him every night.

"I'm not ready to be a mother," Sara blurted.

Shock stilled Jesse as he assessed the situation. He glanced at Sinclair, who bit her lip and nodded, as if sensing his silent question. This couldn't be what he'd somehow jumped to.

But it was.

Sara pulled a sheaf of papers from beneath her shirt. "I spoke with my attorney. She drew everything up, but Doc says you'll want to have time to look through everything."

"Sara, honey? What is this?" Ellie asked as she drew away from Jesse and closed in on Sara.

Jesse remained close, at Ellie's back. He rested his hands on her hips and kissed the top of her head, near the healing bald spot she hadn't tried to hide. A crowd had gathered, as if sensing the tension of the moment. Though no one else seemed to have connected the dots, Jesse was glad his family was here, surrounding and protecting his wife.

Jesus.

His eyes burned as he glanced away and forced a deep, even breath. Ellie would fall apart. He had to be here to make it safe for her to let go. Sara's watery gaze collided with Jesse. She smiled.

"I can't be the mother Ariana needs, but you will be, Ellie." Sara licked the tears near her mouth away and continued. "And Jesse... you'll be the kind of father I would've wanted for her if I'd had a choice."

Gasps echoed around them, but Jesse kept his attention on Sara.

And Ellie.

His wife buckled, but Jesse roped an arm around her waist and drew her close. He leaned down and kissed the shell of her ear. "Breathe deep, Peanut."

"This isn't real. Jesse. These are..."

"Adoption papers," Sara said. "And parental termination paperwork. I don't understand all the legal stuff, but my attorney assured me it was all in order. I trust you can help work through whatever else we need to do. I want Ariana to be a Mason. To be yours."

"Honey, my God." Ellie trembled. "You're already a part of this family. No matter what, you are always a part of this family."

"I know." Sara reached out and took Ellie's hand. "When you hold Ariana, you look at her like there's nothing she can't do. When I..."

Jesus.

"I don't see that, Ellie. I should. She deserves a mom who will slay her monsters and a dad who will kill anyone who hurts her." Sara looked at Jesse. "I'll be that kind of mom someday. I hope. But I'll do it having learned from watching you and Jesse raise Ariana. From a distance. I'm going to NYU. I've registered."

Sobs echoed from behind them. Jesse glanced back as Rhea ran from the gathered crowd. What the fuck? Fallon followed.

Ellie looked up at Jesse. Confusion warred with hope. Sadness.

They'd made love twice so far. Though it'd likely happen again, neither held out hope for a child of their own.

Jesse smiled and let the tears flow. Surrounded by family and friends, he let the woman he loved and those he loved see the enormity of the gift Sara had just given them.

A child.

Ellie turned and wrapped her arms around him.

And sobbed.

He feathered kisses along her temple as he looked across at his brothers. His mother had her head buried in Nolan's chest. Riley clutched Cord. The rightness of the moment burned away another piece of the hell he'd endured.

He had a wife.

He had a family.

Cord smiled and mouthed, "Welcome home, brother."

~THE END~

ABOUT THE AUTHOR

Born in small-town Texas, Cara Carnes was a princess, a pirate, fashion model, actress, rock star and Jon Bon Jovi's wife all before the age of 13.

In reality, her fascination for enthralling worlds took seed somewhere amidst a somewhat dull day job and a wonderful life filled with family and friends. When she's not cemented to her chair, Cara loves travelling, photography and reading.

Newsletter|Facebook|Twitter|Website

THE ARSENAL SERIES
Jagged Edge
Sight Lines
Blood Vows
Zero Trace
Battle Scars
Impact Zone (October 2019)

THE COUNTERSTRIKE SERIES
Protecting Mari
Justice For Angie (November 2019)

Want more of The Arsenal Series? Did you know there are free reads between all the Arsenal releases? Subscribe to my newsletter or join my Facebook group for the first peek at exclusive bonus content.

Links to free short stories in the series can be found on my website at www.caracarnes.com

Made in the USA
Monee, IL
22 May 2023

34290360R00182